THE WAR OF THE WICKED

Fae Crown Book Three

JOY LEWIS

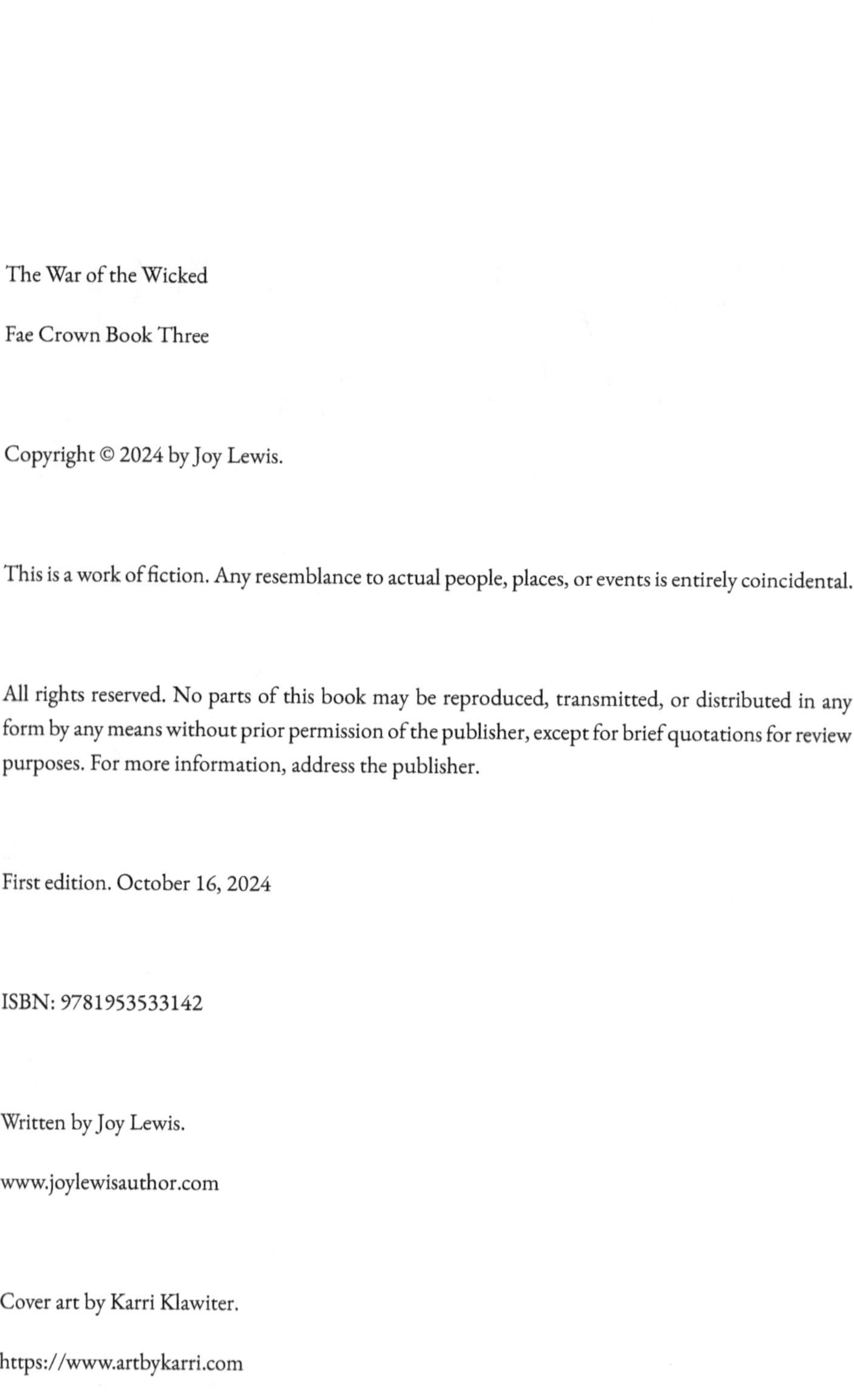

The War of the Wicked

Fae Crown Book Three

Copyright © 2024 by Joy Lewis.

This is a work of fiction. Any resemblance to actual people, places, or events is entirely coincidental.

All rights reserved. No parts of this book may be reproduced, transmitted, or distributed in any form by any means without prior permission of the publisher, except for brief quotations for review purposes. For more information, address the publisher.

First edition. October 16, 2024

ISBN: 9781953533142

Written by Joy Lewis.

www.joylewisauthor.com

Cover art by Karri Klawiter.

https://www.artbykarri.com

CHAPTER ONE

Mikal kissed the hollow of Juras's throat. "Are you sure you don't want me to stay the night?"

Juras swallowed the nest of nerves and emotion inside him. Surrendering to base pleasures tonight would have been too easy.

And he owed Mikal. He'd gotten the tavern matron to allow Juras to board in The Last Chance for a pittance. He hadn't been back to their attic home above Mara's bakery in months.

As he remembered why, Juras's stomach flipped.

"Not tonight," Juras said with no small amount of effort.

Even if his body was wired for his touch, singing for the release that Mikal's words promised, he couldn't. The barkeep disentangled himself from where he'd been perched in Juras's lap.

Mikal hovered at the threshold of Juras's rented room, looking back at him. His gaze hovered at the mouth he'd been hungry to kiss only moments before. Without another word, he left, pulling the door closed behind him and leaving Juras to his thoughts.

Juras's hands ran through his curls as his elbows hit the table inside the small room. He couldn't tell Mikal what was bothering him. He could hardly admit it to himself.

What the hell was he going to do?

What was the right answer?

She's dead. You saw with your own eyes.

But Juras couldn't help but hold to the hope that Anova—his only family left in the world—yet lived.

But maybe he just told himself that because the alternative was too gruesome. Crueler even than the fae who had stolen her.

The truth was that he'd helped kill her.

You really are a damned fool, he told himself.

Juras had helped round up a small band of humans to ambush the fae High King in the border forests when it had become clear that Anova's warnings about him were coming to fruition.

While the High King had been killed that bloody night, so had others. Juras had seen it with his own eyes. Anova had poisoned him to protect their world from his cruel reign. But in doing so, she'd dosed herself with it, too.

And Juras had been the one to help her do it.

Juras fisted more of his hair. She'd gone back to Fae because of *him*.

Leander Wolfsbane.

Otherwise, they'd be on the mainland in another human city by now. Both of them alive.

The bastards would have taken Irbess, Juras reminded himself. But what was protecting a rat hole like this when it had meant his best friend had died in the process?

And, if the rumors and stirrings on the streets were to be believed, this new fae king had his eyes set on Irbess just as much as the last one had.

His teeth bit into his tongue. *Damnit, what had it been for?*

It left him with only one real option: join the fae resistance groups.

But there was one other matter that complicated things. It was the matter of the woman after him and the debt he still owed.

Madam Hinterfell.

He had three choices when it came to her.

Run from her forever. Continue his petty crimes to pay off the abyssal hole he owed. Or allow himself to be recruited to her brothel to pay it off.

And joining the resistance groups wasn't exactly keeping a low profile while Hinterfell hunted him. But he couldn't just do *nothing*.

And he'd be damned before he'd accept the last one as an option.

A knock at his door interrupted his thoughts. Juras threw his head back and leaned into the back of his chair. Mikal was persistent.

But, then again, maybe a distraction was *exactly* what he needed tonight.

His mouth curled halfway up. He didn't blame him. Juras was quite good at this.

"Alright. You win," Juras called to him. He swallowed. His voice sounded strange to his own ears. "Come on. It's still unlocked."

But when the door swung open, it wasn't Mikal. Juras's head jolted up before his body followed suit.

It was a *fae*.

He swept tousled black hair away from his too-perfect face. The corner of his lips twitched into the ghost of a smile when he looked at Juras. It was like he knew who he'd mistaken him for or what he'd meant when he'd called out to Mikal.

There was no better word for what he was.

Beautiful.

Harsh was a close second.

Juras swore. He'd left his knife in the bottom of the dresser pushed into the room's corner.

"What the hell do you want?" Juras said through his teeth.

He smirked at him, and that too was annoyingly beautiful. "Charming. Anova wasn't exaggerating."

Juras nearly fell over. *Anova. Is she …?*

He realized who this was a second later. *It's him.*

"Wolfsbane," Juras breathed and steadied himself on the back of his chair. He hadn't seen the fae since he'd first pulled Anova from their last job here months ago. "It's you."

Before the fae could respond, Juras's gaze shot back to him. "You have no business walking about with her name on your tongue. She went back to Fae for you. And *died* because of you."

Wolfsbane looked at Juras for several heartbeats. The levity on his face slipped, and some hair-raising expression passed from his eyes too fast for Juras to fully see it.

"She's *not* dead." His words were low and dangerous.

Juras stared. It was nearly too good to be true.

He shouldn't take his eyes from the fae, but he couldn't help it. He needed to think and stared into nothingness.

If she's alive and well, then why hasn't she contacted me? Why hasn't she come back?

"And why should I believe you?" Juras's voice was equally quiet. "She hasn't been back. She hates Fae."

Wolfsbane was silent for several seconds. Juras looked at him again. Maybe the words had had an effect on him, he considered with a vile sort of satisfaction.

"Another fae male has captured her and keeps her captive." Wolfsbane stepped forward. "She's in grave danger. I need your help to save her."

Juras stared at the fae.

So, she's alive.

But how?

Was that truly the important part?

Her life was in danger while they stood there. Juras rushed over to his wardrobe where the knife was hidden. With his back to Wolfsbane, he said, "Tell me everything."

The fae didn't make a sound, though Juras felt him watching him. He didn't particularly relish exposing his back to one of them, but he needed to get ready if he was to do this.

Gods, was he actually going through with this?

What choice is there? She'd do the same for me. And has before.

"He wants the crown bound to her," he said. "And he's utterly obsessed with her at the same time. A dangerous combination."

Juras frowned as he dug out the weapon and the strap for it. Nothing about that sounded good.

The crown? As in the fae crown?

But there was something else bothering Juras that he considered at that moment. How had Leander Wolfsbane been able to find him? Not even Anova could have known he'd been hiding out here for the past several weeks. He'd been very careful now that Hinterfell was out for blood.

How had he been able to get past the boundary?

His thumb ran over his pocket, and he remembered what was in it.

Salt. According to the rumors he'd heard, salt disarmed fae glamor. He'd taken to keeping some with him since he'd been thinking of joining the fae resistance groups.

Juras was aware then of the silence that stretched between them. He needed to say something.

He turned, his hands fixing his knife inside the holster he'd buckled to his waist. On the outside, he was calm. On the inside, his blood pounded.

Never trust the fae.

He needed a test. Something that would prove if it was him or not—a test that didn't seem like one.

"It's a good thing she remembered which room we used to rent in this place," Juras said as he tightened the holster.

"Yes," Wolfsbane said. He sounded bored. "It is. Are you ready, human?"

But we never did rent a room in any of the taverns we pulled jobs at. It would have been far too risky.

Especially with our home above Mara's bakery.

Juras's fist released the salt into the fae's face.

At first, nothing happened. Other than the snarl that ripped from his throat.

It was then that his eyes changed from pure black to a strange violet that reminded him of a grackle's feather.

Faster than Juras could react, the fae boy who wasn't the fae boy who he'd seemed to be pushed Juras against one of the walls of his rented room.

"You're not him," Juras said in a gasp as his body hit the wall. When he recovered enough breath to speak again, he said through his teeth, "Who. Are. You."

The fae's face had changed. Although his hair was still dark, it had grown and become unruly. The look in his eyes was wilder than the look of the fae he'd pretended to be before.

I need to get out of this. His mind raced. The weapon was still at his waist. If he could only move his hand and grab it …

Then a stab through the fae's abdomen would be easy.

His mouth hovered above Juras's throat. "Do you want to know a secret, human?"

Juras's skin crawled when he spoke like that. He was sure he didn't.

"Let go of me," he grinded out.

The fae ignored the order and said instead, "I'm the dangerous, obsessive fae." He smiled, revealing his teeth. "And you're going to help me get what I want."

Juras locked eyes with him. He felt himself swimming in his strange violet-shaded gaze. Where the rumors that they knew how to charm humans with a look true?

He needed to focus.

Juras looked at the deadly fae. He had to distract him somehow. It would surely be his only chance.

"I've always wondered." He cocked his head to one side as he looked at the fae crowding his personal space. "Is it true what they say about fae males?"

Juras's gaze flickered somewhere besides his face—leaving no question about what he meant. Or rather, *where.*

The fae's mouth quirked up on one side, revealing inhuman, pointed teeth. What the hell was he doing? Juras felt lightheaded.

"What a foul-mouthed human." His thumb rested on Juras's jugular as his heartrate raced faster. "Wouldn't you like to know."

It was his chance. Juras hoped fae males were as obsessed with the idea of sex as human males were.

Apparently so.

Though he might have had pure strength over Anova in their one-on-one scuffles over the years, he knew he had nothing on this creature in a fair fight.

Too bad for him that it won't be a fair one, then.

He grabbed the hilt of the knife and plunged it into the fae's lower abdomen where it sank past his shirt and into flesh.

Even before the fae swore from the pain, his hand twisted around Juras's wrist. Pressure burst there, and Juras's knife clattered to the floor.

"That was a very stupid thing to do, human," he growled. The fae's other hand shot to Juras's throat.

"Do your worst then," Juras spat. His heart thundered like it knew its end was closing in on it.

No. I have to get out of here alive. I have to warn Anova.

But he couldn't move from the creature's iron grip. He tensed for what he knew was coming: strangulation and the painful death that accompanied it.

But it never came.

Instead, the fae pressed his thumb under his chin, tilting Juras's head up.

The fae smiled at him, though Juras could smell his blood now.

"I'll make you beg to see my worst before I'm done with you," he threatened.

His other hand went to his forehead. Before Juras could move, a flash of silver light sparked above his eyes.

Juras tried to thrash out of his grasp, but with each passing moment, his body grew heavier.

Darkness claimed him seconds later.

Before the human collapsed on the ground in a heap before him, Hellmyr caught him in his arms.

Were all humans this much trouble?

Judging from the few he'd met so far, he knew the answer.

The pretty ones are always the most aggravating, it seems.

Hellmyr shifted the human so he was slung across his shoulder. It had smelled suspiciously like arousal in here before he'd walked in.

Naughty human boy.

A mischievous smile flicked across his face before a grimace replaced it from the pain. His other hand went to his now-wet black-cuffed shirt.

Now the tang of fae blood contaminated the air. What was more, the human had gotten him good. He'd already started bleeding on the floor.

Although the typical human wouldn't be able to tell the difference in the smell of human blood and that of a fae's, his enemies could. They would find him if he lingered here longer.

He'd taken a steep risk coming here. But looking at the young male human slung across his shoulder—his bait—he knew it would be worth it.

This will work.

Hellmyr opened the lone window in the small room and crouched on the sill, balancing the human and Hellmyr's own weight.

A little moonlight later, and he was gone.

CHAPTER TWO

The twin drugs of terror and thrill were caught in Anova's throat. She watched him and wanted everything about him.

Her mouth was insatiable for Cadmus's skin. Everything about him was achingly perfect.

A stray beam of moonlight fell on his hard chest. He made a sound in his throat when her mouth hovered just above the waist of his pants.

"Not yet," he said. The words sounded strained—like he couldn't stand more of her mouth there and also not to have more of it there.

Her heart caught in her ribcage as it thrashed within her. "Oh, really? And why not?"

She was back to her kissing. Their bed's pillows and covers were tangled up in their limbs.

"You know why, Anova," he said. "It's not because I don't want to."

Anova ignored him. They'd only done this once before, but she wouldn't be put off again.

She wanted this. Him.

And *damnit*, he wanted this, too. Wanted her.

Her mouth crooked to one side in a half smile. She knew one method that no male could resist—human or fae. Admittedly, she'd never done it herself, but growing up in a brothel tended to make one aware of such things.

Anova tugged his pants lower, and she swallowed a gasp at what she saw. It'd been so dark last time that she'd barely been able to see him like this.

"Anova," he growled in warning. But, curiously, he shrugged the rest of the way out of his pants.

Before he could catch her hand, she started to trace swirls and patterns on the inside of his thigh.

She swallowed. Fae males were sizeable.

"Anova, we need to talk about—" His words were cut off in a gasp.

She'd bent before him, her hands taking him much too fast for him to complete a rational thought. His hips moved into the motion, and he groaned.

"Anova ..."

"Do you want me to stop?" she asked, biting her lip. She would've.

But she knew why he'd protested earlier. And she knew that it was utter—

Cadmus bared his teeth. "No."

His nails dug into the bed he perched on. Sweat glided down his stomach. She pressed a kiss there before moving her kisses south.

He gasped her name and worked himself into her, just inside the mouth that had been kissing him. He shuddered as she tasted him, and they moved as one.

But before she could bring his pleasure to a height, a snarl erupted from his chest. Faster than lightning, he pulled her up, and his hands closed around her wrists.

His member throbbed near her. He tugged her shirt up some, and his mouth mirrored what hers had done to him. Anova squirmed in his grasp, but her core heated with the promise of what was to come.

"Cadmus," she said in barely a breath.

He pinned her down with his body as he moved. The bastard hadn't let her finish him and now he was using her tricks against her.

She cursed his name out loud. Cadmus laughed at that, and goosebumps rose on her skin.

His hand hovered at her waist, about to tug her pants down, when Anova stiffened.

Cadmus stopped. "Okay. It's alright. We don't have to do this. But the deal is you have to talk to me about it."

She jolted up, but she was moving way too fast again, and it upset her even more. It was then that she caught sight of herself in the mirrored walls of his room.

She saw the pointed ears. The crown. The burns.

Her foreign body.

"Anova, wait," Cadmus said. "Please."

But she was already out of the room. She couldn't be in there. Not with the person who was and wasn't herself reflected back at her.

After she came off the twisted stairwell downstairs, her chest heaving from her escape, Anova avoided the dining hall. Voices rose from the cracked door to the rest of the estate.

It was Nerium, Della, and Maris. She heard the clink of glassware and Della's high laugh.

Since Nerium had rescued them from Eastwoe palace and they'd all reunited after what had happened in the Lost Forest, the three of them had been inseparable. Anova was overjoyed for them, but she couldn't bring herself to let them see her this way.

Ashamed and distrustful of her own body. Uncertain.

Unhappy when she should have been nothing but.

She didn't think she could lie convincingly to them right now, so she passed their company up for the room she knew to be empty.

This time, she knew that Cadmus wasn't coming after her. Her heart thrashed in her chest at the memory of his hands and mouth on her.

Her jaw worked. She'd make him drop the matter. Sooner or later.

Besides, she needed to find more information about something. Or rather, *someone*.

When Anova crossed into Cadmus's study, the walls of texts muffled the sound of her footsteps. She breathed, finally assured that she was alone.

Anova started by pulling the tome of fae tales from the shelf, followed by the text on translating the style of ancient fae runes that typically made her eyes cross without its help.

With both books in her arms, she settled into Cadmus's plush chair.

But dawn's approach was too soon, and, true to the fae whose body she inhabited now, she tired at the feeling of it. When she rested her head against the plush backing of the lounge chair, her eyes remained closed.

Anova was lost. A bloated moon sat in the sky above her, but she didn't dare look at it.

It might stare back at her.

There was something wrong with these woods. They weren't ending.

It wasn't that she was going in circles. She was going on into nothingness.

But there was more to it than that. She was being watched.

Anova turned on her heels. "Show yourself," she challenged, but nothing responded.

You're crazy, she thought. But she couldn't shake the feeling.

She *knew* there was something here.

With a start, Anova began to run through the cursed woods. Her breath puffed in front of her face, and slivers of moonlight escaped past the canopy of trees above her. They fell on her skin like burns.

It was then that she heard the voice—it was the one that had haunted her in her quietest moments for weeks.

"Your debt to me is due, Anova. You're going to pay up, one way or another."

The voice didn't belong to Madam Hinterfell—the woman she owed many gold coins to. No, this was—

She spun on her heels and gathered the vile energy of the blood crown at her fingertips. She would save herself, no matter what she had to do.

The demon Rietvar was behind her, but he wasn't in either his goblin form or the disturbing human one.

The massive silver beast launched himself at her, but not before he opened his maw wide enough to swallow a building.

Anova couldn't move, and his jaws tightened around her in a gulp.

"But luckily for you, you're almost ready to repay me."

CHAPTER THREE

Anova jolted awake, her breaths coming too short for her to breathe properly. She shoved the blanket off her—someone had visited her in the night—and tried to rise to her feet.

Cadmus was above her and stopped her from rising. "What's wrong?"

The sound of a heartbeat thrashing drowned out all other noises. She thought it was her own before she remembered she could hear such things as the heartrates of others.

It was too much, and she pushed the thought away.

He'd been worried about her, though that was clear from his face. He lowered himself to where she sat.

"You were screaming," he said, his lips tight together.

She didn't decide to do it consciously. She hid her face against his chest.

"It's him. Rietvar," she whispered against his skin.

Cadmus tightened his grip on her and made a vow. "He won't get you. So long as I live."

But that was the issue. Rietvar didn't want her dead.

He wanted something else.

Since Anova had brought Cadmus back from the realm of the dead by bargaining with Rietvar, they'd tried to learn what they could about him.

Purveyor of souls. Death.

Whatever name he went by, Rietvar was a creature out of human myths and fae tales. And she owed him.

Not only for the feat he'd pulled to retrieve Cadmus's soul from the afterlife once he'd sacrificed himself for his twin brother—but also for the hasty bargain she'd made with him when she'd thought she wasn't going to outlive a month.

Her stomach churned to remember what he'd made her promise.

"One act of service to me, the nature of which will be determined at a later date."

At the time, she'd been sure she wouldn't see the day to repay it.

She'd been a fool.

She and Cadmus had dissected the bargain's wording in what felt like every possible way. There was practically no hope of determining what Rietvar would ask for. He could ask that she spend the rest of her life trying to push a building to budge a hair-width.

It wouldn't have endangered her life to do so, which was the bargain's only real stipulation.

And yet, it would surely end with her descent into madness.

He could ask that she pluck the moon from the sky for him. He could ask anything of her, and the fact that this entity had so much power over her made her physically ill.

"He said something to me. I don't think it was just a dream," she whispered.

Though she couldn't see his face, she felt him stiffen. "What happened?"

Anova closed her eyes. "He said I'm almost ready to repay him."

The silence that pervaded his study was uncomfortable. Anova wasn't dense. What Rietvar had said wasn't a good sign.

They couldn't afford to interpret it merely as a dream and not a warning.

When Cadmus spoke, he wasn't the fae she knew. He was speaking as the son of the strategist and right hand of the previous High King. The patriarch of the house of Wolfsbane.

Slowly, he disentangled himself from her and started to pace.

"He has a specific plan for you, then," he started. "Almost *ready*," he muttered a moment later. Anova could see out of the corner of her vision that he was staring at her.

"I'm sending Nerium away," he announced.

Anova rose. "Where is he supposed to be going?" She thought back to last night and what she'd heard in the dining room. If something happened to him, she didn't think Della and Maris would forgive her.

She added, "The entire fae realm is looking for us. They'd kill him just to get to me."

With the help of Nerium and Cadmus's fae magic, they'd transported most of the Wolfsbane estate from where it had been in the Sorrelands. It had been much too risky to leave it where it'd been—considering most all of Fae knew where it was after it had become the war camp for the previous blood-hungry High King.

And also considering she was still a target for any fae with a thirst for power.

How am I getting out of any of this?

"We need more information," Cadmus stated. He began to walk towards the doors out of his study. "There's only one place left in Fae where we can hope to find it."

Anova stared at him. She knew without having to ask where Cadmus was speaking of.

The Eastwoe archives.

"He'd be walking into a trap," she said as she caught up to him. "He can't do this. I can't ask this of him."

Cadmus ignored her. Anova gritted her teeth.

Stubborn fae.

She pushed herself in front of him. "I'll go," she said. "I can get inside the archives and get the information that we need."

A look flashed across his face before it was gone again. "It's not you getting inside that I'm concerned about. It's the getting out."

"I would convince him," she said. "Believe me."

Cadmus's expression was inscrutable.

"What is it?" she demanded, though she felt she knew already.

His voice was whisper-quiet. "Is this about what he feels for you?"

Something caught in her throat. That was what he was worried about? "No, it's not. I don't—I told you, I never felt for him that way. Not truly."

Cadmus moved his face so she couldn't see it. "There are those of us who take multiple partners. Your friends have seemed to accept that. Are you sure that's not what you want, too?"

Anova closed the distance he'd made between them. Was that what he'd been worried about?

"Cadmus, I want you—and only you," she said. "I'm not like you. Not like the f—"

She'd almost said it.

Fae.

The skin around Cadmus's eyes tightened. "I think you know we need to talk about that, too."

"Like hell we do," she said, though she said it much less forcefully than she'd wanted to.

"You don't want to talk to me about it?" Cadmus whispered.

The way he'd asked it made her heart stop for a beat. He knew how to undo her in the worst way.

"I don't ... want to think about it," she settled on.

On what I've lost, she thought, but didn't say out loud.

Cadmus's dark eyes flew to her mouth. "You saved me. You survived something set on killing you. You outsmarted Death himself. Is that so wrong?"

Anova swallowed. "Of course not."

Cadmus kissed her neck. His thumb found the edge of her mouth.

"I can show you some things about this ... type of life. If you want," he offered.

Anova stood, caught between the vulnerabilities of her human scars and the mysteries of her new fae body. Her fears and her desires.

Cadmus brought his lips to her collarbone and hovered over a burn scar stretched across the bone. He was careful with it, gliding his mouth over it with barely a touch.

It made her shiver.

He hooked one thumb and then another at either side of her waist. Before, there's been human curves there. Softness—even after her upbringing in poverty.

Now ...

He moved his body close to hers, and a low fire started in her core. He slipped her shirt up and moved his kissing to her stomach.

She gave in, letting him touch her.

It was a good kind of giving in. The kind that made one forget about pesky things like misgivings and thoughts. She arched at his touch.

Her fears wormed their way through the sensations coursing through her anyway, calling her back to the reality of what she was. The strangeness of how she reacted to even the familiar stimulus of pleasure.

When she gathered enough breath to say it, she said, "You first. Let me do this to you. To see ... how a fae body works. To understand the differences."

Cadmus looked like he was on the verge of refusing her—of kissing her until she couldn't think—but he said, "So long as you let me ask Nerium to go."

She agreed.

Sometimes, winning meant giving in, too.

CHAPTER FOUR

"I'm sorry. Nerium is in danger because of me," Anova finally said.

The thought had been clattering around her brain for the past forty-eight hours or so, but she hadn't had the courage to say it to the two of them until now.

Della and Maris, the women who had been her mother's closest friends and who had grown to become two of her own closest, were helping Anova dress. Sunlight had faded from the land moments ago.

Now that they rose on Fae's time, their day was just starting.

Anova stared ahead of her where she'd thrown a sheet over her floor length mirror. She'd done this to all the mirrors in her rooms. It made things easier that way.

Maris was careful not to disturb her burn scars as she straightened the sides of Anova's dress. "He wanted to go. He's wanted to repay you for saving Cadmus, you know."

She looked to the floor. This next part would be the worst.

The zipper that sailed over her skin was cool to the touch, but even so, when it grazed her raw skin, Anova couldn't help the gasps of pain that slipped past her mouth.

Maris stopped. "I thought you said this didn't hurt anymore."

Della's eyebrows came together. "Why didn't you say anything, Nove? We could have gotten some of your pants and shirt out instead."

Anova was silent.

It was stupid. She didn't need to be reminded of that.

She liked her burn scars. They reminded her of being human.

But she liked her dresses more. She liked feeling like the person she'd been before this.

Constrictive clothing had been out of the question—as well as anything that exposed too much of her body. The latter was her own stipulation.

"You're still you, Anova. The outside doesn't change the inside," Della said. "Now, let's get you into something else."

"No," she said forcefully. Anova took a step away from them. "I'm fine. Really."

She could see reflected back in their eyes the obvious lie she'd spouted, but they didn't say anything after that.

Great, she thought to herself. Anova knew when she was being an ass.

Della and Maris were too good for the likes of her.

As Maris styled her hair around the blood crown—another piece of proof that she was irreparably different from the human girl she'd been—Anova's ears burned with the thought of what this night would bring.

"And just what are you thinking about, Anova?" Della asked. Before she could respond, she giggled and said to Maris, "It seems we'd better stuff our ears with cotton tonight."

Anova turned as well as she could without disturbing Maris's handiwork. She scoffed. "It can't compare to the sounds of the dead raising I must have heard for a week straight."

Della howled with laughter while Maris muttered something about purposefully tangling her hair into a knot when Anova saw it.

It was on the other side of her balcony doors, staring straight inside at the three of them.

A part of her scolded herself that she was too jumpy. It was just a crow.

But she remembered something one of her enemies had once done to be in more than one place at once.

No. No, it's not.

Anova startled forward. *It couldn't be. No.*

At one time, Lycasta had given one of her moths moonlight nectar in order to speak through it and see through its eyes.

But a crow? This wasn't exactly Lycasta's style.

The crow stared back at Anova with an inhuman intelligence as it perched on her railing.

No.

Maris was after her for moving in the middle of her work, but she evaded her and flung the door open.

"What do you want?" Anova growled at it.

At first, she felt like a proper lunatic. The moonlight she usually kept carefully away from her fell on her skin. The blood in her veins sang to it, pleading to Anova to dance under its light.

She ignored the feeling as best as she could.

The crow's eyes glimmered like smooth onyx as it stared back at her.

"Get *out* of here," she hissed for emphasis.

She was yelling at birds. What was next?

She was about to close the door and go back inside her rooms when she heard his voice, too quiet to be heard by anyone else.

"Anova."

Breath stuck in her lungs, and her heartbeat pulverized her body.

It sounded like ... him. Hellmyr.

She could feel Della and Maris staring at the back of her, waiting for an explanation. The crow pecked at the railing it perched on.

"Tell them to leave," it muttered. It brought its head back up again. "I'll speak to you alone."

"Why should I listen to you?" she whispered, still not sure why she was masking his presence already.

She needed to get to Cadmus and tell him that their barriers concealing the estate had been infiltrated.

How? Does this mean that others can get through, too?

In the body of the crow, Hellmyr finally responded. His one-visible eye gleamed. "Do you really want to find out the consequences, Anova?"

Consequences. What's going on?

Anova stepped back. No, she didn't.

Her decision was instant. She walked back inside her rooms, shutting the door behind her to conceal what had happened outside as well as she could.

"What was that?" Maris said. She narrowed her eyes on her. "Are you alright?"

"I'm fine," Anova said. "I ... think I'll take a few minutes before breakfast in my bathing chambers. I'll meet you downstairs."

Her two friends shared a look that was barely a look. Likely, they hadn't intended her to see it, but there was much less that slipped her notice as a fae than it once had as a human.

But what could they say? Was this behavior stranger than the behavior she'd demonstrated lately, such as her demanding to cover mirrors and windows for fear of her reflection?

"Alright, Anova." Maris pursed her lips. "But remember what we said," she said pointedly as they left.

"Just tell us when we need to cover our ears tonight," Della inserted before Maris shoved her out the door.

With a smile, Anova promised them she would, and they were gone. She turned to open the door to her balcony again and stopped.

It was open already.

Anova stepped back. Panic threaded her veins like a heady drug. But the smell hit her before she could stop it.

It was the smell of the woods. Pine. Crushed leaves. The crow's body reeked of it.

He sat on the top of her wooden headboard, staring back at her. He was as still as a statue.

"Why—You're—" Anova stopped. There were too many questions to ask here, so her brain settled on the one it deemed the most important. "How did you get inside?"

Hellmyr—as the crow—threw his head back and barked a strange chittering sound that she'd never realized crows could make. He was laughing at her.

"Darling. You don't even lock your doors." He stopped and stared at her with those onyx eyes again. "One would think you're secretly hoping to be spirited off by strange fae males."

Her cheeks heated from her growing rage. Hellmyr knew how to activate it inside her like no one else could.

It was definitely him behind the unblinking, patronizing gaze of this bird.

"But your neck," Anova said in a falsely sweet voice as she stepped towards him. She showed her teeth in a fake smile. "It's so breakable in this form."

Hellmyr—or perhaps it was really the bird this time—crowed at her.

If birds could smirk, she would have sworn he was now. "I've been breaking Cadmus's charms for years. Trust me when I say that it wasn't a difficult feat for me. Even if his magic kept me from walking inside and dealing with him as myself." His head cocked to one side as he looked at her.

"What do you want, then?" Anova demanded.

"Only my throne, my queen, and the loyalty of the entire realm—and beyond it." He picked at his feathers as he said it.

Lovely. He hadn't gained any humility.

He's always been more grackle than fae, though, she thought to herself. Greedy and ambitious. This was probably the truest version of him that she'd seen.

Anova swallowed as she considered what he was really asking beneath all the posturing.

The last time she'd seen him, she'd been clinging to life. And he'd blamed himself for nearly burning her alive.

Even if he'd believed her to be dead at the time. Even if she'd already relieved him of the guilt.

When she spoke at last, her voice was deadly quiet. "It's done, Hellmyr." She looked away from him. "You already know my answer."

What went unsaid was the part of her that bled for his situation.

Doomed to love her—doomed to love someone already in love with another.

Doomed from the start.

He cocked his head to the other side as he said, "But you don't even know what's in it for you this time."

Anova stared at him. What was he talking about? "What are you getting at?" she said carefully.

He hopped off her headboard and landed on top of the swath of covers and blankets across her bed. His head ducked low to the covers, seeming to sniff them.

Pervert.

She was about to wave him away from her bed when he jerked his head up to her suddenly. He looked as if he were smiling again.

"I've caught a human pet just for you. Become my queen again ... And he'll be yours."

CHAPTER FIVE

"**I**'m coming with you," Anova insisted.

"You're exactly what he wants. What happens after he gets you?" Cadmus said.

The crow was still locked in her room, though it was no longer Hellmyr. He'd reversed the magic the instant she'd trapped him in her bedroom.

He was gone from the bird. They'd have to release it soon, but that felt too much like giving up.

Cadmus was stalking through the house, checking the magic concealing the estate.

Anova wouldn't be left behind. It was only his male ego talking, and they both knew it.

Her best friend's life was in danger. She couldn't leave him in the hands of Hellmyr.

But you left him to the streets when you didn't come back to Irbess to pay your debts.

Anova wanted to scream at the voices inside and outside her head.

"I can't lose you again," he said. "Not so soon."

Cadmus's words were soft, but his expression was hard. He didn't stop as he flew from door to door, checking the magic spelling them shut.

Anova beat him to the next one with her arms crossed before her chest.

"This is what he wants," she said. "Us fighting. Divided."

She stretched a hand towards his chest. He wasn't Hellmyr—possessive and unsure. She would remind him of that.

Anova held her chin up. "We're stronger together."

Something in Cadmus's gaze changed. His shoulders slumped forward. His eyes lingered on her face.

"For not the first time, you're right," he whispered in her ear.

Anova pulled him tight against her, and Cadmus threaded his hands through her hair.

His lips hovered at her forehead. She felt him smile.

"How did I trick you into this affair with me?" After a second—too fast for her to answer him—he responded to himself, "No. Don't say it. It would break my hold on you."

Anova pressed a kiss to his lips, full and consuming. This wasn't like it'd been in his bedroom. This kiss was for them both.

Cadmus pulled away from her, still holding her in his arms. His breath tickled her neck when he sighed.

"Is it ever tiring getting exactly what you want?"

"Never," she said.

Cadmus shook his head. "We need to go soon. I've asked Nerium to hold off on entering the archives—"

"He's there already?" Anova's heart jumped into her throat.

Cadmus smiled. "He tends to be fast."

Anova itched to ask him to use some of his magic so she could speak to him—to figure out where Juras was being held—but she held herself back.

The three of them would be more capable of breaking him out together. There was no sense in endangering Nerium's life like that. Or that was what Cadmus had convinced her.

Juras, please hold on. I'm coming.

This was her fault, and she would fix her own mistakes.

And allowing Hellmyr to blackmail her was one of them. She would rectify that mistake soon, as well.

Anova and Cadmus started for the grounds beyond the estate. There was moonlight left to burn still, but they had a night of hard riding ahead of them if they wanted to catch up to Nerium by the next moonfall.

As soon as Cadmus unstoppered the bottle of silver liquid he held out, the creature appeared like a moth to flame. Although, as a butterfly, she might have taken offense to the comparison.

Viridia alighted on the edge of the glass, her mouthpart tasting the air as if in anticipation for the treat ahead of her.

"Hello again, friend," Anova murmured to her. Viridia's head moved towards her so her black-coal eyes met her gaze.

Viridia had been with Anova through some of her worst moments and, along with Juras, had even helped her escape her jail cell in Irbess.

They'd found her after moving their estate across Fae—or rather, Viridia had found them. After breakfast one evening, Anova had walked out to her balcony to find her there, her iridescent green wings fanning out and in slowly in a silent greeting.

From her first journey into Fae, Viridia had been fed fae magic to help them cross the Sorrelands to the Wolfsbane estate as a winged mount. Since fae magic only lasted the night, she'd safely returned to her normal size.

But, as Cadmus had explained, once a creature like her got a taste of moon magic, sometimes they refused to go back. The human world would taste and seem dull to them in comparison.

Cadmus's nose wrinkled. "What's that smell?"

Anova narrowed her eyes at him. Once, he'd mocked her for smelling like a human. She was about to bite back a reply when she realized something.

She smelled it, too. Something reeked of sweat, fish, and earth.

Humans, she realized.

Her heart throttled her throat.

Who was it? Why were they here?

The visions of the children that the previous High King had captured and kept in cages sprang to her mind. Were these more humans captured by the fae?

"Come out," she called to the woods around them. "We won't hurt you."

Anova made to step forward, but Cadmus grabbed her wrist. Before she could say anything to him, a whistle sang through the air.

He jerked her away by the arm just in time for an arrow to sink deep into the earth where Anova had been standing seconds before.

Her attention snapped to the trees around them. At once, Anova pulled free the sword she'd stashed at her waist. Behind her, Cadmus's hands filled with the glint of moon magic.

"Show yourself," he snarled at their unseen enemy.

Their response was to fire an assault of arrows upon them.

Her body knew what to do as it fell into the dance of deflecting their attacks. She protected Cadmus's backside while he did the same for her.

"We don't wish to fight you," she said over the sound of snapping bowstrings and metal hitting metal.

Cadmus caught her eye. Well, *one* of them didn't wish to fight. Anova wouldn't spill human blood unless it was absolutely necessary. Or unless it was Hinterfell's.

It was then that they came at them from the opposite side of the onslaught of arrows.

An ambush, Anova realized. Sweat slicked her shirt to her skin.

A small army of men descended upon them with venom written on their faces and in the way they attacked them with steel.

"Get the male," the one in front growled, a grizzled man that smelled too much like Irbess's docks.

Anova shoved herself in front of Cadmus. "Like I'll let you," she said through her teeth.

She'd fought their likes before. Now, she was trained better than she ever had been as a street urchin conning men out of trinkets in taverns.

Without losing her breath, she parried their steel with her own while Cadmus shielded them from the arrows that still rained down on them.

A thought wormed its way through her brain.

Who trained them? Where did these humans come from?

How are they here?

"Leave now while you still have your lives," she said to them, dodging a stab to her chest. "You shouldn't be here."

"Coming from you, that's rich."

Anova snapped her head in the direction she'd heard the voice, and sparks of fire met her. Flames licked the sword facing her, their greedy fingers tasting the air and searching for her. Heat washed over her exposed skin, and its light burned into her eyes. Her heart kicked alive in her chest as her body trembled with the memory.

Smoke filled her lungs and stung her eyes. She felt the heat boiling the air around her.

It was the memory of being burnt alive.

She needed to get out of the pyre. She needed to show them she wasn't dead yet.

Or she soon would be.

"Anova!"

When she heard Cadmus's voice, she startled. *I'm not there. I'm not there.*

"What in the hells are you?" said the witch.

Alys had lowered her flame-coated sword. Her eyes were wide, and her eyebrows were sharply angled over them as she took in Anova. She watched as the witch's gaze hovered over the obvious.

Her ears. Her face. The silhouette of her body under her clothes.

She took a step towards Anova. In a voice hardly loud enough to carry, the witch said, "What did they do to you?"

Anova's heart sounded too loud that even the humans would have been able to hear it, she feared.

"What did they do to you?"

But that wasn't the question. The real one was, *what have I done to myself?*

Anova stared at the witch she'd called a friend once. Confidant. Accomplice. Enemy.

All that came out of Anova's mouth was, "What the hell are you doing here?"

CHAPTER SIX

"I'm here to prevent a war," Alys said.

"A war?" Anova spat out the word. "You're the only one talking of a war."

Alys looked at her archly. "It's been some time since you were in Irbess, hasn't it?"

Anova stared back at her. Her words had clearly been crafted to rile her. But as her eyes passed over the faces of the scores of humans she'd brought with her, Anova couldn't help but wonder.

What the hell is going on here?

There was too much she didn't know, and she needed to fix that *immediately.*

She's lied before, Anova reminded herself.

She narrowed her eyes on Alys. "How do I know you're not the one fanning the flames?"

Alys smiled at her, though it wasn't benevolent. "And what if I am partially to blame?" Her smile faded. "For decades, fae have stolen us. Enchanted us. Hunted us for sport." Alys's gaze was as cold as sea-wash in a storm. "You know the truth I speak."

Flames jumped along her sword, and Alys walked some steps nearer her. "*That's* why I'm here, Anova."

"Anova! Now!" Cadmus's voice reverberated around the wooded area.

She didn't have to speak with Cadmus to know his plan. They'd been here before, too many times to number.

Too many foes. Not enough allies.

But that was what worked in their favor.

The men were too slow. He shoved himself before her, shielding her from Alys's flames. Cadmus knew she could deal with men. But fire …

That was another matter altogether.

Anova felt the caged animal rouse from its slumber as she called to the power sleeping in the blood crown. She'd have to be careful not to kill them, but she could do it.

As the heat built in her hands, she lunged to create a path for them. It was then that she heard Alys's voice behind her.

"If you value his life, you won't do that."

Anova turned in time to see a strange sight. The moonlight magic in Cadmus's hands flickered and died. In the same moment, one of the men shoved a kick to the back of his legs. The flames along Alys's sword puffed out, though it still clearly hummed with heat as she held the edge of it near his throat. He'd landed on his knees and froze before his skin was scorched and then cut by her blade.

Somehow, Alys had done it.

But he was fast. Too fast for them.

He ducked out of Alys's hold before she could shove the blade into his throat and rolled from them. Anova twisted, letting the power of the crown come to her fingertips.

Even if it made her a monster, she ached to let it entirely free. To consume. To destroy all these men—and then the witch, too.

It was then that the nearest of her foes lunged for her. Except, he didn't try to hit her or slash at her with his weapon.

Something flew into her face. Anova stumbled, coughing, as she felt the magic that had invaded her body wane until it was near-silent. Her knees faltered as the coughs racked her lungs further. The taste of it landed on her tongue, and she realized.

Salt.

A boot slammed into her back, and she choked on the pain and weakness staking their territories within her.

"That's enough," Cadmus growled.

Anova glanced up and saw that Cadmus had been similarly disarmed of his magic and weapons, too.

"Anova may say what she wants of not wishing to kill you, but make no mistake. I harbor none of the same inclinations for any who touch her again," he said through his teeth.

"Hm. Quite a loyal one," Alys observed with raised eyebrows. "It makes sense, given what Anova sacrificed for you. You should feel grateful."

She heard what went unsaid in the witch's words.

And the sacrifice I promised but failed to give to Alys.

The end of the blood crown.

But instead of leaving the crown in the realm of the dead, she'd used it to survive trading her human life for Cadmus's soul.

As if it knew it was being thought about, the blood crown felt as if it tightened around her cranium. It hadn't hurt her as it had when she was a human, but she could never fully forget about its presence when it did such things.

Or, maybe she'd gone fully crazy.

Anova glared at Alys. She needed to end this before it escalated further. "Fine," she said. "You have my attention, Witch. What do you want? If this isn't war, then what is it?"

Alys didn't respond to her. Instead, she looked to the man nearest Cadmus. "Secure him," she ordered.

Anova lurched forward. "Don't you dare touch—"

"Salt," was all she said.

A cloth shoved against her lips, and granules poured into her mouth. She choked against the mountain of salt forced into her mouth, though she kept fighting, blindly attacking the man who had dared touch her.

"Enough," Alys said.

Anova spat what she could on the ground, and though the world swirled around her and her magic was gone for the moment, she kept herself upright. The grizzled man who had forced salt into her mouth stepped away from her.

It could only mean one thing.

Her gaze darted to Cadmus. He was bleeding from a cut along his cheek, and he'd been shoved to his knees once more. His hands had been hastily bound behind his back. Her eyebrows came together. Had they forced more salt at him, too?

He looked as dazed as she felt. It sobered her.

What happened? How had they gotten the better of him?

Alys must have seen the fight in her eyes kindled at seeing Cadmus hurt because she looked at her warily before approaching her. "Anova, listen to me for a moment. I'm not here so we can hurt each other."

"Speak for yourself," Anova said. Any lingering feelings of comradery or feeling as if she owed Alys something had all dried up.

The witch continued as if she hadn't heard that. "What I'm asking is something we both want. But I need to know it will get done. There's too much at stake here."

Alys paused in her speech, and Anova wondered at the expression on her face. It was almost regret. Or perhaps hesitation?

"There are more of us," she said to Anova finally. "We found the entrance to your manor tonight when you left it."

A cold dread gripped her stomach, and she felt as if she spun on a spider's web. It was all too clear what Alys meant. Or rather, who.

Della. Maris.

She wouldn't dare involve them.

"We are not the fae," Alys said. "We are not conquerors. We are angry, certainly. But not unreasonable. Or *cruel*."

And somehow, Anova suddenly knew what this was all about.

"Hellmyr," Anova whispered.

Alys's brown eyes glimmered in the darkness, and despite what she'd said, she seemed exactly like the fae in that moment.

Entirely too sure of what she wanted—and tempted to madness by almost having it.

"Get him to me. This is what I need."

"Why? What do you want with him?" Anova said. She didn't like how her voice sounded. She feared looking at Cadmus in that moment—to see what may have been written on his face from her words.

"Someone must answer for it," Alys said, her teeth bared. "The crimes that your people have committed."

Your people.

Anova wanted to say something to that, but she couldn't. She would have looked the fool in front of all these humans, arguing about what she was when she'd nearly killed them with magic forbidden to humans.

"You want revenge," Anova countered.

"Yes, well. Obviously, I want—"

She interrupted Alys to clarify. "For her. Your mother."

It was too plain to see, and to say she was here for any other reason was a blatant lie.

Alys stared back at her, and an uncomfortable silence crawled between them.

When she spoke again, her voice was much more measured. "Something has to change, Anova. You're aware of that. Whether that's accomplished by negotiations between humans and fae or any other method matters less to me than the fact that the end is the same. Humans can't be made the target anymore."

Anova watched the girl before her.

At one time, she would have had done nothing but agree with Alys's words. And she still agreed with her, at least in principle.

Her mother, too, had been murdered by fae who'd wanted to toy with humans because they were the *weaker species*.

In the end, she was still human inside.

Finally, Anova looked to where Cadmus was still bound. She wouldn't leave him here, and she was about to say that, when he caught her eye.

His lips moved too fast for any of the others to read, or so she hoped.

"Go. Get Nerium."

To cover up the fact that they'd communicated, Anova darted towards Alys suddenly. All eyes moved to her. The witch looked on the verge of calling flames to her weapon again, but she kept it by her side for the moment.

"You can't touch him. Or the deal's off. Or *any* of them, Alys."

Alys's gaze was steady on her. "Get him to me before the next moon."

CHAPTER SEVEN

Anova leaned into Viridia as they cleared the tops of the trees. There's been a sliver of moon magic left in the vial, just enough for the butterfly to grow big enough to carry Anova while they flew.

But day was breaking. She knew it when they lost altitude enough to skim the branches below her, and the tops of the trees scraped at her legs. Below her, Viridia's body changed once more, and Anova fought to keep her grip on her.

"This is it," Anova said through her teeth. She shifted her weight as Viridia became even smaller than a calf. She gave one more peek below her to confirm there was more than a dead drop below them and told her companion, "We fall here!"

If she could have laughed, she would've. She'd said it like it was a decision when the truth was, they'd lost the magic to go on.

When she slipped from Viridia, Anova spread her hands before her as the branches below them rushed to meet her. Wind ripped at her clothes and hair, and she called on the power inside the crown to shield them from further physical harm from falling.

But it didn't work. Anova didn't soften the blow before her; instead, the crown's magic destroyed the tree's topmost branches. Pieces of its wood creaked and fractured as Anova crashed through the upper reaches of the tree. Pain from her burnt skin burst inside her, and she swallowed her screams.

Splintered limbs scraped at her clothes and skin, and a bough slammed into her stomach, stopping her momentum.

Finally, Anova let loose the agony inside her. She slipped from the branch, but this time, she didn't have the fight to stop her fall. Something in her felt like it had broken with the branch.

Anova braced for the impact of the ground against her back.

Instead, the world slowed down around her. Strong, yet slender insectile limbs grasped her. They still fell, but when they hit the ground, Anova didn't break further.

A wordless groan left her lips, and she found she could barely move.

Somehow, even with the pain from her scraped and bleeding burnt skin, the pain in her abdomen was worse. Anova bit back the cries of pain that rose to her lips.

Dawn was flooding the woods around her. She wasn't in the Sorrelands anymore. She needed to move.

But she couldn't force herself to get up. As the air warmed from the sun's slow ascent, Viridia alighted on her nose. She'd fully transformed to her original size.

Her compound eyes seemed to linger on Anova's face in concern.

Anova breathed. No, she wasn't sure she was okay.

In fact, she was pretty sure she was anything but.

"What am I going to do?" she asked between her teeth.

She'd left behind Cadmus, Della, and Maris. Cadmus had wanted her to regroup with Nerium, but what then? While Anova and his fae manservant could attempt to fight back against Alys and her human army now that they knew what to expect, there was another complication.

Juras was on borrowed time.

Hellmyr had made himself perfectly clear. He called Juras a *pet*—and Anova remembered with clarity how Hellmyr reacted to her the first time they'd met. Hellmyr had nearly hunted her through the border woods for the fun of it.

If it seemed like her answer to him was no—well, then there'd be no use for the bait, would there?

Anova forced her body upright, swallowing the groans that wanted to leave her lips. After ensuring the crown was still attached to her—it had a way of securing itself to her head—she found the direction she knew Eastwoe palace to be in.

She needed to save Cadmus. Della. Maris. Juras.

Her breaths came too shallowly. Viridia landed in the nest that had become her hair tangled around the crown.

She needed to stop Alys and the humans. Didn't she?

For Alys, the ends justify the means, she reminded herself. Her teeth grinded against one another in her head when she thought of any of those men trying to touch Della and Maris.

In the silence of her thoughts, another concern returned to the surface of her mind.

There was also her little issue of her debt to the being known as Death.

As she scented something familiar on the air, Anova considered that there was perhaps a way to fix all she needed to with one act.

She looked to the new day above her.

Wait for me, Cadmus.

Please.

Nerium's eyes missed nothing.

They lingered on how she held herself, perhaps piecing together all the injuries she'd sustained when falling from the sky.

And yet, when she explained the situation with Alys and the humans occupying the Wolfsbane estate, Nerium didn't try to argue with her that what she was proposing was too dangerous.

"He won't be happy you're doing this," he murmured.

So, Nerium agrees with me, Anova noted with surprise. But, as much as Nerium liked her, she knew his highest priorities were Cadmus, Della, and Maris.

"I can't leave Juras behind. Cadmus will realize that," she told him.

She hoped it was true.

And, as much as Anova hated to admit it, she'd already proven herself fairly useless against the witch's tactics.

They needed more firepower. They needed the High King.

The question of how she was going to convince Hellmyr to do her a favor when he currently held the cards was something she'd have to figure out later.

Not all the cards, she reminded herself.

She swallowed. As the declared High King of Fae, Hellmyr had seized all the power and status he'd wanted.

But there was one thing left he hadn't been able to steal away.

Anova remembered Hellmyr's proposal and swallowed.

It won't come to that, she thought. All she had to do was manipulate him into driving the humans safely back into Irbess.

Which is something he should want to do anyway, she considered.

Nerium was nearly ready to ride back towards the Wolfsbane estate. Her hand flew to the creature still perched in her hair.

"Wait," she said. "You'll need to get back before something happens to Della and Maris. Since you still have some moonlight nectar spelled to transform her, you should take Viridia."

His eyes rested on her companion for a moment before he shook his head. "I'll find another creature for that." A rare smile flickered across the fae's face. "Keep her with you."

The levity dissolved from Nerium's face a moment later, mirroring Anova's own fluidly-changing emotions. The lives of their loved ones were at stake, so they couldn't afford to waste time.

"Anova," he said, his eyes narrowing at the corners. "Are you sure you can do this?"

"I have to." It was her only answer, and they both knew it.

"If he could, he would kill me for this." Nerium closed the small distance between them. Suddenly, Anova remembered that this fae was just as deadly with poisons and blades as Cadmus had been raised to be.

"And he will do worse to me if you're hurt," Nerium continued. "You can't allow yourself to ever be in a position of serious danger while you're there. Hellmyr is an ambitious little bastard, so he will do what he needs to in order to get what he wants. I don't think I have to tell you what he wants above all else."

Myself—tied to him in the most binding of fae ceremonies.

Anova nodded. Hellmyr hadn't murdered her for the blood crown the entire time she'd been his prisoner as a human.

She had to gamble that he still wouldn't. They had little other choice.

Besides, if there was one thing that she was good at, it was manipulating fae males.

She had to do it even if, this time, her heart was tangled up in it.

"Focus on getting yourself and the human out first," Nerium said. "If that proves to be impossible or unwise, you will slip to the High King information of the invasion. As you said, he will have little choice but to side with us."

Anova agreed with him verbally.

The problem with sides was that there were never just two.

CHAPTER EIGHT

As much as she hated to admit it, Anova didn't have the strength this time to sneak inside Eastwoe palace.

Besides, this was a different kind of breaking and entering.

This is for Juras and Cadmus and Della and Maris, she reminded herself. Too much rode on her for her to fail here.

After she promised Viridia that she would find her again soon, Anova walked to the front of his castle.

Something in the back of her head buzzed. It was the feeling she got when she accessed the part of her tied to the blood crown.

Fae guards lined the front, standing like gray sentinels in the early morning when most of Fae was sleeping. As soon as the breeze lifted behind her, carrying the smell of another fae to them, their heads and weapons raised at once.

She passed the last of Eastwoe's trees filled with will-o'-wisps and dangling moss, coming fully into view of his guards.

"Stop! You'll come no further," the one in front said.

The sun was angled above them. They had only their teeth and teethy weapons. Anova cracked her neck. Despite the pain surging through her from her injuries, she had a suspicion this next part would be enjoyable.

Some of these fae boys had held her at knife point last time.

Anova pushed the power from her hands, and it glowed a searing white as she did so.

Don't kill them. Focus.

She aimed her thoughts at creating a plume of magic—rather than focusing on a single point and creating a weapon out of it. Anova held on to while it grew like a bloated sun until she couldn't any longer.

The magic of the fae crown burst and slammed into their bodies, knocking them together and pummeling them into the ground. The excess magic from the crown continued, hitting the building's delicate exterior. Pieces of decorative stone goblins rained down on her. Anova ran through the smoke and rubble.

She was getting better. Even if some of the palace had been damaged. This was the truest breaking and entering she'd ever done.

Anova giggled at the thought. Maybe she was mad, but if this was madness, then it wasn't so bad.

At least she was funny when she was crazy.

The rest of his palace guards wouldn't be long now. No fae could sleep through that. She'd barely made it through the first section of the palace's halls when she heard him.

"I knew it was only a matter of time before you crawled back to me."

Fae bastard.

Anova turned to see Hellmyr, still much too harshly beautiful than any male had any right to be. His dark violet-black eyes held her gaze like a prison. His hair was unruly like he'd been roused from slumber.

Good, she thought with a measure of malice.

His eyes moved from the crown to her face as a new expression came across his features. "You've gotten ... powerful."

His strange response made her stomach flutter. He liked seeing her destroy things—even his own things, it seemed.

She had no time for his games. She had to know.

"Where is he? Tell me," she demanded.

Without thought, power gathered in her from the crown. If this fae had touched him, she would—

She heard his rabbit-paced heartbeat before she heard the rest of him.
Juras.

He rushed her, running past Hellmyr in the wide hall.

"Anova," he gasped.

Before she knew it, he was in her arms. He smelled good—like sea salt and hickory-lined attics and blueberry vanilla pastries.

He smelled like home.

"Are you okay? Did he hurt you?" she asked him in a single breath. She reluctantly allowed their embrace to break.

"I'm fine, but it—" Juras seemed to process her appearance for the first time. "Anova—"

Somehow, the fae king was still faster than she could process. Hellmyr was suddenly beside them, his hand under her chin.

"Afraid I'm not that kind of monster." With a light touch, he moved her face from side to side. His jaw tightened with a bare twitch as his eyes ran over the rest of her. Seeing, no doubt, the evidence of her new injuries. "But it looks like he is."

Anova pulled away from his touch as she glared up at him. "Cadmus didn't do this. You know that."

"He can't keep you protected?" he said in a soft yet deadly voice.

Her mouth went dry at that. It was a ridiculous conclusion.

"I'm fine. That should be enough," she said and angled her body between her best friend and the fae king. "I'm here for Juras. In exchange for my presence here, he's going free. As we discussed."

"*Nove,*" Juras protested behind her. She ignored him.

But Hellmyr only laughed at that. She felt her teeth grind against each other in her head.

"That's not quite what we discussed," Hellmyr corrected her. He made a *tutting* sound. "Besides, our little discussion at dear Cadmus's estate can't supersede a fae bargain."

Anova stared at him, waiting for his words to make sense. They never did. That's when she felt Juras fidgeting behind her. She turned to see his lips pressed tight against each other. His face was pale.

No. Gods, no.

Juras said, "He swore he was off to hunt you down and even kill you. I didn't—"

Hellmyr smiled, revealing pointed fae teeth. "I can be a very convincing monster."

Anova turned on the fae king. "You didn't. You conniving fae bastard. You didn't make him bargain with you, you—"

His grackle eyes brightened. "Who knew owning humans could be so profitable?"

The latent power sleeping in the crown shot through her like a drug. She would kill him. She would murder him right here in his own halls.

But as she stared him down, her mind provided her the answers she needed.

Trade him to Alys.

Save Cadmus.

Save Juras.

She had until the next full moon to do it, but she'd had less time before.

CHAPTER NINE

His fae servants had apparently cleaned the chambers she'd had when she'd last been here. Everything was as she'd remembered it—too many clothes were stuffed in the closets, every piece of furniture doubled as a lounge, and her windows had been barred to prevent outside entry. Or perhaps escape.

But it felt unnervingly empty without the others who had lived here, as well.

Della, Maris, Alys. Even Sera.

Anova shuddered when she thought of the young human servant. She'd been an agent for Lycasta's grand scheme to poison Anova with belladonna.

Anova would have died, the blood crown would have been passed on to another fae, and it would have made Cadmus's decision to let his brother live instead of himself an easy one.

Only, the last of those three had happened.

She let her head fall into her hands. There were too many fae bargains here. Too many moving pieces and yet all the pieces were far too delicate to manipulate carelessly. It was like trying to throw a ball of glass without shattering it.

"I'm sorry, Anova. I know they lie." Juras was pacing and shaking his head. He stopped and laughed harshly. "I should have known he was lying. It's all he did from the start."

Anova jerked her head up. "How? What happened?"

Juras's gray eyes reminded her of morning mist. Shifting, but not yet transparent enough to see through. "I'll tell you. If you tell me something."

She didn't have to ask. Seconds passed by like that, each of them staring at the other.

But something in her didn't want to break the illusion that things were as they'd always between them. That they were the same people they'd always been.

Juras took a step towards her. His voice was too quiet.

"Anova, I saw you die."

He took another step.

"And I helped you do it."

Anova stared at the floor. In no small part, she'd deceived him to her true purpose on that night. Juras had helped her kill the last tyrannical High King, but she hadn't told him that doing so was likely going to kill her, too.

He must have seen me succumb to the poison.

Cadmus had told her what had happened after Anova had poisoned the king by disguising herself as his lover, Letharia. Hellmyr had stabbed him through, but he'd been too late. The crown had already passed to a then-human Anova.

Cadmus had escaped the battle with a gravely injured Nerium. Some other fae had dragged her from the battle likely to kill her at the first opportunity.

In any case, Juras hadn't seen her wake.

And Anova hadn't gone back to Irbess for him, either. Of course he'd think her dead.

She moved her gaze back to his. Even before her mother had died, he'd been the one she'd been closest to in the entire world. So why was this so hard for her to say?

"I'm sorry, Juras."

It wasn't enough, but it was a start.

It was time to tell him everything.

Juras listened to her story without interruption. Even when she told him how she'd traded her humanity to save Cadmus's life. Or rather, how she'd traded it to bring his soul back after he'd sacrificed himself, thinking that his brother's life was worth more than his after assuming Anova to be dead.

Silence stretched through the room.

None of it was an excuse for allowing him to think her dead for so long. She wanted to buy him a blueberry swirl pastry to bribe him into forgiving her like she used to. She wanted to tell him how she'd gone looking for him in Irbess the night she'd found Alys, but she kept her mouth shut on both accounts.

Juras raised his gaze from where he'd sat down across the room from her in a plush fae-made chair.

He looked at her straight and said, "Those are certainly worse bargains than the one I made."

Anova darted to her feet. "Are they now?" She smiled a fake-sweet smile and said, "Am I the one indentured to a maniacally ambitious fae king?"

Juras mirrored her movement and came to his feet. "No, but at least I don't owe the fae lord of *death*."

Anova couldn't help it. She started laughing hard enough to make her abdomen hurt, but she couldn't stop. Juras had a way of doing that to her.

She'd always considered them cut of the same cloth. Both street rats and thieves that had cut their teeth on the predators living in their harbor city.

Juras had joined her unhinged laughter by then, so there was little hope of her laughs stopping soon. Tears rolled down her cheeks at their ridiculous predicaments.

For once, she didn't hear one of them approach.

The guard was inside their rooms already. She groaned internally that she'd forgotten to lock their doors.

But the look on his face was utterly worth it.

Well, if she scared a few of them, that wouldn't be so bad, would it? Maybe they'd even leave Juras alone.

"The High King requests your presence in his chambers, your Highness," he said when he could finally be heard over their dying laughter. Frown lines were still visible at the edges of his mouth.

Juras's head whipped to her. She wasn't sure if it was the *your Highness* part or the *his chambers* part that made him look at her so.

"Fine," she said when she could speak calmly again. "I'll be there."

She shared a look with Juras. At least it would be a good opportunity to discuss the terms of his bargain.

CHAPTER TEN

After reassuring Juras that she'd be fine alone with him, she still wasn't quite sure she would be.

He'd been the one to first teach her how to harness the magic in the blood crown. And now that evening had settled into early night, he had his magic back.

This is all for Cadmus and the others.

But how was she supposed to save them all?

She'd have to convince Hellmyr to go to Cadmus's estate on the full moon. She could tell him of the attack to goad him into going there, but that didn't mean he'd release Juras of his bargain. She needed to be sure of that beforehand.

But maybe she could be. She swallowed as the guards let her past and she pulled open the doors to his chambers.

"Anova. My little secret-keeper."

Anova's face grew unbearably hot. "Could you possibly put something on?" she growled, looking pointedly at the towel wrapped around his waist.

"Why would I? Assuming you stick to your word, you came here to return as my queen. As the king, one would naturally assume—"

"Stick to my word?" Anova had had enough of where that had been going. She felt her eyebrows lift. "You never said Juras would be *your pet* when I returned."

"What's mine could be yours," he murmured, enjoying the view that her figure made in the dress his servants had stuck her in.

"And I came here to have a civil conversation," she said between her teeth.

"Is that why you're calling to the blood crown's magic?" he asked, his eyes lingering on her hands that had balled into fists.

She stuffed them against her chest as she crossed her arms. Anova sat on the far end of the couch and tried not to look anywhere below his waist, thinly covered as it was.

"What are the exact terms of this bargain?" she asked.

Hellmyr arched his back in a stretch. "Simple. I won't harm you for any reason, and he remains one of my servants. This means he cannot leave the palace unless by my side or with my express permission. Additionally, if I give him a command, he must follow it."

Anova stared. He must have insinuated that he would have hunted her down otherwise.

A simple omission and assumption. He *had* been about to hunt her down—to talk to her. And it was reassuring that Hellmyr still wasn't trying to kill her for the blood crown, though she'd known that by now.

Anova leveled her sights on his face. She thought she knew his answer already, but she had to try.

"And what is it going to take to convince you to release Juras from this ridiculous bargain?"

An evil grin spread across his face. "You could become wedded to me."

I knew it. Still as power hungry as ever.

"So you can potentially have access to the blood crown, right?" Anova said archly. *And abuse it.*

Though no High King or Queen had ever proven it so, there was the possibility that any fae married to a fae in possession of the blood crown would become its second owner. Fae weddings under a full moon were the most binding of contracts. Even though fae often took multiple partners, it was rare for them to marry.

Hellmyr's grackle eyes held her there in a stare. "So you can become my queen forever. No matter who you share your bed with," he said as he moved towards her on the couch. Her heart shoved inside her throat. He stopped, lowering his mouth near her ear. "So you know you're mine."

Heat washed over her skin despite herself.

Out of everything she was willing to do, she couldn't do that. She couldn't risk spreading the rule of the blood crown. Not to the one most likely to exploit it for pure power.

So, she did the only thing she could.

Anova moved so her face was inches from his. As she did so, she pushed her hand against his chest where he couldn't fail to feel the fae-witch magic gathering there.

"Release him," she said in a whisper, "or it's your life."

She couldn't look away from his eyes, and his breath blew into her face when he spoke.

"Do it," he said. "Become my undoing as you were meant to."

Her jaw unclenched as she tried to make sense of his words. *No. No, he's bluffing.*

But her heart told her that he wasn't—or that he perhaps was willing to find out if she would. Her head felt too heavy.

Was it true? Did the curse placed on him by Alys's mother refer to her?

And what did that mean if it did?

She didn't move her hand from his chest when he tangled his hand in the strands of her hair, forcing her lips to his. It was as easy and effortless as tipping off the side of a cliff.

She should have blasted him now that he was vulnerable and distracted. She should have shoved him off her. Her body wanted other, traitorous things. It wanted him.

She wanted him.

No.

With a push, she got him off her. Hellmyr came away without comment, his eyes on her lips still. They flickered back to her eyes.

In subdued voice, he said, "I have an engagement tomorrow in Farstar. I want you to come with me." After a moment of silence, he added, "And the human. Should he want to."

Anova slid off the couch. She wondered why he didn't simply command them both by now. He could, as king.

The very last part of what he'd said occurred to her.

And the human.

For not the first time, she'd forgotten what she'd become. She turned, her fingers brushing through her hair past the crown. The guards would talk anyway, but she could try to look respectable.

As if he could sense the direction of her thoughts, he said, "You know. No matter what you look like, I feel the same. So, you shouldn't count on that to dissuade me."

Anova lingered at the door, wondering what she could say to that. Her hand shook as she was about to grab the handle.

"I'll go. And I'll ask if he wishes to go, too," she said and left.

CHAPTER ELEVEN

When Juras had asked how it had gone, Anova had omitted the bit about the curse and the feelings she may or may not have still felt for the wicked fae.

It did no good to speculate on them, not when her heart belonged to another.

She and Juras rode together on one of Hellmyr's mares through the frigid land of Farstar. He rode ahead of them on horseback, his kingsguard clustered around him. They hung tight to the two of them, as well, making it difficult for their conversation not to carry to all the fae.

Every so often, cold air nipped at her extremities, though his servants had forced coats of white fur on them and cold weather boots. She supposed that pets weren't very entertaining if they froze to death.

"So you know you're mine."

Anova clenched her teeth.

As fae bargains went, the one between Hellmyr and Juras was a fairly straightforward one. But she didn't like the addendum about how he could order Juras to do absolutely anything and how he'd be compelled to carry it out.

Then again, hadn't she traded a similar amount of leverage to the lord of death himself?

Which was worse?

Hellmyr hadn't asked her how she'd brought back Cadmus, which meant that he must have heard rumors or gathered intel on what had happened. But she reminded herself that he and his mother had likely planned on the crown turning her more or less fae from the start when they'd started to train her to use its powers.

And he hadn't bothered to inform her about that tidbit when he'd started training her. Though, at the time, she'd been dying from the blood crown's influence on her.

It had become a seamless part of her. No longer did it send tendrils of pain down her nerves. While it didn't scream at her in her heard when she removed it, she felt a nearly irresistible urge to return it to her person when she had to take it off.

Besides, it wasn't something one should leave lying about.

"You've gotten ... powerful."

Anova stopped thinking of him then. She was doing this all for Cadmus.

Hellmyr's fist punched the air in a signal for the rest of them to stop. The gates to his father's castle rose before them like black thorns growing towards a sky that constantly drifted down snowflakes. Being here didn't sit well with her as the memories from when they were last here came to mind.

She and Cadmus had been invited to the former High King's court ... only to be used as a demonstration why Fae should wage war on the human lands.

Too suddenly, Hellmyr was beside their horse. His dark hair and eyes stood out in a stark contrast to the snow-flecked land around them.

Anova reluctantly accepted his help dismounting from the mare, and as he did the same for Juras, Hellmyr murmured, "And my harem, of course."

Juras's ears reddened and his jaw set, but Anova bit out a response faster than he could. "You wish," she said through her teeth.

Hellmyr shrugged as he turned away. "As you say."

Anova stared daggers at the back of Hellmyr's head as they walked through the halls that his father had formerly thrown the most lavish of fae parties in.

She'd thought he'd abandoned the castle in Farstar on principle—to show to Fae that he wasn't the man who'd sired him and who had kept the realm in an oppressive grip.

So, what the hell was this all about?

As they passed through the halls, a variety of fae moved past them, their heads quickly tilting down in deference when they passed Hellmyr. It was strange. None of them seemed to be guards or more of his soldiers.

When they passed one fae with hair as white as snow pushing a cart of glass flasks and vials, Anova realized they were full of fae magic.

What's going on here?

Hellmyr stopped this one to speak with her for a moment. Anova stared at their lips, trying to read them as they spoke too quietly to hear otherwise, when she heard something else.

"He should have left the pets outside. This is no place for them."

Her gaze shot in the direction she'd heard the words, but all she saw were two fae that had already passed them many seconds ago in the halls.

Likely, Juras hadn't heard them. They were nearly at the entry doors.

It was then that she realized, though all the fae passing them showed deference to the king, their gazes had narrowed or their lips had pinched when they'd seen her and Juras trailing him.

Harem.

Anova bit into the tip of her tongue. She was going to have to talk to Hellmyr about the words he used for the two of them.

But isn't that what I am to him? A possession that he fights with Cadmus over?

Anova had to stop thinking on the words replaying over and over in her head. Juras shot her a questioning look, but they'd all stopped at last.

When they walked into the cavernous room where it had all happened, she shivered from the vile memories. Hellmyr looked at her and shed his coat, attempting to hand the feathered thing to her.

She shook her head at him. "I don't like it here," she said through clenched teeth.

For once, he seemed to sober from her words. Anova remembered that Hellmyr had been a pawn of his father back then—as the heir he hadn't known he'd had and the babe he hadn't killed. Those days, they'd all played parts they didn't relish.

Two fae approached from the other side of the room. The first, she recognized with a start.

The fae lady's yellow eyes felt like they pierced through Anova's core. Letharia didn't seem surprised at her being there—even though when she'd last seen the fae lady, Anova had been declared dead in a haze of belladonna poisoning.

And then there'd been the matter of her escape from Eastwoe palace when she'd freed the witch Alys in the process. Letharia's gaze passed from hers to Juras, at last settling on her son.

"Everything is ready," she said.

"Excellent," Hellmyr responded just as the other fae walked before them.

This one was at once delicately beautiful and yet, the muscles that peeked past their nearly transparent shirt were clear enough. Their hair was silver in the light and cut to their chin, and a pair of purple reflective earrings dangled from their ears.

But it was their eyes that arrested Anova. They were a startling blue, much bluer than those of any human's.

"Anova. A pleasure to see you yet live." Those shockingly blue eyes looked at the tips of her ears. "Though it appears the High King owes me a story."

"Iben," she breathed.

She remembered this fae now. They'd been one of the fae searching her and Cadmus at the previous High King's quarter moon fête.

Hellmyr's head tilted at an angle, and he crossed his arms. "Just get on with what the work I've hired you for, Iben."

He's turned this into some sort of research facility, Anova realized then. *But for what?*

Iben raised an eyebrow at Hellmyr's response but said, "Very well, your Highness."

They backed up several steps so that they were in the middle of the room, directly under the porthole. Moonlight streamed over their skin, coloring it to match their hair.

Iben stretched their hands before them as silver liquid was pulled from the air. She felt Juras tense next to her as fae magic spilled on the floor. He tugged her backward by the wrist, and she followed, eyeing the substance as it pooled in a fat puddle on the floor, nearly reaching their feet.

Her gaze flicked to Hellmyr. What was his angle?

Iben's intent with this magic wasn't yet clear. If it touched one of them, there was no way of knowing what it would do until it was too late. Their magic could poison them if that's what they wished, or the puddle could swallow them up like it was a hole in a thin layer of ice on a lake.

Suddenly, the liquid magic jumped into the air, seemingly of its own accord. It formed shapes and mass and structure until it became something more. It was at once both familiar and alien.

Bodies glistening of pure silver hung in the air, their feet tethered to the ground by the moonlight still spilled on the floor. Though they had the silhouettes of fae, their faces were featureless.

They were at once beautiful and haunting.

It was then that they began to waltz in circles around them. They'd moved into pairs, their silver hands morphing with the backs of their partners while they swirled about the room. As flecks of snow continued to fall, they absorbed into the liquid moonlight upon touching one of the ethereal non-fae beings.

Anova watched, spellbound. Surely this was how myths were made, spun from pure magic into life.

But as she watched, something strange started to happen.

The delicate details of their liquid bodies smoothed until they were less fae-seeming and more swirls of upright water. Legs and arms became silver water spouts.

It started with the sharp details of their hair strands and ended with the primordial puddle they'd formed from. Without exception, the strange non-beings evaporated until they were nothing but a silver mist rising to the porthole above her head.

Throughout it all, Iben hadn't moved from their position, their hands before them, open palms facing the moon above.

Iben opened their eyes, and their startling gaze landed on Hellmyr.

"There's nothing left," they said. "That's all."

Hellmyr's reaction confused her. "Are you sure? You didn't exhaust it earlier?"

This time, it was Letharia who answered him. "This is the first Iben's drawn it out in several nights."

Hellmyr's hands ran through his jaw-length hair. Anova stepped in the middle of the fae. It was time that someone—anyone—explained what was going on here.

"Exhaust what, exactly?" she demanded of Hellmyr.

But it was Iben who answered her. "The moon's store of magic. Or rather," they said, their lips pressing tight together, "its capacity of magic available for us to harvest from it."

Anova stared at Hellmyr as the pieces fell together, and she remembered a conversation they'd once had.

"At the quarter moon fête under the last High King, Leander said that these events were necessary for the flow of magic. That the High King had a part to play in returning the magic to the earth from the moon," she said.

"That's right," Hellmyr had responded. "The wearer of the blood crown typically does hold these celebrations at least once per month. It is said to restore the balance between what our kind take from the moon and what we give back."

Was this some sort of elaborate scheme of his?

Another piece of evidence to show that she needed to wed him? Was this an attempt to guilt her into staying by his side as High Queen and using the crown's magic to draw out the moon's power monthly?

Is this all one of his manipulations?

He'd wanted her to see this—invited her to it. She could see where this was leading.

Even if all these fae were telling the truth, she didn't savor the idea of being used by them.

Pets.

Anova crossed her arms before her chest. "I'm going to need more proof than this," she said to Hellmyr.

One of them—Letharia or Iben or perhaps another fae—had started to say something, but Hellmyr raised a palm to silence them. He didn't break his stare with her.

"And what would that be?" he said.

What would prove to her that the moon was truly running short of magic? An answer came to her then.

No matter what, she would relish this.

"Duel me," she said.

CHAPTER TWELVE

It was an echo of what he'd said to her when he'd found her all those nights ago on the Fae side of the barrier forests. Lost, alone, and hunted for the crown.

"Anova." Juras touched her shoulder and met her gaze.

He didn't have to say it. They knew each other too well.

Are you sure about this?

"I'll be safe," she said, a small smile coming to her lips, "because of your bargain."

In return for Juras's service to him, Hellmyr had vowed not to harm Anova. Or, at least, she'd interpreted it so.

She turned to Hellmyr. "Isn't that so?"

Hellmyr's gaze lingered briefly on Juras. "Yes. I promised that." When he spoke to her again, his predator-like gaze narrowed. "Dueling me will convince you of our situation, then?" His eyebrow arched. "How will I know when you are sufficiently convinced that our magic is running short?"

Ever the bargainer.

She tilted her head to one side. "You'll know. When I concede the fight and to your point." Her eyes passed over his form. "If you can make me, that is."

She smothered the smile that wanted to rise to her lips. Hellmyr's jaw ticked, though he smiled with his teeth at her.

This was a language she was fluent in: baiting fae bastards.

There was no way he could win this. Either he overpowered her with his magic—thereby proving that his claim of the moon's magic running thin was a hoax or at least an over-exaggeration on his part—or she flounced him, proving to him and the other fae here that she was more than a pet or a puppet queen.

And he had to do this all without actually hurting her.

The only way to play games with the fae is to make sure you win no matter the outcome.

Anova supposed this was part of who she was, now. She'd become as conniving a fae as the worst of them.

So be it, she thought.

Out loud, she said, "No weapons, other than those you call upon using the moon. I'll do the same except from the crown. Until one of us is incapacitated or gives up."

"This is unnecessary," Letharia cut in. Her eyes were the yellow of a viper's. "Either you accept the role required of you by the blood crown or you refuse it and allow disaster to come to Fae."

Before she could respond, Hellmyr moved so he faced her alone. "I agree to your terms." His palm shot out towards the others. "Give us space for this," he commanded.

She shed her outer layers over a form-fitting top and her riding pants. She didn't miss how his eyes passed over her form anew when it was more exposed like this, but she stuffed the feelings that rose from that into her aggression.

When the others had lined the walls of the room, Hellmyr started to circle her. Her heart galloped in her chest.

Part of her needed this. *Craved* it.

The volatility of it shocked her, but she couldn't deny the desire now, not when it was right in front of her like this.

"I may be bound by our bargain not to inflict damage on you. But you will know when I've bested you," Hellmyr vowed with a low voice.

His words nearly made her shiver again, but she suppressed it. It was time to show them all that she wasn't to be used. Possessed. Caged.

The magic gathered at her temples first, ready and aching to be released. Hellmyr's deft hands formed spears of crystal out of the moonlight where it fell. They certainly looked like they'd hurt if they hit her.

A new thought occurred to her then.

If she got hurt because of him, would that nullify the bargain that made Juras his servant?

I need to gather more information on fae bargains.

With her thoughts still scattered about her, his first volley came. His crystal spikes shot from his palms towards her, whistling through the air. The breath left her lungs as she dodged the projectiles, and she slid across the floor. The spikes crashed upon it seconds after her.

When they broke, the glass-like fragments dissolved into the air leaving small trails of smoke each. But he wasn't done, not by a long shot.

His dark eyes gleamed in the silver light. Two more crystal spikes hovered in the air above his hands. One by one, he hurled each at her midsection in an easy dodge.

He's holding back, she realized.

All she had to do was prove that he was lying somehow by goading him into using more magic than Iben had.

She needed to be ruthless like them. And in more ways than one.

Anova pushed the magic inside her body to a point on each of her palms. She formed the loose energy into a ball of crackling light. With a thrust, she threw it at Hellmyr's chest just as he tried forming more crystal spikes.

Hellmyr bent back to avoid it, and it dissolved before it could crash into the wall near Juras and the gathered fae watching. He hadn't even broken a sweat to do so, and the spike was already sailing towards her.

Anova growled low as she moved out of its way, causing Hellmyr to smirk.

"If this is too much, we can stop. There are other ways of proving my point."

"Why? I haven't even started yet," she responded.

Anova gathered more of the blood crown's magic in her hands, though this time, her thoughts bent in another direction for its form. Following her intent, it shaped itself into something she was more familiar with.

She gripped the sword in her hands. When the flurries from the wide window above came too close to it, they dissolved into water vapor on the air.

He'd waited for her, and she partially hated even that courtesy. But as soon as she dove for him, a new series of crystal spikes erupted from his palms.

Her feet didn't stop moving as she came for him. Anova used the sword of heat and searing light to block his projectiles, and they broke on contact with her magicked weapon.

Goad him into a true strike, she commanded herself.

Her body spun out of the way of his attack, a feint that Cadmus had trained her to spot early in her opponents. It brought them much closer than before.

When she was near enough to him that her words wouldn't carry to the others, she said in his ear, "If you can't subdue me, how could you hope to wed me?"

Hellmyr's eyes flashed at her as she pulled out of his reach at the last second. In a voice equally as low, he said, "I could make you mine, you know."

"I'd like to see you try," she said through her teeth.

Anova shoved the sword at his shoulder joint. Heat vibrated off it in waves.

He twisted out of the way, at the same time shoving a crystal spike at her upper half like he was trying to pin her down with them.

Something had changed. It no longer felt like they were dueling to prove or disprove a point.

Or, at least, they weren't dueling for the point they'd established beforehand.

Anova's heart danced like the bodies of ethereal fae had. Just one more well-timed strike would do it. She was certain of it.

Light burst behind her eyelids as more magic flowed through her hands to the sword.

She was going to force him to concede in front of them all. And not by a deficit in magic. The moon's energy filled the room like another witness.

She'd pretended to prepare for a strike to his side, but at the last draw of her breath, she pulled back and aimed for his shoulder on his dominant side.

When the magic of the blood crown slashed into him, it would be over.

With fae magic to repair him, it shouldn't permanently injure him but it would be far and away enough to end this fight. He'd have no choice but to surrender, and she'd prove that the moon had plenty of magic for any meddling fae tonight.

And she'd prove that she was more than what they thought her to be.

Be as they are. Sharper with words than with a blade, even.

If he dodged this, she would be much too open. She had to deliver as much a blow with her speech as she did with her attacks.

"I told you," she said through a smirk, "you don't have the power to make me yours." She swallowed. She was playing with fire.

This last part was too much. Too cruel.

But she said it anyway.

"You only have what makes you a monster—your bargains and tricks," she said.

She saw it in his eyes. He was thinking of the same thing she was when she'd said it.

Anova was talking about the curse the witch had placed on him for playing cruel tricks on humans as a child. And the fact that the-then High King had killed one of the last witches over it.

The curse that would haunt his days until he fell in love with a human like the ones he'd previously taunted.

And, by chance, the human who he'd fallen in love with happened to love another.

Her blow never landed.

Instead, a voice more beautiful than any other rang through the awful silence.

"You will be mine. I vow it."

CHAPTER THIRTEEN

One of his crystal spikes pierced through some loose fabric along her sleeve, sending her to the floor and pinning her there.

Anova struggled to free herself, on the verge of ripping her shirt apart just to get back to her feet.

What had happened? She'd been about to land the ending strike to this—

She heard the beautiful voice again, and her thoughts went curiously blank. Her muscles slackened.

"Anova," he said, his body crouched above hers. His index finger tugged her chin up so she faced him. His eyelashes brushed his skin as he looked down at her. "I need something from you."

His face was framed by a halo of moonlight. His firm and full lips twitched with a smile that she hoped was for her. How had she ever dared to fight with him?

"Anything," she breathed. She would do anything to keep him talking—even just looking at her.

A spark of resistance to all this erupted in the base of her skull where the magic of the blood crown usually slept.

No. Fight it, it bade her.

But why should she listen to it? She'd never trusted the blood crown before.

It had tried to kill her only recently.

"I need you to tell me something. I need you to be honest with me. Do you think you can do that?" he said.

"Of course," she promised.

Another voice—it didn't really matter who it belonged to, as it wasn't Hellmyr's—interrupted them.

"Stop this! She's not herself—"

"Be quiet," she commanded them.

That made another smile come to Hellmyr's lips. "You will listen to her," he said to that other person without taking his eyes off her. His next words for her, or so she hoped.

"I need you to tell me how you feel about me," he said.

Anova stared back. "There aren't the words to say." She admitted, "I … I think I *need* you."

Something glimmered in Hellmyr's eyes at that. Sounds of a struggle came to her ears. Who was fighting?

Before she could go on, he said, "What about before? When we were fighting? Surely you hated me then?" He rubbed his thumb along her bottom lip. "Be honest with me or I'll be very cross with you."

Get out of his spell. He's using you!

But she didn't care for the blood crown, so she ignored it again.

Anova's heart shoved into her throat. What should she say to him? Looking at him now, she was embarrassed and astonished that she could have ever tried to attack him.

And yet, she had.

She did as he commanded, thinking back to how she'd felt about him before these moments—*exactly* how.

"I didn't hate you," she admitted to him. Before he could think she was lying to him to please him, she added, "but I wanted to beat you in combat."

"What else is there?" Hellmyr asked patiently. His gaze smoldered more the longer she held it. "What else is it that you want?"

Anova thought of how his body lingered above hers at that moment. She wanted …

"I want you," she admitted in a breath.

"Anova!" The shout was cut off. Who was that?

Well, it didn't matter.

Hellmyr's eyes grew darker in the shadow. His voice was dangerously quiet.

"Would you like to prove it?" he asked. "After all that, I'm not sure I'm so convinced."

"Yes," she breathed. "Let me show you."

Anova's hand curled into his hair as she thought of how she was going to kiss him—and his entire body. Who care who saw it?

But the longer she looked into his eyes, the more she wondered what the hell she was doing. A line had formed between his eyebrows as he watched her back.

The spell.

Hellmyr's spell.

Suddenly, she felt like she couldn't breathe from anger.

A pair of hands crushed into Hellmyr's shoulders, ripping him from where he was crowding her on the ground.

"Get the *hell* off her," Juras snarled.

Impulsive ass decisions like these weren't his province like they usually seemed to be for Anova, but he'd made an exception this time.

His cheek stung from the smack one of his guards had given him from the hilt of a sword and the scrapes he'd won from their resulting scuffle, but he'd finally gotten free.

He'd had enough of watching his friend be ensorcelled by this fae bastard into kissing him. Anova hadn't exaggerated his vileness, and the thought of his bargain binding Juras to him made Juras physically ill.

But he couldn't think about that now. He had to get him off her if it was the last thing he did.

No matter what strange fae magic had given Anova those powers and those ears, she was still his best friend.

Surprise had given him the upper hand, Juras knew. He jerked Hellmyr from her in a single motion, throwing him by his shoulders in the other direction.

Anova stared up at him, seeming to finally realize what had been going on. He felt like he'd taken a punch to the gut. She looked dazed.

They can truly do anything they want, can't they, Juras realized.

He could see the justification behind her hate for them now; he'd always had, seeing as how one of them had killed her mother, but seeing their wickedness up close was another matter.

"*That* was not wise," he hissed behind Juras.

Juras spun on his feet to face the fae king.

Fae king, he thought for not the first time, *how the hell am I getting out of this?*

But he needed to project confidence. Rumors were that the fae could scent fear on the air like blood. If he was going to survive here, he'd best remember that.

Hellmyr's eyes flashed with anger like a cat's, and his teeth showed behind a snarl.

"You dare touch me, human? Or have you forgotten your place?" He cracked his neck like he was pretending to exude calm, but Juras could see the true anger behind his gaze.

"She was right. You are a monster," Juras said back to him. He couldn't help it—even knowing that the consequences were likely to hurt. It was bullshit. "Not because you're fae, either. But because of how you act," he said in his face.

He hadn't realized how close he'd gotten to the fae king.

Hellmyr said, "Monsters do what they want. Take what they want—damn the consequences." The fae smiled at him, though Juras could see that it was forced. "Perhaps you're about to find out what that means, my human servant."

Anova shoved herself in front of Juras before Hellmyr could do anything more.

She'd been a damned fool. The blood crown and what lingered of her human sensibilities had tried to convince her of the truth, but she hadn't wanted to hear it.

Juras had been fighting for her from the start. Those were the noises she'd heard in her delirium.

It was time she showed up and did the same.

The magic came to her grasp easily, like it had been watching and waiting for the moment it would be let gloriously free. This time, the magic of the blood crown formed a whip of light streaming through her hands.

She reared back and let the magic free in a searing strike aimed at his chest.

Hellmyr's hands made a gesture as if he was pulling magic from the air to form more of his crystalline weapons, but a strange thing happened.

Nothing appeared.

So, when her strike landed, slashing past the soft fabric of his clothes to the skin underneath, genuine shock surged to Hellmyr's face. When her whip returned to her hands, Anova saw miniscule blots of red underneath where she'd hit him.

Pale moonlight still framed him.

He tried again to pull silver liquid from the cold light that fell on them, but nothing happened. Hellmyr's gaze darted back to hers, his teeth bared.

Anova's knees felt weak.

It was true. All of it.

The moon was running short of magic for fae to possess. She glanced up at it for a bare second. It was heavy, just past quarter-full, and she knew that it had been waxing rather than waning.

This explained something else, too.

Cadmus's magic had failed during our fight with Alys. It was how she and her army had been able to best us—even on a night with bright moonlight.

Hellmyr said no more as his guards came to clean him up. Some drew their weapons, likely about to arrest either Juras or herself, when Hellmyr ordered them to put them away. Hate was clear as day in Letharia's gaze.

Iben merely watched her, saying nothing and helping no one.

Her stomach twisted into knots.

Fae needed her for this. Letharia had been right.

But the question was: did she want to save it?

CHAPTER FOURTEEN

I t had been days since they'd arrived back from Farstar. Anova felt stuck between what she wanted, what she knew was right, and what she knew would be good for the world.

She and Juras were safe for the moment, but that couldn't necessarily be said about her other loved ones. She cursed herself for not taking the chance to call on Viridia when she'd had the chance to during their journey to Farstar castle.

Anova needed to know that Cadmus was safe. That Nerium was protecting her friends. That Alys hadn't done anything rash since they'd spoken.

Judging by the moon calendar she kept pinned to the wall, she still had under short of two weeks. But she needed to finish this as soon as possible.

Hellmyr hadn't called on her to join him in his chambers since then, and they'd communicated exclusively through his servants. When one of them knocked on their door, Anova answered.

"What does he want?" Anova said without preamble.

The fae servant narrowed her eyes on Anova. "His Majesty requests your presence at dinner—"

"You can inform him we're eating in here again," Anova said archly.

But the servant wasn't done. She cleared her voice and added, "Privately, in his chambers. He wishes to discuss with you the terms of the human's bargain." Her cat-like eyes flitted to Juras for a half-second before returning to Anova.

Air left Anova's lungs. She fell back on the heels of her feet.

Juras was suddenly next to her. "You don't have to do this," he murmured.

After Farstar, it seemed he'd understood exactly how vile Hellmyr could be. And his obsession with owning people like they were prized objects.

She looked at him and lowered her voice. "There's a chance. I have to take it."

I have to get out us both free of Hellmyr.

And, ever since they'd arrived back from their journey into north Fae, a plan had been nascent in her mind.

A plan that would free them both from Hellmyr and one that would deal with the Alys problem. But she had to meet with Hellmyr in order for any of it to be possible.

And maybe even do more than that, if necessary. Anova swallowed, her hand firm on Juras's where it had pressed into her shoulder.

"I'll be there," she informed the fae servant.

The guards parted for her, and she pulled open the doors to his chambers. Her heart thundered with something that she wasn't sure was only anger.

He's dangerous. Too dangerous for such a position of power.

But was it possible? She needed to do something to fix this all.

Anova adjusted the neckline of the dress she wore. The top was made of layers of black tulle that was thick enough so that it was opaque. Mostly.

If she was going to bargain for Juras's freedom, she needed every weapon in her arsenal.

But what if he charms you again?

Her hands tensed into fists at the thought. She would be *no one's* puppet.

She'd been putty in his hands—and in front of them all. It was enough to make the blood crown's magic throb in the back of her skull.

Before her was a table laden with candles with long-burning flames, a roasted duck, glazed apples, and glasses of crystalline water.

She supposed, if magic was running thin as he'd said, it wouldn't be wise to extract some just to make her drunk on fae wine.

Or maybe he finally learned the lesson.

Heat washed over her anew as she smelled him. He had seemingly materialized behind her.

"You would be wise not to touch someone so casually before knowing whether they are your enemy," she grinded out as he lifted a piece of her hair to tuck it behind her ear.

Hellmyr's breath played on her skin when he spoke. "That's never meant much to you before," he purred.

"Maybe it does now," she said.

Anova turned to face him, the power from the crown surging inside her. He was suddenly behind her again, holding a chair out for her to sit in.

"My servants tell me you have barely eaten since we arrived back in Eastwoe. I will see you eat, at least."

Anova glared at him, wondering who had told on her habits and how closely they'd been watching her this entire time, but her stomach won the battle. She shoved herself in the seat.

She had to play this right, but so far, she was being far too emotional.

Hellmyr joined her on the other side of the table, his white shirt open to most of his chest.

Vain thing, she thought, trying not to linger on the sight.

Despite herself, she watched as his heartbeat flickered at his bare throat in a regular rhythm. If she concentrated hard enough, she thought she might be able to hear it.

I could use his tactics against him, she realized with a start.

But for what? She'd have to find his lies and use them to her advantage.

"Once you're done ogling me, you're free to eat," he said as he leaned back, somehow exposing more of his chest.

His smirk was infuriating. He continued talking. "Unless you came here for a reason other than for dinner."

Anova couldn't help the vitriol that crept into her voice. "And how do I know you haven't poisoned it?"

Hellmyr sobered, picked up his knife, and stabbed through one of the duck's thighs. He chewed, slowly, as he held her gaze and swallowed.

Anova averted her eyes. Maybe it was trite to say such a thing when he could charm her at any time, but she wasn't too keen on granting trust freely at the moment.

She started by slicing into one of the apples coated in a thick glaze flecked with cinnamon. Her stomach had started to squeeze itself, and this seemed the safest choice.

"Why?" she said, glancing at him.

He would know what she was asking.

Why did you do that in Farstar?

Perhaps they'd both gone farther than they should've. But what he'd done didn't compare to a little sparring.

It was then that she noticed a thin, pale line on his chest.

He found where she was looking. "The crown's magic tends to leave marks. It's different from ours," he said.

Anova stared down at her food.

I'm sorry, she said in her thoughts. But it didn't come out.

"I did it to prove it to you," he said finally. "Your feelings."

Anova's gaze darted up again. What the hell sort of excuse was that for enspelling her?

"I love Cadmus," she said.

Hellmyr's eyes were dark in the shadows of the room. "Then why aren't you with him now?"

Because I had to save Juras. Because coming here could free Cadmus and my friends.

But she couldn't say any of it. The wavering candlelight fell on his face, traveling along his sharp jawline.

"I am fated to you," he said. "From the moment I was cursed to the moment I wither to dust, I will still be fated to you."

CHAPTER FIFTEEN

Anova's stomach clenched, harder this time. *No. No.*

She had to say the words that made even her ill.

"I am no longer the human you fell in love with," she said as she held his gaze.

She heard it, then. It was a thunderous cascade of a heartbeat. And it wasn't hers this time.

Hellmyr, she thought. Her heart felt like it was being pinched.

"I don't care," he said, revealing his teeth as he said it.

Anova swallowed at that. But there was something else that stole her attention in that moment. As she watched the skin flickering at his throat, she realized something.

It wasn't timed to the heartbeat she'd heard seconds ago. When she focused on the rhythm of Hellmyr's, she could hear it distinctly from this other one.

Someone else was here. Possibly spying on them.

But Hellmyr's not reacting. That means he hasn't heard it or he knows about it already.

Either possibility didn't sit well with her. What was going on?

Anova picked at her food. In any case, she needed to cover up what she knew until she could straighten out this situation.

She'd been tricked in this palace before, and she couldn't easily forget it. And it was time to get down to why she was here.

"I need to know," Anova said. "Is it really happening? It's not a ruse or excuse for debauchery?"

Hellmyr studied her before answering. "You must feel it. The imbalance between the moon and this land. It taints the very air."

She watched his throat for any indication of a quickening heartbeat, but it was curiously steady.

Maybe he's just a psychopath and excessively good at lying.

Anova clenched her teeth. Nothing about this sat well with her.

First, there was an unknown party listening in to this conversation.

Second, Hellmyr was telling the truth—or at least, he considered it to be the truth.

And in her heart of hearts, Anova had to admit to herself that she had felt *something* different in the last few weeks. Whether Fae's apparent degradation was due to her inaction or whether it was all from Hellmyr's hold on the land, well, she hadn't entirely decided.

"What is your proposal?" she asked across from him.

Hellmyr smiled. "Join me in hosting a full moon fête like never before."

"And just what would that entail?" Anova needed to be careful when it came to him. She'd learned to be so. "Groveling at your feet while the rest of Fae drinks and trashes themselves around us?"

"Nothing so dramatic as that, unless that's what you want." The smile slipped from his face. "What I'm asking is simple. Give in to the moon madness—for one night."

She wasn't someone who typically *gave in* to anything. Her hands clenched into fists under the table.

She didn't like this.

For the moment, she ignored his *moon madness* suggestion. They could go mad all they wanted without her. In fact, the fae that she knew needed little help with that.

"We can't just invite all of Fae here." She shifted, her hand hovering over one of her hips where she'd been stabbed. "In case you forgot what happened at the last gathering like it."

His gaze was heavy on her. "Should you agree to this, this fête will be the first in which those participating will pledge themselves to you as their rightful queen."

Anova stared. Full moon or not, he was mad already.

"I am not marrying you at this fête," she said.

His gaze raked over her, seeming to say, *you will soon enough.*

But when he spoke, he said, "That's not necessary for them to recognize you as Fae's queen. You are the holder of the blood crown. Therefore, you are a queen." He leaned back again, allowing moonlight to follow the hard lines of his chest. "Of course, you'll be my queen in due time, but you are irrefutably a queen of Fae."

Anova breathed and allowed herself to think on what he'd proposed.

She didn't relish the idea of fae pledging themselves to her. And she suspected they'd feel the same.

But what if it means they stop seeing me as Hellmyr's pet?

Or as a target?

She swallowed drily. There was another reason she was doing this, and she'd do best to remember it.

Anova leaned forward. "If I agree to this, you're freeing him. Now. No tricks," she said.

Her heart felt like it stopped beating in the seconds before he answered.

Hellmyr looked at her face like he was measuring the emotions she knew were written there.

"Not yet. That will come when you marry me," he said. "But I will agree to this. On the night of the fête, I will allow myself and the human to respell the terms of our deal. There will still be a bargain, but we will reach a new consensus as to what the parameters are."

He arched an eyebrow at her. "Is that not fair?"

Fair isn't a word I would even speak in the same room as you, she thought but didn't say.

"I'm not one to say. I will need to speak to Juras about this," she decided to say.

After all, it was *his* freedom on the line.

After a few heartbeats, Hellmyr said, "Fine. But I will require an answer to my proposal within the night. Speaking of which," Hellmyr said and then paused. The skin around his eyes narrowed. "You traded your humanity to the lord of death, didn't you?"

Anova's stomach dropped like a stone.

"That doesn't concern you," she managed, though she felt blood rise inside her. Did fae blush in anger like humans did? She didn't know.

She didn't feel like them. Flawless. Cunning. Magical.

But she didn't feel like the human she'd once been.

Hellmyr's gaze lingered on what could be seen under the gauzy dress: her burn marks.

"When it comes to you, it concerns me," he responded.

Words fought to be said against her tight lips. The truth was, she needed help. There was a bargain that Hellmyr didn't know about—one much worse than the one he'd mentioned about her humanity. One that he would have laughed at her for agreeing to.

A near-unconditional one.

She could ask him for help. She could ask him for advice.

But when it came to him, there was always a cost. And she feared she already knew what it would be in this case.

Anova returned her attention back her plate just for an excuse to look away from his face.

Cadmus's voice was whisper-quiet. "Is this about what he feels for you?"

She was a coward. She'd not sent Viridia a message to Nerium because she feared what Cadmus would think when he learned that she'd gone back to him—even if it was to free him from Alys's army.

Cadmus. Her throat was too tight to respond.

Something else was happening, however. Suddenly, her stomach roiled like a boat on a turbulent sea. She felt bile rise on her throat.

Anova jumped to her feet, nearly knocking over the table from the force she'd expended. Hellmyr mirrored the movement.

"What's wrong?" he said. Light from his fae magic already played in his palms.

Anova shook her head. She was going to be sick.

She must have eaten too much too fast.

"I'll be fine," she managed to say, but then she clamped her teeth together. She didn't want to give the food an easy escape route—not in front of him.

Anova had already pushed her way through his guards when she realized something that made her feel even more dizzy and ill.

The thunderous heartbeat that wasn't hers or Hellmyr's—their apparent spy and the third member of their meeting—was coming with her as she ran through the halls.

It can't be.

It can't be.

CHAPTER SIXTEEN

I'm a damned fool.

Anova had locked herself in her and Juras's shared washroom. When her stomach had calmed enough for her to speak, she'd explained Hellmyr's proposed deal to him behind a locked door. She'd told him to respond however he'd like when Hellmyr sent a servant to retrieve their response.

Hellmyr had also sent fae healers to their rooms, but she'd refused them each until he seemed to get the idea that she didn't want them.

She'd tried to assure Juras that, though she was sick, she was fine.

Anova wasn't sure if he believed the lie.

Her body shook with weakness when she moved, but she had to know for sure. She had to know if this was happening to her.

Anova forced herself to walk on shaky feet until she got to the long-barred window set into the wall above the wide tub. With a shove, she slid open one side of the glass. While it wasn't enough space for her to haul herself out of—not that there was anything but a long fall on the other side—it was enough for someone very small to fit through.

Her throat stung from bile when she spoke. "Viridia?"

After a moment, Anova fell back against the cold porcelain of the tub. She hadn't yet run a bath for herself and was still in the clothes she'd worn to dinner with Hellmyr.

Anova feared what she would or wouldn't see under her clothes.

Don't be silly, she scolded herself, but she couldn't bring herself to do it. Not yet.

No. She needed to speak with someone first.

Anova's nausea returned when she considered that Hellmyr might have pieced it together already. She focused on her breathing to keep the tide of panic from swallowing her completely.

No. This is all impossible, she thought. There hadn't been enough time.

But I know next to nothing about fae physiology, save that fae and humans look *somewhat alike.*

And certainly nothing about …

Anova couldn't even think the word. She looked up.

A soft weight had landed on her nose. Viridia flexed her wings where she'd perched on Anova's face.

Despite how her body was feeling, Anova couldn't help the wide smile that spread across her face. She held one finger out for the butterfly. Viridia took her cue and climbed from her nose to her offered finger, her mouthpiece tasting the air as she did so.

"I know," she sighed to her. "I'm sure I smell. I'm sorry."

The butterfly's wings twitched like that hadn't been what she meant. She rested her body against Anova's skin, and Anova's heart calmed a little at the gesture.

"I missed you, too," she said to the insect. "I'm sorry I haven't called on you sooner." She bit her lip. She was being an ass again by only calling on friends when she needed something.

But this time, no one else could do what Viridia could.

"Could you find someone for me? I need to track down a moth," she said.

Viridia flexed her wings, her black compound eyes seeming to sparkle in the limited light.

Anova was sure she didn't deserve friends like these.

Anova woke with a start. Darkness still invaded their wash chambers, but she was certain something had forced her into wakefulness.

The feeling was like a fly sitting on top of her head. She blinked and looked to the window. Something was coming.

It was then that she saw a flurry of colors and wings tangled together. The mass toppled over the other side of her window, landing on the bottom of the dry porcelain near her feet.

She could tell by the vivid green of her wings that one of the creatures was Viridia.

"That's enough fighting," Anova said, trying to pry the two winged insects apart. "You're not hurting her on my watch," she told the tiger moth as she pulled it freely from where its limbs had been on the butterfly.

She could have sworn Viridia was glaring at the moth. She sat perched on the edge of the tub, her wings twitching with agitation.

"Maybe if you hadn't have sent her after me like your bloodhound, then I wouldn't have needed to defend myself so vehemently," said the moth in a haughty voice.

Anova laughed. She couldn't help herself.

It was all too ridiculous. In the body of one of her moths, Lycasta glared at her from the bottom of the tub. Even if her voice hadn't told Anova that it was really her, there was no mistaking that glare.

"Stupid human," the moth muttered as it shot back up into the air and towards the open window.

Anova slammed the window shut before she could escape. The laughter died on her lips, and her stomach clenched at what Lycasta had called her.

"Nope. Wrong on both," Anova bit back, parting her hair to show one of her ears.

Lycasta fanned her wings out, exposing the eerie pattern on them as she spoke through the moth's body. "Oh, don't think I haven't heard. You may look like us physically, but who you really are is another matter."

"Nice to see you, too, Lycasta," she said through clenched teeth.

"Is it?" The moth's eyes stared through her.

"What do you think?" Anova blurted despite her plan. "You got what you wanted, and Cadmus paid the price." Her voice came out in a harsh whisper.

Something in the fae lady's demeanor changed, and her voice fell quiet.

"Well. Leander didn't appreciate my methods."

Anova's jaw dropped when she realized.

He left her.

Of course, the fae lady had done all manner of terrible things to merit that. And yet, she was surprised to feel some measure of pity for her.

Tricking Cadmus into sacrificing his own life for his brother's had likely been the only way of making the spell permanent for Leander. The cost of restoring his life would have been too high otherwise.

It had been the only way for Lycasta to have him alive again.

And it had driven him from her entirely.

In her position, would I have done the same? Anova wondered. Her jaw tensed. There was a great deal of things she would never have stooped to in Lycasta's position.

But was that one of them?

Lycasta interrupted her thoughts as she flexed her wings tersely. "Unless you intend to torture me with more dull banter, I'll be leaving now."

"Not so fast," Anova said, catching the moth in the air. Until Anova opened the window once more, she had nowhere to go. But she wasn't about to risk her escaping Anova's sight while answers were so close at hand.

"You aren't going anywhere until you answer some questions," she added with a glare.

"Oh, what could you want?" Lycasta seethed through the moth's body. "According to the rumors and what I see here, you got everything. Isn't that enough?"

Anova ignored what she likely meant by *everything* and said, "I … need some clarification. It's not something I can openly ask about here."

That got Lycasta's attention. Anova bit the inside of her cheek.

Was she giving Lycasta more fuel to use against her? Was this wise?

Anova already knew the answer to that, but she needed some answers.

After a pause, Lycasta said, "What are you talking about?"

How could she say it to her? Lycasta had proven herself more than a silly romantic rival. She was the enemy.

But there was no one else she could turn to. Not for this.

When she spoke finally, Anova's voice was quiet.

"What is a fae pregnancy like?"

CHAPTER SEVENTEEN

Lycasta's moth eyes stared at her long and hard for several seconds.

What had she done? What had she admitted to her?

You don't know, Anova said to herself. *It might not …*

"You haven't," Lycasta said.

She'd been a fool to call on her. But she needed to know. Now.

"Just answer me," Anova bit out.

"It's not like how it is for humans, so pre-determined," she said eventually. "How long it lasts varies in length. But we know because all fae infants are born on a full moon. Sometimes, this only takes three months. Sometimes, twelve."

Anova went still.

"How do you know when?" she said after a moment.

"Sickness, nausea, pronounced moon madness," Lycasta listed with a twitch of one of her legs. "It starts one month in, but it gets worse just before."

"Pronounced?" Anova spat out. "What in the hell does that mean?"

"Don't blame me for your decisions," Lycasta snarled, openly glaring at the window and the promise of getting away from Anova. She twisted the moth's insectile body to look at her again. "It means you'll be more ... attuned to the moon. Or so I've heard it explained."

Anova sank against the cold surface of the empty tub and breathed shallowly as her mind raced through the facts.

She hadn't noticed the absence of her bleedings. Or, rather, she'd assumed the change had been from becoming *one of them.*

The back of her head smacked against the porcelain.

She had to speak with Cadmus. She had to free Juras.

And, according to Hellmyr, she had to save Fae.

Gods, there was so much she didn't know about her own body now.

Lycasta's voice was flat. "Which one?"

Her head jolted up at *that.* "Which do you think?" she snarled.

"Cadmus, then." A heartbeat passed, and Lycasta said, "You have to tell him."

"Of course—" Anova started to say.

"You will only have the one," Lycasta said, interrupting her. "Each fae pairing may mate once in their lifetimes." She tilted her head. "Assuming your body works like ours now."

Anova felt even more ill than she had before. She spoke the words that scared her, more than the words *fae pregnancy* had.

"And the blood crown?" Anova said. "Before, when I was human, it tried to kill me. Will it ..." She couldn't finish the thought.

Gods. What was going on?

Judging from her calculations, it had only been a few weeks. Maybe a month or so. It had happened after she'd made the deal with Rietvar to save Cadmus and accepted the crown's power while giving up her life as a human.

But her body had once been human. Would the blood crown react so violently to their child?

Child. The word made her heart race.

Cadmus.

"I don't know," Lycasta admitted. "But that's the extent of what I can explain for you." Her fan-like antennae twitched in apparent impatience. "So, I'll be leaving now. Before your mad fae king discovers you're full already with another fae's child."

Anova gritted her teeth, ready to bite out a fitting response to *that*, when she stopped herself.

There was something to Lycasta's demeanor that gave her pause. It was in the way she kept looking at the closed window and the way she spoke about Hellmyr.

Because, underneath the taunting and the insults, was a darker, more vulnerable emotion.

She's afraid of him, Anova realized. *That's why she's so anxious to get out. She's afraid Hellmyr will take his revenge on her for tricking him into thinking I was dead.*

A new plan had formed in her mind.

Lycasta had started to flutter to the closed window, but Anova grabbed the moth before she could make the distance. "I'm not done with you yet. I need you to deliver some correspondence."

The bug's legs writhed in her grasp, but Anova didn't let go. "I'm not your delivery pigeon," Lycasta said. "In fact, this whole farce has gotten old. I'm sure you're aware I can phase back into my body at any time, so why don't you quit your pathetic scheme and let us part ways *finally*?"

"But you haven't yet," Anova pointed out. "Or else you would have by now. I watched Hellmyr perform the same magic, and he phased out of the animal's body without having to go anywhere."

Lycasta stayed silent. It was time to make some more guesses.

"There's something wrong," Anova surmised. "You can't. You don't have the magic for that." The moon's magic was fading, after all. It wasn't a stretch to assume that it was affecting fae all over.

She wouldn't have stayed and answered my questions otherwise.

Anova narrowed her eyes at Lycasta. "You're stuck as a moth until sunrise."

The fae lady glared back at her until she spoke. "Your attack hound caught me at a bad time. I wasn't aware of just how much the moon's magic has waned for us because of your negligence."

Anova swallowed at her wording. She'd never wanted or meant to possess the blood crown, but that couldn't be helped now.

What mattered was that she had Lycasta in her power. And she needed something from her.

While she still held the moth that was Lycasta, Anova looked over to her butterfly friend. "Do you think you could keep an eye on her for another night or so?" she asked Viridia.

"I'm not doing your bidding—"

Anova smiled. "Hellmyr would be most interested to see you tonight. In fact, even if I let you go now, I think he would love to hear you're still within Fae's borders after all." With the knowledge that Leander had left her, she could afford to make one more stab in the dark.

"Especially seeing as the two of you have split. It would be easy to guess that Leander is still here, as well. I think I could convince the king to devote more resources to finding him, at least."

She could almost feel the rage lifting in a wave off Lycasta. "You will do no such thing. You will not harm him while I live."

Something in her voice made Anova pause. Her fingers dug into the hard porcelain, and she bit her tongue.

The realization that she would have said the same thing about Cadmus was not an easy blow to take.

Maybe I am becoming like them after all. Anova shuddered away the thought.

"Just do this, and we'll call your attempt on my life even after," Anova said in a dry voice. "All I need from you is to deliver one message. And then we'll be quit of each other. For good this time," she added.

The moth's head moved to look between Viridia and Anova, her gaze finally settling on the latter.

"Fine. But only for the sake of not seeing the two of you again."

Anova almost smiled at that. For once, the two of them agreed on something.

CHAPTER EIGHTEEN

Juras was done pacing. He'd waited for hours to hear more of an explanation from his best friend about what was going on.

She was sick, but it was worse than that, really. Like a wounded animal gone to hide in a den, she acted and looked as if she were dying.

Don't be dramatic, he scolded himself. He'd had enough of dramatics and Fae in general. He feared it was starting to affect him.

What did he say to her?

When he thought of him—his fae master—he couldn't control the searing anger that rose within him like heat from sun-baked earth. His hands trembled with it.

He'd had enough of the ass. He'd manipulated Juras's care for Anova just to bait her here. And he'd let himself be used.

And now, she was ill. If it was something of his doing, Juras vowed there would be hell to pay.

But what can you do against them? You're just a puny, powerless human pet in the fae king's gilded cage.

Even Anova's strong like them now.

Juras silenced these thoughts. They did him no good.

Just as he was about to knock on the door to their bathing chambers again, it swung open.

A pale Anova stumbled out. Juras caught her, barely.

"Anova, you're shaking," he said.

"I'm fine," she said. "I'm ..." She couldn't seem to complete the thought.

She looked at him, gripping his arms that held her. "Juras, I can't do it anymore. I can't seduce him. I can't convince him to free you. I'm so sorry. I can't even be in the same room with him anymore. It's too great a risk."

She was ... afraid. Juras straightened. "What are you talking about? What did he do?"

Anova shook her head. "It's not what he's done ... but what he will do. I can't let it happen. I can't let him know." She stared into his eyes. "He can't charm me again. I don't want to forget Cadmus. Not ever again."

"Tell me what's wrong," Juras said through a tight throat.

"There's been a complication." At the last word, Anova's voice cracked.

Juras looked at her. Her hand brushed against her abdomen, as if searching for something there.

Juras continued to stare at the area. It was hidden under the upper half of her tulle dress.

Fae bodies were typically slim, all lean muscle with very little roundness or softness. This contrasted with humans' bodies. Humans' faces, ears, and bodies had much more curve to them, even if lack of food stole much of the effect for those living in Irbess.

Though they'd dressed and briefly seen each other in the same quarters, as they had for much of their lives, Juras hadn't allowed his stare to linger on how her body had changed out of respect for their friendship and her privacy.

She was, and always would be, just Anova to him.

Of course, it was hard not to notice the burn scars across her skin and the way her face and ears had become sharp like a fae's. But she didn't seem so sharp here.

Though he was a man, and had never been that interested in the female body, growing up in a brothel had acquainted Juras with things that other men wouldn't know so well.

Such as how subtle an early—or even late—pregnancy could look.

He met her gaze. "How long?"

And by who? But he couldn't seem to get that part of the question out.

As if she knew what he really asked, she said, "Cadmus and I … it's been a few weeks. A month. But I don't know how long I have. It's different for fae."

She breathed. Juras allowed her to collect her thoughts and start again. "There's no way to tell when. It could be anywhere from a couple months from now to the better part of a year. All I know is that all of them are born on the full moon," she said.

"And you think it will be the same for you?" Juras said.

The same as a fae. One of them. But he left that part unsaid, as well.

Anova collapsed in the nearest chair, her head supported by her hands as she closed her eyes.

"I don't know," she admitted. "I don't even know if the blood crown will allow it, considering it previously tried to kill me as a human."

After a second, her head jerked up to look at him. "I can hear its heartbeat," she revealed. "I don't know if he has heard it yet, too. This is the first I've noticed it." Her eyes went back to the floor.

He didn't have to ask to know what she was thinking about: what Hellmyr would do when he found out.

Anova had said he'd claimed to be content if Anova had another lover—so long as she pledged herself to him in the most binding of fae contracts.

Juras wanted to snort. The asshole was about as willing to share his mates and land as a lion.

Inside his skull, his teeth grinded together. He was tired of being useless here. Powerless. And even dumb enough to make a bargain with a fae, binding him to this fae unless his best friend submitted herself to him.

Anova was right.

Hellmyr couldn't find out about this—not if Juras still hoped to get himself out of this damned bargain or if they hoped to ply him into helping them save Anova's fae boy and their friends.

He looked at Anova, his family in every way but by blood.

She'd risked her life to come save him from the situation he'd gotten himself stuck in.

From the very start, she'd infiltrated Fae in order to pay off both their debts and keep Juras from becoming Hinterfell's property upon his eighteenth birthday.

Well, it was time to repay the favor.

It was time to best the fae in the only way he could.

CHAPTER NINETEEN

He would trick the fae king.

Juras's heart jumped into his throat as he looked at himself in the mirror. He knew well that what he was preparing to attempt was insane.

But he was surrounded by unhinged, power-hungry fae. It was the only way to *be*, here.

And if he could fight for himself for once, then all the better. He would show them that humans weren't so weak as they thought.

He would save himself and Anova.

Juras had kept his plan from Anova, though the guilt ate at him. He knew she would have objected to it on the basis of his safety, but he had to try.

Anova had kept to her rooms for the past several days. He'd told the fae king's healers that it was a case of food sickness. How long that explanation would hold until he stormed in himself and demanded to see her remained to be seen.

No, Juras had to do something. He couldn't just wait here until the fête, twiddling his thumbs, acting like the human servant he was now, and hoping the fae king would release him from his bargain while Anova participated in some fae ritual.

Each day that passed was another that Hellmyr might discover their scheme or Anova's pregnancy.

He looked back to the floor-length mirror propped inside his room. His brown curls were as unruly as ever despite his attempts to control them. He had what he considered quite arresting gray eyes—well, for a male, at least.

He thought of Mikal at The Last Chance and nearly lost his nerve. Theirs had been a mutually beneficial relationship. Mikal had helped him secure housing after their attic room at Mara's had been compromised. And Juras had done his best to repay him in any way he could.

Mikal was sweet, though there'd never been anything beyond the physical with the two of them.

Before that, he'd had flings here and there. But never anything permanent, as necessitated by their lifestyle and profession as con artists.

It was good, then, that he had this type of experience—one in which the body got what it wanted at the expense of the heart.

Juras's fingers dug into the cold, smooth surface of the glass as he gripped it and looked down into it at the person staring back.

What the hell are you doing? This isn't some drunken ass in a tavern.

In their jobs, Anova had always been the bait. But he couldn't let her be the dangling piece of food anymore.

Get a hold of yourself. Lying comes naturally to you, remember?

It was what he repeated in his mind as he threw a loose shirt over his head and buttoned it to his chest. He was wearing the pants he'd been wearing when the conniving fae had abducted him in the Last Chance. It was one of the only things with him to remind him of who he really was—that he wasn't merely a human servant to the fae king.

He shoved the knife he'd stolen from one of his guards inside his waistband, careful to conceal it alongside his thigh as well as he could.

Juras waited until the fae guard outside their living quarters left to notify his relief. He'd been watching them since he'd been taken here, and most days, the ephemeral time between night's last gasp and the beginning of gray dawn was when the shifts ended for the palace's night staff.

He'd also observed that fae were more apt to sleep in the morning. They sometimes rose in the afternoon and evening, but most of them seemed not to want to waste the night to come by staying up into the early day.

And, he hypothesized, it was when they were weakest.

Juras moved like the wind through the palace's halls. He hadn't gotten to be a sneak-thief by being loud, though he knew that a fae's sense of hearing was much sharper than a human's. Even so, he reached the hall that ended in the king's chambers with his careful timing.

All he had to do was slip inside the doors to his rooms. Undoubtedly, he was sleeping by now. But it seemed his personal guards were much smarter about not leaving their posts unattended until their relief came.

He had to make his move before more of them came down this hall. He was hidden well enough in one of the palace's alcoves for now, but he couldn't stay here.

There was no getting out of it. He had to confront them directly.

His hand slipped into his pocket and pulled out the rolled parchment like the messages he had seen his servants carry on a nightly basis to and from his chambers.

He had to hope that the promise of hearing directly from Anova would be enough.

Juras breathed and left the alcove in a sprint down the hall. At the sudden movement and noise, his guards turned their weapons to train them on him.

"Who goes there?" The eyes of the guard nearest him flicked from what was in his hand to his face again. Her face was twisted in a mask of disdain when she saw that it was him.

"Don't come closer. These are the king's chambers," hissed the other one. Not only did he sound like a snake, but he looked like one, too, with green-yellow eyes that burst from the pupil outwards.

"Wait," added the snake-like one. "This one's one of his human pets." His eyes narrowed on Juras's form, lingering on what was visible underneath Juras's shirt. He licked his lips.

Juras tried not to flinch.

"I'm here to deliver a message to His Majesty," Juras said, barely managing to say the last two words instead of *fae asshole*. "It's concerning the wearer of the blood crown. I don't think he'd want you to get in the way of this."

"Is that so? Well, messengers don't sneak."

His voice came from behind Juras. He spun to see him striding down the hall in the direction he'd just come from. He was wearing a black jacket threaded with gold that hit the back of his legs and a crown that looked as if it'd been made to match Anova's.

A lazy smirk came to his lips when he met Juras's eyes.

His guard raised her voice. "Would you like me to deal with this one, Your Majesty?"

Juras felt like he'd been strapped up by his ankles. This wasn't going his way *at all*.

"I wasn't sneaking," he lied through his teeth.

When none of the fae said anything to that, his guard with the snake-like eyes stepped forward and pushed a blade against his back. Juras felt it softly pierce the fabric of his shirt.

Juras's jaw set as he looked at Hellmyr. "Do you wish to take chances when it comes to her wellbeing? I know she hasn't sent word to you this whole time."

Quick as the tongue of a flame, the fae king was there, too close to him. His eyes took him in as they narrowed.

"Your Majesty?" asked one of his guards.

He ignored them. When he spoke to Juras, his voice was a harsh whisper. "You've been given much too slack of a leash, my human servant."

In his eyes was every bit the loathing that Juras held for him.

"In fact," he continued, "you don't even properly realize you're leashed."

Before Juras could bite out a response to that, Hellmyr moved. In a blur, his hand reached towards Juras's hip. The fae pulled free Juras's stolen knife that had been tucked into his pants' waist.

At the sight of it, his other guard pulled out her weapon. "Assassin filth. Dare you to think you could hurt the king of Fae?" she hissed.

It was over now. He'd done a sufficient job of screwing himself and his chances of leaving this place.

Anova had told him about the human they'd kept locked in his dungeons because her existence threatened *his majesty*.

The feeling in the pit of his stomach told him the same fate would come for him in this gild-over-rot place.

But Hellmyr said to the guards surrounding them, "No." He exposed his teeth as he looked down on Juras. "I'd rather teach him a lesson. Why ruin a servant so soon? The human ones break so easily."

He felt he would be sick then and there. Heat flooded his body at his vile words. His plan had blown up—spectacularly so.

But he would show this fae no one owned him. He'd fought his whole life not to be owned.

It was a foolish thing to do, but it was the only thing left for him to try. His hand shot out to take back his stolen knife, but Hellmyr stopped him by grabbing his wrist. At once, he pinned both of Juras's hands behind his back, and he brought his mouth to Juras's ear.

"You wanted inside my chambers, did you? Then go."

The fae bastard then threw Juras through the doors.

CHAPTER TWENTY

Juras stumbled to the floor. Everything felt hot as a simmering rage boiled within him. He rose to his feet and spun around in one motion, abandoning his half-brained plan.

There was no way he could seduce this monster, no matter what he'd felt at The Last Chance between them.

He couldn't even do it for Anova.

"How did you know?" Juras spat.

"What's that?" The fae king dug under his nails with the tip of the knife he'd taken from Juras.

Juras threw the *note* from Anova on the floor between them. Of course it had been a farce, but he shouldn't have been able to foresee that. Dammit, this fae was supposed to be protective of her, wasn't he?

The knife he'd been holding shot through the paper, pinning it to the floor in a direct hit. Hellmyr looked over to him after he threw it.

"A guess," he said. "And now I know with certainty." He smiled, but it looked wrong.

Embarrassment surged through him. Juras bared his teeth at the fae. "What do you want?"

Hellmyr tutted. "Trying to sneak into *my* rooms and you ask me that?" He cocked an eyebrow at him. "But since you asked." He showed his teeth again. "The power to protect what is mine. A command of fear large enough to dissuade my enemies *and* allies from foolhardy acts. Good help."

The fae king's eyes scanned him from his shoes to his head, and Juras felt as if he were seeing him fully for the first time that night. They stopped at his open shirt.

"Run me a bath, servant," he said. "Hot as it goes."

His smirk could have melted ice.

Are you kidding me?

Suddenly, Hellmyr fell back against his low couch in the front room. When he didn't move, the fae added, "Or we could start with the pigsty in my bedroom." He opened one eye lazily. "That would earn your keep."

Juras kept his mouth shut and stalked in the other direction before he could get himself into worse trouble.

Maybe he wasn't going to be strung up in irons in his dungeons this time, but what exactly did *teaching him a lesson* entail?

Waiting on him hand and foot from dusk until dawn, likely.

He'd gotten himself into this mess and with nothing to show for it but exercises in humiliation directly from the fae king.

Juras entered his bathing chambers and nearly lost his balance at what he saw. He kept one hand on the threshold for support.

It was like a small coliseum. It was all so wasteful.

Juras doubted even the old human king over their lands had a bathroom that even somewhat rivaled this one. What was supposed to happen in a tub the size of a lake?

The answer was painfully obvious.

Probably an orgy.

He narrowed his eyes at the memory of what he'd called him and Anova in Farstar.

Harem.

These fae certainly thought a lot of themselves.

Juras crouched near one side of the pool. It was comprised of several tiers and depths, each bigger one overlapping the smaller one before it. Stairs descended at various levels.

He found the smallest—the pool the size of merely an oversized tub rather than a lake—and turned the faucets for the water lines.

It was the highest level, and it filled quickly with steaming water. The overflow ran to the next level below it in a lazy waterfall.

Wisps of steam rose to his face. A part of him longed to plunge himself inside if only to wade through the cleanest water he'd ever seen.

Through his life, he'd considered a bath a high luxury, and one he'd only ever gotten when he'd lived as a boy with his mother at the brothel.

"Good." When Juras twisted to look at him, Hellmyr flashed his teeth. "See? It isn't so hard to do my bidding."

Juras felt his teeth grind in his head. He'd appeared out of nowhere, his shirt already gone. His clothes had been piled next to him.

When he'd started to step out of his pants, Juras jerked his gaze away on instinct. He wasn't sure why he was giving him so much privacy when the bastard deserved so little. Perhaps it was because Juras knew he was taking every opportunity to show off to anyone and everyone.

In a way, he felt like this would annoy him. Juras smothered a smile at that.

"No longer curious to confirm your human rumors?" the fae said as Juras heard splashes.

Juras swallowed drily. He remembered just then what he'd said that night to Hellmyr before stabbing him in The Last Chance.

"I've always wondered." Juras cocked his head to one side as he looked at the fae crowding his personal space. "Is it true what they say about fae males?"

Juras's gaze flickered somewhere besides his face—leaving no question about what he meant. Or rather, where.

"Is that what you want me here for?" Juras said. "A captive audience to *ooh* and *aah* at it?"

Hellmyr leaned back. Water concealed him below his midriff, but Juras resisted staring for too long should the fae catch him at it. A line formed between his eyebrows, the only evidence of his annoyance.

Good. Maybe he'll tire of me, Juras considered.

Instead, he shrugged. "If you'd like that."

Juras said through his teeth, "And I don't suppose I can leave now, can I?"

"No. You haven't been taught your lesson yet. Not by far." Hellmyr angled his head back to look at something across the room. "No. I think I'll require some of that, though."

He jerked his chin at the polished stone block before a length of mirror. On a gilded platter rested a pile of grapes and assorted berries, ones as fat as he'd ever seen.

Juras walked over and grabbed the plate, his jaw already set for what was coming.

The fae king was intent on showing just how much a fool he'd been by attempting this. It was working.

But maybe there was an opportunity here for something more than humiliation.

He had to try, at least.

"Bring them to me," he said with his eyes still closed.

Juras snuck a glance at the pile of his clothes that he'd left behind. He wouldn't have left it ... Would he have?

"Now," the fae added.

Juras was forced to do as he bade. He had to do better than this.

"Here," he said between his teeth as he placed the plate on the floor within arm's reach. When one of Hellmyr's eyebrows rose on his face, he forced out, "Your Majesty."

But he was still looking at him. His head rested back, and his chest dripped with water as he stretched himself.

Unfortunately, it was true what they whispered about the fae's beauty. Juras hated the lines of muscle so clearly lining his bare skin, leading down paths he didn't dare look. He hated the smirk on his pouty lips about as much.

"It would be improper to feed myself when you're so readily available," Hellmyr observed.

Juras grabbed the biggest berry on the plate and imagined shoving it down his throat.

But he couldn't choke him on a fruit. Probably.

Instead, Juras brought the red berry to Hellmyr's mouth. Despite himself, he watched as it dropped inside, and he swallowed it. His eyes were suddenly open, seeming as vile and bright with malice as he'd ever seen them.

"I have an idea," Hellmyr said. "Until those are all gone, we're going to play a game."

Juras couldn't help himself. There was something about the fae bastard that made him slip easily. "What do you want from me? You could have had them kill me," he blurted.

It was too late to take back, now. It was possible that Juras had planted the idea new—that it hadn't been on the table yet and he'd just introduced it.

But he was tired of this. Of not knowing if he was being toyed with or if this was a test on whether or not he'd live past the night.

Flirt. Dance. Death. Threat.

It all blurred together with this fae.

Hellmyr was suddenly too serious. "An answer for an answer. What is it that you people say?" He pretended to think. "Fair's fair."

Juras narrowed his gaze. "What's your game, fae?"

He smiled. "Easy. I say something. You confirm or deny it."

"And ...?"

"That's it. And I'll do the same." Hellmyr shrugged. "To determine whether I lie or speak the truth is your job. Though I'll do the asking first."

CHAPTER TWENTY-ONE

A cloud of new steam rose from the fae king's bath. It couldn't be so easy as that, Juras reasoned. When it came to the fae, there was always a catch.

But what choice was there? He needed a distraction for his new plan.

"Fine," Juras said, agreeing to play Hellmyr's game.

Without hesitation, Hellmyr asked, "Did you come here to kill me?"

Juras's fingers squeezed the berry before he dropped it into the fae's mouth.

Does it count if I want to now?

"No," Juras admitted, though he was debating it.

Before Juras could dangle the grape above his mouth, Hellmyr's eyes shot open. His hand grabbed Juras's wrist in a tight vise.

A wicked smile spread across his face. "The truth. You surprise me more and more, human."

Juras jerked his hand back to his side. Despite his better judgment, he opened his mouth.

"How do you—"

Hellmyr's eyes gleamed. "You're not that hard to read."

It was then that Juras remembered something. Anova had told him about a habit that the fae king kept.

He can hear heartbeats. If it's clear enough, he can use that to guess a lie from a truth.

As if in response, his heartbeat kicked up the pace.

Hellmyr licked his lips. He seemed to have heard the difference. "Excited that I might lick your fingers instead? Or do you just hate me that much?" His dark eyes danced.

Juras's hands shook, so he shoved them down.

"You wish," he said.

Do better, he commanded himself. *He'll hear the difference.* His eyes briefly shot to the pile of the fae's clothes. *I have to keep calm if I'm going to pull this off.*

There was a possibility that his knife or another weapon was there.

Hellmyr had closed his eyes again as he savored a strawberry that Juras had fed him. "Have you come here to spy on me?"

Juras froze. It was closer to the truth than he would have liked.

He'd originally planned to seduce Hellmyr into altering their bargain—and maybe even distracting him from Anova for the next several days until they could escape this damned place together.

I have to learn to lie to him with more than words.

He was acting much too suspicious. He picked up another berry.

"I'm not a spy," Juras asserted.

Hellmyr opened his eyes. "But that's not what I asked, is it?"

The fae watched as Juras lowered the fruit to his lips. He sucked it in, locking his gaze with Juras's.

His heart wanted to thrash out of his chest. Juras breathed, trying to drive thoughts that weren't helping his case out of his mind.

Calm. He isn't going to kill you. Probably.

"What is it?" Juras spat out. "I told you my answer. No."

But Hellmyr's smile had an edge to it. "When I took you from that place that stank of ale and depressed humans ..."

Juras stiffened. Immediately, he knew what he was talking about.

The Last Chance.

The fae continued. "Well, I smelled something interesting." He paused as Juras shoved another grape at him, a vain effort to get him to stop talking.

His heart couldn't help it. It sped faster, listening to the damned fae's words.

"Not all of us have so refined a sense, especially when it comes to humans. In fact, many fae can't even discern between the smell of human and rabbit blood," Hellmyr continued, despite no prodding from Juras.

He paused. "So, few of us can smell things like human arousal." His eyelids lowered. "When I shoved you against that wall—just before you attacked me to try to get away—I thought I smelled something curious."

The strawberry's juices splattered in Juras's hand, and it ran between his fingers.

"It almost smelled like—"

"No. No, it didn't," Juras said between his teeth.

He should have made his move now to seduce him and keep him from discovering Anova's condition. But something darker had been uncovered within him.

Yes, something had raced through him when Hellmyr had touched him in that room. But it wasn't lust.

"It was hate," Juras said out loud. "You said it yourself—how the two can be so easily confused with another."

Hellmyr was silent. Finally.

He seemed to be thinking as he chewed and swallowed the fruit Juras had been forced to feed him. He tracked how the fae's throat moved.

"Hotter. Turn the water hotter," Hellmyr commanded in a low voice, staring straight ahead. Juras couldn't tell if perhaps he was watching the cascade of water flowing from one pool to the next or staring into nothing. Fae were difficult to read.

Juras's heart calmed.

Yes, that was right. He hated Hellmyr. That was why he'd acted like that. It'd been repulsive to have this fae so close to him—the one who had tricked and used him. The one who had hurt Anova.

As the steam formed fog-like clouds in the oversized bathing chamber, Hellmyr leaned further back, exposing more of his chest as he breathed steam and said nothing.

It was a welcome change.

Now was his chance. As he pretended to take his time selecting more fruit to feed him, Juras moved quickly. The pile of his clothes wasn't far away, but he knew fae had more sensitive ears than humans did.

There was only a small chance that he'd left the stolen knife here. But Juras had to take that chance.

His fingers rifled through the pile, moving aside his pants as his heartrate picked up. He wasn't finding it. It should have been here.

No. It was only ever a weak gamble.

Splashing reverberated through the space. Juras nearly leapt so that he was close to the platter of berries again.

Through the heavy steam, Juras saw as Hellmyr's eyes cut to him.

CHAPTER TWENTY-TWO

Had he seen Juras picking through his things? Or had his elevated heartrate tipped him off?

He had to distract this fae.

"I believe I'm owed a turn," Juras said as he crouched low enough to force the fruit to the fae's lips.

Juras couldn't read Hellmyr's face. This wasn't the wicked fae from before who wore a smile like a snake would've. At least that fae was one he understood.

"Then speak it," Hellmyr said under his breath after he chewed the offered fruit.

There was no promise of truth in this game, so he likely wasn't going to get it. But he needed something to keep Hellmyr's attention away from what he was attempting.

And, if he admitted it to himself, he needed to know *why*.

It had been eating him alive since Farstar.

"Why not kill me? She's isn't going to say yes. Clearly. This bargain hasn't gotten you what you wanted." Juras shut his trap before he could say more.

In his mind, he added more.

To a fae king intent on getting what he wants at all costs, I've proven useless. Worse than that. A liability. A spy.

But the answer was stupidly obvious.

Anova would've hated him for killing Juras.

Somehow, it made Juras even madder. It wasn't rational, justifiable anger. It wasn't even righteous.

But to be kept alive as a pet just because it would have angered the one that he was trying but failing to trick into a marriage ...

The fae king Hellmyr wasn't saying anything. Maybe he was thinking the same thing. Maybe he was reconsidering it.

In that moment, Juras noticed what he hadn't before.

Farther along the stone counter where the platter of berries had been was what looked to be a scattering of seeds on another plate. It seemed another of his servants had cut, cored his fruit, and left already.

And left behind a knife.

What he had to do came to Juras then. Hellmyr still wasn't speaking, so there was a chance that what Juras had said had somehow affected him. He needed to dig in more. Fortunately, Hellmyr had closed his eyes again.

To cover up the sound of him moving, Juras said, "And then there's my initial question. Why not let your guards take me to your dungeons? If you suspected *spying* and *murdering* from the start, why not let them kill me?" Juras's eyes shot to Hellmyr, but he hadn't moved at all. "Or is putting me in my place what you wanted all along, both in public and private?"

Hellmyr's heart hammered, but this time, it was from the words he spoke. He'd already pocketed the knife and made it back to the platter of fruit on it.

"Do you want me to let them," Hellmyr said. It sounded more like a statement than a question.

Juras realized, seconds later, that he was serious. He was at a loss for words. Of course he didn't want that.

But what did he want, really?

The answer was startling. It came to him like a flash of lightning in the night.

I want to control some part of my life again.

But the last part of the thought stuck with him. When had he last had control over his life in a real way? When he was conning assholes in taverns to pay off a debt that would never be paid in full? Or fleeing the woman who wanted to make him another of her whores?

He wanted to stop being the bargaining chip and start being the bargainer of his own fate.

The words that came out of his mouth surprised even him. "I want to not be powerless. I want power," he said through his teeth.

It was the same moment when Juras stuck the serrated edge of his knife against the fae's throat.

Juras wasn't sure how he'd managed it or when he'd decided to really do it rather than entertain it as a thought of fantasy.

One moment, the knife had been tucked in his pocket, and in the next, it was pressed into the fae king's bare throat.

Underneath Hellmyr's skin, his fae heartbeat flickered and bumped regularly against the knife's edge. The knife wasn't a big one nor a sharp one—but that made it even deadlier.

If you had to be stabbed, would you rather it be a clean cut or by a jagged edge?

If his expression was anything to judge by, Hellmyr seemed to be realizing the same, too.

"What are you doing?" he asked.

"Threatening you, fae," Juras said. "You know how that feels, right?"

Hellmyr's head was leaned back at the ideal angle for keeping a knife to his throat, but Juras needed to secure the rest of him. His lower body was submerged in the pool beneath him, so that was helpful, but he could still pull out of his hold with his free arms.

"Spread your arms behind you and keep them apart," Juras said.

"What is this, a search?" Hellmyr said. "You can quite clearly see there's nothing on me."

Juras resisted a look down at his lower body. The fae was trying to distract him back.

"You have no magic now that it's after dawn," Juras continued. "But I can't risk anything."

Juras pinned Hellmyr's arms down by gripping his wrists together and hastily binding them with his belt.

Hellmyr breathed in his face. His eyes had narrowed on him. "Are you an experienced hostage-taker or are you naturally gifted in tying others up?"

Juras crouched behind his head, keeping a steady grip on the knife while putting weight on Hellmyr's arms. Even with a fae's more flexible physicality, he knew it must have strained him.

Good.

"Enough of the games, fae. I need some things from you."

"And I thought the restraining was because of how delectable the grapes were going to get." Hellmyr's taunts seemed to roll off his tongue far too easily.

Juras's blood throbbed faster through him in response. Was the bastard not taking this seriously yet?

He shoved the jagged edge tighter against the fae's throat where a small dribble of red appeared. "That's not how it's going to be," Juras said.

The taunting smirk fell off his face. "What is it that you want, then?"

Hellmyr's puffs of breath moved a curl out of Juras's face as he looked down at his captive fae king. The knife at his throat necessitated them to be close.

"You are going to leave her alone," Juras commanded. "Unless she initiates contact, you do not. Say it."

"How are you going to make me, human? We have a bargain." His eyes smoldered as they looked up at him in a show of defiance. "I can make you do *whatever* I want."

"And yet ..." Juras started to say.

It all came to him, then.

"You haven't," Juras continued. "You haven't, even now. When I could cut open your throat."

The hate had made Juras blind to it. Hellmyr was allowing this. And he was doing it for a reason.

"You ..." Juras swallowed.

Hellmyr's full lips pulled to one corner like he was fighting the emotions within him. Like they didn't agree.

"What do you think you know, human?" he taunted.

Hellmyr's eyes hovered on Juras's lips above him. It was for only a second, but he'd caught it. Juras felt his heartrate bob faster against the edge of the weapon held so tightly to his skin.

Juras didn't think anymore.

He leaned down and kissed Hellmyr on the mouth.

CHAPTER TWENTY-THREE

I t was awful.

It was wonderful.

Juras's hate for himself—for desiring this—lived alongside the searing desire itself.

He kissed Hellmyr deeper, consumingly. His face was upside down of Hellmyr's, so he couldn't see his expression.

So, he held the knife close to the fae's throat. Hellmyr kissed him back. He was sure neither of them even breathed as they tasted each other.

Juras had never had a kiss like this. It made him feel like his head was being held underwater. But he couldn't stop, either.

Hellmyr's bound wrists found their way to Juras's lower abdomen, near where he'd been pinning them down against the floor.

The fae's hands found the flat of his stomach, pulling his shirt higher as they kissed. Juras didn't dare break their kiss to remove it, and Hellmyr's hands ripped the buttons from his shirt in response, allowing them to explore more of his chest. His thumbs traced old scars and circled areas of muscle, making Juras's body move against Hellmyr's touch.

The steam from the hot water below had already stuck Juras's clothes to his skin, but when Hellmyr moved to pull him closer, more water splashed across his front.

His hair was soaked, and his opened shirt clung to his arms, weighed down by the water.

Hellmyr was much too experienced manipulating the body, Juras found. His heart galloped ahead of him, making him dizzy. He moved against Hellmyr's grip on one of his hips, and his thoughts went to other places.

Like how it would feel to plunge in the water. How it would feel to be pressed against him again.

Juras jerked himself up and away from the fae, away from those thoughts, gasping for air like he'd been sprinting instead of kissing.

What the hell had he done?

Below him, Hellmyr was gasping, too. His mouth was red from the force of their kissing. It was then that Juras saw his reflection in the water and how flushed his own skin was. The way his hair curled weakly behind his ears from being half-soaking wet.

Hellmyr's face had an alien expression on it. He'd never seen such an expression on one of them before. His violet-black eyes seemed to gaze ahead at nothing, yet they didn't stop moving. His breath hadn't slowed, and his bare chest rose and fell quickly. His mouth was still parted slightly.

He was disoriented, Juras realized.

Juras rocked back on the floor as he tried to understand what had happened between them.

What the hell did it mean?

What the hell had *that* been? His response?

Juras's own chest heaved. Buttons from his shirt littered the ground. He could feel tears in the fabric at the shoulders, too. He looked up to see the fae staring at him.

His eyes had moved from Juras's face to his body. He looked at Juras's bare chest that he'd ran his hands so freely over seconds ago.

When Hellmyr finally spoke, his voice was muted and odd. "What are those from?"

He was talking about his scars, Juras realized.

The memories readily resurfaced in a black wave within his mind. He didn't wish to talk about that. Not with this fae.

Juras couldn't seem to make his mouth say anything about that, anyway.

Instead, what came out was: "Isn't it about time you make me do something?"

The reminder of their bargain seemed to revert him back to normal, at least. Hellmyr brought his bounded hands to his front, and with a little twisting and a pop of his shoulder, he'd slipped his wrists out of Juras's belt. He rose, water falling from him in a wave, and fixed a towel to his waist.

His gaze was dark and indecipherable. Juras noticed then the bead of blood he'd drawn at his throat was dripping to his collarbone.

"You're right, of course." Hellmyr stepped towards him.

Oh, great. Usually, his mouth didn't get him into so much trouble, but he was breaking a new record for that.

"Is that so?" Juras had pulled free the knife again, ready to both defend himself and stab at the fae.

"Drop it at your feet," Hellmyr said. "*Now.*"

Juras's jaw clenched as the sudden inexplicable urge came over him to move. Without his permission, his body bent at the waist and dropped his one weapon on the floor.

"Let me out of this," Juras snarled.

Hellmyr ignored that. He seemed mostly back to himself, though his unnerving smile didn't quite reach his eyes.

His gaze was greedy on Juras's dripping form. It was then that his smile dropped.

"Catch this," he commanded, throwing a piece of clothing at Juras.

He was compelled to catch it, and he saw that it was the shirt that Hellmyr had been wearing before his bath.

"Don't move," the fae king said as he stalked closer to him.

Juras couldn't. He couldn't even seem to speak.

"You are to report here after dawn every day." The fae lifted Juras's chin, and he found he couldn't fidget out of the way. "You will tell the guards and servants you are being punished for your attitude in the hall. You will tell everyone you are being forced to clean my chambers every day until they are spotless."

"In reality, you will come here daily—unless I say otherwise—and try to convince me of what you want. Of the power you claim to want." Hellmyr brought his face to Juras's so that it consumed his vision.

"Convince me in a week. Or not at all."

CHAPTER TWENTY-FOUR

It was the first day in several that Anova felt well enough to pry herself from a waste basket. She first saw a flicker of motion at her window as she rose in the late afternoon.

Then, she saw her green wings flapping rapidly on the other side of the glass.

Anova jolted to her feet to lift her window and let in the insect. She released a breath when she saw that it indeed was Viridia.

She'd expected her back sooner, but she was relieved at least to see her well and back with her.

"What happened?" Anova's eyebrows came together as he held out a palm for her friend to land on. "Where is she?"

It was then that she noticed something about the butterfly. Now that she'd gained entrance, the rate of her wings flapping had slowly decreased until she held them out on either side of her. She moved slowly, too, taking her time to come to the most comfortable spot of Anova's palm.

No.

Gods, she'd been blind.

"You're hurt," Anova blurted. "Viridia, what happened? Gods, I got you hurt."

At once, Anova dove for the dresser next to her bed that had been painted a striking silver to match the moon. When she found the small glass with a screw-in top, she didn't hesitate to open it.

A small amount of liquid remained inside it—moonlight nectar that one of Hellmyr's healers had previously drawn from the moon to use as a pain-killing medicine. She held it before Viridia.

"This might not fix everything, but it'll help your wounds feel better faster," she explained.

The butterfly's compound eyes seemed to hold Anova before moving to the container. With soft steps, she came to the edge of Anova's palm and stuck her proboscis inside it.

After she drained a few droplets, Viridia retreated several steps back on Anova's palm. Her proboscis nudged the base of her wrist as she held Anova's gaze. Her wings seemed to move at a more typical speed again, flexing and unflexing as she rested.

Anova smiled back at her small friend. "You're welcome. I'm just glad I had something for you. Please, rest here a few days before flying again."

Anova's smile dropped. Something had happened when Viridia had accompanied Lycasta to the Wolfsbane manor to send Nerium a message. She couldn't assume that the message went through.

"I'm so sorry. I should have been more thoughtful about where I sent you," Anova said. "Please accept my apologies for putting you in danger. I'll send the guard for some nectar water."

At that, Viridia's mouth-part twitched and her wings seemed to vibrate with the prospect, as well. The butterfly allowed Anova to put her on a cushion that caught a bit of late sunlight from her window. Viridia fanned herself in the warmth.

Anova breathed. In the days she'd been too sick to move, she'd known it was past time for her contingency plan.

Hellmyr wasn't simply going to let her and Juras go.

In fact, he'd demonstrated that she needed to participate in the full moon ritual to restore the balance of power between the fae and the moon.

And if she didn't participate, Alys's forces could stand a real chance at doing some damage in Fae.

This was a bad thing. Or so she needed to convince herself.

When Anova tried to pace in order to think, her breaths came too short. She supported herself on the edge of the dresser as she regained her breath. She closed her eyes.

And then, there was the fact that she was with child.

One that might not survive to term between the power-hungry fae who held her here and the enigmatic blood crown tethered to her life.

No. She had to stop being paralyzed by her problems. She had to do something.

She had to tell Hellmyr about Alys's coup and the other reason she'd come here. If what happened to Viridia was any indication, the lives of all fae and humans from the estate were in danger. She couldn't trust Alys not to touch them while she waited for Anova to deliver Hellmyr to her.

She had to tell Hellmyr. Even if she implicated herself by doing so.

At least he could send forces to the estate.

But there was something else she needed to do while she was here and still able to freely move about. Anova still needed to do a little digging.

Her stomach protested in a growl. She supposed that there was one small thing that had to come first.

What had he gotten himself into? Juras paced in front of his mirror and considered it all.

He'd stuffed the shirt Hellmyr had thrown at him to wear out of his rooms into the back of his wardrobes. It was a reminder of the commitment he'd made and what was coming after the night.

And there was something to the gesture that made Juras feel as if the shirt was a show of ownership.

"Convince me in a week. Or not at all."

His words had been a clear challenge.

Juras stopped his pacing when he heard noises in the other room. He'd told them, time and again, that they didn't want his servants coming and going through their rooms.

But as he opened the door, the words on Juras's tongue died.

"Anova," he gasped. He raised an eyebrow. "So, you're not dead."

She smirked at his words. She looked about as well as she could look, having lived off fruits roasted until they were softened and bone broth for several days. But at least she didn't look like Death himself.

"Not on your life," she said. Her eyebrows rose. "Besides, I don't have any of my old trinkets anymore. I'm afraid your inheritance is shot."

Juras shook his head. "And here I thought all fae bled and shat gold."

"Sorry to disappoint."

Her smile faltered. It was the only sign of how it must have affected her. Juras cursed his choice of words. He needed to keep his damn mouth shut more often.

"You're feeling better then?" Juras asked, closing the distance between them.

"Well enough." She frowned. "Viridia came back."

"That's good news though, isn't it?" Juras said. "What's going on?"

He hoped Della and Maris were safe and unharmed.

Anova sank into a plush chair and held her head. "I don't know. Lycasta didn't return with her." Her voice sounded small as she said the next words. "And Viridia was hurt. I have no idea what's happening there. But I can't trust their lives to Alys anymore." She looked up at Juras. "I'm going to tell him about her occupation of the estate."

Juras stared back. "And her deal with you? That you'll trade him for Cadmus's life? Don't you think he'll wonder what she's doing at his estate? He'll piece it together."

"I know! I just—" Anova groaned. "What else can I do? I can't risk their lives any longer."

"I know," Juras echoed. His eyes went to the floor like they'd find answers there.

"But there's something else I need to do first. I came here for some answers about Rietvar, and if Hellmyr starts to suspect any of my agreement with Alys, we may not be able to move about so freely," Anova said.

They both knew what that meant. They might be watched every hour of the day. Or they could be sent to the dungeons. It would be justified if the fae king suspected treason in his own house.

"I need to get to the archives without his knowing. Preferably tonight. Or whenever I can sneak inside there."

Juras breathed. He knew what to do. He could be the distraction.

Anova's eyes were on him. His thoughts must have shown on his face. "Juras, is there something wrong?"

I can't tell her what's going on. Not the whole truth of it.

So, Juras shook his head.

Even as he tried to form the words, they scrambled in his mind. Hellmyr's commands still had a hold on him because of their bargain.

You will tell everyone you are being forced to clean my chambers every day until they are spotless."

Everyone included her, it seemed.

Juras's heart felt as if it were held in a tight fist. He hated lying to his best friend.

"I'm fine," he said. "But I did have an idea. I think I can help with the plan."

Anova's eyebrows pushed together. "What do you mean?"

"It seems he grew tired of having a servant in title only and not in actions."

"What?" The word ripped from her throat. "He's truly using you as his servant now? That ass."

Anova rose from her chair like she was off to punch Hellmyr. Admittedly, he would have paid to see that.

"It's not what you're thinking," Juras explained. "I clean his rooms at dawn for a week." Juras leaned against the wall, trying to shrug off what he was really doing and how it made his blood surge. "I insulted him, and some of his guards heard. This is his punishment, I guess."

Anova's jaw tightened. "I still don't like it."

He was reminded for not the first time how quickly Anova had defended him when they'd been children. Even when he hadn't asked her to.

He smiled at her response.

"Well, the situation will work to our advantage now. I can keep an eye on him and ensure he doesn't leave to find you. As long as you can get in and out without being seen, you can get the information you need."

Juras's smile fell as he remembered how, despite his best efforts, he'd been tracked the first time he'd tried to strategize and sneak from their rooms without being noticed. It'd been what caused all this mess in the first place.

"Though, that will be an entire job in itself," he muttered as an addendum.

It was Anova's turn to grin. Her eyes gleamed like they did when she had one of her schemes brewing.

This was why she was his best friend.

"Oh, just leave that to me," she said.

CHAPTER TWENTY-FIVE

Anova hugged Juras one last time before he left to clean Hellmyr's rooms as his servant. His words still echoed in her head.

"We're getting through this. Don't forget that we're doing this for them."

They gave her the courage she needed for this. What was sneaking about the fae king's castle when Cadmus was without magic and the witch's captive?

She had to find some answers here and then come save them. She'd saved them all before, and she'd do it again.

Anova's nails dug into her palm. What she hadn't told Juras was that she needed to use the blood crown's magic to get to the archives undetected.

She didn't like showing him that part of her. When they were together, she wasn't the master of the blood crown or a fae in a burnt body. She was just Anova.

Her hand hovered at her belly as she considered the other issue gnawing at her.

What if this hurts it?

She'd used the blood crown's magic when she'd broken inside his palace, it was true. But when it came to it, Anova couldn't be sure if it had affected what had been growing in her belly.

Anova breathed. *The least amount of it possible, then.*

She crouched to the ground, already smelling the guard on the other side. He smelled of iron and weather-worn leather. Anova peeked underneath the door, watching the far end of the hall outside where it bent to another hall.

With even breaths, she concentrated on what she could make—heat and light.

Not too much. Steady.

A flash of light materialized near the end of the hall. She heard her guard's breath quicken. In no time, he'd left his post to run down the hall and chase her phantom light.

Quieter than she could've as a human, Anova slipped from behind the door. She'd been practicing for this in her rooms. But the real test was at hand.

Anova closed her eyes to better hear and smell.

Distant steps blurred together around her, and smells twined together. When she focused, she started to notice what could have been individual fae closest to her.

None of them were very near to her except her guard.

Now was her chance.

The key that she'd learned to sneaking around fae was to not run or allow her heartbeat to accelerate for them to hear. Otherwise, she would hear or smell his guards before they passed her in the halls.

Anova left this hall before her guard returned. The next one over was blessedly empty as well. Juras's plan seemed to be working perfectly. At dawn, the palace was filled with mostly sleeping fae.

As she passed other rooms—guards' or servants' quarters—she thought she heard the near-quiet noises of sleep. She passed like a wraith through his halls, diverting her course when she smelled a fae coming too close to her path.

The quiet allowed for one other thing. She heard the heartbeat inside her body more clearly than she'd been able to ever before.

It was louder today, not like it had been in the days before.

Sporadic. At times, weak.

Anova swallowed drily. There was something she hadn't told Juras yet. She didn't have full proof of it, so it was only a possibility. But she couldn't even articulate it for fear that she'd manifest it just by speaking it aloud.

The fear that Rietvar would collect on his dues with a stillbirth.

Anova's hand went to her stomach when it clenched in response.

No. Please. It won't be that. It has to be something else.

But what other more perfect way would there be to take his revenge on the human who had tricked him? What more gruesome cost would be there to pay than if she paid with something she could never have again?

This was why she had to find answers here. The fear had grown in the days that she'd been ill.

After Anova distracted the guard of the archives with another flash of light, she slipped in after he'd left his post, careful not to make a noise.

The smell of paper filled her. The scent was stronger now that she had fae senses, and it was nearly overpowering.

Dawn light spread through the small windows near the ceiling, coloring the stacks of documents and books a warm, honey color.

The answer she needed was here. She felt it.

On his way there, not one fae looked twice at him. He was sure it was because he was wearing the set of servant clothes the king had sent him.

As he thought of it, his cheeks heated with anger. He thought he could play power games with him. Well, Juras was ready for that.

Even so, the clothes had their uses. He'd become invisible to them. Juras worked on keeping his heartrate even, though his nerves tangled in his throat for what was coming.

Do it for her. Do it to keep him away.

Hellmyr opened the door before his guards had a chance to address Juras.

"You're here. Finally," he said dismissively. "This room is a mess."

Against his better judgment, Juras stepped inside. "Your Majesty," he said through his teeth, though it was more for the benefit of those listening.

He was starting to wonder if he'd really been conscripted to be his personal maid for the remainder of the week.

When the fae king closed the door behind them, his eyes appraised him and his servant's garb. The top was a rough cotton shirt and the pants were a pair of plain tan trousers perfect for scrubbing in or crawling in the dirt as a gardener.

"Isn't this what you wanted?" Juras said. He stepped into his space.

"No. I want it off." Hellmyr shrugged as if to counteract the seriousness behind his words, but the gleam in his eyes didn't leave.

Juras glared at him. *Controlling, aren't you?* His heart raced.

"I could do that. If you tell me the truth about something you haven't yet," Juras said.

Hellmyr fell against his lounge couch that was more of a bed. The fae's eyes were wary, though he could feel the greed Hellmyr had for seeing the reveal. Juras needed to hook him more.

He needed to keep him here right now at any cost.

"What do you want to know?" Hellmyr's voice was careful. Measured. His eyes flicked across Juras. "And what do I get out of it?"

Juras came to the lounge without invitation. The fae couldn't escape this question anymore.

"I'll ask my question. Then you name your price, and I might agree to it."

"Ask then," Hellmyr said. His expression was impossible to decipher.

Juras breathed. He could do this.

"Why didn't you let your guards take me the first time? After you found the knife?" The more he spoke, the more he had to keep digging this hole. "I could have been trying to kill you. You said so yourself."

Hellmyr's lips came together. "The truth? It'll be expensive." He lifted the shirt's fabric at Juras's collarbone. "This will definitely need to go." His eyes went farther down.

Juras interrupted what he'd been about to say. "The shirt. Along with what I'm going to do to you," he proposed.

His heart throbbed. He was playing with fire and knew it.

Hellmyr's violet eyes were closer to black as he stared, likely considering the deal.

"Fine. I agree to those terms, despite the ambiguity. But I'll give my answer only while you pay me for it. Not before."

Juras responded by unfastening the string at his throat holding the shirt together there. "The truth is what I want, fae."

He threw the shirt over his head, and Hellmyr's eyes traced his bare form, lingering on his stomach and passing over the scars that Juras had refused to tell him about earlier.

"I did what I did out there because I have to maintain a certain image," Hellmyr said.

"Image? Of your being an ass?" Juras said.

"Of being untrickable. Unkillable. Invulnerable. Everyday, those around me test my boundaries. A man isn't killed by a small nick, but it all starts there. They want to see how deep they can cut it," Hellmyr said, his eyes keeping him prisoner. "I may not have the blood crown, but I'm the one who they hail as king now. They'll kill me as soon as I show them it's possible."

Juras moved so he was above him and looking down at the fae.

"You know that doesn't answer what I asked," Juras said. "Your actions make even less sense in light of that."

Why spare me?

Hellmyr licked his lips. "Convince me. And maybe I'll tell you."

Juras's fingers were quick to unbutton most of the fae's shirt, and his mouth found his bare skin at once. His lips moved up his chest, exploring him as Hellmyr had done to Juras in his bath.

His lips moved up his sternum until they found the fae's collarbone. Underneath him, Hellmyr's body turned from resistant to pliable, and though he couldn't hear it like the fae could, Juras felt how his blood raced through him as he made his way along his bare skin.

He heard Hellmyr inhale sharply when Juras reached his neck.

"Are you going to talk or not?" Juras said.

His hands moved in the same path that his mouth had taken, only in reverse. Hellmyr's body responded in kind, moving against Juras's touch. His spine arched when Juras's hands found the small of his back.

Hellmyr's words came out in a growl. "Stop teasing me, human."

Juras pulled away from him. Something dark rose in him—some strange mix of desire, power, and loathing.

"Make me. Command me," Juras said.

Hellmyr stared back at him until Juras's hairs started to rise. Hellmyr broke the moment with a smirk.

"If that's what you want. Fine."

The fae pulled himself out from under him. "Stand up."

CHAPTER TWENTY-SIX

Juras was forced to do as Hellmyr ordered. The dizziness assaulting him was the only evidence of the terror and desire running through him.

Hellmyr stood as well and approached Juras. His voice was low and dark. "You will make no noise to reveal what's going on here to the fae stationed outside," Hellmyr said. "You will resist me until you can't. I want to see the point in which your desires overtake you." He met his gaze. "But I will stop the instant you say. You are allowed that noise. I am not quite *that* type of monster."

Heat grew at Juras's center. He could do little else but nod to show his agreement.

The challenge was on. Juras wouldn't be there one to break first. He would make the fae putty in his hands.

Hellmyr started by completely removing his shirt, allowing the gray silk to drop at their feet.

He did what Juras had done, only he started lower with the kisses he planted on Juras's stomach. He moved up, avoiding the scars decorating Juras's body at irregular intervals. One of his hands hooked along Juras's hip, and quicker than he could realize it had happened, the fae had moved so he was behind Juras.

Juras could hardly breathe as Hellmyr continued to kiss his skin. This fae was too beautiful and his lips were too soft for the monster that he was. In truth, Juras could hardly stand it.

No. You have to show him you're stronger than your desires.
Show him that.

It was then that his other hand found Juras's neck. He tipped his head back, one hand on his throat, as he kissed behind Juras's jaw.

It was a mirror to what Juras had done to him in his bath. Hellmyr pinned Juras close to him with his other arm.

Heat spread through Juras, and all he could think about was how it would feel to have him. To take and be taken by him.

A groan escaped his throat. He hadn't allowed it, though it had been barely audible.

Hellmyr's voice was a breath in his ear. "That's what I thought."

Juras's heart hammered in his throat. *Great.*

That was when a loud knock at his door came. Juras nearly jumped from the noise.

"Your Majesty. Something important requires your attention at once." It was one of his guards.

Please don't let it be Anova. Please.

Hellmyr breathed a puff of air that tickled Juras's face. He didn't move from where the fae held him, and Hellmyr didn't move, either.

I have to keep him from leaving, Juras realized.

A wordless gasp shot through Juras then. "Please," he whispered to the fae who held him.

But when he finally spoke, he didn't speak to Juras.

"Is someone dying?" Hellmyr called to the guard at the door.

"No, but—"

"Is the palace on fire?"

"No, Your M—"

Juras shuddered. While he spoke, Hellmyr had moved his hand to below Juras's waist, resting on top of his pants. It was a sensitive area.

"Then it doesn't actually require my attention, Idier," Hellmyr said to the guard. Hellmyr held him tighter as he whispered in Juras's ear, "Please what?"

"Let me move," Juras whispered.

Hellmyr said back to him in a whisper, "Alright. I release you."

From behind the door, his guard said, "As you say, Your Majesty. My apologies."

But Juras's mouth was already on Hellmyr's.

Please be safe, Anova. Soon, however, his thoughts turned blank but for the searing heat consuming him like a fever.

He had to make this two-sided. He had to make Hellmyr want this as much as he did. To make him weak for a human.

He had to convince him.

Even those thoughts fled as the kiss turned greedy. Hellmyr dug deeper, biting at the bottom of Juras's lip. Juras would make him beg for this, he vowed.

His hands pinned Hellmyr's behind his back as he had in the bath. The fae allowed that, though he wondered if he'd allow this.

Juras's hands were deft and quick as they pulled Hellmyr's pants down his waist and thighs until they fell to the ground.

Juras broke their kiss to stare. His heart galloped.

"What is it, human?" Hellmyr smiled.

"We'll see how long until you're overtaken, fae. Until you beg me for more," Juras said.

"I'd like to see the day a human—"

Juras had dropped to his knees already. Hellmyr interrupted himself with a gasp through clenched teeth.

Juras moved his hands over his member. All his jokes about fae males and their sizes fell from his lips.

He wanted to taste him. He wanted him, and he knew Hellmyr wanted him, too.

The knowledge emboldened him to run his hands over him.

"You will say why, fae," he said. "You'll tell me the truth."

"We'll see—" Hellmyr breathed as he cut himself off and closed his eyes.

Juras tasted him, and Hellmyr's fingers tangled in his hair. He seemed not to be able to help himself but to move to Juras's rhythm.

"So, you can do more than insult with that—"

Juras dug his fingers into Hellmyr's lower back. He felt the fae's knees weaken against him. It was then that Hellmyr started to speak again.

But it was different this time. He spoke between gasps, almost too fast for Juras to catch it all.

"I couldn't have them kill you. But it wasn't just to keep you as bait." He tried to laugh but it sounded forced.

He was close. Juras could sense it.

He would bring him to his knees.

"It wasn't—not because of this, either. Not that I hadn't—hadn't imagined—"

Naughty fae, Juras thought. So, Juras wasn't the only one who'd had these thoughts. Hellmyr had made it sound like it had been one-sided.

Juras wasn't giving up. He didn't have much time before it would be over.

"I did it for a vile reason. Vile because a human shouldn't have such unreasonable sway over the ruler of fae. My decisions." Hellmyr drew a short breath. "Even if you were trying to kill me—"

He gritted his teeth and continued to speak. "Because I can't have you dead. I can't have you hurt. I can't have them touch you. Ever," he said in a growl. "Because I am *weak* to whatever you are. Because I fear and crave what might happen. That you're going to undo me."

Juras could do nothing but take his words in. He'd brought him to a height. He'd gotten Hellmyr under his power.

And he'd done it his way.

But what the hell had he meant by all that?

It was then that Juras was made aware of the incessant knocking on Hellmyr's doors again.

Hellmyr's breathing was too fast. His skin was flushed, and sweat beaded his brow and got into his hair. His eyes shot to the door.

"As I've said, I'm busy," he growled.

But this guard was a different one.

"Your Majesty, the palace is on fire."

CHAPTER TWENTY-SEVEN

The words curling across the books' spines blurred together to Anova. Dawn light no longer filled the high reaches of the windows above her in the archives.

At least she was faster at this than when she'd been a human—though she wasn't sure this quicker pace would help if there were no answers to be found here.

I can't give up. I have to try harder.

Anova shelved another bundle of books and documents that had turned out to be fruitless. As she did so, she considered what she knew.

Previously, she'd found answers about the blood crown and other ancient fae magic in a book of fae tales that she'd pulled from the Eastwoe archives. But that book had since been removed from here.

Even if I had it, there's no guarantee that I'd have found anything concerning the fae lord of Death in its stories.

She thumbed at her chin.

What do I know about him?

The truth was, Anova knew little about Rietvar.

He was a shapeshifter. He traded souls and seemed to relish bargains. He lived in a place called the Lost Forest.

Anova stared at the section of the archives she'd since turned upside down in her search. It contained everything from tomes explaining the burial rites suitable for the High King or Queen to which phase of the moon was best to die under. She suppressed a shudder as she thought of the latter.

No. This wasn't right.

She needed to find answers that others would have overlooked. Lore like fae tales that would have been considered myth rather than fact.

But she'd found curiously few books concerning what the fae thought of the one who shepherded souls from life to death. She returned to the section of the shelves filled with fables to check that she hadn't missed one.

After several minutes of searching, Anova frowned.

There were plenty of fae tales on avoiding Death, though they all seemed thought up to scare fae children into obeying their parents.

It was then that she found one with a tale of how a fae had combined two animals together and taunted Death with his powers. How it was a fable and not a horror story was beyond her.

Sickness swirled in her stomach. She slid to the floor, holding her head tight to her.

They're all monsters.

What the hell was she doing? She'd gotten so far over her head that drowning felt normal to her now.

How was she going to protect this life when she couldn't even protect hers?

Cadmus, I wish you were here. I wish I'd never left you with them.

In her mind, he didn't say anything back.

But something else did. The other heartbeat inside her kicked up a faster pace. She held her breath.

Anova closed her eyes and made a promise to the small life inside her. "You're going to make it. You are."

She would make sure it lived no matter what. Wasn't that worth it all?

Wasn't it worth spending all the time she had here to find the answers needed to protect this? To protect the future that she had with Cadmus?

As soon as she came to her feet again, she saw it. It was a book that she hadn't seen the cover of yet but that she'd exposed in her search among the other tomes.

The book's cover was missing any text, though the image of a wolf was embossed in faded silver on it.

Anova blinked, seeing not the book's cover, but a wide, gaping maw big enough to swallow her whole. She nearly dropped the book.

Just maybe ...

With held breath, Anova flipped through the small binding. It contained only one story, and it had no title to it other than the image of the wolf above it. The more she read, the more her hands holding it trembled.

Long ago in the human realm, there existed a singularly talented human hunter. He was the envy of his peers and faster with a bow than any other. He was better even than the swift and sure-footed fae.

The hunter bragged to his rivals and friends that there was no one better than him. And soon, the young hunter ran short of any to test his skills against. All animals he crossed paths with were fallen with one of his arrows each.

One day, in a glade deep in a wood, a stranger approached him. Though he wore a wide-brimmed hat, his eyes were bright like the sun as he looked upon the hunter.

When the hunter asked the stranger his business, he replied thus:

"Are you the hunter they hail as even greater than the gods?"

The hunter smiled. "They would—if any dared challenge me."

The stranger showed his teeth in a wide smile in return, and under the brim of the stranger's hat, the hunter saw something curious. He was speaking to a man of bleached bones and teeth rather than one of skin and muscle.

But the hunter did not flee at the terrifying sight.

The stranger introduced himself as Death, the best hunter of all living things. Death posed a challenge to the hunter to test the hunter's claim.

The first of them to fell the spotless white wolf that lived in the woods around them would be granted the title of the best hunter as well as a single boon.

If the human hunter won, he would be given power equal to Death's. If Death won the contest, he would be granted the soul of the hunter.

Eager to prove his skills against an opponent worthy of him, the hunter agreed to these terms. Just as he did, a howl broke the quiet of the wood. The hunt began.

Death was the faster of the two, but the human hunter was cunning and knew these woods well.

As Death followed the howls, the hunter broke in a different direction. In little time, the hunter found a den of rabbits he'd discovered in the days before and hid in a bush of blackberries.

When Death realized the hunter wasn't following him, he turned on his path, spitting fire. Death had produced the howls and thrown his voice to sound like the wolf and trick the hunter.

It was then that the hunter found the snow-white wolf pacing the den of rabbits for his next meal. He loosed only one arrow, and it pierced the creature's heart.

But a strange thing happened then. Death appeared, and in the shadow of his wide hat, the hunter saw that he was no longer a skeleton but a man of flesh again. He looked at the hunter with a ghastly grin.

It was true that the hunter had bested him in this test of skill, but Death had wanted this all along. The hunter had won the powers of Death—and his burdens.

The hunter was cursed to the duties of Death, to collect the souls of those passing from this world into the next, and to be forgotten by his friends and rivals alike.

When in a dark wood, the howls of the wolf are to be as trusted as a stranger's smile.

Anova shut the book.

She felt as if she hadn't taken a breath since she'd started reading the story.

As her mother had been fond of saying, there were no coincidences in this world. Anova couldn't afford to start believing in coincidences now.

This must be referring to Rietvar. The details are too parallel.

First and most obvious was the reference to Death. Then there was the wolf—it was one of Rietvar's forms. And he'd claimed an area of woods for his home.

This was it. She had to assume the story was referencing Rietvar. She couldn't afford to assume otherwise.

But then, what does this mean? What does he want from me?

The answer was a sickness in her belly.

The hunter had won the powers of Death—and his burdens.

Did this mean that he wanted another to take the mantle of Death from him? To curse another with the duties of bringing the deceased to the next world?

As Anova considered all the possibilities, her breaths grew more ragged. A cough scraped the inside of her throat.

Her heart raced, and she smelled the air. An acrid smell hung on it.

It was the smell of fire.

CHAPTER TWENTY-EIGHT

"You are to stay here until I come back," Hellmyr said to Juras.

Juras was pushed into the arms of several fae healers. He pried himself off them. Physically, he was fine.

Besides, he wasn't worried about himself. He'd gotten out of the palace.

The sky was bright and achingly blue. It eerily contrasted with the screams that pierced the air around them and the trail of black smoke snaking into the sky.

When the fae king's guard had knocked and told them the palace was on fire, it hadn't quite sunk in to Juras until they came outside and saw it. According to the fae around him, the fire was contained to one of the lower floors.

Hellmyr had lifted him out of the room, and in barely more than a few blinks, he'd dumped him with the crowd outside. He still hadn't gotten over the feeling of being so close to him. Or what had happened before that.

What the hell are we doing?

Juras's attention was stolen. Five seconds into being out in the panicking throng outside, and it was obvious to him. Anova was still inside the burning palace.

He finally processed what Hellmyr had said to him. He grabbed the fae's arm. He didn't care who saw them right now or the insubordination that it was.

"Find her and bring her out," Juras said to him. Some fae was trying to jerk his grip away from Hellmyr, but he resisted it.

He'd be damned if they'd survived what they had only to lose her here.

Hellmyr broke the stare between the two of them suddenly, barking orders at his guards and lackeys. He was running towards the palace.

When they realized what he was trying to do, they tried to stop him, but the fae shrugged them off.

No matter what the hell this was between them, Juras wasn't going to lose Anova. Even if it drove the mad fae king back to her. They could deal with the consequences later.

It was then that a tremor shook the ground. Seconds later, debris burst from the side of the palace, and a clipped scream soared through the air.

Fire. Death. Pain.

Anova's thoughts ran together as she sprinted through the halls. Her blood thundered like she was being bled dry. She was going to die in this place.

No. No! I won't.

But the flames had claimed her once already and made her theirs. They had taken her and left her with their marks.

They were back for her. This time, they would claim her life.

The heat started to come from her center, too. It fled to her fingertips.

This heat followed her orders. This pain was hers. And she would make it do as she wanted.

The blood crown eagerly gave its energy to her. It had waited for the chance to be released.

Anova wasn't sure where she'd been in the palace before, but the magic that formed in her hands, a searing, destructive light, blasted apart the stone walls and structure of the palace.

Before she could change her mind, Anova jumped from the hole she'd made in the building. The smoke in her lungs was replaced by nothing at all as she found she couldn't breathe as she fell.

Protect us!

Her hands spread before her as the heat gathered there again. Even if all this magic was capable of was destruction, Anova would use anything she could to save herself and the life inside her.

Fae were scattered below her like cattle. She screamed at them, though the wind stole much of her voice.

"Go! Get out of the way," she shouted.

After all, even if they were fae, they didn't deserve death at the hands of the cursed crown. But one of them wasn't moving.

He held his arms out for her and called for her.

At the last moment, Anova pulled her hands back to herself, recalling the dangerous magic that she'd intended to use to break her fall, and balled her limbs to her body.

The fae were hard, solid creatures. Anova knew this, but the feeling of slamming into Hellmyr's body was still one that stole her breath and bruised parts of her.

The momentum of her fall sent him back several paces and nearly brought him to the ground, but the fae regained his balance before stumbling entirely.

Still gasping for air, she stared into his wide grackle-colored eyes. She couldn't interpret the expression on his face. She tried to disentangle herself, but he didn't let her.

"Are you hurt?" Hellmyr said, already searching her body for the evidence.

"I'm fine." After a moment, she amended, "I'm not hurt." It wasn't like she'd been *fine* in ages, but that wasn't what he'd asked.

She squirmed to get out of his grasp. It all reminded her too much of when he'd held her for her *safety* in the palace after her belladonna poisoning and her almost-death at the funeral pyre.

As she tried to move and he prevented it, his hand passed over her abdomen. Hellmyr looked at her, his eyes narrowing.

He was about to say something when Juras's voice stole her attention.

"Anova," he called. She used the distraction to slip out of Hellmyr's grasp.

Juras engulfed her in a hug and peppered her with the same questions about her safety—though with the added knowing look that she knew all too well.

"Are you really okay?"

She heard it in the tone of his voice. She squeezed his hand back and hoped he knew what that meant.

I'm okay enough. Thank you.

Hellmyr was staring at them, she realized. She resisted staring back.

Did he find out? Did he hear the extra heartbeat?

Anova shifted, but Juras seemed just as put off. What was going on? What had she missed here?

Chaos reigned around them. She had to find a way to tell Juras about what she'd discovered in the archives and what it meant for her deal with Rietvar. But before that ...

Anova turned to Hellmyr. "What's going on? How did this happen?"

"It's not spread to the structure itself as most of the exterior was built with stone. All my staff and guards are generally accounted for, so likely there are only injuries and some damage to the lower floors. But this was no accident," the fae king said. His stare lingered on her.

Anova was about to tell him to say it already if he were going to accuse her when another noise interrupted them.

Two of his guards dragged a human man by his shoulders towards Hellmyr. On his cheek was a collection of blisters, and his clothes were smudged.

Anova couldn't stop staring. There was no mistake, even with the blisters marring his face. Even his smell reminded her of the rest of them—salt, sweat, and earth.

He was a part of Alys's army.

She held her breath, waiting for him to look at her and show some sign of recognition that would tip off Hellmyr. It seemed Alys was done waiting.

The full moon was still two nights away, and she hadn't yet gotten Hellmyr to the Wolfsbane estate. It didn't matter. Her time was up, and her cover was blown.

One of his guards addressed him. "We found this maggot with his firestarter. He infiltrated our stronghold and set the fire, my lord. He doesn't deny it."

Hellmyr's voice was soft. "Pitiable human man." His sword was out at once. Anova hadn't even seen him draw it.

"I don't converse with monsters." The man looked away, his jaw set.

Using the point of his sword, Hellmyr moved the man's head to face him. "You do now," he said through his teeth. He smiled one of his hair-raising grins. "You and I are going to get to know each other well soon. In fact, I have a feeling you'll want to talk quite freely to me after just a few nights of my dungeons."

Despite the point of Hellmyr's sword digging into the skin under his chin, the man's gaze moved to Anova and Juras.

Her stomach turned. What was she supposed to do? Who were the monsters here?

All she knew was that she was one of them, now.

The man hurled spit at the two of them. "Traitor scum," he said.

Anova saw Hellmyr's jaw tighten. "You *do not* disrespect what is mine." Before she could say anything or stop it, Hellmyr's wrist twisted, and a line of red ran from the man's throat.

Though it appeared to be a shallow one, he'd cut into the man's throat. Anova's head pounded. This couldn't continue.

"I came to deliver a message, fae bastard. Not be cut up while your guards hold me back," he said.

"You'll have plenty of time to speak when I command it," Hellmyr snarled.

He's going to charm him dry, Anova realized. That was why he wanted to interrogate him later. He needed the moon to get the full truth out of him.

Hellmyr will know of my involvement by nightfall.

But there was a worse thought that occurred to her.

Alys is done waiting. What else has she done?

Who has she hurt?

"I'll talk now, you vile thing," the man said. He glared up into Hellmyr's eyes as he said, "'The insects you've stepped on are here. And the moth won't be enough.'"

"What are you talking about?" Hellmyr said. He pressed the blade harder against his throat. "Speak plainly or else. Who is your master? What moth?" His mouth twisted the word.

He smiled. "We humans have no master. Well, most of us." Anova's hands balled into fists when he saw the man glance at Juras. She hadn't even realized her hand had gone to the knife at her waist until Juras grasped her arm. "But you fae only respect one thing—power and magic." The man said the words like a curse.

It happened fast, even for Anova's eyes. The human jerked out of Hellmyr's grasp at the same time that a whistle sang through the air. It was then that an arrow pierced his chest straight through, and the man stumbled as blood gurgled to his lips.

Anova twisted to look for the marksman, but she saw only the paved paths to the gloom forests of Eastwoe around them.

Hellmyr turned to his forces that weren't quelling the fire inside the palace.

"Search the perimeter until you find something. He wasn't alone."

CHAPTER TWENTY-NINE

When Anova walked inside his strategy room, Hellmyr was still issuing orders. Fae rushed in and out of the doorway.

Upon noticing she was there, he locked eyes with her and said, "Everyone else. Out."

She could see the sleeplessness on his face. This was normally when faekind slumbered. Daylight didn't seem to suit them.

The fae around her startled as if from individual dreams. They hadn't quite seen her or realized she'd been there.

Pet, she remembered. She held her ground, watching them as they rushed from the room.

But as much as she enjoyed watching fae scramble around her, Anova knew just how much she shouldn't have been in that room, alone with Hellmyr. There was the steep risk that he'd hear the heartbeat of the life growing inside her.

But it was time. She was done keeping those she loved in the path of danger.

It was time to face Alys with everything she had.

Hellmyr walked over to her. A wide table stretched between them where he normally received reports from his scouts and counsel from his advisors.

"You should be with the healers now," he said in greeting, his eyes roving over her.

"I'm fine," she said. She wasn't really, but talking to more fae healers wasn't going to keep her from seeing flames every time she closed her eyes.

"It's Alys," Anova said to cover up the silence between them. She hoped he hadn't heard the heartbeat inside her. "She's here with men. You have to face her."

"I'm sending forces out all around Eastwoe. They'll follow her trail and expand to the other provinces of Fae if needed."

Anova's pulse raced. "We need to find her on the full moon. That's when your power will be at its greatest." She stopped and raised an eyebrow at him. "Or isn't that right?"

His eyelids lowered as he looked upon her. "Assuming you're able to successfully complete the moon ritual, yes. Speaking of which," he started as he turned away from her, "in light of what's happening here, your debut will need to be another month."

No. Cadmus and Nerium need their magic now, not another month out.

And by then, her fae pregnancy would be another month along.

"We have to try it," Anova said. "We need the moon's power now. Can't the full moon ceremony be done without all of Fae in attendance?"

Hellmyr looked over at her suddenly. "It should be. It's the efforts of both the High King or Queen and the participating fae bathing in moonlight that can facilitate such a large transfer of energy."

"What about the fae already here? Wouldn't that be better than nothing?" Anova pressed.

For a moment Hellmyr evaluated her. "I'm not willing to risk the safety of those that I care about here by inviting all of Fae here right now. And, frankly, I doubt that our numbers are enough without that." He paused and tucked a piece of hair behind her ear. She froze. "But I would be a liar if I said I didn't want to bathe in moonlight with you and try."

Anova shivered from both his words and the promise that the first of her goals had been achieved here. She was already closer to saving them.

"Then we'll join your forces on the night of the full moon after the moon ceremony," Anova said.

Hellmyr said, "It's too soon. We don't yet know her location or even the size of her forces. They could be intending to destroy this place as soon as I turn around."

"But it would be reasonable to assume she's in the Sorrelands, wouldn't it?" Anova said.

"Reasonable, hm?"

Anova stepped back from him. Sweat beaded at her hairline. She could hear the accusation in his voice.

Suddenly, he was behind her. "My sweet, lying Queen. Why might you say that?" His breath tickled her skin.

He didn't have to say how *awfully coincidental* it was that she was trying to order him to send his forces to where Cadmus's estate was.

Anova jerked around to face him again. She felt the energy of the blood crown gather at her hands, though she held its leash.

"Her forces are likely all human. Proximity to the human lands would be reasonable," Anova contended.

Anova used her anger to smother her fear.

It only made sense to guess she was there. But, either way, she'd let too much slip here.

She wasn't sure if her words had convinced him or not, though the mask returned to Hellmyr's face.

"Perhaps," he said. "But the full moon is too soon to go looking for a renegade witch." One of his eyebrows flicked upwards. "In fact, one would almost think she'd expect it—having attacked my hold two nights from it."

Anova breathed.

There was no chance. She needed to go now. A new, desperate plan was all that was left to her.

After she made her excuses to leave, he leaned over a window overlooking Fae. "By the way."

Anova paused at the doorway to look back, but he didn't turn around. "My guards reported something strange last week. A moth was sighted outside the palace, attempting to gain entry within."

Hellmyr turned his face halfway from where he was leaning into the wide window. "There will be a heightened presence of my armed guards throughout the palace for now. This includes the night of the fête. No fae, human, or creature will be allowed in or out that night."

In the tone of his voice, Anova heard what he meant.

Whatever you're planning, my darling queen, you won't get away with it.

CHAPTER THIRTY

The new plan that Juras and Anova had developed replayed over and over in Juras's mind so that he hardly realized when he'd made it all the way to the fae king's rooms at another dawn.

He had one more chance to convince Hellmyr to leave Anova alone for good.

One more chance to convince him to dissolve the one-sided bargain between them.

One more chance before what needed to happen at the fête happened.

There was a strong possibility that Hellmyr knew *something* had happened between Alys and Anova. That part of the arsonist's message had been meant for her.

And then there was what Anova had told Juras of what she'd learned in the archives. Anova believed that there was a chance that Rietvar wanted something to do with her child. Their only consolation when it came to that was that she had at least another two months before she'd be anywhere near due.

Juras's chest tightened. It was all beginning to make him feel dizzy. He practiced breathing evenly as the guards let him in. He couldn't afford to look weak in front of the fae.

Especially their king.

And his *master*.

The arsonist's words came back to him, and his stomach swam.

Traitor scum.

His words had clearly been meant for Juras, as the only other human there. His heart pounded.

He looked up. Hellmyr was dressed not for bathing or lounging or even for his court.

"Eat with me," he murmured, his face unreadable.

The fae stepped aside to reveal the table set in his living quarters. Nearby, a sheer curtain allowed the dim light of early day through. A surprisingly modest amount of food for a king had been arranged on top of it, including what looked to be a small wheel of cheese infused with dried berries, a loaf of sourdough bread, a jar of honey that smelled of cinnamon, and some sliced plum.

"What you mean is for me to feed you," he corrected.

"No. I meant exactly as I said." Hellmyr crossed his arms. His eyes roamed to scowl at the wall. "No one else will. I'm supposed to be receiving the reports of my scouts. Or inspecting the damage. Or ordering my scouts. Or finalizing the preparations for tonight. Or all four at once."

He can't sleep, Juras realized. He saw it in the faint circles under his eyes. He heard it in what he wasn't saying:

"I should be sleeping right now. But I can't."

Juras still couldn't shake the feeling that this was a trick, but he pulled out a chair and sat across from him anyway. Besides, what was the use in resisting a monster who could order him to do whatsoever he wanted?

He could see that they weren't talking about what happened on the dawn of the fire. That was fine with him. Juras could pretend that it hadn't happened, too. The problem was, his body had more trouble.

His heart hammered faster in its cage of bones. Despite Juras's reluctance to admit it, Hellmyr was still the most beautiful and intimidating creature he'd ever seen.

Hellmyr leaned back, closed his eyes, and breathed. "No games. Just eat."

Juras waited for the command to spark something in him—an undeniable urge to follow his orders. When it never came, Juras realized then that Hellmyr wanted him to choose to do it or not of his own volition.

With the knowledge that he could have had him poisoned any time before this—or, indeed, he could have ordered Juras to run himself through with a sword well before now—Juras sliced himself some of the food.

His stomach growled obscenely in response to the stimuli. He would never get used to fae food. In fact, Juras was unsure he would ever get used to eating this regularly. His body reminded him of the cramps of hunger he was used to.

It was always either feast or famine when they'd lived in Irbess. Though, the feasts had never been like this.

In the silence, Hellmyr opened his eyes, picked up a small skewer and speared three slices of plum before dipping them in honey.

Soon, Juras discovered he didn't even care if Hellmyr had poisoned the food. He couldn't put it down.

Hellmyr suddenly asked, "Has that place always been your home?"

Juras's eyebrows came together. "That place? Irbess? Yes."

"Because you have family there?" he guessed.

Juras stared at him. What the hell was his angle?

"There's no one there to extort for my safe return," Juras said finally. "I was there because I needed to pay a debt."

Hellmyr fell silent after that.

Juras didn't like this. Why was he digging into his past?

"And you did?" Hellmyr asked after some minutes. "Paid it?"

Juras looked at him archly. "No. That witch can rot in hell."

He picked at his food. He'd had enough bread to last a lifetime, but the cheese and plums together were undeniably delicious.

His words elicited a dark chuckle from the fae.

Normally, Juras felt he would have bristled at such a reaction from him, but Hinterfell deserved to be laughed at more often.

Even so, this probing didn't suit him. He'd agreed to take a meal with him, not an interrogation.

But maybe he could use this chance. There was still the opportunity to change how tomorrow went.

Why do I care? Alys will get her audience with the fae king. Anova and I will be freed of him. And Alys's prisoners will be, too. What does it matter how we get him there?

Juras started talking before he could let any of this show on his face.

"Anova said the blood crown usually determines who rules here."

"I'm surprised she admitted that out loud," Hellmyr said past a grin. There was an edge to it. "I aim to set a precedent. To prove that Fae can determine who rules itself instead of an object."

"But you do want it," Juras accused. "I know you do."

"Even without it, I prove to them everyday that I'm their king." Hellmyr gestured with his chin to the palace around them.

"An easy thing to say as son of a king."

"Maybe so." Hellmyr shrugged as he ate another plum. "Though he tried to kill me as an infant. Only by my mother giving up any ties to me and giving me to a stranger did I survive past a few days."

Juras ate in silence as he considered this.

It was uncomfortably close to the circumstances of his own birth. Though, he didn't think Hinterfell wanted him dead.

In fact, the birth of a baby ensured its mother continued to remain at the brothel. Juras had heard of very few cases in which fathers of brothel children bought out their mothers' debt to Hinterfell. Juras had never known who his father was, and he preferred it that way.

"And you killed the High King. Your father," Juras said.

"He deserved it." Hellmyr didn't look at him as he said it, seeming more preoccupied with spreading cheese on bread. But Juras thought he saw the look in his eyes change at the mention of the previous king.

Juras swallowed. He was sure he had.

Suddenly, Juras stood. Hellmyr's eyebrows came together. "What's wrong?" the fae asked.

His heart thundered.

Juras pulled off his shirt and draped it over the back of his chair.

"You asked about these. I'll tell you," Juras said.

Was this a part of Juras's act? The one in which he'd been trying to get a fae to fall for him over his pregnant best friend?

Or was this real?

Does it matter? Juras wondered.

Juras traced the longest of his scars, the ones that he had the most of. "But only these," he said. Hellmyr watched and waited in silence.

Juras turned around. He found he could speak about it easier that way. Besides, many of these longer ones spanned his back and shoulders.

"They are what they look like. Lash marks."

Juras breathed. He kept his eyes on the wall opposite him as his pulse raced.

"I got these because I attacked my mother's client," he said. Juras closed his eyes as he remembered. "He'd leave bruises on her after. One day, I couldn't ignore it."

He wasn't sure what compelled him to keep talking, but he did. "The brothel madam punished me with these, but I've never regretted it." He clenched his teeth hard enough to hurt. "I should have killed him."

Juras saw and felt it again—how he'd attacked the bastard who had hurt her. He'd done it perhaps a few months before she'd fallen ill with the sickness that would claim her life. His knuckles ached.

He'd been young then. He wondered if he could have finished the job now that he was more than a scrawny brothel brat.

She shouldn't have spent her last few healthy weeks entertaining that monster.

Juras opened his eyes, willing the images and memories to fade. He moved to grab his shirt to put it back on.

"If you were mine—in the real way—the one who gave you those would be dead," Hellmyr said.

Hellmyr was suddenly too close to him. Juras was near enough that he breathed in his scent—something between amber and the smell of the woods.

"What are you talking about?" Juras said.

He turned around, a heady anger suddenly flooding him. "I *am* yours. You've made it so. Forced it out of me, actually." The words left Juras's tongue too quickly for him to stop them.

But he couldn't seem to shut up. Not about this.

Instead of rising to his anger like he'd wanted, Hellmyr only stared.

"Not anymore, Juras," he said finally. It was strange to hear his name on Hellmyr's tongue. It made him wanted to shiver.

"I revoke our bargain making you beholden to me."

CHAPTER THIRTY-ONE

I t was time. Evening light leaked into their rooms from their thick glass windows.

Anova looked to her bed. The servants had already delivered their clothes during the day. She spread her hands across the light silver-gray material of the strapless dress. The topmost layer of gauzy fabric had crescent moons embroidered into it, spreading down a floor-length skirt that was interrupted by a side-slit. The material was achingly soft to the touch.

It was the color of moonlight.

Suddenly, Anova heard a cacophony of voices outside her bedroom door. The fae attendants had arrived to dress them and make them look presentable to *his majesty*.

She glanced to her mirror as one of them knocked.

"Your Majesty, it is time for us to prepare you for the ceremony." Before she'd even answered, she heard them trying the door knob.

In the mirror, her hand hovered over her soft stomach.

"I do not yet need assistance dressing," she told them. "Tell that to the king. Or, if he wants to dress me himself, so be it. He can come here and do that."

Heat from the crown's magic gathered in her palms but cooled moments later as silence passed. *They must have moved on to Juras's room.*

I should have warned him about that.

She took her chance and undressed. Her skin was scarred and puckered in places where the flames had done their worst. Her gaze didn't linger as it moved elsewhere.

Her limbs were toned and lithe as a fae's were. But her abdomen was as soft as a human's … And more so than was normal for a half-starved street rat.

It contrasted with the rest of her. It would have been evidence enough, had they seen her undressed so.

She clasped the backing of the dress together herself, and it ran over her body like water, falling with and highlighting the gentle curve of her back. White gems glimmered within the fabric at her skirts as she moved.

Am I ready for this?

Moon madness?

There was no other choice. She had to be. She had to give herself to this experience tonight. Or else Cadmus and Nerium didn't stand a chance against their foes.

She would do this for him, she decided.

Anova stepped outside her room to see a gaggle of fae flitting around a red-faced Juras. There were so many that she could hardly see past them at all.

"Leave him alone," she began but stopped herself. Her mouth popped open in a gasp.

They were already done, and damn, they were *good*.

His shirt was made of the same fabric as her dress, and it highlighted his upper biceps and a large span of his chest. It was the same silken silver-gray material and nearly sheer in some places.

His pants were midnight blue and a tailored fit that made her wonder when they'd sized him. Cuffed along one of his ears was a small silver band, shaped into a crescent moon like the ones all over her dress. A hint of kohl had been applied around his eyes, bringing the gray out.

Juras looked away. "It's all ridiculous, but I couldn't stop them once they started."

Anova shook her head. "No, you look ..." What was the right word? She found it a second later. "Dangerous."

He smiled at that. It was something they used to tell each other before a job. Juras nodded at her.

"And you, too," he said. His eyebrows raised. "That dress."

The fae attendants still tried to come for her, but Anova managed to shoo them from their rooms. Their escorts to the celebration would arrive any moment, and she needed to speak with Juras about their plan.

When they'd left, Juras stared at the door.

She shook her head. They were as alone as they could be, considering they were guarded every moment of the day. Anova beckoned him to her room where curious fae ears out in the hall would be least likely to overhear them.

"Are you sure you're fine with this?" Anova looked to the last streaks of daylight leaking through her window. "Even without many more Fae in attendance than were already here, moon celebrations tend to make the fae ... unstable."

Juras looked at her straight. "Unstable? Like they were so sane to begin with." He stopped himself. "Well, except—"

"It's fine," she interrupted him. "I know what you mean."

I know you didn't mean me.

Even if she wasn't sure she was exempt.

Anova pushed that thought away even when another, worse one replaced it.

Am I going to go crazy and lose myself tonight like the rest of them do?

Will I be the same person under this moon?

But she had to try to heal the flow of magic between the land and the moon if they were going to solve things with Alys and the humans. No matter what Alys said about diplomacy, Cadmus and Nerium needed their magic back.

Anova pulled open the top drawer of her dresser. Among dangling earrings and other jewelry worthy of the pet-turned-prized-fae-lady of the king, she'd hidden them.

They were vials of diluted belladonna juice. A sip or two would be enough to render an adult fae unconscious shortly after.

The dosage and its effects were something Anova knew from experience.

Without hesitation, Viridia took to the air and landed on the tip of Juras's nose. His eyebrows jumped up at the sight of her.

"It's good to see you, too, Viridia." He watched as she crawled along the bridge of his nose. His eyes went to Anova. "Do you think she's healed enough for this?"

Viridia seemed to answer him herself when she launched from his nose and hovered in front of him, her wings strong enough to push a light wind into his face as she stared him down.

"Okay, okay, I think you've proved your point," Anova said, offering the butterfly one of her fingers. Instead, she landed in her hair. When she looked in her mirror to see where she was, Anova couldn't help but smile.

She'd attached herself to one of her opal hairpins.

"She looks like she's part of the hairpin," Juras pointed out.

Anova blinked, realizing her insect friend's intent. "You came up with this, didn't you? This would be a perfect way to keep you on me for the night without raising any suspicions."

Viridia flapped her wings smugly as Anova dipped one of her fingers in sugar water to give her a treat.

After rest, fae medicine, and a steady supply of nectar, Viridia had recovered well in the past several days, and Anova was gladdened to see it.

Once they left their rooms, Guards accompanied them on all sides as they walked to the wide hall where the celebrations were to be held. Night had fallen moments ago. Anova felt it in how the air sang around her.

The full moon was rising.

Resting on her hairpin, Viridia flexed her wings among the strands of Anova's chestnut hair. Anova breathed.

They were ready for this.

She caught Juras's eye as they walked. He'd been staring at the lanterns filled with flashing insects. The light of the will-o-wisp-filled gloom forests of Eastwoe filtered through the high windows that they passed. The soft illumination outside made strange shapes on his face as they walked.

What was she dragging him into? Even without all of Fae in attendance, a full moon celebration wasn't exactly safe for a human.

It won't be like how it was when I was here, she vowed to herself.

"Stay by my side," she whispered to him, steadying his arm with a grasp.

She hoped he knew what she wished she could have said in front of their guards but couldn't.

We'll save them tonight.

Juras gave a tight nod. She wanted to ask him how he was feeling, but it was then that their entourage stopped.

As they entered the wide room, the fae that were gathered had all paused at once. They were the same guards, staff, and attendants who she usually saw.

But they seemed vastly different right then. They wore dresses and vests and silk and gauzy shirts. They drink wine and fed each other berries. They moved and laughed at the edges of the room—until they noticed her.

Anova tried not to stare back. The fae in attendance were nowhere near the number they'd had at the quarter moon celebration.

This has to work.

Anova would restore the magic from the moon to the earth and then they'd begin their plan. They'd drug Hellmyr and take him on Viridia's back out of the palace.

With so many of his guards here, it was their best chance, despite the risks.

Hellmyr beckoned them forward. On top of his head was a crown of black feathers sewn together between black gems. Cascading down his shoulders was a black mantle. He wore a charcoal-colored doublet inlaid with crescent moons. They all matched.

Anova looked to Juras as they walked to the center of the ball towards him.

"What's wrong?"

Juras's face had paled. He stopped walking.

"It's you." He shook his head. "I'm sorry—it's just—"

He went back to staring. His voice was small. "Your shadow."

Anova followed his gaze. Light was coming from her. In her shadow were strands of moonlight, moving as she moved and following her as she went.

Moonlight poured like molten silver through the porthole above them.

When she saw it, a strange beating began in her veins.

All at once, she felt how the stars must have. Glimmering. Immense but removed. Powerful.

She needed to feel its light on her, more than anything. She needed to feel the light of the stars, too. She needed it more than life.

Her feet ached to run towards it—to embrace it and bathe in it. To know what it was to be home.

Anova stopped, jerking back from the light. This wasn't her home.

What was happening? It felt like her blood crown hallucinations all over again.

No. No, this isn't me. You won't take me like this.

But as she gazed at the threads of light spilling from around the column that poured inside the room, she felt it.

It was small at first—the feeling of the life within her. But it grew until she could ignore it no longer.

How its heart beat strong and loud for the moon.

"This is what you want, isn't it?" she whispered as she stared at the light filtering inside. As she looked upon it herself, Anova realized something.

The moon was strongest now. If she could harness it and use it to protect herself and the life inside her, then she would no longer be beholden to Rietvar.

What if I lose myself? What am I giving up for it?

There was always a price. But sometimes, the toll was worth the result.

Anova stepped into the blade of the pure white moonbeam.

Juras wasn't sure what he was seeing.

Well, he had been certain seconds ago. He'd walked with Anova into the full moon fête only for the fae creatures to stare mercilessly at them.

Then, she'd started to radiate light.

For a moment, he thought she'd decided not to go through with this after seeing the moonlight.

When she'd stepped into it, something had happened. The gasps of the fae filled the air.

"Anova," Juras said. He started for her, but one of the king's guards grabbed his wrist.

"Stay out of this," he ordered.

A blinding white light flooded the hall. It came from her in a wave like heat from the sun. Anova raised her arms to her crown within the column of light. Her eyes were a pure white, pupilless and unearthly.

Juras locked eyes with Hellmyr.

Is this normal? he mouthed to him.

But by the expression on his face, Juras could tell it wasn't.

A fierce wind kicked up around them, sending plates and goblets from the feast tables crashing to the ground. Glass danced around them like leaves.

A wordless agreement passed between the two of them.

They both cared about her too much. This wasn't normal or perhaps even healthy. They had to do something.

As soon as it had been summoned, the wind died around them and the flooding light faded. But Juras had been mistaken when he'd thought she'd tried to lift her crown off.

Her hands had gone to Viridia in her hair. As Anova held her, Viridia grew to the size of a small horse in the air above Anova.

In turn, the moonlight-fed butterfly plucked Anova where she stood and flew through the porthole in the ceiling.

Around them was a strange quiet. Juras stared without comprehending for far too many seconds.

What is going on? That wasn't our plan. What the hell?

But the answer was all around him. The influence of the full moon had gotten to her. She was fae now, no matter if he remembered that fact or not.

This was who she was, now.

He didn't care who saw. Hellmyr was still staring at the space where she'd been as if transfixed by what had happened. *Or perhaps it's gotten to him, too.*

Juras grabbed him by the shoulders. "We have to go. We need to find her."

Hellmyr's dark violet eyes focused on him, and his expression changed in an instant. He side-stepped out of Juras's grasp.

The fae king turned to his guards. "Accompany us. Ready several of my horses. We're going after her."

CHAPTER THIRTY-TWO

The gloom woods raced past them. Every few breaths, spurs of strange lights glowed between the tree branches above their heads. Their horses pushed away the dangling branches of river willows as they galloped into the soft earth.

Juras had been shoved onto a horse ahead of the fae king and was surrounded on all sides by him and his fae retinue.

As if he'd try to escape the king's clutches *now* when Anova was missing and there were potentially murderous humans about. Juras leaned forward into his mount, a cherry-brown mare with a mane of sleek black hair.

He could feel how the fae around him reacted to the moonlight dappling their skin from the trees around them. A tense energy carried on the air. They reacted strangely to familiar stimuli. Their gazes lingered where they shouldn't have, and they noticed less of what they should have. He could feel their group pull towards patches of unblocked moonlight filtering to the ground.

Juras looked to Hellmyr. The fae king was armed well, and where moonlight hit his body, the silver of twin sword hilts reflected back. His jaw was angled, and it looked to Juras as if he was constantly clenching his teeth as he rode them forward harder.

A strange feeling twisted inside Juras's stomach at seeing the concern for her driving him so mad.

But why should it bother him so? Juras was just as worried. His best friend was in danger—whether by Alys or Anova herself.

And Juras had no real claim to the fae king's attention. Hellmyr was a means to an end—just as Juras had been to him, he reminded himself. He shoved that fact before himself with aggression.

Juras had achieved that very means the other night. He was free of him.

Then why doesn't it feel like it?

There was no time for more thought. Hellmyr's guards in front motioned for them to stop.

"What is it? Speak," Hellmyr commanded them. Even before they could respond, he was off his horse.

His guards stepped back towards him from where they'd surveyed beyond the trees ahead. Their eyes were unfocused, and one of them seemed to sway.

"You should see for yourself, Your Majesty," one said with too-bright eyes.

Juras dismounted. This didn't feel right. He needed to speak to Hellmyr. They were under some spell, and he wasn't sure it was just the moon's.

But Hellmyr was already moving, pushing past his attendants voicing the concern stuck in Juras's throat.

The fae king stalked past the last of the willows as he drew one of his silver-inlaid swords. Juras started after him, his name on his tongue but still trapped within him. On the other side of the trees, he stopped.

It was like something out of a dream.

On a lake as clear as crystal, Anova danced on its surface. As far as he could see, her feet kicked up no ripples or splashes as she moved. Instead of water, it looked as if she danced on solid glass. As she moved, light filled the body of the lake more and more.

The fae guards and attendants started to lope towards the lake. Juras felt the opposite—an insurmountable paralysis.

Anova didn't appear to notice them. In fact, she seemed not to notice much but the threads of light that came from her hands. They faded after her like dying stars.

Juras could do little but stare.

The other fae had gathered at the edges of the lake and must have found it equally as solid as Anova had, for they joined her in their revels of the moon and began to dance.

Juras couldn't stop staring.

She's still there. It's still her.

But the more he watched, the more she looked like their queen.

Hellmyr was right. Juras was just a human. They were kings and queens. Fae and monsters. They were *magic*.

He was just a professional street rat.

Suddenly, the clothes on his back felt heavy, like an ill-fitted costume.

Like he was playing a part in a theater show.

Juras wasn't sure when he'd walked back into the woods. All he knew was that he couldn't remain there any longer.

They were like feral animals and gods all in one.

He leaned against the gnarled trunk of a willow, its whip-like branches draped all around him.

How the hell were they going to get back to Wolfsbane's estate tonight? Time was running out by the second, but Anova held the paralysis poison.

By himself, Juras couldn't do it. His teeth gritted.

He needed to be there for her. She was still Anova.

And he was being an ass, hiding like this.

It was then that he felt his skin crawl. Juras jerked around, but there were only shadows. A sheen of sweat had coated his back.

He breathed. It was time to stop jumping at nothing and try to get Anova out of the moonlight.

I'll have to enlist his help, he realized.

"Tell me, human, whose are you? Or are you out here all alone?"

Juras's back hit the tree as he lurched from the voice. His eyes adjusted a moment later to see a male fae with too-bright green eyes.

Juras couldn't help but wonder if the fae's teeth were sharp enough to tear flesh as he smiled at Juras. The fae's eyes lingered on him uncomfortably.

"Leave me alone," Juras muttered as he turned to walk from him.

The fae ignored him, and he moved too fast for Juras to stop him. His hand hovered above the skin of Juras's throat where his heart raged.

"This is where they usually are. The collars or marks for the house you should belong to," he said. His eyes flitted up to Juras's face again. "But you belong to no one, isn't that right?"

Juras's throat felt too tight to speak through, but he managed after a moment.

"I am no one's," he said.

It was stupid, of course. Juras should have claimed to belong to the most powerful fae—or any of them at all—but to say it felt too much like surrendering when he'd only just reclaimed his freedom.

The fae's eyes seemed to glow with malice at Juras's admission. A slice of moonlight fell past the branches. Juras's hair stood on end.

This fae was moon-mad. There could be no doubt.

He needed some way to defend himself, but he was cornered.

"Then you'll be my pet." The fae flashed him an evil grin as he came closer. "I've heard humans break so splendidly."

"Like hell I will." Juras's teeth ached from clenching them. If he had to go down here, he would fight all the way.

Juras's hand snapped out to rip one of the branches from the tree, but the fae was faster.

"You shouldn't have been out here, a human in Fae during a full moon such as this one. We can't help ourselves what we do tonight," he confided.

His hands were on Juras's wrists, and his grip was iron. He shoved his wrists together in a blink, but not before Juras slammed his head into the fae's.

Stars burst across his vision, but Juras couldn't stop for a breath now. He jerked out of the fae's grasp. He needed to run. Now.

Juras got only three steps away before the fae grabbed him again.

"Normally we make deals with your kind to trick you into becoming our servants," the fae whispered into his ear as he pulled Juras to him.

"Get off me," Juras growled. He shoved an elbow into his stomach.

The fae gasped in a sharp breath but didn't release him. "But I think I deserve some recompense for that alone," he hissed. "Lost little human."

Juras's heart thundered hard, making him dizzy.

The fae's hands were rough on his face as he forced him to look him in his terrible gaze.

"But maybe I'll just convince you to be my slave ... let's say, until you die. And that's all the life you've ever known."

His grin sharpened as he continued to speak. "How magnificently pitiful."

CHAPTER THIRTY-THREE

Juras stared back, aware that he had perhaps seconds before he lost his sense—and possibly his memories. He'd seen it happen too quickly with Anova.

Would he even realize what he'd lost?

Juras didn't think. He hurled a wad of spit into the monster's face.

The monster's grip found his throat and squeezed.

"Little human—"

But the fae's words were cut off.

"You have three seconds to grovel for mercy," came another voice behind the fae.

Juras blinked, and a silver sword gleamed in the limited light. Though it was dim under the branches of the grim willow, Juras clearly saw the dark purple-violet of his eyes shine with something not all that benevolent.

It was Hellmyr.

But it didn't make sense. Why was he here? He should have been dancing with Anova, drinking in the light that was intoxicating to them.

His queen.

The fae's grin turned to a sneer. He released Juras before glaring at Hellmyr. His eyes lingered on his feathered crown.

His sneer faded.

"My king—"

"He is mine. Now turn around and beg for forgiveness from him."

"From him?" The fae's eyes narrowed on Juras. "But he's—"

Hellmyr moved so fast that Juras nearly lost sight of him in the gloom-shadows. His sword pierced the tendons of the fae's shoulder. He let out a screech that sounded as if his blood were being boiled inside him.

Juras found he couldn't speak. It was then that Hellmyr caught sight of his face. He didn't know what he saw there, but he knew he felt like vomiting.

His entire life had nearly been erased.

"Are you fine with my killing him?" Hellmyr murmured.

Juras was far from fucking fine. Would being sprayed in the blood of the fae who'd nearly killed or enslaved him help?

He wasn't sure.

When Juras didn't respond, the fae king's gaze switched back to where the other fae cringed on the ground. He held his seeping wound like a mother would a child.

"Stop that and listen to me." Hellmyr shoved the tip of his sword under his chin. A soft glow coursed through it, touching the fae's skin. He seemed powerless but to look at Hellmyr then.

"You will never return here. You will never approach this human again. Or I will kill you for it." Hellmyr showed the fae his teeth as he vowed it. "And I would *enjoy* it."

Hellmyr removed the weapon. As the glow subsided from the air around them, the fae male staggered to his feet. Without looking back, he ran into the thick gloom around them.

For many seconds, Juras just breathed. Even without a fae sense of smell, he noticed the scent of blood on the air. His wound had left stains on the earth.

Juras looked at the king of monsters before him.

He'd once told Anova that she was unreasonable to hate them just because they were fae.

But the more he lingered here, the more he understood.

The more he felt the same.

For some reason, Juras could say only one thing. "Why aren't you with her?"

"She's safe." There was something strange to his voice as he said it.

Juras backed away several steps. His hands ran through his hair. He felt like he was the crazy one here. Like he was losing his mind.

Why the hell was he acting like this? Juras had known better. This whole time, he'd known the fae were monsters.

Just like you know he's one of them, too.

Any of them could have done any of that. Made him forget who he was. Why he was here.

It was somehow worse than being killed by one of them.

"Tell me what you're thinking," Hellmyr said suddenly.

"You can't guess? With my heartbeat?" It came out less like a question and more an accusation.

"No."

Honesty. It must have been a trick.

"And why do you care?" Juras said. But there was no answer to that, he knew. Juras continued by answering his question. "I'm thinking that it's always going to be too much."

Juras laughed then. Once he started, he couldn't stop.

Hellmyr watched, his eyes dark in the gloom.

"I don't understand."

"You're always going to have the upper hand." Juras's laughs died. "You're always going to be too strong. Too ... overwhelming. Too better."

This was how Anova had dealt, Juras realized suddenly. She'd broken herself into becoming stronger. More than a fae was. It was what this place had done to her.

But he couldn't. If he broke, he would break weaker.

Anova had always been different from him in that way.

He charmed and lied while she lied and fought.

"And what would change that for you?" Hellmyr said.

Juras turned around. "Nothing. Don't you understand? It's what you are. Not what you do. You'll always be in power." Juras laughed. "You had it right before. The servant coming to his fae master to submit to him. That was what you wanted. No, that was *natural* for you."

Hellmyr's eyes stared unblinkingly. Hard. Unrelenting.

"That isn't what I want," Hellmyr said finally.

"What do you want?" Juras spat out. "Why did you do it? You shouldn't care this much."

He couldn't stop it now that he'd started. All his carefully preserved fear and anger was leaking out of him.

"This isn't normal." Juras's hands flew to his scalp as he continued talking. He needed to stop talking. "I'm nothing here."

He looked at Hellmyr. He'd gotten what he'd wanted; he'd seduced the fae king for his freedom and Anova's.

Then why did it feel like this?

Hellmyr narrowed his eyes. "I'm more interested in what you want."

What?

It was such a ridiculously simple question, and yet, he struggled with it.

Juras wanted to get out of here. But he couldn't, not when doing so meant he'd turn tail back to his hide-hole in Irbess like the coward he'd been this entire time.

He couldn't leave. But maybe he could escape.

He could lose himself.

It was odd, considering he'd been so afraid of that exact thought only moments ago. But he wanted to forget it all right now.

Juras didn't answer verbally. Instead, he brought the fae close by pulling at his cloak. His hands slipped into the fae's wild raven hair until they formed a cage at the back of his neck.

Too quickly, Juras's mouth was on his.

It was exactly as he'd hoped. It felt like drowning.

It was dark. Easy. Numbing.

He tasted like sweet berries, and he smelled like hickory. After a moment, Hellmyr seemed to thaw out. His hands explored Juras's stomach under his shirt. Suddenly, their kiss broke, and he pulled Juras's shirt off him.

Juras pushed the fae against the rough bark of the willow, tracing the edge of Hellmyr's lips that were swollen from their kissing. He pulled Juras's ear to his mouth to whisper.

"Because you undo me, and I'm afraid of that," Hellmyr admitted.

Juras didn't let it settle in the air between them. He didn't stop to process what the words meant or why he'd said it now.

Juras moved Hellmyr's head so he could kiss him again. Losing himself to the sensation of Hellmyr's mouth on his meant he couldn't think.

Juras didn't want this. And yet, he wanted it most of all.

He pushed deeper, and Hellmyr's hands gripped either side of his hips in response.

"Tell me what you're thinking," Hellmyr whispered in his ear when they paused to breathe.

"That I hate all of you. And that I hate myself for thinking it," Juras panted, surprising himself with the words.

He could feel Hellmyr's smile when the fae pulled him back to his lips. Juras's hands found Hellmyr's wrists and pushed them against the tree, holding the fae king there. But he couldn't stop the heat that spread through him.

It made him want to do terrible, wonderful things.

No, Juras realized. He hated that he wanted this.

He lost track of time then. The stars might have moved around them a thousand cycles for all he noticed.

It was then that Hellmyr stopped kissing back. Juras pulled away to look into his eyes, but the fae's blinks had already slowed to a close.

Hellmyr slumped forward.

CHAPTER THIRTY-FOUR

Anova spun like a puppet on a string. Something inside her was happy to be pulled along by the force that moved her so.

She was barely aware and yet much too aware of everything.

A bloody waltz. Gifts for a mad king. The moon spell.

Memories burst through the surface of her moon-addled mind, breaking the enchantment on her.

But there had been something else there—something behind the haze of the moon intoxication.

It'd been him. She'd been dancing ... with him.

Cadmus.

Anova's eyes darted all around her. She was in the grove of a dark wood that looked to be somewhere in the gloom forests of Eastwoe.

Where are you?

Anova found herself in the middle of a crowd of twirling and writhing fae that she didn't recognize. She touched her face and found it wet.

She'd been crying.

What's going on? How did I get here?

But she needed to find Cadmus, first. She was certain she'd just been with him.

When she came to her feet, she realized they were all on the surface of a lake. Anova stared into its depths that were pierced by stark moonlight in places. She didn't dare test the strength of the strange magic that made the water like solid ground.

Did I do this?

She put that thought of her mind. Questioning the magic might break it.

As she started to move through the crowd, none of the drunken fae appeared to notice her break from the spell. But as she neared the edge of the lake where the land began again, more and more of their heads stopped and stared at her.

They were waking.

Watching.

She felt it then—primal feelings that ran together inside her like rainwater and earth. The moon was heavy in the sky, calling to her, needing her to celebrate it.

It was saying her name.

Anova. Anova. Anova.

Anova's palms slammed against her ears. She didn't want this.

It wanted to fill her with its burning, searing, wonderful light.

No. NO. My mind is my own.

She needed to get away from the moonlight flowing across her skin and tainting her mind. She wanted to rip her skin from her bones just to stop it.

She started to run then.

Where was Juras? Hellmyr?

Gods, what had she done?

Humans aren't safe during a full moon in Fae.

How many times had she been hurt on a night like this one? How many times had a fae, drunk on moonlight, tried to hunt her?

Damnit, she knew better than this.

A strange feeling came to her then. She felt it in the wind that blew between the trees. How their leaves shifted.

They sounded like whispers.

Anova's head snapped in the direction the whispers came from. She was going mad.

Wasn't she?

Suddenly, she felt Hellmyr and Juras.

Juras must be safe, then. If not, Hellmyr was well aware of what she'd do to him. It was then that she heard the thundering of heartbeats.

It's them.

Anova slipped among the slender trees of the gloom woods and saw something she didn't understand. Juras had pushed Hellmyr against a tree.

They were kissing.

In the seconds that followed in which she couldn't move, she started to puzzle it out until it made sense.

Juras had volunteered himself to the fae to keep Hellmyr away from her and from finding out her secret. Anova's hand hovered over her belly.

She owed Juras for that.

But she had to talk to him about this. She had to understand how far it went. How far he'd gone for her.

And their time under the bloated moon was running thin. They had somewhere else to be.

She wasn't sure how, but the trees had led her here, and as Anova considered the problem at hand, she felt a strange urge blossom inside her.

Anova held her breath and allowed her heartrate to slow. She had to be covert lest Hellmyr realize she was there. When she came to the other side of the tree, the magic danced inside her. It was the crown, and it was drawing power from the earth, she realized.

Her body knew what to do before she did. The magic inside her ran from her, jumping from the tree's frame to the fae on the other side of it. She needed not to hurt him, but to remove him from the situation for a few moments while she spoke to Juras.

Or, that's what she told herself, at least.

Before Hellmyr slumped to the ground, Anova appeared and caught the fae.

She couldn't quite believe it. Before, she'd only used the crown's power to destroy. It was normally a twisted, sick thing that wanted to sear through her veins. Her leashed mountain cat with claws that mauled.

But she hadn't hurt him at all, it seemed. Dizziness circled her, but so did giddiness at the control of her power.

She looked up into Juras's face, and in his eyes was someone she didn't quite recognize.

Juras just stared. "What did you do?"

"I don't know how," she started. "He's just—knocked out."

But Juras was still staring. Well, it had seemed a good idea before.

"Anova, what the hell happened back there? What's going on?" he finally said.

As she considered how in the world she'd answer that, Anova placed Hellmyr on the ground. He looked oddly at peace in his sleep. It didn't suit him.

Juras didn't wait for her to respond. He began to laugh, though not in a joyful way.

Anova's hands found his shoulders. A pit had formed in her stomach.

"What happened to you?" she whispered.

She knew the signs of hysteria. Something had happened here tonight. And she'd let it.

His laughs had died. "Nothing happened," Juras said.

"That's a fucking lie, and you know it." She moved so he couldn't avoid her.

"And when have you been a stranger to fucking lies?"

Anova's heart hammered faster. *No. Please, Juras.*

But those words didn't leave her. Instead, she said, "Just tell me what happened. I'm sorry for ... tonight."

I don't know what I did under the moon. I don't even know what I'm apologizing for. Her teeth clenched.

Out loud, she added, "I shouldn't have let you be here."

A short, bitter laugh escaped Juras's throat. "Let me? The fae queen lets me in her realm, is that it?"

She didn't know this Juras.

"What are you talking about? I'm not some *fae queen*. You know that, Juras."

His gray eyes were piercing when he looked at her. "You could have fooled me."

"I'm still the same person." But her voice came out barely more than a whisper. If she couldn't convince herself, how could she convince him?

Juras turned from her then, shifting past the willow branches.

"Juras—"

"If you really think that, then tell me." He stopped and looked halfway at her. "What were you doing an hour ago?"

Anova didn't have an answer.

She still didn't have an answer when he said, "Don't follow me."

And left.

CHAPTER THIRTY-FIVE

Minutes passed. Anova knew not how many.

She was still staring after him when she felt she could move again.

Of course I'm coming after him. He'd be hollow-headed to think otherwise.

Despite the firm words she said to him in her head, Anova felt she left her heart behind her as she ran after him in the gloom woods.

She could still catch up to him. Hell, she could still smell him as his earthy scent wound through the trees. Juras's words rattled around in her head as she followed his trail.

Anova stopped. She shivered, though it wasn't a cold night.

His words ran through her, over and over.

"And when have you been a stranger to fucking lies?"

Fae queen.

She'd become what she'd despised. She was one of the things that had murdered her mother.

Something out of the corner of her vision moved then.

She hadn't smelled or heard anything. Anova jerked around but saw nothing except streams of moonlight between the trees. It fell between branches, slicing through them to the ground.

Anova's blood ran cold as ice as she finally saw something among the gloom.

A familiar hissing double-voice called to her.

"Jumpy, are we?"

A scream stuck in her throat. *This isn't real. This isn't real.*

It's just the moonlight.

"Oh, I'm very real."

Malor's eyes were as red and malevolent as she'd remembered. His antlers threw shadows as he shifted.

"No," Malor continued. "I'm as real as ever, Anova."

Before she could move, he stepped forward and touched her face.

Gods, was he?

"It feels real because this is in my head." Anova shook her head and backed away from him like that would dispel the illusion. It didn't.

She hadn't had a hallucination from the blood crown since she'd been human. But this was surely another of them.

"Not so. I'm here because you've accepted me." Malor's voice raised the hairs on her arms.

"That doesn't make sense. I saw you die," Anova said between her teeth.

"Haven't you guessed what I am yet?" Malor tilted his head so his antlers were highlighted in the pale light. He closed the distance between them again. "Or do you not want to know?"

"You're part of the crown," Anova whispered.

Malor had always seemed to her a being more of magic and spite than one of flesh and blood. But this ...

"Erion gave much to make me physical," Malor said. "Until then, I'd been a mere voice in his head."

She hadn't heard the previous high king's name in so long that it took Anova a few seconds to realize who he'd meant. And then, the rest of what he'd said hit her.

This must have been how he'd gone crazy, she realized.

She backed away further and hissed, "What could you want from me, you devil?"

"Now, that's the problem here. You're the devil. We are one and the same." Malor cocked his head to one side. "The pitiable human is right."

Anova raised her voice in the gloomy quiet. "No, he's not,"

But he was gone.

And so was her hope of finding Juras, she realized.

A wordless yell tore through her. None of it made sense.

No, it does, something in her argued. *The problem is you don't want to face it.*

She was tired of what or who she was supposed to be. No matter what Juras said to her—no matter if he wanted to never see her again—he'd been here because of her.

And he'd been the closest thing to family she'd had for years. She needed to find him.

She needed to help Cadmus.

She needed to fix *everything*.

Her fingers dug against her scalp as she sank to her knees. She didn't want to look through the shadows anymore in case they took other forms like High King Erion himself, dead as he was.

"Juras," she whispered, but she knew he was gone from here.

And he doesn't want me by him anyway.

"What the hell have I become?" she said, too quiet for anyone else to hear.

Just then, she felt a soft touch at her forehead. Anova looked up to see Viridia, small and flexing her wings where she sat on her.

"At least I can still call you a friend," she said in an admittedly weak voice. She held out a finger for her to climb to.

We have to go from here.

Without thinking on it further, she knew what to do. Anova held her other hand out to a pure white moon beam.

I need something to feed you so you can grow strong again, my friend.

The light poured, turning to liquid silver before her eyes. Anova held her breath.

Somehow, she'd learned this. Fae magic. It wasn't like using the crown—it didn't build in her body to the point of bursting.

The magic felt cool to the touch. Viridia alighted on her other hand and drank her fill of it.

As she grew in the air before her, Anova knew what to do. Even if he didn't want to see her anymore or even care what happened to her, she cared for him.

She said to the butterfly, "Find Juras. Keep him safe. Get him out of here, please."

Viridia, now as grown as a horse, nuzzled Anova's palm. Her tiny ebony hairs rippled in the breeze.

A moment later, she turned from Anova and galloped into the thick gloom faster than Anova could run.

Thank you.

CHAPTER THIRTY-SIX

Anova's heart pounded until she found Hellmyr.

She needed him to live. Despite how much of an ass he could be, he didn't deserve to be left alone and unconscious on such a night when moon madness filled their veins.

And without him, there would be bedlam. It was possible there'd even be a civil war to find the next ruler of Fae.

But there's a real reason you can't have him die, a voice inside her said.

It's because you'd be the replacement.

Anova ignored this thought as she checked his vital signs. His pulse was regular, and he was still unconscious.

Not that it matters now that it's impossible to get there in time tonight.

Viridia was gone, and not even a horse would get them to the Wolfsbane estate before the sun rose again.

Anova curled into herself next to him on the ground. It was then that she remembered what had happened on the lake. She'd been dancing with Cadmus—or rather, a shadow of magic that looked like him.

They'd moved in a pattern like the waltz they'd danced on the morning she'd woken as a fae. When she'd known he was alive again.

She'd cried when the dream had ended.

Her fists trembled. None of it mattered now. She'd given up her only way back to him.

And after tonight ...

Did Cadmus believe she would come back for him? Had Nerium told him?

Would Alys hurt them for her failure tonight?

What wouldn't she do to him? To all of them?

She swallowed the sobs inside her, but her shoulders shook from the force of holding them back. There was a life inside her, dependent on her, and she couldn't even protect that.

Soft footfalls broke into her thoughts. Anova jerked herself upright on the ground, her heart tumbling inside of her.

It didn't smell like a fae or human. Her breath froze in her chest when she saw.

The creature's lavender eyes were on her, too. After a moment, the unicorn padded closer, her eyes not leaving Anova's except for a brief glance at Hellmyr.

After a moment, she continued closer. She remembered Hellmyr saying that unicorns didn't like those who had unpure hearts.

But she didn't appear so bothered by his presence now, stopped as she was before the both of them. The unicorn lowered her head until her snout touched Anova's forehead.

Anova didn't dare move in case she startled her. It was then that a strange thought occurred to her.

Your name is Nemesia.

Anova frowned. She knew it to be true, and yet ... How had she known?

Nemesia moved a step away, and Anova came to her feet, barely breathing. Quietly, she said, "Where have you been? This is your lake, isn't it?"

Nemesia's gaze moved to the trees and back.

"I'm sorry." She breathed. "They're here because of me. I hope you weren't driven from your home."

But something in her eyes changed. Had Anova misunderstood?

She tried to remember what she'd learned about unicorns. She knew laughably little.

"Can I ... help you?" she tried again.

When silence met her, heat prickled at the back of her neck and she shifted her footing. She was alone in a wood talking to an animal of myth.

This was an intelligent creature, certainly. But that didn't mean the unicorn could understand her words. Right?

Anova's hand moved to Nemesia's sleek hide. She was warm. Anova listened to her heartbeat, trying to time the strange and inhuman rhythm.

Nemesia's heart beat faster at her touch, but she didn't pull away from her.

"Is this what you want?" Anova said. Her hand moved to where her mane spilled, tumbling over her pure white body. "You're beautiful," she whispered.

Nemesia moved so she was in the path of the moonlight, her eyes still on Anova. Her heart sped up again.

Anova stared. Could she want ...

Suddenly, she knew what to do.

Her other hand collected the silver light in her palm, and she closed her eyes.

I want to grant Nemesia's wish, she thought.

She had no idea how any of this worked. But before she could reconsider, the moon nectar had spilled to the unicorn's hide.

The air shimmered between them. Nemesia whinnied and backed up by several steps. Anova gasped.

As the unicorn raised on her back legs, something grew from the moonbeams pouring on her. Small stubs from her back formed into wings, silver like the moon and larger even than Viridia's.

It was the most magnificent thing Anova had ever seen. She'd become a thing of myth.

A winged unicorn.

Nemesia kicked at the dirt and locked gazes with Anova. This had been what she'd wanted, she realized. With careful steps, Anova came by her side once again.

Juras couldn't stop running.

Around him, the woods flickered with strange lights as he sprinted. He couldn't be sure, but he felt they watched him. They blinked, moving between distant trees and fading before he could see them better.

A chill ran up his spine. Was this the magic of the fae? Or something else entirely?

His body wanted to quit more than anything, but he couldn't afford to stop. Noises in the bushes sounded, getting closer.

His stomach dropped when he considered what it could be.

No. He didn't want to think. Not about him. Not about any of them. But the thoughts crashed through him anyway.

What if that rabid fae came back?

Hellmyr had injured and humiliated the other fae, making him vow never to return. But Hellmyr wasn't here now.

Well, he would fight him. Kill, even. He was no fae's plaything.

Never again.

Juras's head shot up. The disturbance came from the direction he'd been heading in—away from the noises.

Her spindle legs flicked off the highest branch above him to float to the ground with a grace that was impressive for her size.

"Viridia," he croaked. Juras had never felt happier to see the butterfly, even if her present form unnerved him still.

He approached her, one of his palms stretched towards her. Her black compound eyes watched, only breaking contact for her delicate head to move into his palm.

"I'm sorry," he whispered. "But I need to ask a favor." He lowered himself so his face was at her level. "I need to get back to where we came from. Do you remember it?"

He didn't belong in this wretched place. He never had.

If Anova did, well then that was her business now.

She wasn't the Anova he'd known.

CHAPTER THIRTY-SEVEN

The air nipped at Juras's feet and fingers as it rushed past Viridia's delicate wings. He thought he'd left his stomach somewhere on the ground below. Every time he looked down, his last meal bubbled into his throat.

Breathing out his nose helped. As did not looking down.

The air was colder up here. At least the moon's bloated light revealed more of the land around them.

"She sent you, didn't she?" he asked the magicked creature.

Of course, she didn't answer. She didn't have to, either.

Anova was somewhere below with her kind. He'd done his part and gotten the fae king's attention off her.

What had happened that night wasn't her fault, a part of him argued. He'd been the one to wander from the lakefront.

The wrong place at the wrong time.

Too bad all of Fae was the wrong place if you were a human.

And somewhere below was Hellmyr, drugged by Anova's new magic to be brought to the witch Alys. A swallow scratched his throat. This was the right decision.

This was how he got out of here alive. No matter what his fool heart felt.

All they do is trick and manipulate, he reminded himself.

He couldn't afford to believe that Hellmyr had real feelings for him. He was in love with Anova.

All Juras had been was a distraction from what the fae king couldn't have. Juras had known that from the start.

As he stared towards the horizon where the human realm slept, something happened. His vision dipped to the side suddenly, and air left him as his throat tightened around a silent yell.

And then, they were falling.

There was little Juras could do besides cling to Viridia. Below him, her body shrunk, her wings losing the air that had they had soared through only seconds before. Soon, her body squirmed from the weight of Juras, and he knew what he had to do.

She was smaller now than a foal, and he'd have no choice in seconds.

He jumped.

The tree below him carved off bits of his skin as he fell through its branches. All around him were flashes of moonlight, sky, and the ground rising beneath him. The yell in his throat never left him.

The world stopped, and pain burst against his side. He was suspended a few feet above the ground when he'd smacked into the branch that had blocked his fall. Juras breathed through his nose for several seconds, trying to will his heart to stop falling, too.

He couldn't tell in this darkness whether they'd even left Eastwoe yet. Juras cursed his luck.

At least nothing seemed broken.

They were right, he realized. *This moon magic is running thin—and on tonight of all nights when it should be most powerful for them.*

He didn't dare look up into the sky to see it, though the moon's strong beams illuminated the sparsely wooded area well enough. Something below him made his breath catch.

A worn pack had been hung by its single strap on a low branch of a tree nearby. Underneath it was a rudimentary hunting bow. Someone else was here.

Juras didn't move. Motion caught his attention in his periphery. Viridia, small as a regular butterfly again, alighted on his arm. Her eyes were bright as she looked to him and then took to the air again so that she landed on a branch just out of arm's reach.

As he looked to where she'd landed, he saw it then. The fae who the pack must have belonged to.

In water just deep enough to be called a river, his head emerged. Water clung to his hair, revealing the sharp ears that parted them.

Juras stilled in the tree. The fae hadn't seen or otherwise detected him yet. An idea sparked within him, dark and risky.

But it would be riskier to continue like by foot until another fae found him and tried to make him his brain-addled prisoner.

Juras decided then. He'd had enough of that.

As soon as the fae's head disappeared under the water again, Juras moved. He couldn't stop himself from making noise, so he worked quickly. Luck was on his side this time, and Juras found arrows in the pack. After grabbing the wide hunting bow, he crept to the water's edge.

A soft, featherlight pressure landed on his shoulder. If his nerves hadn't been so string-tight, he would have smiled.

"Okay. You can stay," he mouthed to Viridia.

She opened and closed her wings, once, in response.

He'd have to find some sugar water for her when he could afford to stop moving towards the boundary forests. Somehow, he didn't feel so alone with her.

He positioned them behind the brambles of the thick bushes that lined the riverside. In the shadows, he tested his ability to draw an arrow and nearly broke the bow in the process.

Juras's hands slicked with sweat. His eyes flicked to the river. The fae emerged downstream, but his eyes didn't leave the water. He appeared to be searching for something.

The fae dove into the water again, and his body moved like a fish even when he swam against the current.

For not the first time, Juras cursed their perfection.

Too soon, the fae broke the surface of the river again. Juras had no time to practice it anymore. He drew one of the arrows he'd taken from the fae's pack and stepped out of the brush, aiming it at the back of the fae's head.

"Try any magic, and I'll release one. We'll see who gets who first," Juras announced.

He kept far enough from the river bank to make sure he wouldn't be ensorcelled by fae magic. According to Anova, such magic needed direct contact. Even so, he needed to be close enough to make the threat count.

"Dying by my own weapon? How crass." The fae looked back at Juras when he said it.

Recognition shot through him, and he saw something similar bolt through the fae at the sight of Juras.

Juras couldn't help it. He nearly fired the arrow when he saw who it was.

"You're him. Wolfsbane," he murmured.

"Yes," the fae said carefully. His eyes tracked the nocked arrow in the bow that Juras still held.

He wasn't going to lower it so easily.

Even so, Juras blinked in surprise. This didn't make sense. "Anova said you're supposed to be—" Juras stopped himself.

He was being an idiot.

Wolfsbane completed the thought for him. "Leander, not Cadmus." Something in the words made Leander's mouth tighten. The expression was gone in an instant. "And you're one of Anova's ... friends." He'd said it like the word had only just occurred to him.

Like he'd meant to say *human servant*.

Juras still didn't lower his weapon. Even if they knew each other, that didn't mean they were on the same side. That had been proven to him too many times lately.

Leander's eyes were still on the bow Juras had stolen from him. Neither of them had moved an inch in their conversation, though Juras's arm ached and trembled from holding it. And he was sure the fae saw that.

The time for acting like this was a casual conversation was over.

"All I need is a few drops of magic imbued with the intention of returning her to the size of a steed." He'd learned how it worked from Anova. He motioned to Viridia with his chin as he spoke. "Enough to last until the boundary forests. I'll even leave you your weapon—so long as we get what we need, of course."

Leander Wolfsbane stared back at him.

When the fae finally spoke, the words came out through a smile. But Juras felt like shivering.

"Fortunately for your neck, it appears we have a mutual goal. In payment for not dispatching your head far from the rest of you, you'll take me to the boundary forests, too."

Leander stepped fully from the riverbank and continued speaking. The smile had fallen from his face. "Just don't threaten me again. Is that a deal, human?"

CHAPTER THIRTY-EIGHT

The cool night air brushed against her face. Anova held Hellmyr in her arms, funneling into him moonlight magic to keep him unconscious.

What she was doing would be an act of war between the two of them. Anova tightened her grip on him to keep them both on Nemesia.

He'd trusted her tonight. But he'd already proven to her the trust they'd had between each other had been fractured well with hairline cracks.

Too soon, the trees where she knew blocked the estate emerged on the horizon ahead of them. They were close.

The Sorrelands ran underneath Nemesia's wings. A land bountiful and empty.

She kept her gaze on the copse of trees that would best hide them as they descended. As she whispered to Nemesia where to land, memories of a different dark night haunted her. It had been the night she'd come back into Fae after escaping jail in Irbess.

Then, too, she had been on her way to save Cadmus. Except this time, it was up to her and her alone to free them all.

As Nemesia landed, her feet graceful upon the earth, Hellmyr still didn't stir. What would she have said to him if he had woken by now? There would have been no words. She kept one hand on his shoulder as she led Nemesia through the wooded area towards the field of flowers signaling the Wolfsbane lands.

She hoped it would all be worth it—that there would still be lives to save here.

Anova suddenly felt their frenzied heartbeats before hearing the rest of them.

Erratic. Excited.

Anova deflected the worst of their arrows with a wave of the crown's magic. Nemesia whinnied behind her but didn't buck off Hellmyr, blessedly.

"Enough," she snarled at the men in the woods around her. "You are weak to try this. Take me to her or die here. Either way, I'll find her."

They emerged around her, men like the ones she used to trick in taverns, like the constables who used to hunt her, like the ones who used to give her coins when she'd once begged for them.

"Prove he yet lives first, and that you are not a fae wearing another's face sent to trick us."

It was a valid concern, she admitted to herself.

The one who spoke wore the most knives and bows strapped across his body. Surprisingly, he was only a few years older than she was, and despite that fact, he seemed their commander. She would have once called men like him handsome.

Now, she kept one eye on him because the others seemed to respect him. If something happened and she needed to cut loose these boys, that would be the chain link to break.

Free the head, and the body would follow.

She breathed. *That* was definitely the thought of a fae.

After they saw that Hellmyr still lived, and she subjected herself to the effects of magic-nullifying salt for a moment, they led her to through the trees draped in wisteria to the Wolfsbane manor.

It seemed, once again, their enemies had taken it.

Anova parted from Nemesia just as they left behind the woods. The men made the unicorn nervous, and besides, Anova didn't want her caught in Alys's plans.

As the grand doors of the entry hall slammed behind them, the men carrying Hellmyr started forward to the heart of the manor while others, including their captain, tried to usher her to another room.

"Where are you taking him?" Anova stopped. The human men behind her shifted, their weapons coming to their hands.

"They are taking his *fae Majesty* to the negotiations room." Their captain came before her, blocking her vision of Hellmyr with his body. Derision was clear in his voice from the way he'd said his title.

"Where he goes, so do I. Until I get what is due to me," she amended at the end.

Without Hellmyr, she had no bargaining power, or at least that's the reason for staying with him that she told herself.

But their captain relented, and she was walked through the manor that she knew too well. As she was escorted through, she noticed more and more humans, some of which were women.

Her skin crawled. It certainly seemed Alys was ready for a war.

Her escort party arrived in the study moments after Hellmyr's procession did. He was left in one of Cadmus's chairs, head lolling to one side and his chest slow to rise. A human guard had been stationed to him.

Even so, he looked vulnerable. More than she ever remembered him seeming.

This was the wrong way to bring him here.

But when the answer could have been no—or even when the answer could have been to lock her in his dungeons for her treason against him—what choice had she had?

Anova stepped forward. Alys was in the middle of the library, speaking to the captain of the men.

"Where are they, Alys?" she called.

"They're alive." She spared a look at her, her eyes lingering just a second too long on the blood crown before returning to meet her gaze. "Your friends are safe where they are."

When she returned to speak with her captain again, Anova couldn't hold it inside her anymore. The energy of the blood crown flooded her veins, coming to her hands. The others tried to stop her, but the attack was already in motion. The sounds of their swords drawing became the accompaniment to her dance.

Strangely, it was of Hellmyr who she thought as she pulled a crystalline spear of ice from nothingness. This was how he'd fought her just before ensorcelling her.

The shard arced through the air as she dodged the men grappling for her. She'd long ago become faster than them—even as a human girl.

"Then show them to me," Anova said. Her crystal weapon hovered in the air as close to Alys's throat as she could get.

Her captain's blade was at Anova's throat in a similar fashion, but she didn't care any longer. Ever since she'd walked inside the estate, Anova had had a terrible feeling in the pit of her belly.

A feeling that she was already too late.

Alys's smile was frigid. "As the fae wishes." Without breaking their gaze, she ordered her men to bring them all to the study.

It seemed that's all she was to Alys, now. Anova should have taken the moment to investigate Alys's forces for a weakness, but she couldn't seem to concentrate from her anger at the witch.

Well, she'd done her part for humanity. And Anova had to admit that Hellmyr didn't hold a candle to his father's cruelty when it came to humans.

As the humans pulled a table from the dining room to the study for the negotiations to follow, Anova considered that there was a possibility that things could change tonight.

Or, Hellmyr will stir, and he will kill them all out of anger and confusion.

But she wasn't so sure that would be the worst thing.

And then, he'll move on to me.

"Anova!" By the time she turned to see Della, she'd already slammed into Anova with a breathtaking hug.

"I'm fae, not invulnerable," Anova muttered once the other woman had relented. She winced from the force.

Even so, she couldn't keep the joy from spreading through her at seeing her and Maris enter the study surrounded by armed humans.

"Are you okay? Did they hurt you?" she asked Maris under her voice.

But she wasn't paying attention to her. She was looking at Della whose eyes were on Anova. Or rather, whose eyes were on Anova's middle.

Anova didn't breathe. These two knew her too well. She couldn't have been showing—not yet, anyway—but something must have tipped her off.

Our hug, she realized. *She must have felt a bump.*

In the moment between realizing that she had a bump and finding the words to say to Della, Anova saw something. Her gaze had wandered to one of the high shelves of books in the study. On top of one like a trophy was a jar with a lid tight on it.

Inside was a bright, unmoving moth.

Something was deeply wrong here.

Anova's stomach cramped. Undoubtedly, the unmoving moth in the jar was Lycasta. The words of the man who had started a fire in the Eastwoe palace came to mind.

"The insects you've stepped on are here. And the moth won't be enough."

They captured her after I asked her to deliver a message to Nerium here. That must have been when Viridia got hurt, Anova realized all at once.

Is she …?

Anger surged through her like a different kind of magic. Not even Lycasta deserved that. Alys wasn't here to talk with Hellmyr peacefully. No, this was already a war.

And she'd been too dull to see it.

Or too unbothered by the idea, she considered bitterly.

At the same moment, a voice soared through the study.

"You told me she was *dead*."

Each of his words voice cracked like thunder. It was Cadmus.

The look to his eyes was wild and more furious than she'd ever seen. His clothes had been torn and frayed in places, and rings lined the skin under his eyes like he hadn't slept since she'd seen him.

It took several of her men to restrain him from getting to Alys.

Anova's head snapped to the witch. "What the hell are you playing at, Alys?" She was already lurching towards her, magic surging to her fingertips.

"Get back," her captain snapped at her, his sword raised as he placed himself between her and Alys.

But Alys stepped out of his protection to face her again. "You can see he's not harmed. None of them have been." Anova could barely register anything outside of what was in front of her, but she heard Della and Maris reunite with Nerium somewhere in the study. They'd separated the women from the fae.

"That remains to be seen," Anova bit back. For the first time since he'd been brought forth, she allowed her sight to linger on him.

His eyes were already on her.

Anova's breath was stolen for moments.

It was like that morning that she'd seen him for the first time after learning she'd saved him from death. It was like he was the only other person in the room.

They tried to break his mind.

Nerium had reached him with the girls a few paces behind them. The men who had restrained him had allowed their grip to slacken now that Cadmus wasn't fighting them tooth and nail.

With no small effort, she broke their stare to glance back at Alys. "Why have you done all this? The real reason, Alys," she emphasized.

For mere seconds, a strange look flickered across Alys's face. "Answer me something, first."

Anova realized that the strange look was sincerity. She narrowed the gulf between them by several steps. Her words were a murmur like they weren't in the middle of a crowd of spectators.

"Have you sided with them so completely?" Her eyebrows lifted towards the crown. "With that?"

Anova didn't have an answer.

It was then that she noticed two things. First, men had lifted Hellmyr from his chair and were spreading him on the negotiations table.

Second, Nerium was speaking rapidly in Cadmus's ear, one hand like iron on his shoulder. Della was at his other side, her face white. Maris was pulling her back. Cadmus's mouth moved too fast for her to read it, but he was clearly arguing with the other fae.

She felt as if her stomach had dropped.

His gaze refocused on her, on her belly, and in his eyes was a curious look. He seemed to stop breathing.

It was fear.

Della told him, she realized. *But why now? What's going on? Why is he afraid?*

Sweat beaded at her forehead and coated her back. Something awful was going to happen here. It was then that she noticed Hellmyr's shirt had been removed.

Anova's voice caught in her throat.

"You wanted to know the reason?" Alys said, her words too soft for what was happening around them. "To change the world. To stop the atrocities. Even if it means committing one more before they all end."

It was a promise and a threat.

Out of her cloak, she pulled a knife that glinted when she moved.

And she slashed its length along Hellmyr's open chest.

CHAPTER THIRTY-NINE

Juras kept away from Leander as Viridia rose through the low-hanging clouds of Fae. The soft, moonlit landscape underneath them would have been beautiful to him if he hadn't ever set foot on its land.

But he supposed that's how the fae were themselves. Beautiful but terrible.

Juras considered what it would be like on the other side of Fae again. He couldn't go back to Mara's. Hinterfell had been watching it.

The Last Chance was tempting, but no matter how easy it would be, he didn't want to go back there.

Mikal wouldn't ask questions about where he'd been or what had happened, he knew. Just as he hadn't before. Not like someone else Juras knew.

Not about his scars, his history, or his life.

Those things couldn't be trusted to anyone else. That was clear.

He felt the stunning cold of the metal before he felt the iron grip on the rest of him. Behind him, Leander had produced a knife and was holding it to his throat. He couldn't move.

Juras laughed, and it was a bitter thing swallowed by the thin air around them.

Somehow, he'd broken his record for being a trusting fool.

"Of course," he said. "Go ahead and rob me. Every last thing I own is on me now. Clothes and all."

But Leander didn't move. He was quiet until he said, "All I want is for us to land up ahead. I'll take my bow and arrows. You can have your mount back and be on your way to leave this place."

Juras stared ahead of them.

He was damned tired of these creatures. "Why the feign? Why insist you wanted to get to the boundary forests, too?"

"You wouldn't have agreed otherwise," Leander said in a flat voice. "I could tell."

As they landed and Juras saw where they were, he was forced to agree. Among the greenery and showy displays of flora, a fae manor sprouted from the ground. But, even from a distance, he could see that it was crawling with humankind.

This was where Alys's army was stationed. And, if Anova had been successful, it was where she, Hellmyr, and the others were having their so-called peace talk.

The fae look-alike took his pack, including his two weapons. He worked quickly, fixing the bow to his back and his previously hidden knife at his waist.

Before he could disappear into the night, Juras stood in his way. After a stunt like that, he wasn't just going to let him go. "Why," he said dully. "Why did you want to come here?"

Leander's hand nearest his knife twitched. But it remained there. "I know of the situation my dear brother has embroiled himself in, though quite honestly, I'm not here for him. Someone else I care about is here. Undoubtedly as a captive." He shifted out of Juras's path, shifting his gaze away at the same moment. "Even if I never wanted to see her again. I have to know she's ..."

He didn't have to complete the thought. Even so, Juras didn't get it.

From Anova, he knew the terrible story of the fated love gone wrong. Lycasta and Leander.

Lycasta had manipulated her way into having this twin live while the other died for him. It didn't seem to be a decision Leander agreed with when he'd discovered the truth.

"She betrayed you. She orchestrated Cadmus's death," Juras contended. "How can you choose that?"

"Because I can't let her die for nothing." Leander stopped, closed his eyes, and admitted through his teeth, "Because it's not a choice."

The fae didn't wait for Juras to respond to that. He'd disappeared into the trees like a shadow. Besides, Juras wasn't sure he could have responded. He stared after him.

It's not a choice. Leander's words echoed in Juras's head.

But life was nothing but choices. There was always a choice.

Despite this being his home, the fae had nearly left this land for good. That had been a possible choice. So was rescuing the lying she-fae who would be happy to kill Cadmus and Anova if it meant her own lover would benefit.

Juras was at Viridia's side. If he didn't want to get caught in this mess, they needed to leave now. Irbess was close.

There is always a choice, Juras repeated.

His eyes squeezed shut.

Hellmyr doesn't care for you like that. Not like he does for Anova.

But what if he chose to ignore that? His heart galloped at the possibility—at the hurt he would allow for himself.

Well, that was a choice, too.

His nails punched into his palms. Hurt was certainly a choice.

He whispered to Viridia to wait for him until dawn before he ran to follow the path that the fae had taken.

Juras had found Leander in moments. He'd been stalking the property like a cat before its quick-footed prey.

Crouching in the brush near him, he held one of his hands out. "The bow. Or the knife."

Leander looked at him. "Leave me before you attract them."

"You need help," Juras said. It was obvious. Even though he was a fae—quicker and more powerful than the men surrounding the estate—there were many more of the men.

His pride was going to get him caught.

"I don't need *your* help." Leander's voice made it clear what he thought of Juras's abilities.

Juras wanted to laugh. Instead, he pulled an object from his pocket and tossed it to the fae.

Leander stared at the ring in his palm. "When did you get this off me?"

Juras was going to miss that one. He'd really considered selling it to his favorite fence in Irbess. But this was perhaps an even more valuable use for it.

"I don't know. I think I'd rather you tell me," Juras said. "Was it when you were feeding Viridia moon magic? Or was it when you threatened me with your sharp fae knife? Or was it when you were complaining how bad I smelled?"

Juras smiled. It had been none of those moments, but he didn't want to spill all his secrets in one night.

But the fae didn't seem to think it so funny.

Juras continued, "I've been sneaking in and out of places since I could walk. I've been fighting since boys started taking bets on who could beat me the best."

Leander only looked to the ring. Perhaps he was thinking the same thing—how much this would have made Juras's life easier if he'd continued with it to Irbess.

Or maybe he wasn't. His kind were often difficult to read.

After a moment, Leander fixed the ring on his finger and pulled the knife and its leather sheath from his waist.

"I will abandon you as soon as you become a liability, you know," he said.

"Do you think I would do differently?" Juras asked.

"There are no magical wards here. Only a generous barrier of salt," Leander explained.

Together, they'd taken down all the guards on this side of the estate without any of her other men realizing. After they'd piled them in the bushes, Juras had realized they made a surprisingly efficient team.

Juras stared until he explained further. "I could break the line," Leander said, pointing to the scattering of it like snow at the base of the manor, "but it will nullify my ability with magic for a time. I'd rather not risk it right now. The witch seems fond of the stuff, but she didn't bargain on a human breaking in. Only fae."

"I'm useful now, is that it?" Juras said, crossing his arms.

"It appears that way," Leander said, and Juras wasn't so sure if he was joking or serious.

Even so, he did as Leander instructed and cleared a section of the salt from the base of the manor. After, Leander led them straight to the tree that leaned nearest a high-set window looking inside the manor's study.

Juras's blood thundered through him. This was where all the action was.

They'd already traded all the information they knew between them. Juras had revealed Anova's deal with the witch to bring her Hellmyr in exchange for releasing Cadmus and the others safely.

Leander had told Juras how, despite their apparent split, he'd been tracking Lycasta's movements for some time since King Hellmyr had been hunting them both. He'd truly intended to leave Fae for those reasons, but he'd changed his mind when he saw what Lycasta was involved in.

In the study below, Alys's men had surrounded them. Anova was there, as were Cadmus, his manservant, Della, and Maris. Juras stared. He hadn't seen those two from The Rosebud in some time, and it was admittedly unnerving seeing familiar faces in such a place.

"Cadmus," Leander murmured as he looked down on them. "How could you get involved in this?"

The fae almost looked disgusted. Juras wanted to tell him how he was needlessly involving himself in the situation, too, but he refrained from comment.

It must run in the family, Juras considered silently.

It was then that he saw a strange thing on the top of one of the bookshelves filling the room. Juras's stomach lurched. There was no mistaking what was inside that jar.

The moth within it looked dead, like a macabre warning to the others. There was no question that it was Lycasta.

Leander had already pulled out his bow and nocked an arrow along it. But his hands were trembling too much to keep it straight.

Juras stared. He wasn't sure he'd ever seen such a thing from one of these creatures.

Except, Hellmyr trembled for me. Juras pushed that thought away with violence.

Something told him Leander's trembling wasn't from the exertion of holding the arrow in place. It looked like Leander planned to break the glass of the window with his first strike, strike at the jar to shatter it open, and then jump inside the mayhem below to save her.

If there's a life left to save, Juras thought.

As if he could hear Juras's thoughts, Leander spoke in a nearly inaudible voice, "I have to try. I have to make sure."

Juras's voice was low when he responded. "Let me."

A strange sound floated to the branches above them. He'd made the somber fae laugh.

"You're a terrible aim," Leander said to Juras after his laughter had subsided.

"No, I don't mean that." He happened to agree with the fae. "I'm going in there anyway. Break the glass, I'll jump down, and then I'll help you get out your she-fae. But you'll need to cover me."

"Why would—"

But Leander must have seen why at that moment.

For seconds, they both stared into the study below. The deal was going south. And then Juras saw it.

A knife flashed in the witch's grip. Hellmyr's chest had been bared on the table before her.

Something in Juras screamed.

He growled to the fae, "Now! Do it!"

He didn't wait for him to break the window. There was no time anymore.

Juras leapt.

CHAPTER FORTY

G lass rained around Juras as he hit the ground. Leander's arrow sailed above him, having beaten him to the window by seconds.

The world was chaos around him. But that's the way he tended to like it when he was breaking and entering.

Juras didn't look at where he wanted to—he couldn't if he wanted to rescue this she-fae. And he still wasn't so sure what his plan was.

It wouldn't be long before one of the witch's men got to him. Though he wasn't at the center of the commotion, he was sure he'd been noticed.

Juras lurched to his feet where he'd landed at the base of the gigantic bookshelf. He wasted no time, kicking away books from their homes as he locked his feet where they'd been. He used the shelves to propel him higher along the steep climb.

Below him, the bedlam continued, but the world was silent to him in those seconds. He'd been made for work like this, and in no time at all, his clammy fingers had found the jar at its height. Its slick surface nearly escaped his grip. The moth didn't move.

That was when the sound of tearing flesh seared the air.

In an instant, his world changed. He fell from the bookcase, landing among the shards again.

She stabbed him. She's hurting Hellmyr, Juras thought with a frenzy.

Juras couldn't focus for the anger suddenly inside him. His hands were trembling like Leander's had.

He needed to do something. But what? There was too much already going on.

Hellmyr's blood splattered nearly to the ceiling as she made a narrow cut along his neck. Not deep enough to kill. But she wasn't done.

Save him, he yelled at himself. *No matter what!*

He understood what Leander had meant now. This was no choice at all.

In his fist still was the intact jar with the limp moth at its bottom. Leander's eyes were on him, now. Maybe even his arrow point.

This, too, wasn't a choice.

The fae would understand, even if he hated Juras for it. And he most certainly would.

Juras placed the jar fully in the small bag that he'd slung across his back before entering the dwelling. It jostled against Juras's borrowed knife.

Leander was going to do him a little favor.

"What are you doing?" Anova yelled at the witch. "Stop it!"

She was carving him open. Her men tried to hold Anova back, but she slipped easily out of their hands.

Hellmyr was going to bleed out on the table before them.

And it was all her fault.

"Hold her back," Alys commanded as she readied her knife for another incision.

But Anova couldn't be stopped. Magic readily ran to her fingertips, answering the demand she shouted to herself. She felt Cadmus moving from the other side of the room, too.

He was yelling her name, and there was a crash somewhere. It all became white noise to her.

Anova was going to kill Alys with her own hands.

None of this was what she'd agreed to.

But it might as well have been, a dissenting voice sniggered inside her. *You brought him to her on a gleaming platter.*

It sounded like the crown's phantom, Malus, but she shoved that thought aside. She had no time for delusions.

Someone else was running to him, and she realized a second too late that it was Juras. Her heart wasn't done strangling itself inside her chest. She fought to breathe.

What's he doing here?

She shouted Juras's name, but he didn't seem to notice. He'd almost made it to Hellmyr and Alys.

It was then that Hellmyr opened his eyes.

"What—" The rest of his sentence was a gurgle. He spat blood, and his eyes happened to rake across his body fully then. He tried to rise, but his limbs had been tied to the table to keep him sprawled there.

His gaze was frenzied, and it bounced between himself, the walls, the humans, the witch, and Anova.

Anova felt gutted—as if it were her being carved apart by a witch. He was *confused.*

He finally focused on Alys, likely the only piece of the puzzle that made sense to him.

"Release me, you witch," he seethed. He was pale.

Alys smiled, though there was no joy to it. "Welcome to the night of the dead moon, Fae King," she announced to him.

But he hadn't seemed to listen. Sweat had beaded at his forehead, sticking some of his raven locks to his face. Without deciding to, Anova had started running for him again.

"Let him go." The words dragged out of her.

When she spoke, Hellmyr's gaze froze on her. "You ... you ..." The words were hardly loud enough to carry to her, but his tone was enough to turn her stomach.

He'd finally understood how he'd gotten there, bound and bleeding.

"Hellmyr, I didn't mean for—" she'd started, but Hellmyr had already moved on.

He was staring at Juras where he'd nearly made it to the table. Anova's hairs stood on end.

It was a look of pure hate.

He'd realized that they'd betrayed him. That, in a moment of rare vulnerability for the fae king, they'd drugged him and delivered him like a prize pig to Alys.

Juras had had the benefit of being human—and thus seeming to Alys's men one of them. But it hadn't taken long for them to realize that he wasn't their ally. They stopped him, pulling him back by his limbs. One of the men threw a punch to his gut, and Juras doubled over in pain.

"In truth, it wasn't your blood specifically that I needed, Fae King," Alys said to him. She stepped before Hellmyr to redirect his attention to her. He bared his teeth at her, and the hate poured from him.

She continued, "The blood of any powerful fae would have done. Of any magical being strong enough. But I will not spill innocent blood. We are no monsters."

He snapped at her. "And killing monsters is no crime at all, is that right?"

But Alys didn't respond. She said something else entirely. "Do you remember her? Do you remember her face when you look on mine with such revulsion?"

Just as Hellmyr's lip pulled back seemingly to fire off another retort, he stopped. He didn't even seem like he was breathing.

The change in his expression was disturbing. A new paleness had spread across him.

His voice was low. "That wasn't my choice."

Anova's stomach turned. Alys was referring to her mother.

"It wasn't, no," Alys agreed. "But you remember that fae lord pleading to your then-king for retribution when she *damaged* you. For sparing your life when others had called to end it."

She wasn't done. Anova wanted to shout at her to stop, but she couldn't seem to speak.

"You remember ensorcelling humans and how much fun it was turning a child into a torch that'd die when burnt to ash. You remember this."

Hellmyr only stared back.

"And to think, your only punishment was to be cursed to love a human." Alys blinked, seeming to realize something then. Her lips parted.

Hellmyr's face also changed in a strange way.

His eyes were on Alys, though not in a glare. No, it almost seemed like he was begging her to ...

To what? Anova didn't understand.

"Don't say it." His voice was hoarse. "Not now."

But Alys wasn't looking at him anymore.

"Ah, that's the one." Her face softened. "The human you are fated to by the curse."

Alys was staring at Juras.

CHAPTER FORTY-ONE

Juras didn't understand, though he had up until that point. Anova had told him about how Hellmyr, the human-hating fae, had been cursed from a young age with the destiny of loving a human.

It'd been meant as a punishment for cursing humans carelessly in their lands. It was why he was hopelessly in love with Anova.

His mind repeated the last two words.

With Anova.

But everyone was looking at him.

No. This wasn't supposed to be. Hellmyr thought of him as a distraction. A novelty. A runner-up prize.

Nothing more.

And yet, Hellmyr looked afraid. The fear shifted to hate in the span of a blink.

"Hellmyr." His name was a plea on Juras's lips.

No. He'd tricked and drugged him. Juras was the reason so much of the fae king's blood was on the floor.

Juras slipped through the grasp of the men holding him and ran for the fae king.

"Let him go," he shouted over the others. But before he could get any weapon out, something started to happen.

Their gazes moved from Juras to something just above him. Men, fae, and witch alike focused their attention on the spot. Dread crawled like a slug in his belly.

Juras looked up.

Anova watched it materialize like a shadow cast by nothing. First, it was barely more than a dark glimmer on the air.

Then came the smile.

Suddenly, Cadmus's voice was calling her name over the chaos. But the sound was cut off.

Anova and her allies were pushed to the floor by an unseen force. When she craned her neck from the ground, her stomach dropped.

It was Rietvar.

He was in his human-like form, his silver hair pushed behind his rounded ears.

Anova wasn't near ready to see him again. Panic started to claw up her throat, threatening to spill past her lips. She hadn't yet formed any plan for him or really learned much about the one called Purveyor of Souls.

That was, except the fae tale she'd dug up in the archives. But looking at how real he was now, Anova was hard-pressed to think that it meant anything to this creature.

She was out of time. Her heart throbbed like it could escape. Anova had to get them out of here.

The smile stayed on his face as, with a wave of his hand, he forced Anova and the others closer to the floor from where they'd started to struggle.

"Your guests will have to wait to assault me, I'm afraid," he said to Alys. He cocked his head to one side. "Unless you mean some of them as refreshments."

But Alys didn't rise to the bait. "You will recall that you aren't to hurt any of the others here. Else you renege on our deal."

Any of the others. Anova's stomach clenched. The second part of what she'd said hit her then.

Alys had bargained with Rietvar. She wouldn't have believed it if she hadn't heard it with her own ears. Anova had known that what she and Alys had before—something very much like friendship—was long since gone.

But this ... Anova didn't have the words for it.

"Of course not," Rietvar said, though his eyes flashed in the light. "You've done well, little witch." After he turned from Alys, he considered Hellmyr. "A prime specimen."

The fae king bared his teeth at him, though his chest heaved too deeply for him to be fine. One of the humans had staunched the bleeding at his throat, but he didn't look better for it.

Anova couldn't let this happen. She blurted, "Don't hurt him."

No matter who Hellmyr loved, and no matter who had Anova's own heart, she couldn't let him be sliced open again right in front of her.

Rietvar's gaze darted to her. "And Anova." His smile for her was fake, and it made her want to rip her skin from her bones. "The soul thief. I hope you've enjoyed the dreams I've sent you."

"What do you want?" Anova countered. She wasn't here to play games.

But Rietvar's coal-black eyes darkened further. "You will see, I promise you that."

Alys had stepped between them. By the hold of her shoulders, she seemed almost uncomfortable with their conversation. It made Anova's stomach squirm.

"The deal, deal-maker," she said as if reminding him.

"Impatient, aren't we?" Rietvar grinned, but it was gone a second later. "Very well. As am I."

Hellmyr had paled further. Red blood had dried brown into his clothes. At the sight of Rietvar, chest rose and fell rapidly. The Purveyor of Souls approached him, and his fingers turned into claws as he pulled at the bandaging at Hellmyr's throat.

"I accept the lifeblood of the moonchild in payment," Rietvar said.

The fae king's screams echoed through the room as red splattered from his chest. Rietvar had raked his elongated claws across his bare skin.

Anova struggled against the force holding her to the floor. Hellmyr didn't deserve this. No one did.

He didn't deserve what I did to him, either, said a voice inside her.

"Let him go," she said through a ragged breath.

Suddenly, the magic in her body exploded from her. She was running for Rietvar, and no force of magic or man could have stopped her.

She was going to strangle him.

"And Anova, my soul thief," purred Rietvar. He tilted his head, and she saw how Hellmyr's blood still stained his hands. "You're coming with me." He focused his gaze on her stomach. "As is the child due to me."

"You will not touch her." Cadmus's words came out in a snarl. Several men were holding him back.

Due to me. Rietvar's words echoed in her head. A deep fear had burrowed into her throat.

She wanted to throw it up.

Due to me.

Sometime, she'd stopped running. The magic had died in her palms.

"No. How—" The word clogged her throat. One hand formed a fist while the other went to her stomach. "This isn't yours."

The faces of their captive audience stared back at her.

"It's what I require for our bargain." Rietvar stalked around the table, blocking her vision of Hellmyr. "If you recall, you owe me one act of my own choosing. The only stipulations were that it not hurt you and that I would collect payment sometime over a month from our agreement." His words were simple. "The child will be mine, Anova."

"Not this." The words dragged from her throat. "You don't get this."

Rietvar's black-pit eyes were on her as he stepped closer. "Then I will take you now."

At Rietvar's back, Cadmus leapt for him, the expression on his face like a beast's. He left behind him bleeding human men.

His hands had gathered moonlight fire that danced angrily in his palms. He was going to kill him.

In his eyes was a desperation she didn't recognize. They'd promised each other to live—that they'd live and not sacrifice themselves anymore—but Anova had a horrible feeling that he'd left behind their promise in that moment.

"Cadmus," she yelled, but he didn't falter.

Rather than looking behind him at his attacker, Rietvar stared straight ahead and showed his teeth. "Amusing, but it's past time for the deal to be done."

Too much happened at once. Rietvar snapped his claw-like fingers, Hellmyr began to writhe in pain, and the beams of moonlight flooding the room faded. Darkness filled the area like a pervasive shadow, and the noises coming from the fae king quieted too quickly.

Anova felt it inside her like a bubbling pool of bile. Something terrible had happened.

The dancing light in Cadmus's hands died just as Rietvar picked up a long blade left by one of the men. Even so, the son of the former High King's battle strategist didn't stop. Cadmus pivoted so that his body blocked Rietvar's access to Anova.

But Rietvar was faster and stronger than she could understand. In one motion, Rietvar pushed him to the ground and planted the blade into his shoulder, pinning him to the floor.

A scream ripped from Anova's throat. She rushed forward to do something, but a numbness spread through her where once magic had.

"He's done it. The moon is—" A gasp of pain stole the rest of Cadmus's words. Anova's hands trembled where she tried to keep the blood from pouring out of him, but there was little she could do without magic or supplies.

No. They hadn't fought this hard just for it all to end here.

Somewhere outside the maelstrom that was her thoughts, she heard Rietvar's voice. "Now. Just one more step to take, and the ritual will be complete."

Anova's gaze darted up. She needed to get Cadmus out of here. She needed to get them all out—

Rietvar held another blade above the heart of the fae king.

Hellmyr wasn't moving anymore.

CHAPTER FORTY-TWO

Juras wasn't sure what the hell was going on anymore—inside him and around him—but the blade lunging for Hellmyr's heart was a dead certainty.

The lord of death, the being called Rietvar, was going to kill Hellmyr. And not even fae magic could repair that.

A dissenting voice inside him argued that he might already be beyond all efforts, but Juras ignored this.

Even though his guards had abandoned him by now, Juras knew he couldn't make it to Hellmyr in time to stop the attack. And even if Juras did, what could he do? He was just a human.

But there's something even a weak human like me can do.

Manipulate.

Faster than he'd thought he could move, Juras dove into the bag slung across his body, found the glass jar, and held it high above his head as he aimed it at the ground. The moth inside didn't move.

This is not a choice, he reminded himself before squeezing his eyes shut to do the deed that he'd certainly curse himself for later.

Before he shattered the glass, he heard it. It was a whistle on the air, barely noticeable in the chaos unless you were waiting for it.

Juras opened his eyes just as Leander's arrow pierced the wrist that held the blade above Hellmyr's chest. The creature in a human's skin howled, his fingers twitching with pain as he pulled out and crushed the arrow with his good hand. Leander's aim had been true.

He'd hurt the lord of death.

Even if their allies didn't seem to have their moon magic anymore, it seemed regular weapons worked just as well on him.

Rietvar's smile was gaunt and hair-raising as he looked to the broken window where the arrow had come from. "You will regret that."

If Juras had blinked, he would have missed it. One moment, the human-like Rietvar had been standing above Hellmyr's body. It only took him seconds to lunge forward so that his arms became front legs that supported his beastly frame.

This new creature was something between a bear and wolf, and several sizes larger than either. Juras suspected that his maw could swallow a few men whole.

Sweat slicked his palms now, so he shoved the jar into his armpit. He needed easy access to it so Leander would remain loyal to their cause. He was sorely aware that his cover wouldn't last long, and, as he ran to the center of the room, he grabbed an abandoned sword.

Some paces away from him was Anova. She was holding her fae boy. He couldn't do anything for them right now.

Hellmyr was in worse shape, and that had to come first.

Just before he got to Hellmyr, the witch Alys moved between him and the table where he'd been left.

"Get out of my way," he shouted at her. The sword in his hand was a comforting weight. Could he take on a witch?

"You might not agree, but what's happening here is important for humans," she said.

She truly believes in this hellscape, he realized.

"Oh, give up the righteousness already," Juras snapped. "What's happening here is only important for your vendetta."

Her eyes were like a winter night. Cold. Logical.

"He kidnapped you to steal her heart, didn't he? Do you feel so little self-worth that you idolize them so violently for their beauty and pretty words?" Alys shifted her head, making strands of her dark hair fall from her face. "Or is it because you feel you owe him reciprocation?"

"Neither," Juras said between his teeth.

"It's a spell. Not like true love," Alys said to him. Even through her face softened, light started to build in one of her palms. She was going to force him away with magic. "You'll be—"

The air seemed to leave her lungs as another body tackled Alys. Della got her to the ground through a flurry of limbs.

Maris surged forward to help Della pin the witch down. "Get your fae," she managed to say. "We'll buy you some time."

Juras's heart couldn't help but tangle up in his chest. They hadn't seen each other in months, and they were still looking out for him, one of the brothel brats.

He didn't deserve those two.

After he threw the glass jar back into his pack, he cut the binds tying Hellmyr to the table and surrendered the blade to the ground. There was no time for it, but he had to bandage the worst of his wounds before hauling the fae king across his back. His knees nearly buckled from the weight, but he couldn't give in to the floor quite yet.

Beyond his immediate surroundings, destruction reigned. A fire had caught along several of the bookcases, and though Rietvar had been punctured with more arrows, he couldn't see any sign of Leander in the tree outside the broken window.

Juras's stomach plummeted further when the white beast turned around, his claws scoring the floor as he darted back towards them.

It seemed their cover had ended.

Some paces away, Anova and Cadmus's manservant crouched over the fallen fae. They all needed to get out of here—*now*.

It was then that heat blasted at his back, and he nearly dropped Hellmyr. Maris was beside him in a moment, her cheek bleeding and her chest heaving.

Juras turned to see Alys with the sword he'd abandoned in her hand. Every few seconds, slick flames traipsed across its length. The light dazzled his eyes in the darkened room.

Della was on the ground, her throat just in reach of the magicked sword.

"Drop the fae," Alys said, her voice strangely void of emotion.

There was no saving them both, he saw. Without thinking, Juras sank to his knees, gently sliding Hellmyr to the floor as he did so.

Juras's hands trembled.

Hellmyr might have been a manipulator, but Juras had been worse. He'd used Hellmyr's feelings for him to bend him into vulnerability.

Just so we could sell him to a witch.

The witch approached.

"Hold him," Alys whispered above him. Rietvar was almost back to her side. Juras could already see how his claws elongated once more.

He would puncture his heart clean through.

Something in him raged at the thought, and he did something he'd never thought he'd do. Juras flung his body in front of Hellmyr's slack one, his teeth bared at the witch above them.

"What I feel for him is real," he snarled at her. "So don't patronize me and tell me it's because I feel guilty. You're going to have to go through me first."

At his words, Alys froze. But Rietvar didn't.

The creature known as Death lunged for them both.

Cadmus's breathing was labored, and despite her efforts, blood continued to soak from the wound. Anova knew it fully then.

The source of fae magic was gone. Rietvar and Alys had done something to block the moon's influence.

Her hands slicked with sweat. Even though his strength was surely waning, Cadmus gripped her hands with too much ferocity, and his eyes held hers in a prison.

"I thought you were gone," he said in a strange voice. "I dreamt of your death so much that I started to believe it." He shook with anger. "And when she let slip the same thing that I'd seen in my dreams ..."

Nerium was beside her, working as best as he could on the wound without magic. His voice, too, was strangely affected. "She kept us in the underground training room. The witch left us no lights except when her men sent us food."

Anova stared. She'd been a fool to trust Alys's word that she wouldn't harm them. And she'd put them all in further danger by bargaining with her.

But what other choice was there?

It was then that her attention was stolen by a blood-curdling howl. Rietvar, in his creature form, was bounding back towards the center of the study where they were all gathered.

Her heart dropped. Juras's body blocked Hellmyr, but Rietvar would tear right through him to get to Hellmyr. A shuddering breath escaped her.

How were they getting out of this? She had no weapons, no magic, and nothing more to bargain with. Everyone she'd ever cared about seemed to be bloodied and gasping for life before her.

But she couldn't stand by and let them die before her. As if in response, the life in her stomach fluttered.

They were getting out of here alive.

Anova's hand gripped Nerium's shoulder. "Can you support his weight on your own? Can you run with him?"

"Anova. No." Though he was too weak, Cadmus said the words like a command. Like he knew what she was about to try. "I'm not going to lose you to him." He paused. "Not either of you."

Her throat nearly closed as she said to the holder of her heart, "I'll keep my promise. But only if you keep yours."

Beside her, Nerium nodded in response to her question. That was all she needed to know. She rose too fast, and the world spun around her.

Alys and Rietvar might have blocked the moon's influence, but Anova had something more than fae magic running through her veins.

The memories of the blood crown's destruction ran through her mind, warning her as she rose to her feet. The malice inside it bit at her, and her throat tightened as, for a moment, she let the hate for their enemies fill her like tavern swill.

The crown's magic flooded her senses, distorting time for her. All at once, seconds passed by too quickly and slowly.

I can't hurt Juras and Hellmyr. I need control.

I can't let its hate poison me.

"Die, human, for this wicked moon child."

Rietvar raised one of his claws to maul Juras below him. At the same time, the energy inside Anova escaped from her in a light brighter than the full moon.

Heat and light flooded the room, but Anova was already moving. She had to trust that Nerium would get Cadmus out. While the brightness had blinded her for the moment, she'd memorized where she needed to go.

Muffled noise buzzed in her brain. She found Della and Maris when they joined hands with her, and Juras a moment later on the floor.

She had no words to tell Juras that perhaps the fae between them was past help. In the smothering light, they ran together.

CHAPTER FORTY-THREE

"We need to stop." Nerium said to them all. "The two of you need treatment."

"No. I can go farther," Cadmus said, but it sounded like it hurt him to speak.

Juras couldn't stop. In his heart, he knew he was afraid to check the pulse of the fae supported between him and Nerium while their group of fae and humans ran. Hellmyr was still unconscious, and his bandages were soaked.

Anova had provided them the cover they'd needed to escape the Wolfsbane estate, but Juras didn't need fae hearing to feel that they were being chased.

There weren't typical signs of being hunted: crushed twigs and leaves behind them or arrows snapping into trunks.

No, it was a feeling like a caterpillar crawling along the back of his neck. They were being watched and followed in these woods, but not by the men who had infiltrated Fae.

Death was after them.

The old fae helping him carry Hellmyr stopped their progress, and Juras was forced to acquiesce.

Della and Maris helped him spread Hellmyr across relatively flat ground. He brushed away leaves and forest detritus until he could no longer delay the inevitable. Silently, Anova joined him in bandaging the worst.

"Nerium, do you think you can heal him? He's not doing well," Anova said in a too low voice. She was moving between the two injured fae.

"I'm afraid that's not possible."

Juras's gaze jerked up. Someone else had responded.

Standing on a branch of an oak high above their heads, he stared down at each of them. Leander's wandering eyes stopped when they came to Cadmus, clutching at his bleeding shoulder.

"Hello, Brother," he said lazily. "I see you've destroyed my personal library."

Despite the pain he clearly held in his body, Cadmus forced a sharp smile back at him. "We both know at least half of those were there for hoarding, not reading."

Lithe as a cat, Leander jumped from the branch to the earth.

"It seems I'm not the only one with the habit, however. You've amassed quite the collection of humans." Leander's hand hovered over the sheath of a sword he'd surely stolen from one of the humans occupying the Wolfsbane estate.

"Speaking of which." The fae took a step towards Juras, and his eyes gleamed as he tilted his head at him. "You've played me like your fiddle too long, human." He bared his teeth. "Hand her over. Or else."

Anova stepped between them. "Enough veiled threats. You aren't going to hurt anyone here," she said to the fae.

Juras sidled up next to her and shook his head. That was all it took for her to back away. He felt her eyes in the back of his head.

Juras swallowed. The last time he and Anova had truly spoken, he'd told her he hadn't ever wanted to see her again. They needed to talk.

Instead of lingering on that, Juras grabbed out of his bag the jar he'd retrieved from the Wolfsbane estate and tried not to think of the moth inside it as anything other than a bug.

It didn't work.

"You'd have done the same," Juras spoke, though his throat felt dry when he said it.

Since when had that been an acceptable excuse?

Leander's reflexes were faster than his. He'd grabbed and opened the glass before Juras had pulled his hand back. As the insect fell out, wings limp and unmoving, it morphed into the fae lady.

Her skin was a pallid bronze, and her ringlet hair stuck to her head in places. He wondered if it was from sweat or blood.

None of them spoke as Leander lowered her to the ground where he'd held her in his arms. A vein in his jaw flicked as he looked her over.

"You know what this means. You've felt it," Leander said. His gaze shot up. "Your mate will have to do this, Cadmus."

Anova stepped forward, her gaze shooting between the fae brothers. "No. It can't be true."

Cadmus said, "The ritual Rietvar and Alys initiated—it stole the moon from the sky."

"What do you mean?" Juras blurted. None of this made sense.

The moon couldn't simply vanish. Certainly, the moonlight was gone now, but ... This was ridiculous.

Leander leveled him with a gaze like a snake's. "Just as I said. Death has taken the moon with him to his realm. It is dead, and with it, all fae magic." Juras didn't miss how the skin around his knuckles tightened. "The only one of us with a drop of it is the possessor of the blood crown. And the witch. So, the human's life is forfeit to me unless Lycasta can be saved. Now."

Juras's stomach twisted, but before he could open his mouth, Anova had rushed between them.

"If I attempt this, you'll leave Juras alone?" she said.

Leander stared back. "If you save her."

Anova didn't wait. Lycasta might have been her enemy and the reason Cadmus had thought he'd needed to sacrifice himself, but this was more important than her grudge.

Was she going to let the fae lady—if indirectly—claim another life she cared about?

No.

Even if it meant trying to heal her with the blood crown's magic.

The fae lady's breathing was ragged and shallow. Anova's hands shook as she followed Leander's instructions and tried to let the magic find what was wrong instead of allowing her emotions lead the healing.

Clear your mind. It doesn't own you.

Without choosing to, she remembered when she'd last attempted to heal Lycasta. It had gone about as well as she'd wanted it to, which was horribly.

"Rein it in," Leander commanded.

Anova withdrew her hands. She'd nearly started to burn Lycasta's already marred skin. Her nails dug into her palms.

She needed to do better. Anova forced the blood crown's magic back through her fingertips. It felt too blunt for such a precise job as this, but she had no choice but to try. Juras depended on her for it.

The thought of her best friend and their fight almost made the magic in her hands turn into a destructive force once more. Lycasta's breathing hitched underneath Anova's fumbled healing. She was doing it again.

"Move aside," Leander said sharply. "You can't control yourself not to kill her."

"She can do this." Suddenly, Cadmus was next to her. Anova's gaze jerked up as she looked into his face.

Cadmus's normally taunting eyes met hers. This time, in them was a look that melted her. Her throat felt too scratchy to speak, and instead of trying that, she squeezed his hand.

When she returned to her work, she noticed something else out of the corner of her eye. The three of them were all crouched above the unmoving fae lady Leander had laid on the forest floor, and Cadmus had already backed away to give the healing some space. But she hadn't missed how his brother had lingered on their intertwined hands.

Anova felt a small flutter in her stomach as a gentle light roved over Lycasta's several bruises. Leander wanted this with Lycasta.

He can't, even if I can heal her, she realized. *Even though he wants to.*

From what fae lady had said, Leander had left because of her actions leading up to Cadmus's death.

It was clear to any being with eyes that he still cared for her, however.

This was a different kind of heartache, she realized. What did you do when the heart wanted to both forgive and to forswear?

Anova drew in a tight breath. The magic that lived in the crown darted from its resting place and out of her grasp like a snake underneath leaves.

"Broken rib," Leander said through his teeth. "Playing with more than magic, this witch." His eyes flitted to hers. "You need to be able to stabilize it without harming the organs around it."

She swallowed. That was more serious than stitching together bits of skin here and there.

But before she opened her mouth to voice this concern to Leander, she stopped herself. He was leaning over her, spreading some fae-made salve into a gash along her cheekbone. The tension was still visible in his jaw and shoulders, but he was tender with his hands. She could see how he needed to do this for her.

To do something for the fae who'd stolen his heart, whether he liked that part or not.

She led Cadmus to believe I was dead.

But she did it for him.

The skin around her knuckles paled from the pressure of holding her fists tight. Anova hated Lycasta for selling her to another fae, for turning Cadmus against her on the night of the full moon fête, for poisoning her, and for too much else.

She *hated* her.

But, somehow, she was her. She knew the fae below her—she'd been her before.

To save the one she loved, Anova had killed, lied, and cheated. In Lycasta's place, Anova would have done little differently.

It had happened without her realizing it. The blood crown's magic had jumped from her grasp and straight into Lycasta's center. Suddenly, the fae below her inhaled a sharp breath, and color filled out her face once more.

"You did it." Cadmus's tone was low and reverent.

Even Leander seemed stunned for a moment. Anova pretended not to notice how his eyes flew to her briefly, and she could almost see him struggle to reevaluate the burnt, odd human-fae that his brother had picked for a lover.

The moment passed, and Leander returned to his work. His hands moved even faster than hers could've as he checked her vitals. But Anova could see her regular pulse thrum at her throat and knew that she would wake in time.

It would still take her days or even weeks to fully heal, as Anova was fairly certain she'd only stabilized the worst of her injuries, but she couldn't deny what she'd done.

I saved Lycasta.

Was it the right thing to do?

The thought made her woozy, though she considered it might have been the blood crown's magic running through her that caused the feeling.

"Anova." Juras had said her name like a plead. Her head jerked up, and she could hear it from here.

It was a rhythm like a dancer on a tightwire.

Hellmyr's heart was failing.

CHAPTER FORTY-FOUR

Juras helped Anova rip the rest of Hellmyr's clothes from his tattered body. The part of Juras that would have reacted to such a sight was buried somewhere deep within him.

Lacerations and other injuries were spread across his body. Juras, along with Della and Maris, had done his best to staunch the worst of it all, but he'd been in the room when it had happened and knew.

Hellmyr had lost too much blood. Rietvar hadn't finished the job, but he might not have needed to.

Stop it, he chided himself. *Anova can heal him.*

While many of his wounds appeared to have clotted, the fae's overall condition had suddenly deteriorated. Juras was no healer or doctor, but he didn't have to be to see that Hellmyr's body was giving in to the trauma.

His breaths were coming faster and shallower by the second. Sweat slicked Juras's hands as they moved across Hellmyr's skin.

The fae felt like he'd been held under a lake for a few hours.

"Anova," Juras said again. His throat tightened around her name.

"I'm trying, Juras." Light and heat flared unevenly from her fingers as she said it, but she didn't stop trying to push the magic from her body.

Hellmyr's head had lolled to one side, and Juras could clearly see how sluggish his breaths were. He still hadn't regained consciousness.

Juras watched as Anova tried to save the fae who had become so entangled in their lives. When had all this happened?

He hadn't had time to truly process what the witch had said about Hellmyr and his curse. Juras wanted to deny the validity of what she'd said—that Hellmyr was fated to somehow love him—but he couldn't.

Something in him had recognized it as a truth. Perhaps it was in the way Hellmyr had released him from their bargain despite it being against the fae's better interests. Or maybe it was how he'd shown him a vulnerability that Juras hadn't deserved to see.

No. It was in the way Hellmyr made him feel.

He's still fae. He's still manipulative. Controlling. Power hungry.

Unbidden, Juras remembered what he'd said to Anova before they'd parted last. The words sat heavy on his tongue until he blurted them to her.

"Anova, I never wanted this. I know now that you didn't, either. You didn't choose this."

A breath seemed to leave her. "Juras ..."

Before Anova could say something, Juras caught her eye briefly and continued. "You're still Anova to me. No matter what you look like."

Her gaze flicked back to Hellmyr, but he could see it in the way her shoulders slumped forward. For several seconds, she didn't speak. The light from the blood crown's magic touched his face.

The only sound between them was Hellmyr's fast and shallow breaths. He fixed another layer of bandaging around his throat where red was beginning to leak again.

"I should have tried to protect you more." Anova's fae eyes flashed in the dim light as she looked to him. Her hands had started to shake. "They tried to hunt me the first night I crossed into Fae. I should've—"

"It's okay." Juras's hand had found her shoulder. "We survive, remember? It's what we do."

The light of her magic caught on the glimmer of moisture along her eyelids, but when she spoke, her voice was filled with snark. "Even if it means flirting with my prison guard to steal his clothes, right?"

Juras couldn't help himself. He laughed. "It was easy. He was practically starved for some attention, the poor man."

He was about to remind her that at least his flirting had served a purpose then—to deliver her sorry butt out of Irbess's cells—when her smile twisted into a grimace of shock.

A hand had grabbed Anova's wrist and was holding it at an angle that looked painful. Hellmyr said through his teeth, "That's enough of your attempts."

Anova jerked her hand out of his just as Cadmus pulled her from Hellmyr. Cadmus angled himself so he was between them. "Don't lay a hand on her."

"Or you'll cut me up more?" Hellmyr's eyes were pits of black.

But she slipped from behind him to face the fae king. "Hellmyr, we're not trying to hurt you," Anova said.

He laughed, and the raspy sound raised Juras's skin. He was awake, but had Anova truly healed his heart? Hellmyr's face was pale and gaunt like Death's.

She started again, "Hell, please—"

"Don't pretend this isn't what you wanted a little, my dear Anova." His words had an unfamiliar edge to them. His lips pulled back in an aggressive smile. "That this"—he gestured to his cut throat—"wasn't by design."

Juras couldn't stand by any longer. The blood in his veins pulverized him, punishing him for his inaction but also for the thought of what he was about to do.

"It wasn't. We didn't want this." Juras caught his eye and said what he'd been trying to. "I didn't want this."

The memory of Hellmyr's lips on his haunted Juras. It had been the moment when everything had unraveled between the three of them.

But he hadn't meant it to be an act of manipulation.

He'd *wanted* to kiss Hellmyr.

The admission was as disturbing to him now as it had been before, but that didn't change the fact that it was true.

Hellmyr stared at him, and what Juras saw there unnerved him. "You wanted an escape." Hellmyr moved towards Juras, and he found he couldn't move.

It was the truth.

"Don't you dare hurt him." Anova's voice sounded too distant. Juras backed against a tree as Hellmyr, still looking as lively as Death, approached him.

Hellmyr smiled and spoke to her without looking away from him. "Do you see me hurting him?" His bare chest, scored with claw marks and covered in bruises, rose and fell too fast.

Quicker than Juras could process, Hellmyr's hand flew to a pocket at the front of his black pants. He pulled free a small glass bottle and shattered it between his forefinger and thumb. At once, a shimmer descended around them in a dome.

"Magic," Juras said a breath. "But—"

"Previously harvested from the moon. For some privacy." He took one last step. Juras had nowhere else to go. They were nearly touching.

What was going on? His heart pounded like it could leave without him. "You need to heal more." Juras's voice was too quiet.

Juras wasn't sure why, but Hellmyr started laughing. Gusts of his breath pushed Juras's curls from his forehead.

"I thought I was going insane," the fae said. "I'd already discovered who I was to be cursed to. I could live with it even if she didn't choose me, I thought."

Hellmyr's expression changed suddenly. "But then I found you. The madness didn't start immediately. No, it was gradual, like the flooding of a ship." For a mere second, pain raced across his face. "I couldn't stop thinking of you. I couldn't stop thinking of someone else having you like that tavern boy." His eyes narrowed. "Or someone else owning you—your creditor."

"I realized that Anova reminded me of you before I knew you." Hellmyr's lips parted to reveal a sneer. "Fate's cruel, small lesson. It was my own actions that caused you to be in Fae. I'd damned myself, just like before."

Just like he caused the witch to curse him in the first place. Cursed ... to love me, Juras thought.

His heart twisted within his center. *He* was supposed to be the punishment. And, Juras realized, he was playing his assigned part well so far.

To Hellmyr, it would have seemed that Juras had been sent to torment him. He'd seduced and then betrayed him, letting him be drugged and then handing him off to the enemy.

"This wasn't supposed to happen," Juras said in a too weak voice. "I'm sorry."

Ever so slowly, Hellmyr's fingers reached out and raised Juras's chin so their faces were nearly touching. For seconds, a strange emotion passed through the fae king's eyes.

Juras's heart raged in his chest, but he kept still.

"But it did," the fae said as his sharp teeth showed.

He tried to jerk out of his grasp, but the fae was too strong for him. It wasn't until Hellmyr's injuries made him falter that Juras could move again.

He shoved himself out of the fae's grasp as the fae's chest heaved. What the hell was going on here?

"What do you want from me?" Juras managed to say.

A new sheen of sweat had coated Hellmyr's skin. A sudden, brief laugh burst from his lips—only to die a second or so later.

"What I want," he said, "is revenge for this." Hellmyr's hand found the side of Juras's face as he spoke. His words and touch were soft, but Juras felt unable to move from him. "I promise you that, if I outlive what has been done to me tonight, you won't want to find me."

The tone of his voice as he uttered the vow made Juras want to shudder. There was no bluff here. No empty words.

Too quickly, Hellmyr withdrew his hand and took several steps back.

Under the shadows of the moonless night, he continued. "Because, one way or another, I will end this curse. Even if it destroys me to do it."

His eyes hardened, and there was no ambiguity left in what he'd said.

He wants me dead, Juras realized.

A brief moment of pain crossed Hellmyr's features before the shimmer in the air dissolved. He was gone with it.

CHAPTER FORTY-FIVE

"You need to sleep. Having magic doesn't mean you don't need to rest."

Anova's fingers jerked to the knife at her hip and then relaxed when she saw who it was. Cadmus didn't miss the gesture, however.

"I'm fine," she said, though she didn't have to read minds to know that he wasn't convinced.

She'd told Nerium that she'd take watch for the next few hours since she wasn't sleeping anyway. Her lips pressed together.

He snitched, she realized.

The early hours of the day folded strips of golden light across the trees of the Sorrelands. It had been three days since Hellmyr had disappeared. Even with her new fae senses, she hadn't heard or seen any sign of him since that night that he'd woken in the middle of her healing him.

He'd used bottled fae magic to speak with Juras and then left. Juras had been strange since, though she could guess why.

Learning that one of the most powerful and manipulative fae had been cursed to love you wasn't easy to reckon with.

Even so, she felt there was something more to Juras's mood.

They were traveling to a safe house that Leander had established when Hellmyr had been hunting him. Anova hated not knowing what to do next, but she had to agree that they needed to get somewhere out of the woods of the Sorrelands.

They were too close to Rietvar's domain.

Her thoughts were interrupted when she felt her hair being moved to one shoulder. A moment later, lips found the back of her neck as he trailed kisses down her skin.

Anova shivered into Cadmus's touch.

"Can I convince you to sleep?" he whispered in her ear from where he held her on the ground.

Anova stared forward, calculating her resolve. Now that he was awake too, she had even less reason to fall asleep. Between fleeing through the Sorrelands and trying her hand at healing the fae and humans traveling with them, the two of them had barely gotten a moment to themselves.

She shook her head.

But he was already down to kissing her back where her dress exposed her skin. Anova couldn't help but shiver at his touch despite herself. Her skin heated.

Before she could lose her resolve further, she crossed her arms and straightened. "This won't work," she told him. "I'm not going to fall asleep. I promise you that."

Cadmus paused for a moment before she felt his sigh across her skin.

"Anova. I'd thought I'd lost you only a few days ago." His voice was strained when he spoke next. "I was convinced of it for *weeks*."

"And now, as ... you're carrying my child, I can't. I can't sit by and watch you hurt yourself. Not anymore."

Before she could respond, he pulled her body against his, moving her chin so her eyes met his behind her.

"When was the last time you slept?" he murmured. "Be honest."

Her eyes swept away from his. He wasn't going to like the answer.

"I can't really remember."

He inhaled sharply, but she didn't look at his face. She wasn't trying to deprive herself of sleep, but ...

"You need to rest," Cadmus said. "You forget, fae are used to not having magic during daylight hours anyway. I can protect you without it—for a few hours at the minimum." He snorted. "If I couldn't do that at least, my dead father would find a way to disinherit me from the beyond."

But when she didn't respond, said, "What is it?"

She swallowed and finally met his gaze again. The memory of Death's voice ran through her thoughts.

"I don't want to see *him* again," she whispered.

"Anova." Cadmus pulled her tight to him so that her face was buried in his chest.

In their embrace, she allowed herself to feel what she'd balled up inside her since she'd discovered she was pregnant.

Her body trembled with the fear of being hurt—of the life inside her being hurt and others she cared for, as well—but also of the fear of what was going to happen in a few months. Anova still wasn't sure if she was more an imperfect, human-like fae or something else entirely.

What does it mean for our child?

She held Cadmus tighter. How were they going to protect this life from the lord of death himself?

She trembled with the loneliness she'd felt when she'd found out. She felt it like a weight inside her.

"I'm sorry I wasn't there." Cadmus spoke the words through his teeth. "I should've ..."

Anova shook her head. "I should have done more. I should have tried to get you out sooner."

Anova startled when he laughed, but he only held her tighter. "You save four prisoners out from under a witch and Death's noses during their ritual, and you haven't done enough yet."

She paused, and she felt it in the way he held her that he noticed the slip, too. They'd forgotten Hellmyr.

"I shouldn't have tricked him into coming." She couldn't look into his eyes for this part. "I wasn't sure he'd agree to come otherwise. I couldn't lose you."

"I know. I'm still sorry."

He held her tighter while letting the quiet fold around them like another embrace. Carefully, Cadmus traced patterns into her back until she felt the muscles there loosen, bit by bit.

"Are you sure I can't try to convince you to sleep?" he murmured.

Her heart pounded as she suspected what he meant, but her eyebrows rose in mock skepticism. "And how does one *convince* another to sleep?"

His thumb found the base of her throat as he whispered against her skin, "Do you doubt my abilities?"

"Maybe I do," she said brazenly, though her heartrate picked up higher.

Cadmus moved his other hand down the front of her dress, raising bumps on her skin where it was exposed. "I think you need a demonstration," he said.

A trail of sweat lined her back, and she swallowed as the desire for him built in her. She caught his mouth in a greedy kiss.

"Are you well enough for this?" Cadmus asked when they parted.

Anova nodded. Around them, bugs fluttered on the air. Their thoraxes pulsed with light.

Even without the moon, magic was in everything in this land, including in the fae beside her.

Cadmus's eyelashes brushed his cheeks. Anova reached up and moved his dark hair from his face.

"Have I ever told you how breathtaking you are, Cadmus Wolfsbane?" she asked.

Cadmus's smile hitched up on one side. "Not often enough."

"Well, I shouldn't have. Your ego is already dangerously oversized." She shook her head.

Cadmus brought her hand to his mouth where he kissed it. "That can't be the only oversized thing about me, surely."

Anova stared him in fake shock before she smirked back. "I think I need to check that."

Her mouth caught his by surprise. Before she'd decided to, she'd shoved him down and straddled his body against the ground.

She devoured his kiss, hungry for his touch. After a few seconds, she'd stripped him of his shirt. Anova pulled back to breathe for a few seconds, but what she saw made her heart jump into her throat.

His ribs were too visible for the Cadmus she'd remembered. Her hand brushed against one of them, but he caught it.

"I'm fine, Anova. So long as you're alive." His gaze turned wicked. "Besides, I think there's something owed to me. By now, I believe I have the right to claim this"—his hand roved along her back—"as mine."

His last words came out in a gasp as Anova grinded her center over his through their clothes.

Anova gave a wicked smile back. "Claim? What, you think you've caught some sort of untamed animal?"

Cadmus looked back at her, and his gaze was greedy.

"That's exactly what I think." His hands were like iron on her thighs, pinning them against him.

She struggled to move from him, though he was too strong for her to do much but squirm. Her center heated at his touch, and she was sure he felt it.

"I want all of you. No, actually," he corrected himself, "I want you—and everyone—to know that you are *already mine*."

Anova's eyebrow raised. She schooled her body into a stillness, though it wanted to do anything but remain still.

"Is that so?" she asked in a breath.

His fingers raced along her spine until she shivered. He took the chance to try shifting her dress higher above her abdomen. When she froze, he stopped.

"What's wrong?" He tensed beneath her.

"I—I don't look the same." She stopped herself. There was an insistent throbbing beneath her.

Cadmus cupped her face in his hands. "You are the same Anova to me, no matter what. I would properly see what is mine." He paused. "So long as you live, you will always be the one my heart is fated to."

Cadmus pulled his hands from her. "But your wishes are also mine, Anova. I will always respect them."

Her heart throbbed, and heat roiled through her. She leaned back, enjoying the feeling of them against each other like this.

After a moment, she rocked forward so that her hands raked through his hair. Cadmus closed his eyes at her touch and breathed her in.

Her eyes traced the burn scars that danced along her legs, marking her as something strange. An imperfect fae.

She moved her gaze to her stomach.

Not too long ago, she'd been a half-starved brothel brat of the streets. There'd been no home for her except where she'd had a blanket on the floor. Anova closed her eyes, letting breath fill her up and the muscles across her body tense and then loosen.

Something that was a little bit of both of them grew stronger within her with every passing moment.

Something that was only possible after all they'd braved to save each the other's life.

Mine.

Her gaze slipped from her stomach to his beautiful, peaceful face.

Yes, he was hers, as well. Her chest rose and sank faster and faster. She would claim this pairing of theirs with all her body.

And with *every part* of herself.

Cadmus's eyes were closed still, and he looked nearly like he was dreaming. She started to remove the layers of her clothes. Beneath her, he was patient and still.

When she was done, she leaned down to kiss him as the heat spread through her.

CHAPTER FORTY-SIX

Nausea stirred in Anova's belly, ripping her back to consciousness.

She'd been sleeping against Cadmus's uninjured side when she suddenly jerked up to stumble some feet away. Her stomach hadn't stopped twisting, and as she doubled over in the bushes, she emptied what little was left inside it.

"I've got you. You won't fall," Cadmus said.

At once, she could feel Cadmus beside her, holding her upright as best as he could with his injury when her legs started to weaken. She noticed a strange, barely audible noise around her then.

Anova blinked back sweat from her brow and realized that the noise was coming from within her mind.

The blood crown, she realized. *But I haven't had hallucinations from it since I was human.*

The world danced around her as Cadmus kept her upright. Shakily, she wiped her face. The whispering sounds she'd thought she heard were gone.

But there were other noises instead.

Cadmus positioned himself between her and where the noises originated with a blade already in his hand. The blood crown's magic surged through her at her call for it.

"You can come out, now," he snarled at the woods around them.

Her heart pounded. While she'd been sick in the bushes, she hadn't noticed them approach them. All she could smell was vomit, and her blood pounded too thickly through her for her to hear her enemies' hearts.

Had they gotten to the others already? Della, Maris, and Juras?

A group of ten or so men emerged from the woods around them, all well-armed with bows and blades. "Surrender as our captives, and we'll spare you."

Cadmus's lip raised in a smirk. "Captives? Do you think fae keep captives?"

Before he was done speaking, Cadmus had started for them. Those in the front of their party scattered and focused their strikes on his injured side.

"Give it up," said one of the humans through his beard. "Looks like one of our boys has gotten to you already."

Anova moved faster than any of them, diverting and snapping arrows as she moved around Cadmus. Although her body worked like a machine to defend them, her mind was faster.

These humans weren't at the estate, she realized. *Rietvar was the one to give him that wound, not another human.*

There was only one real explanation, but she hoped she was wrong.

Even with just one functioning arm, Cadmus was still beating them back. But to prove her theory, she needed to get close to one of them.

Anova turned and threw one of the knives she kept at her waist. It barely missed their archer who had been hanging back from the others, but Anova smiled all the same. This was what she'd wanted.

As he dodged the thrown knife, she rushed him and grabbed one of his wrists.

He bared his teeth at her. He looked just old enough not to be called a boy any longer. "Let go of me, she-fae."

"Where is she?" Anova demanded. "Where is the witch?"

He glared at her. "Enough of your fae nonsense."

She saw it in his eyes. He hadn't come here with Alys. He didn't even know what she was talking about, likely.

It's started, she realized then.

She had nearly twisted his wrist to stop him from firing any more arrows when she felt Cadmus's heart pound much too fast behind her. Cadmus had been driven to the ground while three humans crowded him. One of their blades had pierced his wound again, and her stomach cramped at the sight of the pain on his face.

"Cadmus!" Anova shouted.

"I wouldn't, if I were you," said a voice in her ear.

It happened too quickly. Anova tried to jerk out of his grip, but a sharp point jabbed into her stomach in response. She stopped moving then.

He'd let her go, but in turn, he held ready an arrow aiming at her center. It was too close to dodge.

"I saw you sick in the bushes, you know," he revealed. "You vile things look like women, but you're not."

She felt his grip shake, and she barely breathed.

A wave was beginning to wash over her. Numbing. Consuming. Searing.

He wasn't done whispering to her. "If I end you here, I can end another fae monster, too. Two with one arrow," he said. She heard him swallow. His voice shook to match his grip. "Two less to kill us."

This time, the screams came not from her own lips but from somewhere else. They grew to a chorus. Over all of it spoke a double voice that was uncomfortably familiar to her.

"Poor, little human. In your haste, you've found a real monster."

Malor appeared before her, the dawn's light bending around his antlers. His red eyes revealed no inner humanity.

He smiled before ripping out the human's throat.

Anova was on the ground. Blood covered her, she discovered when she touched her cheek. His arrow had never fired.

The human was on the ground, too, and a pool of red was spreading from where his throat had been into the earth underneath.

Malor watched her from where he stood above her, his hands painted with what he'd done. He smiled as they stared.

"Get away from her," Cadmus said somewhere behind her. But Anova found she couldn't move as Malor crouched to her level.

"What do you want from me?" Anova's throat scratched when she said it.

He pointed at her heart. "That's the wrong question, Anova. And you know it."

Her tongue was too heavy to speak, but her blood raced through her. She would fight this illusion if that's what it took to keep him out of her thoughts for good.

Before she could move, however, he'd disappeared from her sight.

All that was left where he'd stood was the light of the new day streaking through the leaves above them. She felt she'd be sick again.

It was then that Anova was scooped from the ground and into Cadmus's arms. He moved almost too fast for her to see around them.

"Cadmus, you're hurt," she said. Now that she had a personal view of it, she could see how much worse his wound had gotten from their fight. His entire shoulder had been slashed up where the men had been aiming for the spot.

Her stomach turned with the thought. "You can't carry me like this. Put me down," she commanded.

"Malor is alive." He sounded like he was speaking only to himself. "If he survived, then what the hell does that mean?"

"Cadmus!" She tried to free herself from his hold, but his grip was iron. She squeezed his uninjured arm with perhaps more force than was necessary. "He wasn't real."

Cadmus stopped as if hearing her for the first time since Malor had appeared. The world stopped whirling around her. She saw the bodies of some of the humans that had attacked them and realized they weren't far from where they'd fought. He'd been testing the perimeter to find the direction Malor had gone in.

But he must not have heard or smelled any trace of him, Anova realized.

"What are you talking about?" Cadmus's dark eyes focused on her.

"It was an illusion. Like when I'd used to have hallucinations from the blood crown. He wasn't real," she repeated to him.

Cadmus stared at her before his gaze moved to the boy that Malor had massacred. His broken bow was underneath his body. While he looked, yet more blood came from him.

Illusion or not, Malor had been an animal.

As his eyes moved back to her, he said dully, "That is real."

Anova didn't have an answer for him—at least not one that was sane to say out loud. Malor's words to her on the night of the full moon came back to her.

"Erion gave much to make me physical. Until then, I'd been a mere voice in his head."

But Erion was dead. Even if Malor had always been tied to the crown, he'd been physical before.

Hadn't he?

Anova was saved from having to respond to Cadmus when a shriek shot through the morning quiet.

Cadmus lowered her to the ground, his eyes scanning her before he set himself between her and the noise. But what emerged from the trees beyond them was only Nerium, Della, and Maris.

Della's face went as white as a sheet when she saw her. She gasped her name and almost fell before Nerium steadied her.

On his other side, Maris said, "Anova, your face!"

She remembered then that the human's blood was still on her. She felt ill but managed to shake her head. "It's not mine."

"We've been found." Nerium's eyes bounced around the carnage spread about them before settling on Anova and Cadmus. "Are you hurt? Either of you?"

"I'm fine, but Cadmus has been," Anova said.

"It's nothing." Cadmus shifted so his injury was less visible to them. He added, "We were attacked by a band of humans while on watch. We may have more company in the vicinity."

The hair on the back of her neck raised as he spoke. His words referred to the possibility of more humans, but she knew he was thinking about Malor still.

Suddenly, Leander appeared behind the others. Knives were already in his hands. "What's going on? There's blood in the air."

"We're moving." Cadmus stepped forward while pulling her away from the humans littering the ground. "This location has been compromised."

Leander's eyes focused on his brother's wound. "We should head east. There's an apothecary just within Eastwoe. We'll need medicine for that, and it'll be faster than bumbling around in the forest for herbs."

She could see Cadmus's jaw tick. "I'll be fine. We need to keep moving. Eastwoe is too close to the palace, which is too much of an obvious place for the witch to attack."

"I'm afraid it's necessary. Leander's right," Nerium said. "It would help ease the burden on Anova to heal us constantly, too." All the fae looked to her when he said it.

For some reason, the human boy's words came back to her then.

"If I end you here, I can end another fae monster, too. Two less to kill us."

Anova looked into Cadmus's face. His expression softened a degree while they stared, and she knew that he was deferring to her decision in that moment.

Even if she knew there'd be a conversation later about what exactly had happened before the others had appeared.

Finally, she said, "Let's go."

CHAPTER FORTY-SEVEN

"In our world, this would be enough, you know," Maris said as she passed Nerium a spear of rabbit thigh.

He cocked an eyebrow at her but accepted the food. It was roasted to a gleaming tan, and she'd even seasoned it with wild herbs.

Anova watched as Nerium bit into the meat and knew with a certainty that it was over for the rabbit.

Warm thyme drifted on the air, and the heat from the coals warmed her feet. Anova knew she should feel more at ease—or at least, like they'd stopped running from shadows for a moment. She'd been practicing her own version of a fae barrier. It trapped the smell and smoke from their low-burning fire as well as the sounds of their voices.

But she couldn't rest. Leander and Cadmus had left earlier in the day to find the apothecary run by the woodland fae.

She tried to remind herself that they were capable enough not to need her clumsy magic. During the daylight hours, they were used to not having the moon's power, anyway.

The rest of them had camped at the edge of a field that gave way to the gloom of the forests of Eastwoe. Even during the day, light beetles and ghost glows often played through the trees here.

Though it was warm, Maris and Della had built a low fire to cook the rabbits that Nerium had hunted for them. The three of them sat across from her and Juras. She'd last seen Lycasta some hours ago, but that suited her fine.

Juras nudged her. A quick but subtle smile had spread across his face. She followed his gaze to the other three across from them.

"If we were on the other side of your fae forests, I could make you mine with food like this." Maris shook her head as she ran water over her smudged hands.

"I am already." Nerium's eyes shifted to hers as a smile ghosted along his lips.

Her ears reddened, and Della giggled next to her. Maris's eyes flew from Nerium's as she spoke. "You're not used to eating meat. Of course you like it."

Anova smiled at the last-second modesty.

"Human men are fools," he purred at Maris and Della. "They do not know what they have."

Juras shifted. "Don't lump me in with them."

Anova and the other women laughed. After a moment, Juras couldn't help but join in. By the end of it, her belly ached from mirth. Quiet followed as the coal fire gave off soft, irregular glows that came from its heart.

"You can't eat again, can you?" he said under his breath. Juras hadn't missed it, then.

Anova watched the remaining wood blacken further as she considered how to answer him.

"My mother used to tell me that she often couldn't eat anything but ginger root when she was pregnant with me." Anova smiled. "She didn't even brew it into tea. She chewed it whole, apparently."

She leaned back against the stump she'd settled against where she sat on the ground. Talking of her mother reminded her that she'd never gotten justice for her murder. Now that she was one of them, she was supposed to be as powerful and cunning as them, but she still hadn't made any more progress on finding her fae killer than when she was human.

Anova released a shaky breath and asked Juras, "How did you get away from her?" One of his eyebrows arched at her until she added, "You know who I mean. Hinterfell."

Juras was silent for too many seconds before he said, "I left behind the loft. I knew she'd look for me there after my eighteenth birthday." Anova knew he was remembering the same thing—the threat Hinterfell had made to force them against their will to work at the Rosebud.

"And then, after everything that had happened that night in the border forests ... Well, I didn't think you were coming back," he finished.

Anova stared forward. "Back when you thought I was dead."

Back when you thought you'd helped kill me, she said in her mind, though the thought stayed there.

"I rented out rooms at inns when I could afford it. Mostly, I couldn't," Juras continued. "Then, towards the end, Mikal let me stay at The Last Chance ... in exchange for my company for a few nights."

He shrugged at the fire like he was talking to it and not her. "It wasn't so bad."

Despite his words, a lump formed in her throat. She'd promised to come back for him. And while it hadn't been her intent to stay in Fae, she remembered well those days after she'd acquired the blood crown.

Those had been days of running and not sleeping—or sleeping in empty houses. Of waking up in a cold sweat to discover no one there but herself.

Of feeling nothing but fear and the emptiness that had hollowed her chest. Of the feeling that she'd been betrayed by one she loved.

Before she'd decided to do it, her arms were wrapped around Juras's frame. She pulled him tight against her like doing so could take her back to that time to fix everything.

Her heart thudded too loudly for her to hear his. For all the charm that Juras had, for the show that he put on for others, Anova could see the signs of what was underneath it.

"As long as I'm alive, you won't be alone again. As long as you can stand me," she whispered with a half-smile.

Slowly, like first light pouring over the night's frost, his arms came around hers. His curls pushed against her cheek as he held her back.

"Do you remember the days we didn't say our names?" His words were barely audible.

Anova swallowed. Of course she did.

Those days had turned into months.

Years.

But, back then, their aliases had been their names. There'd been no other choice.

"Yes," she responded.

"I never want to go back to that. Not between us," he said.

She nodded, not trusting her voice to remain even. Juras was, and always would be, her family—even if their blood wasn't shared.

But when they pulled apart, Juras had a strange look to his face. He shifted.

"Anova, there's something more I need to tell you."

Her gaze shot up before he could continue. She'd smelled something familiar on the air past the trails of thyme, smoke, and roasted meat.

Something that didn't belong at all.

But there was no sound of a heartbeat with it.

"What's going on?" Juras said.

Nerium had already risen to his feet, too. She stared at him and saw that they'd both scented it. But she still didn't understand.

It was one of the humans who had attacked them days before. He stepped into the clearing then. Along his neck was a scar like his head had been stitched back to his body.

She could have never forgotten his face after what had happened. It was the archer boy from the group of human raiders.

Her stomach turned. He hadn't been alive when they'd left him.

He smiled at her with his familiar face, but another voice came from his throat when he spoke.

"Hello, Anova. I have a message for you."

CHAPTER FORTY-EIGHT

"Leave. Now." Nerium had moved faster than Anova could track. He'd put himself between them and the thing that looked like the human boy but wasn't.

"Or what?" His eyebrows lifted barely. It didn't match the young man's face. "You'll kill the Lord of Death with your bare hands? Or a kitchen knife?" His eyes flicked to Maris where she gripped the knife she'd used to butcher the meat.

The blood crown's fury ran through Anova. "We'll do more than that, Rietvar," she threatened.

Rietvar gave a light laugh. "No need for that, my dear. I'm not here corporeally." He smiled. "No, I just needed to borrow a form that you'd listen to."

His words made Anova want to vomit.

"Reverse what you've done to the moon, and we'll talk," she said.

He ignored her. "Imagine my surprise when I found this." His fingers ran over the human's throat. "Impressive work, Anova. I mean that."

Anova didn't answer. She couldn't

"You're getting stronger. You'll serve me well, soon." His eyes hovered over her belly.

She wanted to rip his throat out once more just for the gesture.

"I'll destroy you before you touch me or this child," she said through her teeth.

He chuckled. "Despite my more mundane forms, I am much too powerful even for you." His eyes snapped from Anova to the human women and he shared a sheepish smile. "Even in this body."

He started to pace, and she was reminded of a wolf circling prey.

Not yet fed. But waiting for the opportunity.

Anova shifted to keep herself between the monster in their midst and her human family. If it came to a fight, their only chance was for her and Nerium to keep him occupied long enough to give the others enough time to escape.

Emotions tangled in her throat. On their own, she knew they wouldn't be sufficient.

She watched him move, the only noise coming from him the soft sound of boots pressing against leaves. In the human's chest was a silence.

She had to keep him speaking long enough for her to find a way to get them to safety. Even if it sickened her to entertain his schemes, she needed to do this.

"What did you do to the moon?" she said.

"What do you think? What do I do?" He smiled and answered himself. "It is dead. It exists now in my realm."

So it's true. Anova hadn't quite believed it despite the evidence in front of her.

"But why?" she asked. She remembered back to when she'd tried to bargain for Cadmus's life. He'd rejected the blood crown on the grounds that he had ultimate power already. "What could you hope to gain from it?"

"It's what the witch wanted in our bargain." His brow creased. "Are you done with your interrogations yet?"

She ignored his question. "And you got what you wanted." Anova's stomach turned.

Had he? Had he killed Hellmyr after all?

"So, so close." He tilted his head as he stopped his pacing. "I almost have. Despite the witch getting everything promised to her."

He stepped towards her.

"That's enough," Nerium said.

Rietvar smiled at him. "How many decades old are you, fae? Or is it more … centuries?"

Nerium didn't answer, but she saw how Maris's knuckles grew white from the tension of holding her butcher knife.

"Sometimes, it's the oldest ones that are connected to it the most. The moonlust. I wonder if you are one of them." Rietvar's teeth slipped past his lips. "I wonder how much longer ones like you can go without it."

Anova stepped to the side to draw his attention away from Nerium. She didn't like where this was going, and it was time to put a stop to it.

"That's enough, Rietvar. Why are you here? What's your message?"

Rietvar licked his lips.

"I offer you one last chance to ensure you make good on your part of our bargain," he said to her. "Come with me to my realm, and you and your child will remain safe. Stay in this wretched land …"

Rietvar's eyes locked onto hers, and she was reminded of the human who'd tried to kill the life growing within her just days ago. "Remember that I'm taking your child. However, you do not have to be alive for that. Necessarily."

Anova stared openmouthed at him.

Something in the back of her mind sang to her like a lover.

Kill him. Now.

"You bastard." The words were dragged through her throat. Anova ran for Rietvar, the blood crown's magic eager inside her.

Rietvar was still smiling when, with a wave of his hand, he forced her to the ground.

Anova looked to Juras and her other friends. "Run!"

Nerium had already grabbed a blade when he'd started for him. Rietvar didn't even look at him. Before he got close to his borrowed form, the blade clattered to the ground just before he forced the fae down with it.

Unshed tears stung Anova's eyes. They'd never had a chance.

"This is why your kind so often bores me," Rietvar sighed. "Predictable. That is, until you are driven to the brink. Then it becomes interesting."

He picked up Nerium's blade and pointed it at Anova's throat.

"Our bargain prevents you from harming me," she reminded him through her teeth.

"Only in that the act itself can't hurt you," he corrected. Something flashed in his eyes as he looked on her.

Would he truly kill her to rip her open and take their child?

It happened in a blink. Wings the color of shimmering emerald flew into Rietvar's face a second before a fae fell from the trees above them.

Lycasta's sword planted itself straight through the human's neck. Momentum slammed them both to the earth. She was still straddling his back when his head twisted to look at Anova.

Oddly, this body didn't bleed even though it ripped and broke along muscle and tissue.

"Don't forget that I offered you sanctuary. I get what I want, Anova. Always."

The life was gone from the human's eyes once again as Rietvar left the body.

CHAPTER FORTY-NINE

"I don't understand," Anova heard herself say.

"There was no forced entry. They were simply dead," Leander said.

The singed smell of drowned coals laced the wind around them, but there was something else on the air. Yet it wasn't quite a smell.

After observing the behavior of those around her, specifically the fae, she realized what it was. Tension.

For what felt like the first time since they'd fled the Wolfsbane estate and started running, all those in their group had dropped what they'd been doing to listen.

Cadmus hadn't left her side since he'd learned what had happened in their absence. Even now, after they'd circled the area dozens of times for any remaining sign of Rietvar, his eyes still bounced between the shadows made by the trees around them.

Lycasta was sitting with her head propped against an oak. She hadn't said much after banishing Rietvar from the dead boy's body. Two moths played in the air above her, and Anova wondered if she was able to control them without the aid of moonlight magic.

Anova didn't mind this version of her so much, except that the fae lady's motives were more opaque to her than ever. Viridia had reappeared with Lycasta, and she suspected the fae lady had been searching for her. The butterfly rested on a low branch above them.

"But what killed these fae?" Anova asked, her eyes flicking from Leander to Cadmus.

The two had found the woodland fae's apothecary, though they'd returned empty handed. But that wasn't the worst of it.

The shop had been filled with dead fae.

It was Lycasta who answered her. Her eyes remained shut. "You heard the abomination. The moon's gone."

Juras squinted at the fae lady from where he sat next to Anova. "And that means ...?"

Nerium completed the thought. "All fae have a connection to the moon. It serves us by granting its power to us when its light is visible and unobscured by the sun. But, there's more to it than that. Many fae believe it grants us life."

Anova's stomach twisted. She couldn't help but remember what Lycasta had told her the night she'd found out she was pregnant.

"All fae infants are born on a full moon. Sometimes, fae pregnancies only take three months. Sometimes, twelve."

What's going to happen if we don't undo this ritual? What happens if the moon is truly dead?

Anova couldn't speak.

Cadmus said what they were likely all thinking. "Its absence will kill fae."

"We should assume this, going forward." Nerium's face was grim when he said it, and she was reminded of Rietvar's veiled threats.

"It's also why we should change our course to Eastwoe palace," Leander said.

"No. Are you kidding?" Anova laughed, but it wasn't a sound of joy. "He hates us."

At the same time, Juras shot to his feet and said, "We aren't going there."

Leander looked at Juras and revealed his pointed teeth in something between a sneer and a smile. "And you have a better plan, sneak-thief?"

"Your safe house not good enough anymore?" he said.

"My safe house doesn't have intact magical barriers. Or medicine." She couldn't help but notice how Leander's eyes flicked to hers for the barest of seconds when he said the words.

Her eyebrows came together. They needed medicine for Cadmus's shoulder. She hadn't sustained any real injuries from their battles against Rietvar and the humans.

The heartbeat inside her that wasn't hers quivered again, and she realized with a swallow the likely true reason they'd gone to the apothecary in the first place.

Her gaze jumped to Juras's, and she saw that he'd realized what Leander had meant, too. He fell quiet.

"This is all assuming Hellmyr is alive," Anova pointed out. "My healing wasn't exactly complete."

"Another reason we should consider scouting the palace, at least," Leander said. "It will complicate matters if the fae king is dead."

Anova resisted a shudder from his callous words, though she couldn't quite deny the truth in what he'd said this time.

Cadmus surprised her by adding, "It goes both ways. Now that the moon's absence has nulled our magic, he would be a fool to deny joining resources considering the situation his kingdom faces. Fae is under invasion in more ways than one." He raised an eyebrow. "Well, as long as he's living."

Anova shook her head. She'd be the voice of reason here. Even if they were trying to do this for her, the risk was too high.

"Even if Hellmyr has what we need and the other way around, he won't agree to working alongside us on principle," she said. "We're just as much enemies to him as Rietvar or Alys."

The fae fell silent around her, and she felt they were all remembering the way Hellmyr had regarded her and Juras when he'd woken on a table, his chest being carved open under a bloated moon.

Anova breathed as she considered it herself. Somewhere in the middle of it all, they'd become mortal enemies. A pain in her chest reminded her of her part in that.

"He may be the recognized fae king, but there is another. A de facto second ruler of Fae." Nerium looked to Anova. "Out of all of us here, you know her best. Would the king's mother agree to a truce between our parties in service of fighting Rietvar?"

For a few moments, she considered it. Letharia had recognized and even fought against the corruption of her lover, the former high king and Hellmyr's father. She'd taught Anova to control the blood crown when it had been eating her alive. And she'd come to an agreement with Anova when she'd wanted to spare the life of her assassin.

So long as our reasons are worthy enough, Letharia could be convinced.

But she'd also hated her more and more each time Anova had placed Hellmyr's life in danger. And this time was worse than all the others, she knew.

Finally, Anova said to them, "Letharia will listen to reason."

She hoped.

Around them, the woods passed in a blur with the occasional glow streaking through the branches; the will-o-wisps played in the air, oblivious to the crises that Fae seemed to be facing from every side. Her breath froze in her lungs at the sight.

They must be their own magic, she realized.

Cadmus squeezed her hand. She'd started to slow down to watch them.

"We can stop and rest if you need," he said. His words carried on the wind.

She shook her head. "No, we need to keep moving forward."

Every dark night that passed was another that more lives were taken. Every day that passed, Rietvar got closer to what he wanted.

The others were spread in a semi-circle with the humans at their center as their group crossed the woods of Eastwoe. As they passed through the trees, she tried to maintain a loose barrier of magic insulating their scents and sounds from the area surrounding them.

She'd even done a moderate job at repairing some of Cadmus's new-old wounds. Her abilities with the blood crown's magic were nothing compared to what the dead High King had done with it, but she was improving most days.

She *had* to.

Her gaze snapped to the side when she sighted sudden movement, but it had come from within her barrier.

"Leander's over there," she told Lycasta when she'd caught up to the two of them.

Lycasta ignored the remark and looked at Cadmus. "Can I speak to Anova? Alone?"

Cadmus's eyebrows lifted. He looked to Anova, but she was too shocked by her request to do anything but nod.

"I'll be with Nerium," Cadmus said to Anova, though his eyes were on Lycasta still.

It was clear what he meant by the words: *I'll be watching.*

Anova felt much the same. She'd already started to regret agreeing to be alone with her.

Though she'd managed not to kill Lycasta during her attempt at healing her broken rib, that didn't mean that the desire wasn't at least a little there.

She suspected the feeling was likely mutual.

"What is it?" Anova asked.

"There are certain signs you need to be aware of," Lycasta said. "Things you should pay attention to."

"Signs?"

"Signs your body is ready to give birth," Lycasta said.

Anova stared at her. She wasn't sure what she'd expected from her, but it hadn't been this.

"You said all fae are born on nights with full moons. So unless Rietvar ..." Anova stopped talking.

"Unless you truly are as dull as I'd feared, I think you know what could happen," Lycasta said as her lip lifted. "Even if you don't understand our biology."

"Not really," Anova snapped back at her. "In case you hadn't noticed, none of this has happened before. How could I know?"

But, as she said the words, she acknowledged that she did know.

In the silence that filled the air around them like a second barrier, Anova whispered after a moment, "It could be a stillbirth."

Within her heart of hearts, Anova had known this already.

"You need to be aware of the symptoms. Even if you are still months from when it should happen, you no longer have the moon's fullness as a guide." Lycasta stared forward. "Increased pain. Nausea." Her eyes flicked to her face. "A craving to feel moonlight. Those are the most common signs, though your body will tell you in no uncertain terms when it's time. Listen to it, and you'll know."

As she digested the information she'd given her, as somewhat vague as it was, Anova glanced at her. Why should Lycasta want to help her at all?

An answer occurred to her.

"If this is an attempt to repay me for what I did for you after we left the estate," Anova said after some minutes, "you should know I did it for Juras."

The words had come out strange. They didn't have the biting sarcasm Anova usually adopted when talking to Lycasta.

Soft, intermittent light from the gloom woods around them passed across Lycasta's bronze skin. The brown waves of her hair were perfectly arranged about her face. She was as beautiful as a doll.

No, more than that. She was like a fae goddess come to life.

All Lycasta said before she left her was, "I know."

CHAPTER FIFTY

They entered Eastwoe proper around midnight. Anova considered once again how different this world was to the one she'd been raised in.

In the human lands, the witching hours were for sneaking and stealing, and certainly not for treating with potential allies.

But, as every plan that Cadmus proposed, this was a strategic decision in more than one sense. This was the time the greatest percentage of fae were likely to be awake, and it coincided with the biggest meal of their waking hours.

If this was to work, they had to approach Hellmyr's stronghold not as enemies but as peacemakers. Cadmus had argued that it was imperative they signal their intent primarily through their actions.

Because they might not get to exchange words before Hellmyr shut them out.

Letharia will see reason, Anova reminded herself.

All she had to do was get to her.

Pain twitched in her belly at the thought of what they were risking here. *We risk more by aimlessly moving through Fae,* she reminded herself, though the reminder helped little.

Anova was at the head of their group with Cadmus and Nerium holding torches on either of her sides. There wasn't really a soul among them who could be counted as friendly towards the fae king anymore, but she had the best chance of breaking the barrier.

She now knew how to find the evidence of magic around her, and she saw the shimmer of Hellmyr's barrier clearly once the palace was in sight.

Anova had once walked into Eastwoe palace without difficulty, though she suspected that was because Hellmyr had spelled the barrier to allow her—or perhaps any human—safely through it.

After all, both times that she'd come here on her own, he'd been expecting her.

That's because it was a trap both times, she considered. The thought didn't particularly make her feel better about their plan, but they had no better option.

The palace was as she'd remembered it. Wrought iron roses twisted around each other, forming the walls around the palace. Even from this distance and in the sullen darkness, she could see the outline of the carved goblins perched on their sullen posts all around the structure.

The wide, central window where Lyrin had nearly been left to die stretched above the main entrance. From the other side of the barrier, she couldn't tell if they'd yet been spotted by Hellmyr's guards or not.

"What do you think?" Cadmus moved a few strands of her hair behind her ear.

She walked closer to it, and her hand moved over the barrier. From experience, she knew that Hellmyr was fond of magic that blocked not only the entry of outsiders and their arrows, but also that which blocked out sound, too.

There was only one way to speak with Hellmyr and Letharia. "We'll have to break through it," Anova said. She touched it, and it was as solid as a wall.

She could force it apart, she figured. She'd broken fae barriers before.

Anova swallowed as she remembered the last time she'd used the blood crown for that purpose. It had been when she'd needed to cross from Irbess back into Fae, and she'd paid a high price for her clumsy effort.

The attempt had stolen days of her time.

But that was when I was human, and the blood crown was killing me, she argued with herself.

"Lycasta," she called as she walked to her. "How did you get through his barrier before?"

Lycasta leaned against a pole holding a lantern. She didn't even bother looking at her, even when she called her name. "The human girl. I gave Sera reserves of magic to weaken the barrier from inside."

"Yes, but I actually meant when I ordered Viridia to retrieve you."

Lycasta looked at her suddenly. Her expression told Anova that she should know the answer to her question already.

"It was open for me. A small area," Lycasta finally responded.

"What do you—" Anova stopped herself and blinked.

Just before Viridia had dragged the moth that had been Lycasta inside her bathing chambers, she'd experienced an odd feeling.

I did it. I opened Hellmyr's barrier for them—just for a second. Anova felt dizzy. How could she have used magic without realizing it?

As she went back to examine the palace's barrier, Anova noticed something that made her pause. There was an odd smell on the air—a mixture of animal scents that didn't belong on the empty streets of Eastwoe.

It was faint, however. Anova looked to the palace before them. Was she smelling that from the other side of the barrier?

A feast perhaps?

She noticed something else strange, then. Anova reached out and stopped Juras from walking right into her. Della and Maris had left him by himself to speak with Nerium.

He'd been so focused on pacing that he hadn't even seen her. She knew him well enough to know the signs of stress in him. "What's wrong?" she asked.

Juras jerked his gaze up. "Nothing. Sorry. Don't let me distract you."

Her eyes went to his hands, but he'd already shoved them under his armpits. He'd been shaking.

"No, I know something's wrong," she said. "What's going on?"

He turned away from her. "Go back to your work. Break through the barrier. I'm fine."

"Bullshit." Anova shoved herself in front of him once more. When she spoke again, her voice was a rough whisper. "I thought we agreed no more of this."

Juras's eyes darted between hers and the palace. "This is what's best for everyone else, but I'm not going inside."

An ache pierced her heart at his words. She'd been the mastermind of their plan to kidnap Hellmyr and she'd told herself that doing so had been a necessary evil to save Cadmus, but she hadn't bargained on it hurting Juras, too.

Then again, things had seemed somehow easier when she'd thought it was her that Hellmyr was cursed to and not Juras.

Anova stared at him. "You can't do that. You'd be hunted out there. You've seen that, Juras."

"I'd be hunted in there, too," he said back in a rough voice.

She shook her head. "Hellmyr may be an ass, but ... he'll need to see reason. Besides—"

"He promised to kill me if we saw each other again," Juras said in a rush.

"What?" The word was wrenched from her gut.

Hellmyr was wicked. Manipulative. Ambitious. Wildly possessive.
But this ...
He wasn't this.
"He wants to rid himself of the curse ... by ridding himself of me."

His words chilled her. *That* sounded like Hellmyr, and it made her fear for Juras's safety. Hellmyr had always been haunted by the witch's curse and the events that had led to it.

But to promise such a thing is a new low, even for Hellmyr.

"Anova!" Cadmus's voice shot through the air.

Anova smelled it, then. It was the scent she'd noticed earlier—but she realized what it truly was now. It was a mask for another scent.

"Behind me," she shouted, but the humans had already surrounded them.

They were outnumbered by dozens. Her heart hitched in her chest. They'd covered themselves in animal furs to trick their fae sense of smell. It was too cunning not to be Alys's handiwork.

One of the men had already grabbed Maris by the wrist. Fury rose inside Anova like a dark storm cloud.

The magic of the blood crown ran white-hot through her, and she formed a spear on the air seconds before firing it at the heart of the man who'd touched her friend.

It hit him square in the shoulder, inches from a killing shot, but he went down all the same.

Behind her, Lycasta and Leander each fought off a group of men by themselves. Nerium was busy protecting himself and Della from three men in wolfskins, and Cadmus hadn't left her side since the humans had appeared. Juras was holding his own for the moment, though she knew she needed to keep one eye out for him.

Especially since he'd apparently decided to sacrifice his own safety for theirs. Anova returned her focus to what was happening in front of her as Cadmus hissed in pain. One of the humans had struck him on his good side.

Sweat ran down her back as she forced another spear of heat and light and aimed this one at the man who'd struck Cadmus.

"Leave this place! If a war is what Alys wants," she said through her teeth, "then she should face me herself."

The man glared from the other side of a steel blade. "We fight for no one but ourselves. We're here to reclaim what's ours by right: the tariffs making our people poor and the lives your people have stolen but not repaid.

Your people.

She wanted to say that these were *her* people, too. That the lives of her people had been taken by the fae, too. Like her mother.

But none of those words came out of her throat.

Instead, she said, "The old High King is dead. There are no more tariffs."

"Tell that to the fae soldiers who collect it monthly still," he said.

Hellmyr wouldn't have allowed that, she argued in her head, but an explosion across their heads broke her focus.

White shards of rock had been flung through the air, some sharpened and others as blunt as stones. Most of their projectiles missed them, but then she saw their true purpose.

At first, many ricocheted off the glint suspended in the air, making the invisible barrier visible where they hit. But as she watched, cracks started to flash into existence before fading like lightning bolts.

They weren't merely rocks. They were chunks of salt—and they were using them to shatter the fae spell.

Though moonlight had already been harvested to cast this magic in the first place, allowing it to function without the moon's presence, it wasn't immune to the corrupting effects of salt.

"They're going to break it apart," she gasped to Cadmus.

If the barrier failed, more than these humans would take advantage of it. Alys's entire army would flood the palace.

As another blast of salt soared above their heads at the same time that a scream pierced the air behind her. She twisted to see what had happened, and her stomach dropped.

Juras had been driven back against the barrier. Blood was splattered across his front, and the white salt dust had fallen on his shoulders. He'd taken a deep slash along his face that leaked red through his hand as he stumbled backward.

His eyes darted from hers and back to the figures wearing cloaks of predator and prey animals alike crowding him. He showed his teeth at them.

Juras is a survivor, she told herself. But she couldn't stop thinking about what he'd said to her moments ago.

"He wants to rid himself of the curse by ridding himself of me."

Her gaze darted to the central window set in the palace's façade just beyond the barrier, and she thought she saw a shadow move.

No, she definitely had.

Her teeth clamped together.

Fated to him ... and you'd let him die before you?

There was no choice left to her, now. Not if she wanted to save them all.

Just as one final siege of salt rained down against the magicked wall, a fault appeared like the tear of a great mountain.

The barrier blinked before splintering down the fault.

"Not without us." The words were dragged from her throat as the blood crown's destructive magic burst from her like the sun.

CHAPTER FIFTY-ONE

Everything was light and heat.

Panic rose in Anova's throat like vomit. She was being sacrificed to the fire once again. It had come back for her, hungry and cheated of a burnt body.

This time, it would take every last bit of her life—and the one growing within her, too. The old burns along her legs seared already.

This time, she would melt.

A familiar double-voice hissed over the flames.

"Do you want to die here?"

Malor touched her cheek.

"It's a simple question."

A body was pushed in front of her. Anova blinked too rapidly as dizziness assaulted her. There weren't any flames here. Malor was gone.

Cadmus crouched low before her, defending her.

"You *will not* touch her," he snapped at an oddly shaped bear. She realized too sluggishly that it wasn't a bear but a man—a mountainous one, but a man all the same.

Her mind registered the world around her too quickly and too slowly all at once. She remembered why she was here.

"My little brother. I found his body mangled in the woods near a doused fire." The man's face had been painted red. "Yet, he wasn't killed by an animal, man, or even a fae."

The bear-man lunged for them with an axe weapon, but Cadmus was too quick for him. He twisted the man's arm that gripped the lower part of the weapon, their faces close enough to touch.

"Cadmus," she gasped, but a new pain was washing over her. Low in her belly, the pain sat like a goblin.

"You will leave this place and never come back," Cadmus spat in his face. With one final twist, he freed the axe. It spun into the air, past the glimmer barrier.

But the man pulled from his sleeve a hidden knife the size of his pinky finger. His gaze passed over hers as he moved, and a dark emotion writhed in his eyes like a flame.

"Only a monster could have done that to my brother."

Anova froze at his words. She couldn't seem to think or, at the very least, move.

Monster.

Before Cadmus could try to block him, an arrow landed in the man's throat, and he collapsed before them.

Leander shouted across a sea of bodies, "They're coming!"

Cadmus steadied her as he nodded in thanks to his twin. Before more enemies found them from the fights around them, he said to her, "Can you stand? He's right. If we don't do something, they'll overtake the palace."

"I'm fine," she gasped. She looked up to see that she'd gotten them through the barrier and near the palace, but for a price. The humans' army was still pouring inside the barrier from the crack they'd made from their salt barrage.

Anova's gaze stopped on Cadmus's bruised face and bloodied clothes. He'd done so much for them—both her and the future child within her.

She needed to end this, but she'd need his help once more.

"Can you cover me? Just a little while longer?" she said.

His eyes smoldered at her. "Only until one of us stops breathing."

A swallow stuck in her throat at his words. Wordlessly, they got into position beside one another. Without even using his blade, Cadmus hurled a man out of his path towards Anova and into another fight.

Anova raised her hands and faced the fracture in the barrier above the fighting. A quick glance across the area revealed that all their group had made it inside—though her gaze stopped on Juras for a second.

At the same time, relief and trepidation mixed within her at the sight of him. There was no sign of Hellmyr or his soldiers.

She had to trust that her allies could hold their own for the moment.

The fracture was barely visible higher up, but she could see it better the more she concentrated. She stopped breathing as she readied the magic within her. She'd done this before without even realizing it.

It should be easy.

While the blood crown's cursed magic flowed through her freely, she wondered at the man's words. In her mind's eye, she watched him die again.

Only a monster.

"Do you want to die here?"

She'd already chosen to live despite what it'd made her into—that had been the condition of using the blood crown to preserve her life.

She'd already chosen, so then why had she faltered when he'd said that?

A final series of twinkles appeared on the air as the magic in her finished sewing together the barrier. In her focus, she'd lost track of the battle.

Among the bodies still standing, a dead quiet had blanketed them.

Cadmus was still shielding her when Hellmyr's guards swarmed them. Quick swords lopped the heads off those struggling on the ground.

"Excellent. Now that you're done repairing the damage you've wrought, you can be punished for attempting to trespass in the king's palace."

Anova's gaze snapped up, but it was merely one of his head guards, sneering at her from the other side of a steel blade. Each of their party had been met by the pointed side of one, though she was thankful none of them were among those headless on the ground.

"You mean for preventing an attack on the king's palace," Anova corrected for him just as the sound of skin striking skin thundered through the air.

"Don't touch me," Lycasta hissed at one of the guards. Red bloomed across one of his cheeks where she must have slapped him.

Heat rose in Anova. They needed to stop this from escalating. Fast.

But he'd already shoved a boot at her, sending her to the ground. Some distance away, something gleamed in Leander's fist.

A weapon.

Anova blocked the path of the guard that seemed to be in charge. "You'll want the king." She tilted her head at him. She knew how things worked here, at least. "I'm sure he wouldn't be very happy if he missed this."

But even as she said the words, her heart hammered faster. What would Hellmyr say once he saw them? What would he do?

She might be putting them in a worse situation by summoning him.

But the face of the guard was impassive. "The king isn't here." Without breaking eye contact, he said to the other guards, "All survivors go in the dungeons. Kill the ones that resist."

The rest of her party looked to her and Cadmus, and she kept outwardly calm for them. They weren't here to war with Hellmyr and the fae aligned with him. But she couldn't seem to get the guard's words out of her head.

The king isn't here.

Did that mean he was gone from the palace? Or something worse?

As the edge of a sword nudged her forward, she saw another guard try the same with Lycasta where she was on the ground. The fae lady twisted out of the way.

"Letharia," Anova blurted at the guard. "Summon me the king's mother."

"I don't have to listen to you," he said back, and Anova realized that her power here had waned since freeing herself of this place.

Do they know what happened? Has Hellmyr been here at all?

Her stomach sank.

She'd never seen this fae before in her life despite living at the palace for some moons. Once these guards marched them inside the palace on the other ends of their swords, there'd be little chance of speaking with them as equals from then on. Her mind ran through all the names and faces she'd come to know there.

"Unferth." She spun to face the rest of his guards and called out, "I would speak with Unferth."

He'd been one of Hellmyr's highest in command—and one of those that had acted decently towards her without Hellmyr's prodding.

The guard's sword found her exposed neck. "You'll do as I say *now* or I'll open your throat."

"Like hell you will," Cadmus growled, but two other guards had already trained their swords on him.

Heat spread through in her veins as the blood crown's magic responded to the threat before her. A fight wasn't what they needed—but it would be what these fae would get.

"You'll release them to me, Argus. Unless you forget our lady's orders." Suddenly, Unferth had appeared next to her fae guard. His words didn't leave room for doubt.

"I did not, but perhaps you did," Argus hissed. "No visitors. No intruders."

"As Letharia's appointed commander, I have the final say on who is a visitor or intruder," Unferth said. His fae eyes flashed in warning.

After a moment, Argus lowered his weapon, and the others did the same.

As Unferth led her group inside the palace, Argus called to him, "Lady Letharia should clarify these differing orders herself, Unferth. Your chain only stretches so far."

The light of lanterns hanging in the halls of Eastwoe palace passed over Unferth's russet skin as he walked them into the palace.

"You have thirty seconds to tell me why I did that," Unferth said without preamble through his teeth.

His words had barely carried, but his actions were clear enough. Despite what he'd said to Argus, they were walking towards the dungeons.

He didn't trust them, either.

This was a test. Depending on what she said, they'd be held as prisoners until Letharia decided they were worth checking on or Hellmyr arrived. And that assumed he'd want them out of his dungeons.

Or...

Anova considered why Unferth had deigned to intervene at all.

Certainly, he'd been one of Hellmyr's commanders and was more familiar with Anova, Juras, and the others who had briefly lived in the palace. But that didn't mean they'd been on friendly terms, even before Anova and Juras had left with Hellmyr.

It didn't make sense for him to risk his authority on them. Anova thought back to their conversation outside the palace. Her heartbeat picked up.

"I'm sure you've seen it. This land is dying. We're here because we need to work together." She paused. His reaction would tell her what she needed to know. "Unferth, I need to speak with Letharia."

"That's not possible," he said after a moment.

"It will have to be possible." Cadmus walked on her other side and addressed Unferth. "We can't stand separately against both the tides of the human war and the one who stole the moon."

Unferth's jaw moved. "You've walked into a situation you know nothing about."

Anova's heart galloped ahead of her. She'd already figured it out.

"Answer me honestly, then," she said, darting ahead of the king's commander to block his path. "Hellmyr hasn't been back since the night of the full moon."

Unferth didn't say a thing, but the hand covering the hilt of his sword at his waist twitched. His heartbeat betrayed him by telling the truth.

Her guess had been right.

Though she felt Cadmus's eyes bolted on her in concern for her safety, she stepped closer to the fae commander. This time, she didn't ask the question on her tongue, but he answered anyway.

Unferth's nod was subtle but unmistakable. He'd been covering up this up to prevent a coup.

Letharia was dead.

And, at the most vulnerable it ever had been, Fae didn't have a ruler.

CHAPTER FIFTY-TWO

"An assassination?" Cadmus asked. There was hope in his voice.

But Unferth shook his head. "When I went to Lady Letharia's rooms one evening before nightfall to update her on our search for the king, she was already gone. All that was left of her body was an outline of bolete caps. A natural fae death."

Anova's gaze jumped between the faces of the fae gathered in Hellmyr's war room. Cadmus, Leander, and Nerium were looking at each other while the only evidence of change on Lycasta's indifferent face was a narrowing of her eyes.

"Could you clarify?" she asked Cadmus.

"Fae may not wither and age such as humans do ... but we do eventually," he said. "The oldest of us have returned to the earth at the end of centuries. Otherwise, we die from poisons and drownings and all other causes that humans do." He frowned. "But a natural fae death is slow. Letharia wasn't old enough for that, and neither were the fae in the herbal shop."

Nerium caught his gaze and said, "This is Rietvar's work."

"The others don't know about it yet," Unferth said across from them. "I have kept it secret to avoid a revolt for the kingship."

Leander gave a nod. "It seems you're very nearly on the verge of it now. Haven't you found any sign of him?"

"Not since these two left with him the night of the last moon." Unferth's gaze was heavy on her and Juras. His arms crossed against his chest. "Does the blood queen and her attending care to explain that?"

Anova swallowed. *Blood queen.*

For the first time since they'd entered the room, Juras spoke. "We told you. Rietvar and the witch Alys are working together to target him."

Unferth stared at him. "And you brought him to them. This is on you, then." He shook his head. "I should have listened to Argus."

The temperature of the room raised.

This isn't going how it needs to, Anova thought.

"And yet, your inaction has weakened your position here, and by extension, the entire fae realm," Lycasta said. "The humans are only getting more aggressive. This palace is a plump bird in the bush, oblivious to the cat staring down at it."

"Would you have had me make the announcement?" Unferth's eyebrows raised. "Sow more chaos?"

"You are missing the point." Lycasta's delicate eyebrows raised to match his as she tilted her head. "A *leader* would have been helpful. There was chaos enough out there already without them knowing about the king's mother."

"Chaos enough?" Unferth laughed, but it was joyless. "I suppose a would-be murderess knows enough about chaos to lecture the king's commander on it." He stepped closer to her. "I remember the days we hunted for you, moth tamer. He'd have had us kill you, had you not hidden so well." His lip raised in a sneer.

"That's enough. We came here to face a common enemy, not to trade threats," Anova said to the room. "Hellmyr is absent from his throne. Letharia is dead. We are at war. The reality is that, all of Fae is at risk whether we fight or not. If we accomplish nothing here, we risk losing everything."

She breathed. The words had started so quickly that she'd surprised even herself with what she'd said.

But she knew what needed to come next, even if she felt like a stranger in someone else's body when the words came from her mouth.

She locked eyes with Unferth. "The balance of power between yours and Argus's hangs by a thread here. Deny me, but he is eager for bloodshed." When he didn't respond, she moved her gaze to them all. "There is one who could claim the authority needed to helm an army against Rietvar and the invading humans without more blood spilled."

Anova felt the heavy truth of it within her and heard the words as if someone else spoke them.

"I will lead in Hellmyr's stead," she said to them all, "so long as I have your support."

The room fell quiet for several moments, and she felt a fool.

Who was she to claim this authority? She'd always rebuked the blood crown's title—High Queen of Fae. Such absolute power was a poison.

But what if this can be something different?

It was this garish hope that had encouraged those words from her mouth, she knew.

Cadmus's hand squeezed her fingers before he dropped it and stepped to the table next to her. "It goes without saying that I stand beside you, no matter what."

Anova swallowed. She knew she shouldn't have doubted it, and yet ... Not too long ago, they'd plotted to kill the last fae claiming the title that came with the crown on her head.

"The leader of Fae will need an advisor, even if just provisionally." For a second, Nerium's eyes gleamed in the dark. "I'm with you, as well."

She smiled at the fae. "I would be glad to have your help. Both of you," she said as her gaze went back to Cadmus. She felt a weight lift from her.

To her surprise, Leander spoke up next. "This is our best option. I'm only surprised you didn't try to seize power earlier."

Anova accepted his support with a nod. She looked at Lycasta, leaning against one of the room's few windows, but she didn't meet her gaze before her friends spoke.

"Do you truly need to ask?" Maris said, though her eyes smiled. At the same time, Juras slammed one of his hands down on her shoulder. "Let's do this."

But Unferth was still staring at her, silent.

She believed her own words. If they were going to avoid an insurrection—not only in the palace but across all of Fae—they needed a ruler not only with some claim to the kingship, but also the support of Hellmyr's strongest followers.

To have one and not the other meant risking civil war.

Finally, he said, "If the kingship is what you wanted by coming here, you would've claimed it already and slit my throat. So, I guess I trust you, Blood Queen. That is, on the condition that you find the fae king and bring him back."

"We should find the witch first," Cadmus said. "She's the key to stopping Rietvar, returning the moon to the night sky, and calling off the humans. Hellmyr can't do that."

And he could be dead, Anova thought but didn't say. He had to be alive.

Cadmus was right, though they needed them both.

"I'll find them," Lycasta said. "I'm the only one who can now that we can't rely on fae magic. Anyone else would only waste time."

Anova considered her words. Lycasta was the one for the task, certainly. With her trained moths, she was uniquely suited to this in a world without moon magic.

But could she trust her with something so important?

She'd nearly died trusting her before. Anova had promised herself never to make that mistake again.

Just as the *no* nearly came off her tongue, Anova realized something else as she looked at the fae lady. They shared a strange and bloodied history together, though Anova had always been able to, at least retrospectively, understand Lycasta's motives.

But lately, she hadn't been acting as Anova had predicted. It was almost as if she were trying to reconcile with her and Cadmus.

She was caught by Alys when I asked her to deliver a message to Nerium. But it wasn't as if she were bound by oath or magic to complete the task. It would've made more sense for her to flee when she saw the estate was occupied.

Was she ... trying to release them?

It would have made more sense regarding the severity of her injuries.

And then there were her words to Anova in the Eastwoe woods.

Anova spoke before she could change her mind. "I'll leave it to you. But we can't afford failure, so you're not going alone."

Red stained Lycasta's cheeks, but before she could speak, Leander said, "I'm going with her."

Lycasta was silent, but her gaze darted to his face. He didn't look back.

"Alright, fine then," Anova said.

She felt more comfortable knowing Leander would accompany her, if only to support her against the witch.

If it's possible to bring her to us at all.

Anova wasn't convinced, but they had to try.

"I'm coming, too," Juras said suddenly.

After declaring his support for her, he'd remained at the edges of their conversation, watching the rest of them argue.

Anova's throat tightened around his name. "Juras—"

He looked between her, Lycasta, and Leander. "I won't be a burden. Or, if I become one, leave me behind."

Leander had already nodded in assent, but the matter wasn't settled yet. Not by far.

Juras was human. She might have trusted Leander and Lycasta to help them save the fae realm, but she wasn't a fool. They'd leave him behind as soon as they caught any sign of him not keeping pace.

Perhaps even before then.

Anova stepped close to him and dropped her voice. "Juras," she pled.

He's going to try to kill you. She didn't say it, though. She was sure they were both thinking it.

He was her friend. Despite the title she'd adopted of temporary leader, this was not someone she ever wanted to command.

But Juras held her gaze. "You know I have to find him. Besides," he said louder, "I think I'm the only one who can. If he can be convinced, this is the way."

In her heart, she knew it was the truth. She grasped his hand.

"Remember to come back alive," she whispered.

Juras simply smiled.

"I've been good at that so far."

CHAPTER FIFTY-THREE

"You've betrayed our kind to let a *human* take the throne."

Argus and his most ardent followers were on the lawn before Eastwoe palace. Anova had hoped to settle the matter privately—or at least without an audience.

Unferth and Cadmus were on either of her sides. She knew she had the former to thank for such a bloodless transition of power and the latter for keeping her relatively sane throughout it.

Many of the fae within the palace such as the servants and the king's guard recognized her. For the others that didn't know or trust her, it had helped that they'd presented a united front with the rest of Hellmyr's staff.

Until now, that was.

While see saw the smolders of anger in Cadmus's stare at the other fae and related too well, Anova resisted the feeling. Anger could be useful here, certainly, but she had something else in mind.

She gave a light laugh.

"And where is this human?"

Argus showed his teeth at her. "Don't trifle with me. I know who you are and what you were."

She looked upon him without any mirth left on her face. "Then you know what I've done to get here." As Anova stepped forward, her dress's slit revealed some of her burnt legs.

Such a disfigurement was a rarity among the fae, and she knew by now that the juxtaposition of her fae features and such a glaring flaw caught them off guard.

She noted his eyes on them. "And you know what I'm willing to do."

Just as conning was, politics had turned out to be all theater. It made her feel more comfortable with it than she perhaps ought to have felt.

He didn't respond to her, instead turning to the fae at her side. "And you, Unferth. You kept the death of the king's mother from us all in order to supplant her with your chosen ruler."

At this, she was silent. The eyes of the palace staff were on them.

It was true—even if Unferth had kept the matter quiet to prevent Fae from delving into chaos.

"My *chosen ruler* is King Hellmyr. This is not a usurpation," Unferth said. He raised an eyebrow. "Or did you have a different king in mind, Argus?"

Argus's jaw flicked with suppressed anger, though his voice was even. "I want what's best for Fae."

They'd struck a nerve, it seemed.

"The Blood Queen is on the side of Fae," Unferth shot back.

Anova pointed to the barrier where it flashed at her gesture. She'd spelled it to allow all fae to come and go. "If you prefer the company of humans wearing wolfskins, then leave."

The eyes of the fae behind them bore into Argus. He must have noticed, for when he spoke, he spoke to them.

"Follow her if you must. But he's after her. The moon thief and creature of the black night." His eyes traveled back to Anova. "I refuse to stay and wither into nothingness when he steals my soul. I'd rather die out there."

With those words, Argus and his company passed through the barrier. They left nothing behind but a glimmer where their bodies disappeared beyond the magic.

Anova turned to the palace's staff behind them.

"You should join him if you think the same," she declared. "Servants, you owe no debt any longer to repay. This is no trick."

It started with a couple of their cooks. They slipped quickly through the crowds and sprinted behind Argus's army without looking back.

Next came a heavy portion of their guards. They took their time picking through the other fae, some of them giving sidelong looks at her as they passed. As they left, more of the palace's staff filtered to the barrier in small groups.

It happened only within a few minutes. When the last of those who wanted to leave passed through the barrier, she counted their losses in her head.

They were left with half of the fae they'd started with, with the greatest loss to their armed guards and those who had come from their training grounds in Westvalde. Most of them had seemed to agree with Argus or perhaps they believed they could improve their chances of survival on their own.

They'd retained most of the others such as their kitchen staff and stable hands, though even there, too many had left. Surprisingly, all the servants had stayed.

Maybe she shouldn't have been surprised. Other than Hellmyr, those were the fae that had known her best here.

In truth, she hadn't expected so many to desert, though perhaps she should have. After all, Unferth had been keeping Letharia's death a secret when their company had walked in and appeared to seize the throne in opportunity.

At least those who remain trust us, she considered. *I hope.*

It would have to suffice.

Nerium intercepted them in the halls of the palace and nodded to the commander of the guard beside her. "Your scouts have found something, Unferth."

Anova's heart hammered. "Is it Hellmyr?"

"Not him. A band of humans is fighting the fae who live in Eastwoe's woodlands."

"It's not something I'd consider under our circumstances normally, however ... Assuming our help sways the woodlanders to join us here, we could use the bolster to our forces." Unferth looked to Nerium and said, "Argus took more than his share of the palace's fae, most of which were our guards."

"But can we afford to expend the resources?" Cadmus's eyes flicked to her when he said it. He looked back to Nerium. "This may be war, but we need to fight the generals. We need Rietvar and the witch."

"Ah, you misunderstand me." He held one finger out. "The scouts were adamant that a strange cloaked figure is leading these humans. The human's face slipped into view enough for them to confirm the description. Young. Dark braided hair. Likely female."

"Alys," Anova breathed.

There could be little other explanation. She'd finally showed herself.

Juras, Lycasta, and Leander had already left, but she realized then that Alys might have left a trail for them to follow across Fae. Despite herself, she was still underestimating the witch.

Anova asked Unferth, "We have enough guards to spare for this?"

"Not really. But then again, we don't need a wall of guards to win this one." Unferth's sharp gaze sized up the other two fae with them, though he still addressed her. "How much experience do your strategist and advisor have in the tactics of infiltration and hostage taking?"

Cadmus's smile was wide. "I think I like this one."

CHAPTER FIFTY-FOUR

Juras kept utterly still—or as still as was possible on the back of one of Lycasta's oversized moths. Closing his eyes helped him forget a little bit about the open air below them.

They'd left Eastwoe just over a day ago, and they'd made considerable progress since then. As the chill seeped into his toes and fingers, Juras knew without having to look where they were heading. Lycasta's moths had found a strong lead for the fae king going north.

His plan drummed in his chest like a second heartbeat, but he kept himself calm as he listened in on the fae riding moths near him. Their words were low, but up here, anything so much as a gasp carried.

"Why did you do it? You still haven't answered." It was Leander's voice.

Lycasta said, "It matters not. I wasn't successful."

Too many seconds passed before the other fae said anything back. "If you think that a foolhardy attempt to rescue Nerium and my brother would earn my forgiveness—"

"I did it because I wanted to," she said.

Something cold traveled from his extremities to his center. He hadn't given much thought to why Lycasta had been so bruised when they'd retrieved her from Alys's forces.

She tried to save them.

His stomach twisted at Leander's words.

"It was a dangerous thing to do." The words were soft and almost too quiet for Juras to hear, making him doubt if he'd heard Leander right.

Just then, he remembered the fae's words to him before they'd broken inside the occupied Wolfsbane estate.

"Saving her is not a choice."

No, he wasn't so sure of that. It would have been abundantly easier for the both of them to leave Fae and never look back. All of what Leander had done that night had been a choice.

But didn't that make his actions more powerful? More meaningful?

It was the fact that he could have turned away from ever seeing her again despite what she'd done—from not knowing if she'd lived or died—that made Juras certain of it.

Juras wondered when he'd stopped thinking about Leander and Lycasta and started thinking about two others. Going through with the plan he'd formed would be a similar kind of choice.

Fraught with risk and dangerous.

But it would be his choice to make, and not because of a magicked fate or out of obligation.

Juras pretended to come to, stretching and scoping what was visible on the horizon before them.

After a few more minutes of silence, he said to them, "I'm going after him alone. We all know where this trail heads." His gaze hovered on the stone fortress nestled among the snow-coated pines.

Farstar castle.

"You want us to leave you?" Leander said. "You're just—"

"Human. Yes. If he yet lives, I'm also the only one who could convince him to come back." Juras looked to Lycasta. "Go find the witch. That's who you need to bring to Eastwoe. We don't have time to find both otherwise."

"He's right," she said to Leander. "The witch's trail will be harder to find, and we need her." Her tone sharpened at the mention of Alys.

Leander's eyes bore into his, but he nodded.

Less than an hour later, they'd landed. His moth's feathery antennae twitched in the cold when Lycasta approached them. Snowdrops melted on her bronze skin as she shoved a fur coat at him.

Juras accepted it without thinking, feeling the shock written on his features but trying to hide it.

"You have one day until my moth returns to me. She waits here," Lycasta said.

He wasn't quite sure what to make of this fae lady anymore, so he settled on a nod. He looked at Leander as they mounted the oversized moths again.

"We'll meet at Eastwoe," Leander said to him.

Before their moths disappeared into the white sky above him, the words slipped out of Juras's mouth.

"You were wrong," he called to Leander. "It was a choice."

Leander looked down at him, but he couldn't hear if he responded back. They were gone in seconds.

Snow blanketed everything, and even in the daytime, Farstar's skies were an opaque gray. Juras thanked the snow for its brilliance. He was well over traveling through the woods in darkness and seeing things in the shadows.

Here, there was nothing but stillness and quiet.

Unfortunately, it left him too alone with his thoughts.

Is this the right thing to do?

The logical, survivor voice within him was loud to answer.

Hell no, it's not. He wants to murder me.

But he supposed he was well over doing the *right thing*, too.

And then there was the cold possibility that what he'd find would only be a corpse. He couldn't linger on that, though. Not if he wanted to keep pushing forward.

The snowfall was slow at the moment which meant that he'd be able to track his way back to the moth waiting for him.

Soon, the trees thinned enough for him to sight the black gates of Farstar's castle. Juras looked up to the spires rising above the high wall that pointed to the snow-laden clouds above. Something odd caught his eye along one of the castle's towers.

Most of the castle's stone exterior was remarkably bare. Looking at it from a burglar's perspective, this made it nigh impossible to scale and break into.

A single balcony and glass door had been built into the side of the tallest of them. Judging by appearances, it seemed to be an addition to the original structure.

Undoubtedly, this had been Hellmyr's design.

As he looked, a swallow caught in his throat. It was nearly invisible to his eyes they'd nearly drowned in the whiteness of his surroundings, but it was clear enough for him to know it wasn't an illusion.

There was a wavering lantern flame on the other side of the glass. His heart galloped faster as he realized; he was here. There was no sign of any other life, though.

Juras walked to the gate, acutely aware of how exposed he was now that he'd left the pines. No fae magic or barrier stopped his approach, and he freely touched the gates and stone walls to ensure he hadn't missed one.

Heavy on the black metal was a complex fae lock. Juras lifted it in his palm, peeked within its several keyholes, and turned his attention elsewhere.

While he was a fair lockpick, he didn't relish the idea of spending a few hours with this lock in the snow. No, he considered as he looked up, there was a faster way.

The stone walls that were connected to the metal gates might not have been scalable, but there was a glaring oversight to the castle's security in plain view.

Juras shook his head. *Fae. Always worrying about the wrong thing. Like appearances over functionality.*

The gates themselves—two metal monstrosities—curled with the designs of various plants. He could identify only a few of them such as moonflowers, lavender blooms, and snow crocus, though it mattered little.

They'd each be excellent foot and handholds. He looked between the metal to see no visible guards posted on the other side of the wall. The structure looked abandoned, but in his bones, Juras knew *he* was here.

After wrapping his hands in Lycasta's cloak to protect them from the frigid metal, he began his work.

Cold bit at his unprotected face, and the farther he went, the more his muscles strained against his progress. After one of his hands slipped on a metal rosebud, Juras stopped his ascent. He clung to the gate and breathed heavily.

He was less than a body length from the top. Juras blinked against a scattering of snowflakes that had landed in his eyelashes.

The castle loomed in his sight before him. Still, no guards had appeared.

Just as he hauled himself the remaining distance to the height of the gates, a short whistle snipped through the air. The sound was followed by a shift in the snow below him.

Though it was buried up to its hilt in snow, there was no mistaking that someone had thrown a blade.

Juras blinked as his brain caught up with the information. It was planted on the other side of the gate right where he would have landed once he'd jumped from the top.

The sound of his voice was profane against the quiet.

"I'm not here to fight. I'm here to work together against him."

Silence was his only answer.

The frozen wind moved around him, urging him to action, but he couldn't seem to budge. There was no one on the grounds of the castle.

In his inaction, the whistle sounded against the deathly quiet again. This time, he knew what was happening—someone was throwing weapons at him.

His heart pounded. Juras slipped down the metal gate, allowing the chill living in the metal to invade his bones. Flecks of snow dust flew from him as he landed against the padded ground. He was almost to his feet in order to run to cover when he saw where the second blade had landed.

It was right next to the first one on the other side of the gate, so close to its brother that it had dislodged the first into the snow.

He looked to the lantern on the other side of the balcony door above him. The light from the flame flickered like someone had passed in front of it.

A warning.

And a dismissal.

On his way back, Juras stomped through the snow to keep his legs warm and because it was the only thing that seemed to help his mood.

Fine, then. Let this place rot for all I care.

He knew he was being childish, but the day was waning, and he had no solution to this problem. The others were depending on him to bring the missing fae king back.

No longer veiled behind clouds, the sun had slipped nearly to the horizon.

As Juras retraced his steps back to the moth awaiting him, he noticed a scent on the air that hadn't been there earlier in the day.

He barely noticed it even now, but it couldn't be mistaken. It was a campfire.

Humans.

This place was far for Alys's invasion to have come, but he had sighted from the air a distant coast past Farstar's thick pine forests. Perhaps they'd sailed there.

The invasion is progressing faster than the others realize, he considered.

By the time he found the moth awaiting him, her large compound eyes staring silently down at him from her perch, Juras knew he'd gotten closer to the humans. The wind had since died, so it was easy to tell it came east of where he was.

But this wasn't his fight, was it? Hellmyr had demonstrated that much to him.

What did it matter if this realm was taken by humans? They were his people, right?

As he slumped forward, Juras's head softly hit the bark of the tree. The snow had started to melt in his boots.

Those aren't my people.

His people were his family. Della. Maris. Anova.

Fae and human alike. He'd come to find that, when it came to family, things weren't so black and white.

And his newer fae cohorts didn't deserve to die, either. Nerium. Leander.

They were just trying to protect who and what they cared about.

But they'll all likely die or live as prisoners if the humans win this war.

Juras carefully picked his way through the snowy woods, walking where the coating was thinner to reduce his tracks. In the stillness, he heard voices.

Juras stopped breathing to listen, though the words were clear and carried well.

"It happens tonight."

It was Madam Hinterfell.

CHAPTER FIFTY-FIVE

Bent trees and flickering bugs blurred past Anova as she pressed close to the horse she'd stolen from the palace's stables.

After her advisors and commander had tried to keep her from assisting on this mission, she'd waited until they'd departed and promptly ignored them.

In theory, she agreed with Cadmus, Nerium, and Unferth.

Why risk her life when the others would be enough? They weren't attempting to win the battle necessarily—just to take their commander.

The only problem was, the commander in question was Alys.

And the only way to fight against magic was with the same. They needed her help.

During their strategy meeting, she'd located a watch tower a short distance from where the battle had been reported.

Once there, she'd monitor the situation and help as needed. It would provide her easy access to those on their side that would need healing. Anova frowned at that thought. It was true that she'd been able to save Lycasta, but they still didn't know if she'd done the same for Hellmyr.

A painful knot formed in her stomach, and she gripped the reins of her horse in her palms harder.

What would happen if they brought him back?

He would work alongside us against Rietvar and Alys, she answered, though she didn't know if this was intuition or hopeful thinking.

Her eyes scanned the gloom woods around her. The sounds of the battle were faint, but she could tell they were skirting the edge of the fighting.

She hated going behind Cadmus's back, but she was no puppet figurehead. As soon as these fae thought that, she'd find a knife planted in her spine.

And she wasn't going to let any more of her companions get hurt because of her.

Her barrier followed her like a protective shadow, muffling the sounds they made and blurring their forms to shadow as her horse ran among the trees. Peeking through the branches were golden strands of sunset.

A sudden, familiar smell was lifted on the breeze to her. Anova slowed her horse from a full gallop to a light tread until they could stop.

Anova didn't dissolve the barrier insulating them until the second, making the other rider nearly collide with them.

Cadmus pulled his mount's reins hard to divert him from their path. His eyes snapped to hers in shock. Her cheeks reddened at being caught and the near-collision. She supposed all the practice had made her barrier more effective at masking her presence.

"Anova." The breath whooshed from him.

In truth, she barely recognized him by sight, so she was glad for her fae sense of smell. Black smudges ran along his cheeks, obscuring his features. His hair and ears were concealed under a wolfskin cloak.

His surprise had quickly turned into something else. He stepped down from his horse and pulled free the wolfskin. "What are you doing here? We agreed this isn't safe."

But she'd pieced together something, too. "You didn't tell me you would be the volunteer infiltrating their rank. This is much more dangerous than my mere presence here. Besides," she said, stepping off her horse,

"I couldn't let you risk your life without my help. Without anything but sticks and stones."

He moved a few strands of her hair between his fingers. "Sticks and stones? You could give your war strategist a little more credit than that." For a moment, she saw it in his dark eyes past the disguise. It was the fae he would've become had his father lived.

It was the part of him that lived for war.

Or, maybe that part is always there, she realized.

As she stared, his fingers moved from her hair to her cheek until his thumb brushed against the edge of her bottom lip.

She lifted an eyebrow, though her heart raged even at that small touch between them. She kissed his hand and pulled it from her face. "No distractions. Why did you have to be the one to risk your life?"

"I was the one who came up with the plan. I couldn't ask one of the others to do it," he answered, the honesty plain on his face.

Anova couldn't argue. Instead, she said, "I know there is a watch tower nearby. I'll monitor things from there so I can help you as needed."

"Alright," he said, seeming to come to terms with the fact that she'd find her way there regardless. "I'm sending you some of our spare guards."

She wanted to point out that they didn't have *spare* guards. They barely had guards at all, but she let him do this for her.

"Cadmus." Anova stole his hand again to squeeze it. Her stomach felt painful and balled up at the thought of him facing her. "Be careful. She can be dangerous."

"So can I," he murmured, looking at her sidelong.

She pulled him to her and kissed him. When she pulled back for a breath, she whispered against his ear, "That's one reason why I love you."

"Are you sure it's not entirely the reason?" he smirked, tracing her collarbone.

"There are too many," she said seriously. She closed her eyes in his embrace. "Just come back alive."

He kissed her forehead before helping her back on her horse. He looked like a specter of the night as he left her. "And you, Anova. I mean that."

Before he disappeared in the gloom woods around them, he added, "There should be a way light hanging from the top of the watch tower. If you need help, I want you to use it."

After he'd left, Anova borrowed magic from the blood crown to disappear into the trees, as well. Its magic thrummed through her.

At least in this life, she could become one of the things that haunted the woods instead of the poor, helpless girl in the fae tales stumbling through them.

We're coming for you, she promised to Rietvar and Alys.

As she rode the rest of the way to the watch tower, Anova frowned in the direction of the setting sun. Already, she could see stars in the darkest part of the sky.

With the assistance of her fae senses, the starlight would be enough to see by, but the coming night felt wrong without the moon. Her stomach knotted further at the thought of it absent from the heavens, enough to want to make her vomit.

Focus on your mission. She breathed to calm herself. She was there to support them so Cadmus could pull off their strategy safely.

When she arrived at the tower, guards were already stationed at its base. She dismissed more than half of them to return to battle, established a thin barrier around the area, and climbed the stairs to its peak.

A wide window overlooked the lands stretching across Eastwoe. From this height, she could even see some of Farstar's snowy mountains to the north. When Juras, Lycasta, and Leander had left, they'd started towards a lead going to Farstar.

Be safe, Juras. Please.

In disgust, she looked to the moonless evening sky that was quickly being overtaken by total night. If only the others had magic, she'd feel better about his chances.

"It's a traaap," someone said a sing-song voice.

Anova jumped as she twisted to see a familiar specter behind her. "Malor." She grinded his name between her teeth. "What do you want?"

"I'm not here because I want to be." He crossed his arms as he hissed the words in his double voice.

Her heart was still thundering from his appearance. "Then you've been assigned from the afterlife to torture me?"

His lids came low over his red eyes. "You know I'm not in the afterlife, Anova."

She shook her head. This was just an illusion. Nothing more.

But, dangerous as interacting with madness was, she had to ask him. "What do you mean? Are they walking into a trap?" She looked out over the battle.

She could see their forces join the fray, though from this distance, it was difficult to tell who was who. Somewhere down there was Cadmus, hopefully infiltrating the humans to get closer to the witch.

"I'm only telling you what you know," he said. He walked towards her, and the dying light touched his antlers. His red eyes squinted at her. "Don't you know by now?"

"Why do you keep following me?" Anova snapped as her back hit the wall next to the window. None of the fae on the ground guarding her seemed to have noticed anything amiss.

"I'm not following you," he said. "I'd say quite the opposite."

Her hand went to her belly as pain twisted there. She raised her voice. "Get away from me now, I'm warning you, you wretch."

Malor stopped. His face hardened and pain seemed to course through him. She thought it was from the epithet she'd called him until he stumbled to the floor and pulled himself into a ball.

It was odd seeing this powerful, enigmatic creature be reduced to such a state.

A sudden pain stabbed through her, insistent and disorienting. Anova's hand slipped from where the gripped the wall and she slumped to the floor.

She realized it wasn't a new pain. She'd been feeling it all along, intermittently.

No. It can't be.

Anova looked to the sky, expecting a bloated moon. Her nails clawed the wooden floor as a groan escaped her.

No. The moon is gone. It's gone. It's gone.

Her eyes snapped apart as a bead of sweat ran between them. Malor was nowhere to be found.

"Help! Guards," she called.

No one answered.

Shakily, she lifted herself some until she was sure her voice could be heard outside the window. Before she called again, she looked over the side directly to the ground below. Her guards were gone.

She lowered herself to the floor again as her reality crashed down on her. It was happening.

It's too early. More sweat ran down her body. *It's too early.*

It was too early, even by fae pregnancy standards, but denying what was happening had gotten her here in the first place.

The moon. The moon.

It was a constant chant in her head, which made it difficult to think about anything that didn't have to do with the moon. Anova sent a flare of magic at the way lantern that hung on an iron ring on the exterior of the tower. It caught only a second before it blew out.

Again and again, the flame failed. Panic clawed up from her belly and into her throat.

Remember. Remember what it was like.

Though Juras had been born before her, she'd been at The Rosebud for a handful of other births. Mostly, she'd been out of the room during the deliveries, but she remembered what it had looked like afterward.

Another short, stabbing pain flashed through her abdomen. She shrugged out of the cloak she was wearing over her dress and shoved it under her. Anova gritted her teeth as the urge to push overcame her.

A scream ripped from her throat.

CHAPTER FIFTY-SIX

At the top of a tower above a battle that raged between the folk she belonged to now and the ones she'd come from, Anova held a tiny body.

Anova's own body and mind were numb.

The baby in her arms hadn't ever cried. Not even magic from the blood crown had seemed to help that.

She felt the presence climb the stairs to her tower before she saw him. She didn't look up when she spoke to Rietvar.

"You're too late." Her voice was strangely even despite what was in her heart. "She never lived."

She could feel Rietvar staring at them. Blood had soaked into her dress and cloak. Her hair was tangled throughout the blood crown on her head. She wasn't sure how much time had passed with the two of them on the floor after the delivery.

She was sure she should have been doing something else other than sitting there, but she couldn't find it in her to do so. On the floor near her was her stained blade. She left it alone.

Lycasta had been right. About all of it.

All fae were connected inexorably to the moon's power and were born on full moons. Though her face was soft like all babies Anova had seen—human or otherwise—their daughter had the thin, pointed ears of a fae.

Anova's hand cupped her small head. She had a shock of dark hair that reminded her of Cadmus's. She'd already memorized everything about her face, from her button nose to her arched lips.

Now that there was nothing for Rietvar to collect for their bargain, Anova supposed he would take her life in recompense.

Get up. Fight. Go!

But the voice telling her these things was easily ignored.

Rietvar's coal black eyes stared forward. He was in the form that most looked like a human or fae, but there was no mistaking the void of a heartbeat that lived in his chest.

Finally, he said, "Do you release your child to me?"

Anova felt something where her heart should have been. A desperate, striking pain. She couldn't move or speak.

How could she mourn something so much that she'd never even had?

Why had she lived from almost dying so many times when the one in her arms had never even had a chance to try living?

Anova kissed her head and closed her eyes before her vision blurred with tears. She hadn't yet spoken her name out loud, but it needed to be said.

"Good-bye, Elissa," she said.

I'm sorry, Cadmus. I couldn't save her.

Another dawn rose over the land when Anova could stand again. The food and water stowed in her supply bag had been long exhausted.

Sooner or later, the body either got what it needed or it quit.

It was these primitive needs that drove her from the watch tower and the thought that she didn't yet know what had happened in the battle. Their plan seemed so far away now, but there was one fact she couldn't ignore. She hadn't helped them as she'd promised.

The possibility that she'd lost two of those she loved in one night made her stagger forward despite the weakness in her body.

She needed to know. She needed to find Cadmus.

She needed to do something.

But nothing will bring her back, she thought.

Anova closed her eyes as she lowered herself to the last step of the tower. She could barely hold herself upright, she realized. No evidence of her guards remained—not even a body or drop of blood.

Where are they? Cadmus and the others should have been here by now, she considered.

The only answer was a grim one. They couldn't. The battle had gone south.

Her knees nearly betrayed her again. She could hardly walk, but the dryness on her tongue told her she couldn't stay here and wait for them.

Anova would have to get through the gloom forests and back to the palace on her own. She started forward, loping through the trees for nigh on an hour, until she collapsed.

CHAPTER FIFTY-SEVEN

Juras's breath froze in the air.

Why. Is. She. Here.

He'd gone crazy. He'd hit his head against the metal when he'd fallen from the gate. He was having a nightmare.

But none of those things were true.

Juras's hands shook. Panic and other painful emotions threatened to seize him as her voice now melded with old memories. His scars ached.

Why is Madam Hinterfell here?

Apparently oblivious to him being in the vicinity, Hinterfell hadn't stopped talking.

"Now that their magic has been neutered, the cover of night will only benefit us."

Another familiar voice spoke. "Where are the guards? Isn't this their king?"

It was Bron. Juras's fingernails pressed too hard into his palms. The urge to hurt something was strong within him.

Bron was what remained of her favorite hired muscle after Anova had accidentally killed Strego with the blood crown. Though neither of them had exactly been a friend to Juras, he had a special kind of hatred reserved for Bron.

When Juras had been younger, Bron had been among his first bullies from the streets of Irbess.

"He's dismissed them all, or weren't you listening to me?" It sounded like Hinterfell had rolled her eyes.

Juras had guessed as much, but it wasn't a good sign that she knew this. *She's been here for more than a few days, it seems.*

It was only good luck that had prevented their paths from crossing until then.

And then the obvious hit him: *She's here for Hellmyr.*

Hinterfell was still speaking. "Remember, you have to work quickly. You'll carry all the bags of oleander brush through the servants' tunnel to the cellar. This way, we bypass the need to enter through his gates and expose our mission. Once there, you will spread it then ignite the brush so it burns through his cellars and seeps through the floors."

Her laugh was short, though it bounced through the trees.

"Paranoid things. With no windows and hardly any doors, there will be no venting it out, either. By the time he finds where the fumes are coming from, it will be too late."

"But how are you going to distract him from that?" Bron said. He could almost see his eyebrows pinch together.

"Leave that my part to me, Bron. Suffice to say he'll be busy enough with a few of our flaming arrows. It may even catch something on fire on the grounds, and we thwart his fae sense of smell this way, too. Smoke will already be in the air."

Just as the woman herself was, her plan was coldhearted and effective. A chill traveled down his spine that had nothing to do with the falling temperature.

He was no expert on poisons like Anova was, but he knew enough to realize the brutality of her plan.

First, they were going to trap Hellmyr in Farstar castle and distract him by presenting an assault from the outside. At the same time, they were going to fan noxious fumes through the floors.

And Hinterfell was right. There were few windows outside.

If their plan went as she'd outlined, the castle would become his tomb.

And there was the real possibility that Hellmyr was weakened enough by his injuries from Rietvar that he might not survive even a botched assassination attempt by these two.

He's not your concern anymore. He's made that much clear.

He needed to leave. Now. Their words spelled death and misery, and he knew Hinterfell enough to know her capable of such things.

You'll never see him again if you leave now.

His heart thundered wildly in his chest. The heart was a fool thing, but he found he couldn't ignore its song.

Destroy their plans and leave. That's all.

Hellmyr wouldn't even know he'd done it, but he didn't care about that.

Before he'd decided to, Juras edged the perimeter where he'd heard them until he found faint tracks leading to an area dry of snow under several trees.

Piled on top of quilts were bags full of not only traveling supplies such as canteens of water, clothes, and cookware, but others full of nothing but dried plant brush. Seed husks, wooden stems, and thin browned leaves were packed inside. Scattered through the piles were brittle, flattened flowers that looked to have once been a vibrant pink or red.

The debris looked dry enough to enflame even without a spark.

Juras's stomach turned at seeing her murder instruments, but his mind was already working. There was an easy solution here to stop them—and maybe even turn them back to where they'd come.

First, he dragged the sacks of dried oleander brush off the quilts keeping it from the cold, snow-packed ground. After grabbing their water canteens and popping them open, he started to flood the noxious kindling until all the debris was soaked through.

Two birds. One frozen stone.

When the last reserves of their drinking water fell from their canteens, Juras tossed the containers aside and moved more snow from the area against the bags for good measure.

With any luck, the water he'd poured throughout the bags of oleander would freeze in a matter of minutes.

Though the plant material would still be poisonous to consume, it would be many days before it thawed and then dried out enough to be used as kindling for Hinterfell's plan.

Juras was about to leave the area behind when his hand casually brushed against the hilt of the short blade at his waist. A smile came to his lips.

"I hate to tell you this, but you're not as scary as you think yourself," he declared to the person standing some paces behind him.

Without another word, Juras twisted around in time to dodge the knife coming for him that Bron had thrown. It landed in the snow behind him with a *thunk*, and he wasted no time in snatching it into his other fist.

Bron sneered over at him. "We'll see what you think when you're a prisoner of war."

Juras locked eyes with him from the other side of his blades. Bron had taken out another knife, and he looked forward to stealing that one, too.

"I think you're quite generous." Juras smirked. "But I only have the two hands. What will I do with another of your weapons?"

Despite his words, Bron wasn't his big prize. He was still fishing.

He wasn't dull. With her dog unchained like this, Hinterfell lurked about. The only question was when she'd choose to make herself known.

"You talk too much for a whore," Bron said, showing his teeth.

Juras felt his cheeks stain red and the anger surge from his center, but he knew he needed to control his emotions if this were to work.

He circled Hinterfell's guard and tracked the path of his feet without looking at them. When he'd moved to the side of the clearing that he'd needed to, he stopped.

Time for a little baiting.

"And how would you know that?" He raised an eyebrow. "Hinterfell pay you in girls?" Juras smiled. Before Bron could get an answer in, he said, "I'm not surprised they don't make a peep when you're in bed with them. You never stuck me as the type to know how to use complicated equipment all that well."

"You little—"

Before he was done talking, Bron rushed him.

Bron's knife stabbed at him in a series of dangerous volleys, but Juras knew this dance already. It was one they'd played out too much for him not to know the steps for it.

The problem was, Bron had remained the same Bron who had once pummeled his face and stomach on the streets.

Juras had not.

Instead of taking the shot Bron expected him to take by trying to stab or kick him back, Juras ducked from under his wide reach. In one motion, he rolled across the ground and kicked one of the bags at him. Pieces of oleander bush flew at him and scattered across the thin snow between them.

His disgust was nearly comical as it bounced across his features. It was an easy dodge for Bron, but Juras had gotten what he'd wanted. He just needed one more little opportunity.

"You'll regret that when you're owned by her," Bron growled.

"And how does it feel, Bron? To be owned?" Juras jerked to his feet as his smile twitched.

Bron's eyes snapped to Juras a second before he closed the distance between them again. "Better than you'll feel after I'm done with you," he said, but Juras could tell from his tone that he'd hit another nerve.

He couldn't lie to himself. It felt good to taunt Bron like this.

Maybe too good, he considered. In his twisted joy, one of Bron's swipes had cut him. He couldn't tell if it had drawn blood underneath his clothes, but he hadn't meant to take any hits during their dance.

Bron's cruel eyes lingered on the place where his knife had frayed Juras's sleeve. "Is this all you are? A poison and nectar-fruit tongue?" He sniffed. "There's nothing under your surface but a broken boy."

Yes, Juras tended to be good at this—using his words to twist and bend the will of others according to what he wanted. The talent had served him especially well in his conning days.

But the fear that Bron was right had already been inside Juras before he'd spoken the words.

It was what halted his movements enough for Bron to nearly get a lethal strike at Juras's heart. Though he stopped him, he'd forgotten Bron's brutish strength. Even with two crossed blades protecting him, Bron's knife had slid to the crux, too near its intended target.

"I should have killed you when I had the chance," Bron whispered into his face. "She told me I could, you know. Do you think of me when you look at the lash scars?"

Despite the cold night draped around them, beads of sweat ran down Juras's back as he huffed in the harsh air. They traced the scars Bron spoke of, and his memories threatened to break him in that moment.

I will not bend to you.

This next part would hurt, though he hoped not too badly.

Juras leaned forward, a smile still on his face as he looked up into the eyes of one the monsters that'd haunted his past. At the same time, he angled the blades in his palms, effectively moving where Bron's knife was pointed on his body.

"Maybe you're right, Bron. Maybe I'm nothing but broken. But the truth is ... I'm not afraid of you anymore."

As Juras said the last words, he set many things into motion. He pressed closer to him, taking a slice from Bron's knife along his shoulder as he forced his foe backward. In his seeming surprise, Bron didn't notice the pile of oleander that Juras had driven him towards, and he lost his footing into the plant detritus behind him.

Panic visibly held Bron for precious seconds as he realized what he'd landed in, but that wasn't where his attention should have been. With all his bodyweight, Juras drove the point of his long blade into Bron's throat where he'd fallen on the ground.

"That's enough, Juras," came a familiar voice.

The bait had worked.

CHAPTER FIFTY-EIGHT

"There was no need for that."

Hinterfell's words were strident, but not unduly so considering Bron was dying before her.

Juras smiled, though the expression felt grimmer now than before. "Wasn't there? Bron and Strego never so much as pissed without your say-so. I'd wager that you'd ordered him to kill me."

"You know me better than that, Juras," Hinterfell said over the sounds of Bron's death gasps. "I don't waste resources." A frown pulled at her features when she looked upon Bron.

He'd left the sword in his throat to keep him pinned there, but as Juras watched him, he was starting to feel that a faster death might have been in order.

His remaining blade was a comforting weight in his palm. He needed to deal with Hinterfell before he gave in to any distractions.

"Then what was that?" Juras's eyebrows lifted.

Hinterfell ignored the question. Night had fallen properly by now, and she carried a lantern that looked to have been lit from their campfire. She lifted it gingerly to better see the ruined oleander spread around them.

The light of the lantern flickered across her body as she moved, illuminating the strands of thick fur from some animal that she wore about her neck. Her braided hair ended in a jeweled brooch that looked like a bee, though its stripes were made of red gemstones rather than yellow ones. He could have sworn the tiny red jewels that were its eyes followed him as he moved.

"You've cost me more than you know here, Juras." Hinterfell's gaze settled on him. "But, I am still willing to accept a trade of your service at my brothel in exchange for transporting you from out of these warlands."

First came the shock. Then came the fit of laughter. "Get one thing straight today. I am never going back there." The laughs dissolved on his lips. "Even if my life depended on it."

"By killing Bron and obstructing our goal in this place, you owe me an even greater debt than the one your mother saddled me with," Hinterfell said.

The mention of his passed mother made Juras's heart gallop fast enough to make him dizzy. He took a moment to collect the breath inside him so his words came out even.

"You will leave this place. Now." He still felt the weight of the blade in his hands where he'd driven it down. "Or else Bron won't be alone in the snow tonight."

He could see the way her hand tightened on the lantern's handle at the threat. Her thugs could no longer shield her, and she appeared to have realized it.

"Oh, Juras. You seem to be forgetting that you belong to me." Hinterfell's eyes were depthless in the dark. "You will work for me until I judge the debt you owe me is repaid."

Heat gathered inside him. He was going to end the nightmare tonight. Here.

Bron hadn't expected Juras to do it, but Hinterfell knew he was capable of spilling her blood tonight just the same.

"You will never own me." The words came from behind clenched teeth as he lunged for her, aiming for the monster's heart.

"If you hadn't nearly killed your own father, I wouldn't have been able to touch you," Hinterfell said as Juras knocked her backward. She'd managed to block his attack with the only thing she had left to shield her, the small lantern.

Juras stopped. "Father? What are you talking about?"

Not only had her words been nonsensical, but he also couldn't understand what she was doing. She was on the ground, and she should have been fleeing now that he had a clear strike for her vital areas.

But she'd remained where she was, and her fist had circled the end of her braid. She slipped the jeweled brooch off the last of her hair.

"I told you, you belong to me," she said.

As she said the words, the thing that had been a brooch glimmered in the amber light of the lantern and took to the air. The jewel-studded metal became a striped, insectile body. Its red eyes saw him as diamond wings carried it faster than he could track.

On the other end was a deadly sharp and golden pin.

Juras darted out of its path, but it was too late. It had landed on the side of his neck where he felt a brief, piercing pain.

"Paralyzing venom," she answered for him. Juras felt himself stumble into the snow as anger and panic rose in his gullet.

The red-jewel bee landed in her palm as she continued talking. "It's not real venom, of course, but a tidy bit of fae magic trapped in a simple hairclip. Traded for it a long time ago." She shrugged. "The one I got it from said it had only a few uses in it, and I'd planned to use it to capture the fae king. If I bring their king back to our lands alive, I'll have more bidders than for just his head. So you see, using it on you was quite the risk."

She looked down at him. "That was the part of the plan you didn't hear." She turned her attention back to the now-unmoving brooch. "It appears my luck has finally shown itself, however. At least one more use."

Already, he couldn't move the majority of his body. But he found that if he concentrated enough, he could still speak.

"Fae will come back here and … kill you," he managed.

"No. No one is coming. We were watching your moth friends." Hinterfell's face softened. "They are well gone, Juras."

She'd started gathering what could be salvaged from their packs. Bron was dead on the ground next to him. He envied the poor bastard.

"You didn't realize that client of your mother's was your father? The rough one?" Hinterfell said. When he didn't reply, she continued. "She was always his favorite. Brutal man, though."

There was no mistaking who she meant. It was the one who had used to beat his mother. The one he'd received lashes for attacking.

She's lying. She's trying to upset me.

But she wasn't done speaking.

"He was going to buy the rest of your mother's debt to get the both of you out of The Rosebud. Jayna knew enough not to say anything about his rough touch, but then you went and laid hands on him. Naturally, he gave up the thought after that. Brutish. But he paid on time, every time. Extra even, when the situation called for it. Too bad he never came back after Jayna's passing."

Juras wanted to vomit.

She's lying, a part of him still chanted.

But there was no reason for her to lie anymore, he realized. He could do nothing, now.

Out of her and Bron's packs, she pulled free an extensive length of rope. She was already crouched in the snow next to him when his mind remembered what was happening in the present.

There was too much in what Hinterfell had said. Physical sensations were easier to decipher, even if they were painful like the knot she was forming at his wrists with the rope.

"Tersius will be happy. I never have enough males for his appetite. He's never met you before, but I think you're just his type."

She'd said it like she was proposing what they'd eat for lunch and not who she was going to sell his body to first.

It was over.

"Anova was always too tenacious. But you …" Her hand held the side of his face. "You know better than to defy me, deep down. You'll do well." Her voice quieted. "Give it some time."

Shock for her strange sympathy ran through him, and he suddenly remembered Bron's last words to him.

"There's nothing under your surface but a broken boy."

Why did they all expect him to roll over and bear it?

In defense of his life, he'd *killed* Bron.

But that wasn't enough to be taken seriously. Not by Hinterfell. To her, he was still the same boy who ran from her on the streets.

There was little strength left in his body that the magic hadn't sapped from him. But there was enough left for this.

"I will *never* be yours."

Moisture gathered at the base of his mouth before he spat it at her face. Astonishment stormed across her features as the spittle ran along her cheek.

"Insolent *wretch*." Hinterfell grabbed a tuft of his curls enough to pull his head back. She wiped the spit from her face with the back of her other hand.

"I may not be wasteful," she whispered. "But that doesn't mean I'm forgiving. You don't need all your fingers to work for me."

She picked up his knife from the snow. He tracked what she did with it until he couldn't from his angle. The tip pressed delicately along his cheek. "Just a pretty face."

No. No!

But the paralysis spell weighed down his limbs too much for him to do anything.

She removed the knife from his field of vision at the same time that she jerked his bound hands against the ground.

Frozen air caught in his throat as he held her eyes. He would make her remember this just as much as he would.

Broken he may have been, but not cowed.

It was then that a voice roared through the sullen and silent trees.

"Don't you *dare touch him*."

Hinterfell didn't even get a chance to look up before her body was thrown against a solid tree trunk.

Juras couldn't believe what he was seeing.

He was wearing a simple black cloak that engulfed his frame. Light from Hinterfell's abandoned lantern provided just enough illumination to see him.

His eyes were a wild, dark violet. He seemed thinner than he'd remembered him, and a long, mottled-red scar ran across his throat.

It was Hellmyr.

CHAPTER FIFTY-NINE

The first sensation Anova felt was shuffling legs that were too weak to carry themselves. The sun dappled its light on a slow-moving creek before her.

Someone had thrown her arm over their shoulder. Anova jerked back when she saw who it was.

"What are you doing here? What do you want with me?" she demanded.

But Malor's red eyes only stared at her. His face was unreadable.

Her hand went to the blade stowed at her side. The previous several hours washed over her once more, and her grief was as fresh as it was when she'd first felt it.

I couldn't save her.

Tears brimmed at her eyes, but she couldn't cry here. Not now.

"You knew," she accused him. "You knew what was coming, and you did nothing."

"I told you it was a trap," Malor said in his double voice.

"You said it like you meant the battle between the fae and humans," she said. "And because of you, she's ... she's ..." Anova thrust her sword at Malor, but he wasn't before her anymore.

She whirled and found him standing a few paces away from her. "Fight me," she growled at him.

"You're not fit to fight," he said, his gaze barely flickering over her form.

She knew she was pathetic in her blood-stained dress, but she didn't give a damn right then.

"I want to fight," she said through her teeth as she lunged again. "Aren't you a blood-thirsty creature? I know you hunger for this."

But he was gone again. She wiped a sheen of sweat from her forehead, and she ignored the phantom pains in her abdomen. There was no child there anymore.

"Fight me, damn you!"

Again, he appeared paces further away from her. His eyes were dull even as sunlight glanced on his face from the creek. "Do you blame what happened on me?"

"Yes," she gasped. "I do. I don't care that you're an illusion conjured from the crown." She stabbed forward. "I know you knew and let it happen."

But it was in that instant that her gaze was caught on the languid creek ahead. She jerked her arm back in the last second to stop her assault.

Standing before her in the water's reflection, as still and calm as Malor had been and in his place, was another her.

Anova stared, waiting for the reflected image to make sense. Despite her wishing it so, this wasn't a dream—even in her nightmares, she was never in pain like this.

As she stared longer, she remembered Malor's strange behavior in the moments before her birth labors had started.

He cowered in pain.

Anova stepped back, her sword forgotten as it slipped from her fingers to the grass. Malor still hadn't flinched. Her hand went to her mouth.

"You're ..." Anova stopped herself as she remembered a conversation they'd had recently.

"What could you want from me, you devil?" she'd hissed at Malor.

"Now, that's the problem here. You're the devil. We are one and the same."

"But you're a part of the crown," she finished. "Not *me*."

"I am a *function* arising from the artifact," Malor said. He'd finally started to walk. His form disappeared altogether from the water. "But it is not the blood crown that has a will. A memory. A motive." His claws closed together in a fist. "An anger. These are things given to me by its wearer."

Anova remembered when Malor had appeared and mutilated the human boy who'd nearly killed her and her unborn child.

I'd wanted to rip out his throat.

That was me.

She stepped back again as she saw him clearly. "You're the worst parts of me."

Malor smiled at her, and the expression was hair-raising. "So close. So very close." He tilted his head, and his antlers threw strange shadows before him.

"All that I am, Anova, is what you hate of us."

She knew that he meant herself by *us*. His red eyes consumed her vision, and in them, she saw the monster who'd let her child die out of willful ignorance.

She saw the girl who had refused what she was and the body she'd been gifted for a second chance at life.

She saw herself.

"No," she gasped, stumbling backward. Malor watched her with a dead expression. "No," she repeated.

"You still want to fight, then?" Malor crouched as he flexed his claw-tipped hands. "Then destroy the spell within the crown that gives me life. Fight me."

He moved faster than she could blink. Anova ducked out of the way of his onslaught, rolling into the grass. One of her arms glanced off the cold steel on the ground, and she grabbed it.

Is this what she wanted?

Yes. I want whatever this is to stop haunting me.

Her blood ran through her at the thought even as pain and weakness knotted together inside her belly.

For an illusion produced by the crown, Malor was undeniably strong. He ran for her again with nothing but his hands as weapons, and when she stopped him with her blade, she could barely hold him back.

"Blame me for it, then. Blame the dread wolf's actions on me. Kill me for them if that will quell your troubled mind," he sneered.

"I ..." Anova drove the blade in her hands forward, but it glanced harmlessly off his antlers.

Of course I want to be rid of you. The thought stayed in her mind.

Her sore body supported her, but only just. Tears threatened to blur her vision, and she wiped them off with a shove of her hand.

She was the solid one here, not him. This was her body. Her mind.

Her.

Anova threw down the sword. When she spoke, her voice came out too quiet.

"No. I don't want to fight, Malor."

Every time that Malor had appeared, she'd needed help. Every time, she'd dismissed him as a specter to torment her or remind her of what she'd done to attain the crown.

"Why do you keep following me?" she'd said.

"I'm not following you," he'd said. "I'd say quite the opposite."

I was the one who summoned him, she realized. *Each time.*

They'd been calls for help. And something—the fae part of her, the part that was attuned to the blood crown—had answered.

She said, louder, "I want your help."

"Lies," he hissed.

"You know they're not," she said, shaking her head.

But he'd picked up her sword, his eyes gleaming like rubies. Her heart jumped into her throat from the sight of its sharp edge.

"I don't," he snapped.

When he came for her, her sword shone brilliant in the daylight, raised for a fatal strike to her heart.

"I accept you," she gasped. "You aren't bad or evil."

The strike to her heart didn't come. Anova threw her arms around Malor's frame, and her sword landed in the grass. She sank to the earth as she tugged her knees closer to her in an embrace.

She thanked her strong arms and legs for carrying her when she'd wanted to give up, her burnt skin for protecting her, and even the pain in her lower body for reminding her that she yet lived.

She thanked her fae senses for keeping her safe and, lastly, the magic that had become as much a part of her as her blood was.

"Can you help me?" she whispered.

When she finally opened her eyes again, she was no longer at the edge of a meadow intersected by a creek in the Eastwoe gloom woods.

Anova stepped forward into the memory.

CHAPTER SIXTY

The age was a different one—Anova couldn't explain it, but she felt it in the air somehow. These woods were different from the Eastwoe gloom forests, too. A handful of fae were gathered around a lake, and the moon had newly risen into the dark sky.

To one side of the lake was a human woman, chained and on her knees. When the wind moved her dark hair out of her face, she recognized her, though she'd never seen her before. This was Alys's mother, the witch who had died by the king's orders after she'd cursed Hellmyr to fall in love with a human instead of ending his life.

It was then that she noticed Malor and High King Erion behind her. Her heart bolted at the sight of fae tyrant she'd murdered even though she knew him to be long dead.

This is Malor's memory. Nothing more. Erion isn't alive.

But she couldn't quite curtail the emotions within her.

The High King motioned to one of his fae guards who then separated from the others and came to the opposite side of the lake.

High King Erion was speaking. "You will lend us the use of your witch magic tonight, and in return, I will consider sparing your life for what you've done to Gleehart's boy."

He means Hellmyr.

She stared at Erion and wondered if he'd ever suspected that Hellmyr was actually his son by Letharia.

He'd have killed him if he ever seriously thought that, she reminded herself.

Alys's mother responded, "You lie plainly, Fae King. You decided to kill me when you heard what I was. But that is not on my conscience." Her eyes—Alys's eyes—stared through to him. "Why are you trying to tear apart the barrier between our worlds?"

The fake mask that she remembered Erion to wear slipped back into place, giving him false joviality. "I merely wish to speak with one of our great fae ancestors." His smile widened. "Besides, you are in no position to refuse."

"I can always refuse, mighty fae lord. So long as I have breath in my body, I have a will."

Anova had been wrong. Her eyes might have looked like Alys's, but they were different. Unlike the fire in her daughter's, they were clear and calm like an endless sea.

She knows they haven't found Alys yet, or they'd be using that to force her to comply.

"You'll do as you're told," said one of the kingsguard. He'd jabbed the point of his swordstaff against her back where she crouched.

"No, she's right," Erion said to his guard. "She has the free will to refuse. It's the lives of those dock humans on the other side of Fae that will be the price for her choice."

Anova's jaw ached as she gritted her teeth. Was this truly only a memory? Or was this something else?

"As you wish," Alys's mother said with a grave face, "but recall that I warned you. The risk that more than your visitor enters this temporary gateway is very real."

"The dead sleep," Erion said. "They are not to be feared, witch."

The High King gestured to his fae on the other side of the lake. It was then that Anova recognized this area. It was the Lost Forest, Rietvar's domain and entrance to the realm of the unliving.

Temporary gateway? Anova frowned. It hadn't seemed so temporary to her when she'd stumbled upon it after acquiring the blood crown.

Temperamental, perhaps, but that was another matter.

Moonlight pooled under the fae's hands while the blade of the witch's guard nudged her to act. Her hands filled with her own magic, and light circled partway around the perimeter of the lake.

Lastly, the High King held out one of his hands. He didn't wait for moonlight to touch his skin as magic jumped from his palm to join the rest of the stream.

"Princess," he called. "I call you from the realm of the unliving. Reveal yourself now."

Clouds slipped along the belly of the moon, but nothing more happened. The quiet of the woods bore down on them.

Erion seemed to speak to himself. "This is the lake in which the princess drowned." He raised his nose. "There's no mistake. The imprint of her death is on the air, even after all this time."

Anova realized which princess he meant just as mists rose from the lake and a blurred form stepped through them. It was the fae princess who had first worn the blood crown, the one from the fae tale and the one who would summon Anova to this very lake years later.

Her bones felt chilled as she saw her pale visage again. Her blonde hair fell along her waist, parting only for her delicate fae ears. A pair of sapphire eyes stared back at High King Erion.

They were a matching pair, each with the same artifact upon their heads.

"First princess of the blood crown," he said in greeting as the magic still surged in his palm. "What a pleasure. I am High King of Fae and master of the blood crown."

Her blue eyes turned icy in the silence.

Finally, she said, "I know who you are, Erion. I have seen who you are through my dreams, as well as all your predecessors. My crown has revealed it to me."

Erion's eyes lingered on the copy of the crown on her head. "The real one rests with me, Princess. You'll do well to remember it."

Her pale eyebrows lifted. "You cannot threaten what's beyond your control."

The High King smiled. "As enchanting as your presence is, I have summoned you here for a reason, Princess." He angled his head to the side. "Tell me the secret—"

"There is no secret to my crown you do not already know," she interrupted.

His smile didn't falter, though she felt something in the air around them change.

What secret? What is he talking about? she wondered.

"And yet, the crown behaves differently now than it has in all the years past that I have been its master. That is its secret, Princess," he said with forced friendliness.

More clouds passed across the dark sky, some barely skirting the moon. Sooner or later, one would pass before the moon and obscure it, possibly breaking the spell as it was supported in part by moonlight magic.

It was into this uneasy silence that the fae princess spoke again.

"The blood crown pains you now because your end is before you, Erion. It senses that the one who will kill you will soon cross into Fae." Her blue eyes became slits. "Its new master is nigh." She said the words with a barely concealed disgust.

For a rare moment, something like unbridled fury passed through High King Erion's gaze. When he spoke, however, his voice was as tightly controlled as she remembered it.

"If you do nothing but lie, you are of no use to me." He shouted to the others supplying magic around the lake, "End the spell."

The witch and the other fae stumbled backwards when the magic in their palms dried. The light from the stream of magic faded, and its absence bathed the area in shadows again.

High King Erion pulled his palm away last, though the specter of the fae princess stepped towards him on the lake before he did.

"What happens next is largely uncertain, except for one fact. Your hubris tonight will have consequences to come, High King Erion. You have opened a door that ought not to have been." Her voice faded just as she did.

Veiled moonlight fell into the glade as a cloud finally obscured most of its bloated mass. The night remained unnveringly quiet.

"Your orders, Your Majesty?" asked the fae. He'd walked from the other side of the lake.

Erion's eyes were still unfocused when he gave the order. "The witch. Kill her."

Anova hadn't yet looked away when the fae guarding Alys's mother impaled her through her back. It was a quick death, though she wondered if that was due in part to the witch seeming to give up.

Even during the witch's last labored breaths, the High King was lost in thought, seeing things not obvious to her. At last, he looked up sharply.

"None can know what happened here. Kill the rest, Malor."

The first of his two guards was down instantly as Malor leaped from the king's side, his claws raking through the exposed skin at the guard's neck. The second, the one who had volunteered his magic to contribute to the summoning spell, only looked from the mess Malor was making to the High King.

By the time he realized that his master had ordered his death in front of him, it was too late. Malor had taken the first guard's bladestaff and thrown it at the remaining guard's neck.

It missed by a few degrees, though not in a way that saved him. The force of it drove him to the ground.

Before the memory faded and the lake surrounded by trees disappeared, she heard a chilling voice laughing on the air.

It was one she knew.

The dread wolf, Death.

CHAPTER SIXTY-ONE

It was like witnessing an angel of destruction—deadly, beautiful, and efficient.

Juras still couldn't move in the snow, though he wondered if that was less due from the fae magic from the bee sting and more from the shock of seeing Hellmyr.

Amber light from Hinterfell's fallen lantern gleamed along his steel sword. It slashed along her face, right underneath her eye like a long tear drop.

"Wait," she gasped on the ground before him. Blood trickled savagely from the wound on her face. "I have knowledge of who wants you dead. You'll want to know that."

Hellmyr bared his teeth at her. "Everyone. Now shut up."

His quick gaze flicked to Bron's lifeless form and back to her. "That one's past my influence, so you'll bear his punishment, as well."

"It wasn't just our king—" she started.

Hellmyr slashed across the front of her chest. Though it didn't look to have gone deep enough to kill her outright, the grimy snow underneath her was staining redder by the minute.

Madam Hinterfell took in a shaky, uneven breath. On the earth, she scrambled back some paces until her back hit the tree he'd thrown her against earlier.

It was strange to Juras. It was as if she hadn't believed that Hellmyr was out to kill her before this moment. Her face was almost unrecognizable to him.

"I shouldn't have trespassed on your lands. I shouldn't have plotted to kill you. Take my supplies. Take my poisons. Take the information I have. Take my business in Irbess." Her eyes sparked. "All the women and men you could want to please your Majesty. For any purpose."

"Enough," Hellmyr shouted, and a terrible silence fell like the trees themselves had heeded him. "Do you think me daft enough to be placated by anything that you could offer me?" The limited light bounced off his bloodied sword. "You're in Fae now, and the rules you play by are *mine*."

The words were enough to send a chill down Juras's back. All fae were proud. He supposed it was only natural seeing as the closest comparison to these creatures was the plain and brutish humankind.

But a fae king?

A human's failed attempt on his life was surely the worst insult. But the thought didn't make sense with Hellmyr's next words.

"Threatening my mate"—Hellmyr's hands ran through his hair—"touching him—"

Hinterfell looked to where Juras was, her eyes wide and confused as her lips pulled back. "Juras isn't ..."

"You will not speak his name," Hellmyr snapped back.

Juras realized belatedly that the first slash he'd delivered to her, the one to her face, mirrored where she'd grazed him with his own knife moments ago. He'd cut her the second time where Bron had hurt him across his shoulder to his chest.

He blinked. It was all intentional.

He still wants you dead, the logical voice inside him reminded Juras. *He's just too proud to suffer an injury to anything he considers his.*

Hellmyr bared his teeth as he continued to speak to Hinterfell. "I have beheaded my own for far less than you've done tonight, but your fate is not in my hands. It belongs to another."

A second blink, and he was crouched by Juras's side. "I should have checked earlier. Are you hurt?"

Juras's mouth seemed to be too dry to speak, so he shook his head instead. It was true enough.

What was going on here?

"Not untouched, however." Hellmyr's eyes raked over his form further until they seemed to settle on the slashes on his face and shoulder. "I don't have any medicine with me, so these will have to wait a bit longer."

"They're fine," Juras said. He looked over to Hinterfell. They shouldn't turn their backs on her, but she seemed paralyzed by shock that the fae king was crouched next to him in the dirty snow.

Hellmyr noticed his gaze. "I meant it. Her life is yours. What do you want to do to her?"

Many words sprang to Juras's mind.

Kill.

Mutilate.

Terrify.

Humiliate.

Imprison.

She'd tried them all with him. But, when he sat with the power to make any of these options a reality, there was only one thing he really wanted—other than never seeing her face again.

Juras looked over at her when he spoke. "No matter how, I want her never to return to The Rosebud."

Madam Hinterfell seemed to crumple against the base of the tree with relief. Most likely because he hadn't said words like *kill* or *torture.*

Before Hellmyr stood, he removed his own cloak and tilted his head at him. "May I?"

Juras wasn't sure what he meant, but he nodded without thinking. He couldn't really fight anyone off as he was right now.

While Hellmyr spread his cloak over Juras, insulating him more from the cold, Hinterfell started talking again. He suspected her jaw had finally loosened from the rest of her head in shock.

"The deed is secure with the judge of the ninth district of Irbess. Take my ring to show as proof of ownership of the business," she said. She lifted her fist where a golden ring stamped with her initials was fixed on her forefinger.

"You should thank Juras for sparing your life," Hellmyr said as he stood and approached her.

While she pried the ring off, her hands hovered near her hair. Juras couldn't put his finger on why the gesture seemed strange until it was too late.

Hinterfell had used it as cover to slip the jeweled bee from her braid. It darted into the air, too fast for Juras's eyes to track it.

"Get away," Juras gasped into the cold night. "It has paralyzing magic."

"Thank him?" Hinterfell stumbled back to her feet. "I don't thank my whores. I've found it makes them feel too entitled."

Before she was done speaking, the enchanted brooch had landed on Hellmyr's shoulder. Two things happened at once.

Hellmyr's thumb and finger crushed the bee's metal wings together while his other fist grabbed Hinterfell's wrist.

"You should always thank your betters," Hellmyr said between his teeth. He forced the glittering bee's stinger straight into the vein at her wrist.

"You knew—" she started to say, but Hellmyr interrupted.

"Don't you remember the fae child that was with the one who traded you this?" Hellmyr laughed as Hinterfell's body went slack. "Don't use my father's inventions against me. He taught me how they worked—better than he taught the humans he sold them to."

He slipped the golden pin out of her vein just as she collapsed entirely. The bee became a brooch again when he held it in his palm.

"Finally." Hellmyr slipped the brooch into his pocket. He spoke to her slow-breathing form on the ground. She looked to be out cold. "It's useful to know how your tools work. The dose can be controlled by holding it."

Juras hadn't quite recovered from Hellmyr's sudden appearance—let alone all that he himself had done here and all that had happened. His brain sorted through the questions until his first one returned to his lips.

"You're alive," Juras managed to say.

In the snow, his steps were made audible as he crossed the area.

"That's a tale for later," the fae king said.

The light from Hinterfell's lantern danced across his skin in strange ways when he plucked it from the ground. Juras's eyes caught on the scar that lined his throat.

It was odd to see one of them with such a mark. He knew that, in part, it was because of him. Bottled in his throat were all the words he hadn't said after that night.

Yet, all his fool mouth could say was, "You don't have to ... put on this act anymore."

"Act?" Hellmyr stiffened.

"That I'm something more to you than ... an inconvenience. Something cursed to you but also owed to you."

"Owed to me." Hellmyr's voice was hollow. He stepped towards him as a note of anger entered his voice. "That may be how they've made you think, but this world is not theirs. I will not choose that."

Juras leveled his gaze on him. "Then what do you choose?"

"Is it not obvious to you?" The wind stirred the strands of his raven hair.

"I don't understand," Juras heard himself say. "Saving me is not ... optimal for you. You should've been relieved to see me dead or gone. *You should have wanted to kill me yourself.*"

Hellmyr's face turned from the light as he grimaced. "I thought, by pushing you away, I could smother the fear. Fear of losing myself to a force beyond my control. Fear of losing you by keeping you away first."

He laughed again. "Idiot." He sobered too quickly. "But pushing you away only drove me to the arms of insanity instead. I became the monster in the castle humans tell tales of." His fingers grazed his throat. "Even more than the ones who gave me this."

Juras's teeth clenched. "Including me, right?"

In the dark, he looked over at him. The shadows made it hard for him to see his face, and the fact rose bumps on his skin.

Slowly, Hellmyr closed the distance left between them. "The nights after I came here—after I dismissed every living soul from this province—I thought those were my last nights. I wanted to be alone when I died like a spider curled under leaves."

He pulled out the jeweled bee and looked upon it. "This is the first bit of magic I've felt since the night they blackened our sky. Other than the night, some days later, that I thought was my last."

His eyes narrowed on the bee like he was talking to it and not Juras. "I saw things I shouldn't have been able to. Things that happened when I was not aware. A bloodbath. And a human risking himself, over and over, to save one wretched life."

Hellmyr shoved the brooch back inside his pocket. "And yet, I was still that monster, even tonight. Still suspicious that anyone could give themselves so selflessly." He closed his eyes. "Without being cursed to. Without wanting power. Without ulterior motives."

Juras thought of not only Anova but also himself. They'd both seduced him to get what they'd wanted. From what he knew of Hellmyr's past now, it seemed clear to Juras that love had been a thing ruled by trade or control in this fae's life.

He shook his head and admitted to it. "But I did come here with another motive to find you."

Hellmyr smirked. "And you think wanting to save this land and the lives of those within it makes you as wicked as a fae monster?"

Despite all that had happened there, Juras felt a mischievous smile play on his lips. "But does desiring the heart of one make me wicked, as well?"

Before Juras could say anymore, he was in Hellmyr's arms.

Dark lashes brushed his skin as he looked at him. "Only one way to tell." His grin dissolved to something more serious. "Though its effects should wear off before morning, there is a way to remove the magic's toxins faster."

Juras's heart hammered faster. "Then I want to try it."

Hellmyr looked around them at the tatters of Hinterfell's failed assassination attempt, at her unconscious form, and at the cold body in the snow.

"Not here, though," he murmured.

Before Juras could so much as shudder, they were off through the woods. White, untrodden snow stretched around them and weighed down branches above them. He felt like he was in a fae tale as Farstar castle loomed above the trees.

"I want to ask you something, Juras." Hellmyr wasn't looking at him anymore. Starlight reflected on the white snow around them, coloring in his face past the shadows.

His stomach swam at the new gravity. He didn't think he could handle another surprise tonight.

"Ask it," Juras said, too quiet.

"You know my answer. My choice. But you never said yours." Hellmyr still wasn't looking at him. "No matter a spell. No matter what I want. I am not so wicked that I would force another to be with me. There is no obligation for you to ..."

Juras stared at him. How could Hellmyr have such doubts?

He was the most beautiful thing in Fae. Man or woman, fae or human, what being could resist him?

But that's not why you want this, he considered.

No, his beauty was unnerving, but beauty wasn't what drove Juras to the most frigid, remote corner of this land.

He couldn't help the laugh that escaped his lips. Hellmyr watched but didn't say anything. Just before he suspected that the fae would self-implode out of not knowing what he was going to say, Juras spoke.

"Everything about you is choices, isn't it?" Juras smiled. "I like it." He joined him in looking out at the snowy woods flying past them. "Do you know what's odd? Despite the wickedness, I feel like I can be myself with you. No more or less."

Finally, Juras said, "Yes, I choose you, too."

At his words, a spark seemed to light in Hellmyr's eyes. "Are you ready for me to remove the bee's spell?"

He breathed. It couldn't be worse than the sting, could it? "Yes," he said.

Before he could prepare for it, Hellmyr's lips were on his. It was unlike any kiss he'd experienced before.

The way his mouth moved on his felt both pleading and softly urgent.

He acquiesced to his unspoken request and kissed him back, just as deeply and greedily as if it were the first time doing so. Hellmyr freed one of his hands to cup Juras's face.

He threw his arms around Hellmyr's neck in the same instant that he realized he could move his entire body again. Juras broke their kiss, and his sudden laugh created a puff of steam in the cold air.

"You *liar*," Juras accused him joyfully. "You just timed the spell's end with your supposed cure."

Hellmyr's smile was slow but consuming.

"As they say, wicked."

CHAPTER SIXTY-TWO

As Anova moved through the gloom forests with the help of Malor, the smell of rotting flesh assaulted her senses. She soon found what she'd overlooked just off her path in the day before.

They were the bodies of her guards, though they seemed to have been dead for longer than a couple days. Even more curious, their chests had been hollowed out, though there was no evidence of blood, and a faint smell clung to them that wasn't fae or human.

It reminded her uncomfortably of the dead human boy that Rietvar had used to speak to them. *No blood. No heartbeat. Just a walking body.*

As she left the corpses behind, she heard the frightened heartbeats of several rabbits still in the area, and her theory was confirmed.

Rietvar's work. They were in the chests of my guards so I'd hear their hearts. It was a trap all along.

His influence likely also explained why none of the others had come to her aid. The thought worried her further when she considered she still hadn't found Cadmus or evidence of what had happened in the battle that had been a farce.

She remembered their scouts' description of the human leading the battle, the one they'd taken to be Alys.

"A strange cloaked figure is leading these humans."

None of them had seen this human close enough to confirm their identity absolutely.

The farther she picked through the gloom woods, the clearer things became.

All the humans who had attacked them after they'd left the Wolfsbane estate had been acting without Alys. While this could have been a logistics issue—she was a witch, yes, but she could only be in one place at a time—in many cases, they seemed not to know who she was.

Rietvar's words to her during one of their conversations came back to her.

"You got what you wanted," Anova had said.

"So, so close," Rietvar had responded. "I almost have. Despite the witch getting everything promised to her."

It was evident in the way that he spoke that, beyond their bargain on the night of the full moon, the two weren't working together. In fact, Rietvar seemed to hold a certain amount of contempt for Alys.

This was all Rietvar's doing to draw us out.

Anova considered the possibility that Alys had abandoned her war.

Or that the witch was dead. Anova's stomach turned at the thought.

When she rested for a few breaths farther along the creek, she thought as she drank from the faster-moving water.

She spoke out loud. She wasn't entirely sure Malor could hear her thoughts when he was a physical being and not just in her head.

"High King Erion created the gateway known as the Lost Forest," she said. She realized now she'd assumed it had existed as a quirk of Fae for all of time.

"Not intentionally, but yes. In part," he said as he picked leaves out of his antlers.

"It's possible to open it ourselves, then. Without Rietvar," she said. "And maybe even seal it to keep him from appearing here again."

Malor seemed almost bored. When he spoke again, it was a strange thing to hear his hissing voice speak in such a sarcastic tone.

"Would I have shown you such things otherwise?"

Anova squinted at him, but her annoyance dissolved a moment later. She laughed. "I have only just started to understand the things you do, you creature. So, forgive me for questioning you."

Malor looked away. Despite what he'd said about not having his own motive, memories, and emotions except what had come from her, he seemed to be becoming more and more a separate being and less just an extension of the blood crown's power.

While the thought scared her, she didn't allow herself to linger in the fear. The blood crown's magic was a strange thing, and hating it had only driven her to ruin. It was as if the curse inside it was fed on her own hate and fear of it.

"It will be an issue, then, if Alys isn't alive," she said to herself. She stopped herself. "The other fae. The gate was opened with magic from a witch, the crown, and the moon." She jerked her gaze to Malor. "Do you know if this will work without using fae magic?"

Malor stared back until his sharp fangs were exposed in a smile. "Does it matter if you don't have the choice?" His smile slipped. "The answer is *no*."

"*No* it won't work?" she said.

"*No* I don't know. I've had enough of this."

Malor stood up. Why—she didn't know. He could seemingly disappear and reappear at will, standing or not.

"Wait," she said as she stood to stop him. "I need your help. I can't continue without more rest. With me slowing us, we'll waste many more days."

He'd at least stopped to listen to her, so she continued, "There should be scouts nearby. Or someone friendly to our mission, at least. I want you to find them and bring them back to me—so long as they are on the side of Fae."

After a moment, Malor said, "As you wish."

When she blinked again, he was gone. Anova pulled her canteen from her bag to fill it with more clear water before resting against the smooth trunk of a desiccated tree. She called her barrier around her once more and gave in to a light sleep.

Anova jerked awake with the feeling that someone was inside her barrier with her. Her heart calmed somewhat when she saw that it was Malor and not some worse creature.

"They plan to kill the witch within the hour," he said in greeting.

Anova didn't waste time with questions other than to ask the distance, direction, and whether to expect a battle.

Now that she'd replenished with water and some scarce hours of rest, her legs supported her more easily, and she was able to sustain a quick pace. In a rare fit of cooperation, Malor explained the situation to her by showing her a vision of what he'd seen.

A small retinue of fae guards from Eastwoe palace had cornered a clearing in the far edges of the gloom woods. A makeshift tent, draped in leaves and brush, had been fashioned against a leaning tree growing along the area.

Malor, apparently not visible to those around him, had entered the tent. Inside it was a small human with braided dark hair. Half-eaten food and other supplies had been scattered about like a windstorm had hit. Salt and dried herbs carefully lined the inside perimeter. Empty vials and other potion materials such as dried plants had been left at the foot of her blanket.

Alys's face was clearly visible as she slept, though something was wrong. Sweat soaked every part of her skin from her forehead to her dampened clothes. Her breathing was labored.

As Anova's vision snapped back to her own, she realized Alys had been sickened. By what method, she didn't know, but it appeared her fae guards didn't need their weapons to kill Alys despite having drawn them.

When she came upon the encampment of her fae soldiers, however, she saw two faces that hadn't been in Malor's vision. Their group had hidden themselves well in the trees, though that likely wasn't necessary considering Alys's condition.

Anova nodded for Malor to leave her for now—she'd have to explain him later—as she allowed the barrier shielding her from sight to dissolve in the air.

At once, most of the fae turned from observing Alys's tent to where she'd appeared in their midst. They'd drawn their blades on instinct, and she admired their quick reflexes.

Leander and Lycasta stopped mid-conversation to draw their weapons, as well. Collectively, she felt their eyes on her form and the bloodstains across her dress.

Did they notice how the shape of her stomach had changed?

Leander was the first to react with something other than a stare. "We've searched for you for *days*."

Lycasta cut him off prematurely and took a step towards her after lowering her knives. "You need to go back to the palace."

The fae lady's eyes were on her too much for her not to have realized what happened. Her gaze was uncomfortable, but Anova didn't falter.

Her hands went to Lycasta's arms. "Where is he? Is he alive?" She shifted to look at Leander. "Does he live?"

"Cadmus lives." Lycasta slipped out of her grasp. Anova believed that the two of them shared a look of mutual understanding at that moment, but it may have easily been Lycasta wondering if Anova was still sane.

But, at that moment, Anova didn't care. Relief stole the strength from her legs, and she nearly stumbled. Lycasta steadied her before quickly removing her hand. "Like I said. You need to go to the palace to be looked at. You and ..."

Lycasta stopped herself at the look that must have been on Anova's face. She couldn't quite talk about it yet, so Anova pretended she hadn't noticed what she'd nearly said.

You and the baby.

One of the fae guards from the palace approached them, though wisely keeping his distance. He announced, "The archers are in place. They await the command."

Behind Lycasta, Leander nodded. "It's time, then."

"We can't kill her," she said to him. Her pulse throbbed faster. Didn't they understand? "We don't have much time to save her. She's not well."

"Killing her could reverse the spell they created to blacken the moon," Leander said. "It's the only way."

"You've got it wrong," Anova told him. "I can prove it, but we have to save her first. She's dying as we speak."

This time, Lycasta looked at her with open incredulity for her sanity. "You realize she's head of this war, don't you? You know what she's done to all of us."

Anova stared back at the fae lady. "There are some who've done worse who don't deserve to die, either."

When Lycasta didn't respond, Anova pushed past her. This would be up to her, it looked like.

I guess she hasn't changed after all, Anova thought with bitterness. It didn't matter if those two were on her side. She would stop the archers by herself.

It was then that Lycasta spoke up behind her. "Tell the archers to stand down." Anova turned in time to see her ask Leander, "Do you still have the herb medicine from the palace?"

He nodded at Lycasta before adding, "Though I would hazard a guess we'll need the abilities of our Blood Queen to have any real effect."

His gaze swept to hers as his voice lowered. "If we're letting her live, I'm assuming you have a plan."

"Only if she lives," Anova emphasized. "So you'd better bring your best herbs."

CHAPTER SIXTY-THREE

"You don't know what happened to her?" Anova asked Leander. "This doesn't make sense."

The sound of Alys's uneven heartbeat worried Anova. Their fae guards had carried her to a cot within one of their tents where the two of them had helped stabilize her condition.

Anova had refused Leander or any other healer to look at her. Alys was undeniably in worse shape, and she'd requested their efforts on her first. Though, she had accepted a change of clothes from Lycasta.

She helped Leander by pouring more tincture that he'd made from the supplies they'd brought with them.

"I don't." Leander's eyes didn't leave his work where he continued grinding Valerian root for another dose of sedative. "At the battle between the woodland fae and the humans, Cadmus infiltrated their ranks to take her hostage where she was allegedly leading the charge. The only problem was that it wasn't her."

The skin around his eyes wrinkled, and he pulled back his lip in disgust. "It wasn't even human—a live one, anyway."

Just like the guards at my tower.

Anova stared. He hadn't mentioned this yet. "Rietvar. It was all his trap, from start to finish."

Leander glanced at her but didn't say anything.

"And Juras is in Farstar. Maybe he's avoided Rietvar's ploys, at least. If he isn't dead." She glared at Leander, though she didn't think he saw it.

Anova hadn't quite let that fact go. They had much to do here, but as soon as they revived Alys, she was going to send their forces north to retrieve him.

She sighed. It had most certainly been Juras's idea.

I told him not to launch himself into danger like that.

After a moment, she looked up and asked him, "How did you find Alys?"

"When we arrived back in Eastwoe following the witch's trail, we found the others searching for you and joined their efforts. It's been days since that alone. I still don't think Cadmus has slept," Leander said. He frowned. "He won't be happy we aren't immediately taking you back. Anyway, we happened to find her scent while looking for you. She was in this state when we found her."

They hadn't yet identified the cause of her sickness, though Anova had done her best with the crown's magic to treat her symptoms.

The strange thing was, her vitals had stabilized with one exception: her heart.

Anova twisted around when a strident gasp pierced the air. Alys's eyes had flown open, and her fists grabbed at the sides of her cot. Her back arched in pain.

Anova and Leander were by Alys's side at once, and magic from the blood crown was already spilled from Anova's hands and into her body when she looked up at her.

"Oleander," Alys gasped. Her eyes were wild and scared as she looked at them. "You need to—"

Her words were cut off in another gasp, and Anova realized her mistake. It wasn't an illness or infection that was weakening her—it was poison.

"I didn't recognize the signs," Anova said in disbelief. They'd been right in front of her.

She blinked. A life was at stake; now wasn't the time to study her failing. She looked up at Leander, scholar of literature and the natural world.

"Tell me what to do," she nearly begged.

"The poison is attacking her heart," he said between his teeth. "Direct your magic there. You can try to fortify her heart's strength, but what really needs to happen is purification of the toxins."

For a moment, he locked eyes with her above Alys. "But *be careful*. The organ is easily damaged, but not so easily repaired," he said.

Sweat ran between her fingers as she placed them on top of Alys's tunic. The witch below her had fallen back against her cot, twisting in pain every few seconds. With such proximity to it, she could feel how her heart stuttered forward.

"I don't understand," Alys barely managed to say. Her eyes were clenched shut again. "You should want to let me die. So much effort."

"Alys." The word came from Anova's throat almost involuntarily. "You're not going to die here."

Alys shook her head. Sweat had stained into her tunic, spreading from her neckline and her underarms. "You misunderstand." She laughed, but the sound was clipped. "The other way around, I would have wanted it. For the person who was killing my race without lifting a finger."

She knows what the moon is doing to the fae, Anova realized.

Anova tried to focus solely on the magic's path within Alys, but the words slipped free from her. "What is going on, Alys? Why were you here?"

The witch underneath her touch flinched. Anova scolded herself from pushing the magic to her heart too aggressively.

After she regained her breath, Alys said, "I was trying to intercept him. What he was doing disgusted me, and I let it show too much." She gritted her teeth. "I was a fool and met with him alone to speak. He poisoned me with oleander tea."

This doesn't sound like Rietvar, Anova worried.

"Who? Why?" she said before she could stop.

This could be her only chance to get answers, and she couldn't afford to waste it.

"My captain." Alys's dark eyes opened to meet hers. "The young one you met at the estate."

Anova tried her best to concentrate. She was close to purifying all the toxins, but she felt she was pushing the witch's heart too hard. Her pulse sped and fell back, catching up on itself in intervals.

It was a dangerous dance.

Alys closed her eyes once more. "After I realized ... after the night of the full moon, I met with my armies intending to disperse them, but I couldn't control them anymore." Her fists grabbed the sides of her bedding harder, and she seemed to swallow another wave of pain. "He's been their leader ... ever since."

Her last words ended in a gasp just as Anova heard the sound. For the briefest second that she could spare, she looked at Leander. They both knew.

"No. *No,*" Anova said to him like that would fix it.

She'd purified the toxins, but at a cost. She'd pushed Alys's heart too hard.

"Tell me what to do. Tell me what to give her," she said to Leander again, her hands flying from Alys's chest to the medicines by her bedside for some cure. But Leander just shook his head.

Alys was fading.

She was on her own.

Anova didn't think—there wasn't time for that anymore. She grabbed one of Alys's hands. It was bathed in sweat, but she clung to it.

The truth had nearly died before, and she wouldn't let it happen again.

Alys needed to know.

"Before your mother died, the last High King brought her to Fae to use her for a spell to speak the dead," she said. "By combining their magic, they did the impossible, Alys."

Alys didn't respond, and her heartbeat was only going slower.

"Do you understand? He forced open a gateway with her magic, and it was left open. It became the Lost Forest." Anova squeezed her fist harder and placed their interlocked hands upon Alys's chest.

"I need your help, Alys. I need you to help me heal you. Because if you don't—if you don't, there won't be a way to fix this. Rietvar can and will come back. And the worst part is, he doesn't have to. Fae itself is already dying. And each of our kind is killing the other while it happens."

Tears had started to stream down Anova's face, but she didn't bother wiping them. Nothing mattered now but what happened in this tent, and she'd failed.

Anova couldn't seem to let go of Alys's hand. She'd realized too late the antidote to hate was humility.

"I won't leave you," Anova whispered when there was no response. "I promise." Her other hand went to her mouth to silence the sobs that wanted to come free from her.

This time, she wouldn't break it.

After a moment, Leander stood and left the tent. She understood it as a gesture of privacy.

The two of them had been molded from the same earth, and Anova felt the loss deep in her chest.

We should have been working together to better this world. Anova's jaw trembled.

It started as a twinge in her palm where it was pressed against Alys's. Anova wiped the moisture from her eyes with the back of her other hand. Even with clear vision, she didn't believe it.

A light had sparked where her heart was, underneath their interlocked hands. Alys's magic was warm where it touched against Anova's skin. Her breathing was labored as it began again.

Anova jerked herself into action. She pushed more of her own magic through her palm where she held Alys's hand.

Carry this energy, she shouted in her mind at their connection. *Carry it and save this life!*

A gasp broke the still air. Alys shot up in her cot as Anova released her hand.

Alys's hair stuck to the sides of her face from sweat. Her hands went to her chest as she gasped, "It's gone. The poison."

Her wild eyes landed on Anova. "Anova. You brought me back. Somehow." They went from Anova's giddy face to her stomach. Something in her eyes changed.

It was shame. It'd been in her words when they'd tried to save her before, but it was written too plainly on her face now.

She's seen what happened. And realized her part in how it came to be, Anova guessed.

Anova took her hand.

"We fix what we can, Alys. As long as I have your help in this."

After a few seconds, Alys squeezed her hand back.

"I should have realized before. I was such a fool." Alys shook her head. "It didn't start with oleander. The poison was already in my heart. I am sorrier than I can say, Anova. For everything."

"I accept your apology. Besides, I was just as much of an ass." Anova smiled. "They should really be afraid of us working together."

The corner of Alys's mouth moved up in a devious grin to match hers. "They should."

CHAPTER SIXTY-FOUR

They arrived on the lawn as afternoon sunlight streamed through thin clouds. Anova had never felt more relieved to see Eastwoe palace as she was then.

She and Alys had shared passage on the back of one of Lycasta's moths while Lycasta, Leander, and their fae guards had shared the others. During their journey, the two of them had shared stories and information freely.

As they spoke, their plan came into focus.

It's possible. We might just be able to do this.

Even so, there was only one glaring flaw: their formula was missing fae magic, nectar of the moon.

We'll figure something out. We have to, Anova thought.

As Lycasta's moths graced the earth, the guards stationed around Eastwoe palace came to them. After verifying who they were, they started to help their group from the backs of the moths.

Just as a guard helped her feet to the ground, Anova heard the sound of swords unsheathing.

"It's the witch. Their commander," shouted a fae guard. "Restrain her!" The command rang out through the area as more guards rushed to their group.

Anova's teeth grinded in her head, but before she could reprimand the guard for the assumption that he could give such orders, Leander had appeared between the guards and where Alys was still on their moth.

"This is the Blood Queen's guest, and as such, she will be treated with respect. You will replace your weapons," he said, "unless you wish my brother to have more practice fodder for his attempts with the bow."

His eyes gleamed with the promise to carry out the threat, and maybe even some glee to do so, but all those who had drawn weapons did as he'd said without another word. Before another fae could do it, Anova extended her hand to help Alys down.

Alys hadn't said a word yet. Anova would have been a fool herself to think that a lifetime of festering wounds and prejudice concerning the fae had been healed with a little reconciliation, but instead of reacting to the other fae's threatening gestures, she merely thanked Anova for her help.

A disturbance in front of the palace's entrance caught Anova's attention. The doors rumbled behind two fae as they exited the palace.

"I don't care how many we need to take from the kitchens to put on as temporary guards. Train them for an afternoon, and they'll do fine for the moment. We need more for the search teams."

It was Cadmus. Unferth was beside him, running to keep up with his gait. They hadn't seen their group yet.

"Kitchen hands? We sit exposed here," Unferth argued. "Kitchen hands won't fight off her armies, especially assisted by the dread wolf's tactics."

"I will fight them off myself, then," Cadmus snarled back. "You haven't seen what I can do. Send them all."

Unferth's eyes finally focused on what was downwind of them, and he stopped to stare at their group. Cadmus jerked his gaze up moments later.

It was like no one else existed to him.

Her heart felt like it'd been shot with poison, but she relished the feeling so long as it meant she got to see him.

The soreness in her lower half and in her very soul cried out, but she ignored these feelings as she started to run to him.

He beat her to him by a wide margin and swept her into his arms. His kisses trailed her neck until she could take it no longer. She kissed him back on the mouth as he held her.

"Anova—" He couldn't seem to complete the thought.

"I know," she said back. "I know."

His hand grazed her stomach. It must have felt different, for his grip on her changed. Soft. Questioning.

Anova shook her head in the hollow of his throat. It was all the answer he needed.

After the past few days, she'd thought all her tears had left her body. She was wrong.

He held her tighter.

After nightfall and more than one bath, Anova had shared their nascent plan with the others.

Juras still hadn't returned, but their scouts had reported that an army of humans larger than they'd seen yet was marching through the Sorrelands. They'd likely arrive in Eastwoe in a day, and to the palace in only another after that.

As they were now, it would be enough to overtake their forces.

They couldn't afford to wait any longer.

Surprisingly, it had been Alys's idea on how to deal with the human invaders peacefully. Once they returned the moon from the realm of the unliving to theirs, they would have enough power from moonlight nectar to put them all under a fae sleeping spell and end the war in one night.

The hard part would come before that, however. Anova shook her head in her room's mirror. If she didn't believe it was possible, then it wouldn't be.

Simple as that.

Cadmus helped her into a silk dress with a soft, pleated skirt. He wore a silk gray shirt that matched her dress and black tailored pants.

They left to meet the others in the war strategy room. As had been all the others before it for too many nights, it was a dark night. Nothing but faint starlight filtered through the windows along the walls, so the servants had lighted lanterns throughout the palace.

She was glad to see nothing alive in them.

Della hugged her upon entering, which was how she knew that she, Maris, and Nerium were already present.

"You don't hug fae queens, Della. Not in front of their people. It undermines their authority," Maris said when she sat beside her at the wide table.

Della frowned and nodded, but Anova went over to the two of them and hugged them both with one arm. "Stupid rules get broken. Or at least here, they do," Anova said.

"I'm sorry, Anova. And Della, too," Maris said. "I shouldn't have."

Maris's embarrassed smile broke off when Alys entered, cloaked and shadowed by Unferth. Anova pulled a chair out for the witch to sit next to her.

"Thank you, Anova," she murmured.

The others knew that she'd arrived with Anova and on friendly terms, but it was an entirely different thing to be sitting at the same table with one they'd considered a mortal enemy a night ago.

Leander sat on Cadmus's other side just as Lycasta wordlessly claimed the seat next to him. She watched their interactions for a moment and tried not to draw attention to the fact.

Leander was speaking quietly under his breath, too quietly even for her fae ears to hear his words. She'd at first assumed he spoke to his brother beside him, but she saw that wasn't the case when Lycasta nodded at him. A moment later of this quiet conversation, and a side-smile slipped onto her face.

It wasn't her business, so she didn't pry, but she squeezed Cadmus's hand when she noticed that he'd seen the same thing.

"I want him to be happy," Cadmus explained too quietly for any other ears to hear. "He feels he doesn't deserve it. Or his life."

Anova frowned at the thought. No matter the complicated history between the four of them, she wanted the same for them both, she realized.

Unferth interrupted the thought. "Now that we've all had a day to sit with the information, we have tonight to construct our plan to stand against the dread wolf and save our realm."

Unferth nodded to Anova. She breathed to steady her nerves before speaking.

"As you all know by now, High King Erion created the gateway to the unliving realm known as the Lost Forest. Our issue, however, is that we cannot freely access this gate to step inside Death's realm whenever we choose. Alys and I have experienced ourselves that only those that Rietvar wishes to enter his domain can do so. But," she said, holding one finger up, "we have something we didn't before. We have the directions for the spell that created the gateway."

"Intriguing claim. I see you've kept my seat warm, *Blood Queen*."

Hellmyr's voice carried through the room and over the heads of the gathered as he stepped fully inside.

CHAPTER SIXTY-FIVE

"But sharing our strategy table with mortal enemies is going a little far, don't you think?" Hellmyr said in completion of his thought. Juras walked in beside him, and Anova rushed to his side.

"You live," she breathed. Her eyes narrowed. "You told me you weren't going to risk yourself unnecessarily."

"Oh, believe me, it was all necessary," Juras said with a rueful smile. He was suddenly serious. "*Unnecessary* risk? Is this a phrase you really know, Anova?"

Anova resisted the urge to pinch him or worse—considering they stood before a group of some of the most powerful individuals across their two lands combined—and beheld Hellmyr. In many ways, he wasn't as she remembered him.

A long, jagged scar ran along his neck where he'd nearly died. And then there was his appearance next to Juras. Hellmyr had emerged holding his hand while his other had hovered over the handle of his sheathed blade.

"You owe me a story," she whispered to Juras, though Hellmyr hadn't missed the whisper as he looked between them suspiciously.

"I think we all owe each other one." Hellmyr's eyes narrowed on Alys, and the temperature of the room seemed to drop.

Anova moved herself between them to break his gaze. "That's enough. We're all on the same side. So long as you're with us, too," she said.

Hellmyr's flickering gaze was so fast she'd nearly missed it—nearly. He looked to Juras, though he hadn't seemed to notice. Anova swallowed.

It seemed he'd accepted the witch's curse. He certainly seemed less murderous. She hoped this was the best thing for Juras, as well.

Time will tell.

"We are on the side of Fae," Hellmyr said at last. "I don't think that my allegiance needs to be questioned in that regard, but here we are."

Unferth had stood upon his king's arrival and hadn't sat again yet. She realized he was giving up his seat for his king, but Hellmyr didn't seem to care.

Anova did her best to ignore his stubbornness. It was a boon that they were all here and agreed. *Loosely,* she added in her mind.

"Excellent," she said, refusing to rise to his bait. "We can proceed, then." She addressed them all again. "As I said, we know now that High King Erion caused the rift between the living and unliving realms known as the Lost Forest. It was from the combined use of magic from a witch, fae, and the blood crown, and recreating the spell is how we cross into Rietvar's domain on our terms. This is how we close the gateway permanently."

"How can you be so sure?" Hellmyr's eyes were sharp on Alys. "How can you know you aren't playing into the plans of his commander?"

Alys didn't look away. "I have nothing to hide, Fae King."

Even Juras didn't look at all comfortable with the witch's presence. Before the anger rose in her at the time they were losing by bickering like this, she stopped herself.

"This wasn't her plan, Hellmyr," Anova said. "So, your suspicions are null. Can we continue?"

"You still haven't revealed how you have knowledge of this." Hellmyr's violet-black eyes drank her in. "It isn't a crime to be curious, is it? I was in my dear, murderous father's employ as a guard for some time. Never did I hear of him doing such a thing."

She could see that he was trying to trust her, perhaps for Juras's sake, but that didn't matter to the annoyance she'd buried in her at his words.

If he only let me speak for more than a moment, he'd know, Anova thought.

"Because you weren't there. As I recall, you were nothing but Gleehart's spoiled youngling at the time." Malor tilted his antlered head from where he'd appeared behind Anova.

Except for the two that she'd told already, Cadmus and Alys, the rest of the room collectively jumped from the sight of Malor and drew their weapons.

Hellmyr swore and shoved himself in front of Juras. Through his teeth, he hissed, "Never thought I'd see you again, you freak."

"Get away from Anova," Nerium ordered as he and Leander started from separate sides to flank Malor. "Cadmus," he snapped when he saw he hadn't moved to help them.

"Enough," she said. "Malor is on our side."

"Erion's puppet could never be on our side," Leander said. There was a strange look in his face that she didn't recognize.

It was then that she saw how the blade in his hand trembled, ever so slightly.

Cadmus stood and placed himself before his brother. "Calm yourselves. He won't hurt anyone here. I've seen myself how he is under Anova's control."

Leander's dark eyes were erratic. "You would join with … that?" Betrayal was clear in his voice.

"It's not the same," Cadmus said. "Malor is a manifestation of the crown's magic. He is a tool of the wearer's will and little more."

"He killed us, Cadmus," Leander said through his teeth. "You were there. Or don't you remember?"

Cadmus stared back at the fae who was his mirror image. In a too-quiet voice, he said, "How could I ever forget?"

The others had all replaced their weapons, and most had taken their seats again. Without another word, Leander left the room. Lycasta followed a second later.

Nerium mouthed something to Cadmus. Only after several seconds did he nod to his unspoken words.

Anova sank back into her seat. This wasn't going quite how she'd envisioned it.

At least they're listening now, she observed, though the fae still present couldn't seem to keep glancing at Malor when they thought him not looking at him. But in truth, if she was going to form a plan, they needed his memories to help them.

Alys pulled back her hood as she leaned forward to take the table. "As Anova said, the spell requires the combination of different magic: mine, the kind produced by the blood crown, and fae magic. Nothing less will do."

Across from her, Nerium said, "We don't have access to ours without the moon. Considering the blood crown is an artifact made from witch and fae magic together, will Anova's contribution suffice?"

Malor's red eyes didn't blink as he answered, "What you know as the blood crown is distinct from the parts that made it. The spell will not work without fae magic in its pure form."

Anova said, "We've already thought of a solution. We simply need an extraction of moonlight nectar, even if it was originally harvested for another use like a barrier or weapon." She nodded at Unferth. "There should be some that the healers have reserved, at least."

But Unferth's face was grave. "Despite our survival, the battle between the false witch and our side resulted in many casualties for the unallied fae. Those that we could save, we saved, but the cost was high for our supplies."

Cadmus's head jerked to his. "There was some reserved for Anova. I'm positive."

For the baby, she realized. Her stomach squirmed at the thought.

Unferth's jaw flexed. "Gone. I suspect we have thieves."

Anova's hands ran through her hair. "How? This is a palace of fae. *How is none left?*"

Hellmyr broke the silence. "They are frightened of dying in their sleep. They are frightened of turning to leaves in the wind upon morning light."

He stood. "On the night of my mother's death, her soul passed enough strength to me to keep me alive. I should have died that night, but I see now why I didn't." He slipped a small object from his pocket.

The amber light gleamed redder along the rubies embedded in it. It was a brooch that resembled a red and black striped bee.

"Count me in. But only if I get to repay Rietvar a favor."

Hellmyr's hand ran over his scarred throat as his mouth formed a devilish smile.

CHAPTER SIXTY-SIX

"And that makes a third," Alys said.

At once, Juras was on his feet. "I didn't go all the way to Farstar so that beast could finish what he started."

Anova noted how the skin around Hellmyr's eyes tightened a degree at his words. But when he spoke, he was all wicked fae king as his teeth showed. "It's the beast who should cower, darling."

Before this could go further, Anova caught Juras's eye. "I know what you feel, Juras. But I think it would have had to be this way, regardless." She turned to the rest to explain the second part of their plan. "In order to undo what has been done to the moon, we will need every element with us of the bargain-spell Alys and Rietvar originally made."

"In witch magic, it is called annulling," Alys said as she continued Anova's thought. "First we need access to the moon, requiring us first to get to the realm of the unliving. Second, we need the blood of a powerful being of magic to reactivate the spell. I counted on that being Rietvar himself, but if it were somehow possible to avoid a confrontation with the dread wolf, I don't think much would be needed from another source. The ritual was activated well before ..."

Alys trailed off unhappily.

Hellmyr raised an eyebrow. "Witch's blood not cut it, is that it?" He sighed, leaned back, and stared at the ceiling. "Fine. I get it. What worked before would be ideal." His voice turned sardonic. "Just know you're not getting enough this time to drown in it, witch."

"Then I'm coming, as well," Juras said. His hands hovered over the knives sheathed at his waist.

Hellmyr straightened. "You're most certainly not. I can only die in so many ways."

"It's not possible," Alys said before Juras could argue further. "Forcing our way into Rietvar's realm with this spell will take a great deal of energy. Each participant will have to expend all the magic they can give and will only be able to focus on bringing themselves." The witch stared at Hellmyr's brooch. "Frankly, I'm doubtful when it comes to the depth of magic stored in that, but we have no other choice, it seems."

"Anova briefed me on this already. Based on what we've seen of their side and how Rietvar's mind works, we think the moon will be attainable as a physical thing. A small trinket or something to represent it," Cadmus said next to her. She looked at him and wondered where he was going with this. "With three focused on opening and closing the gateway, another should be tasked with guarding the moon, seeing as how we're taking it from the Lord of Death himself."

Alys crossed her arms over her chest. "There simply isn't enough magic to get you through to the other side. You've as much potential for magic right now as him," she said, pointing to Juras.

"I can easily pull my weight on the way back," Cadmus said.

"You have to get there with us first," Alys said.

"Cadmus," Anova murmured to him. She held his hand under the table and looked at him. In his face was an unspoken need.

Anova looked over to the witch. "We could try, couldn't we? It would be obvious from the start if the spell doesn't have enough power for all of us to enter his domain."

Something in Alys's expression changed. "Alright. We'll try with us four." She threw another look at Cadmus across the table. "Remember, your only goal there should be to attain and guard the moon."

There was something else unspoken in what she'd said, however. Something full of remorse and understanding.

She knew it well.

The night before they all left for the woods where the Lost Forest was hidden, Hellmyr had announced a great feast in the hall below to celebrate his return, the announcement of his true mate, and a turning of the tides in the war.

She knew it was all political theater and that hosting a party was likely one of the last things he'd wanted to do that night, but it was important for them to see him as their king again. Anova and Cadmus had made a brief appearance—long enough to see Juras blush either from the fae-made wine he'd sampled or all the toasts made to him.

She hoped he and Juras would be happy together. Juras seemed to be a good influence on him, and, if she knew anything about Hellmyr, it was that he was protective of his lovers.

Juras had told her what had happened between him, Bron, and Hinterfell in Farstar. They'd made a pact between the four of them—Della, Maris, and the two brothel brats—to return to Irbess as soon as it was safe enough and liberate those still at The Rosebud.

Anova walked to one of the windows inside her old suite where they stayed. Faint stars glimmered over Eastwoe, but much of Fae was dressed in a thick shadow. She wondered where the human armies were within their forests even now, plotting to save their fae heads to bring back home with them.

Hate had spawned this war, and they would need something else to end it.

Cadmus's hands found her bare shoulders as he pulled her to him. He didn't speak as he held her, seeming to be content with just that.

After some silence, Anova said, "Do you think she'll be there?"

She couldn't look at his face, so she stared out into the dangerous beauty of a darkened Fae night.

"I think so," he said in a quiet voice that hardly left his throat. "Somewhere." He squeezed her harder.

"I hope she's sleeping peacefully like you were when I found you there." She closed her eyes against his skin. His heartbeat thrummed against her, and she cherished its rhythm.

Some moments later, she whispered, "We can't ... bring her back, can we?" Her heart twisted to ask the question, but she already knew the answer.

Souls that passed from this life to the next didn't belong here. Alys had reminded her of that, gently, before the meeting.

A drop of moisture hit her head, and it was only then that she realized Cadmus was crying silent tears. He wiped hers from her face.

"No. But to sleep isn't a bad thing, Anova."

CHAPTER SIXTY-SEVEN

By the first rays of the new day, Anova, Cadmus, Alys, and Hellmyr left on horseback. Flying by Lycasta's moths would have been faster, however, Anova had enough difficulty concentrating on a moving barrier large enough to keep the four of them absolutely unseen and otherwise undetectable while riding on a horse.

In the air, covering at least two giant moths and their passengers, she trusted herself less.

Besides, she hadn't seen or spoken to either Lycasta or Leander since they'd left their strategy meeting.

Unferth and Nerium were officially their commanders in charge while the four of them were absent, but Anova would have felt more comfortable knowing they had the support of those two, as well.

"I should have warned him about Malor. I'm sorry," she said under her breath to Cadmus behind her as they rode.

"Don't be. It's my fault." He added after a pause, "I should have anticipated his reaction. I felt the same."

Anova stiffened at his admission. Under the High King's direction, Malor had killed many people. She should've expected it, really. He had every right to the hate Malor—whether or not he was a specter of magic or a flesh and blood creature.

"But I've long since vowed to accept you. *All* of you," Cadmus said as he interlaced his fingers with hers. "Besides, odd as it sounds, I am grateful for Malor. I know it's what kept you alive during those days."

Anova nodded in answer. Some responses didn't need words.

Ahead of them, Hellmyr held a fist in the air and slowed the horse he and Alys reluctantly shared.

"What's going on?" Anova shouted to them. They'd only just crossed into the Sorrelands less than an hour ago. Though they were searching for an approximate location, this was too soon to be the Lost Forest.

But it was then that she noticed it, too. Once she smelled it, the stench was unignorable.

Cadmus steered their horse close against the other one as he spoke to them. The fae king had already drawn his blade. "Did you leave the barrier at all? For even a second?"

Alys shook her head. She'd smelled it, too. Anova could see the disgust on her face.

It was the smell of rotting dead.

As their two horses picked carefully through the gloom woods, Anova was the first to see any sign of the bodies. She clapped a hand over her mouth.

Hellmyr hissed under his breath at the sight. Cadmus pulled her closer as he held his blade before them.

It was Cadmus who first recognized them. "Argus's band," he said as he looked up at Hellmyr. "The ones who left after Anova took command of the palace."

Anova kept them close to the other horse to keep the barrier strong between them. Her jaw ached from clenching it. Some of them had been cooks. Stable hands. Peaceful fae.

"The men did this. It was the army led by their new captain," Alys said between her teeth. "I recognize the style."

"We should go," Anova said. It felt uncomfortably like a trap. Even if it wasn't, it meant their enemies were too close for them to stop.

Anova's barrier didn't fail them as they rode farther inside the balmy spring forests. Afternoon sunlight fell past the leaves of conifers above them. Suddenly, the forest yielded to cleared lands.

They stopped their mounts. As far as Anova could see stretched fields and rolling hills.

"We passed it," she said, but she was shaking her head. She turned to face the others. "The lake should have been there, even if the gateway wasn't open."

"You're sure it wasn't closer to the forests edging the boundary?" Hellmyr asked.

"No, she's right. Much farther, and we'll happen upon Wolfsbane estate. It was well before it," Cadmus said.

"Either way, we have no choice but to track back another way to find it," Alys said. She looked to the sky past the thin barrier protecting them.

Anova knew what they were all thinking. They didn't have another day to spare. The human armies would be upon Eastwoe palace by then. In another, Fae could be taken and those they loved killed or stolen as captives.

"Are you certain the lake exists without entering the gateway proper?" Hellmyr asked.

"Yes," Anova said. "Entering the Lost Forest is … different. It's a shift. The sun will stop moving overhead, and shadows will flee you. But the physical—the trees and lake—will always be there. Just as they existed before Erion started his spell."

"Then we have no choice," Hellmyr said. "We'll have to split into two parties to find it."

"They'll find you without my barrier," Anova said.

"We have to risk it," Hellmyr said. "It's the only way to find it in time."

But Alys was shaking her head. She thought it was at what they'd said until Anova followed her gaze over the trees.

"Over there," she said. "Hovering over the tree tops. You should see it better than I can."

Surprise caught in her throat. It turned to concern a moment later.

An oversized moth fluttered over the trees in the evening light, but there was something erratic to its movements.

"Let's go," Anova said. She'd had enough observing.

It has to be them.

The closer they rode, the more Anova debated removing their barrier. If this was truly an ally of theirs helping them, the four of them and their horses would be undetectable.

But the memory of the fae bodies piled in the forest stilled her hand. Their enemies were here, whether they saw them yet or not.

The scents of the forest turned at once to an overwhelming mix of different animals. As if they'd been summoned by her thoughts alone, the sounds of humans shouting and firing arrows filled the air.

"Stay close," she shouted to them as they galloped nearer the heart of the fray.

It was as she'd feared. As they approached the men wearing animal skins, she saw clearly who they fired at.

Upon the moth's back were Lycasta and Leander. Cadmus's muscles tightened behind her.

Why were they here? If they'd intended to escape Fae, they were still a distance away from the boundary line. She realized a possible answer then.

But first, she needed to do something.

"Bring us closer to them," Anova said. "As close as we can get without stepping on humans."

They pressed closer to the humans on the ground. Archers fired arrows at the moth's wings, and there was evidence that they hadn't evaded all. Some arrow shafts had partially buried themselves in its delicate, white wings. When they were close enough, Anova raised her hands above her head as searing light pushed from her palms.

To Anova's eyes, nothing seemed to have changed. Leander and Lycasta continued to fire back at the humans below, but the humans on the ground ceased. They started to circle the area in search of their enemy.

To them, it would have seemed they'd disappeared from the skies.

"Don't strain your magic too much, Anova," Alys said. "Remember what we need to do."

Anova shook her head. The witch would understand that she had to do this. She fired a single ball of white magic into the sky above them to get their attention.

Each of the great moth's wings was wider than a man was tall, by far. When it perched in a conifer above them, the wind it produced was almost enough to knock Anova from their horse.

Leander jumped down first.

"Nerium told me your plan," he said to Cadmus. "And the task you faced finding a place named for its elusiveness." His eyebrows rose as he closed the distance between them.

Cadmus said, "Are you sure you weren't just making sure I lived to repay you your book collection?"

"You should have asked for our help, thick-headed fae." Leander embraced his twin. After a moment of apparent shock, Cadmus returned the gesture.

Leander's face screwed up as he seemed to think about it more. "But you still owe me that, so yes. Make sure to come back."

As they parted, his eyes traveled over the others, stopping at Anova's gaze last. "And the rest of you, as well," he said. "The realm of the unliving is a quiet, ethereal place. The dead should not bother you there for they are lost within the worlds of their dreams. But be careful of Rietvar."

"You're just south of the spot. We'll lead them from here to protect you while your barrier is down," Lycasta said.

Anova nodded her thanks. She and the others had separated from Cadmus and Leander to give them some privacy during their conversation.

Once, she would have called herself a fool for trusting these two so.

She realized she was glad she'd started to as the four of them left in the direction that Lycasta had indicated. Above her, she saw the white form of a moth disappear into the darkening sky.

CHAPTER SIXTY-EIGHT

It was as Anova had remembered it, with some exceptions. The lake felt harmless, and the day had passed instead of standing still. Their shadows were long on the ground.

The four of them had spread out evenly along the perimeter of the lake.

"Remember, focus on making your magic meet those on either side of you until we've circled the lake. The gateway sleeping there should activate then," Alys said across from her. She looked over to Cadmus. "Try to receive the magic of those around you."

"Have you done something like this before?" Anova called back to her.

Alys shook her head, and Anova swallowed. It was just as well.

She spread her hands out as the others did the same. The blood crown's magic surged readily through her at her request, and searing light spread from her hands. Some distance away, Alys's witch magic flowed in waves from her, and when their magic met, she could feel the difference.

It was an energy that felt controlled and measured compared to hers. The blood crown's energy was all fire and heat, unsteady and dancing, while Alys's magic was like a series of echoes. It felt greater with each wave that slid against her notice.

Anova breathed in deeper as she realized how her own magic responded and grew. Headiness tried to overtake her, but she focused on accessing the well of magic before her and spreading hers to the others.

When she could feel nothing in response, Anova looked up. Hellmyr held the enspelled brooch between his thumb and forefinger. A soft white light radiated from it and through his other palm. If she concentrated, she could feel its influence, but it was hard to notice past Alys's flood.

Between them, Cadmus stood with his palms to the sky. His eyes were closed, and she could see the strain on his face, but she felt only emptiness from his direction.

"It's not working like it should," Alys called.

Her eyes were wide. Anova heard it then—the screams. They bounced off the trunks of the trees surrounding them and filled the air with terror. No birds or animals appeared, but a wispy mist started to rise from the earth.

Somehow, Anova knew they were the screams of the fae princess who had died in the lake. Despite no apparent disturbance, the lake's water had started to push and pull against its shores.

"We need more," Alys said. "Now!"

Anova felt for the soft energy held in Hellmyr's palm and closed her eyes. She remembered how the moon felt on her skin on a dark night. She remembered how it had felt to bask in its glow on the last night it'd been full. She remembered dancing on the surface of water to celebrate its coming.

Hellmyr's moonlight magic traveled through the stream she and Alys had started. Her heart pounded with joy at the feeling of the moon. The fae princess's screams had quieted.

Anova opened her eyes and saw Cadmus had opened his, as well. He stepped back from the lake and mouthed some words to her.

"I'm sorry.

Tell her good-bye for me."

Tears had started to cloud her vision. He'd never seen his daughter, and he never would.

Something fell forward from her like rain drops left in tree branches well after a storm has passed. It had the outline of a fae, but it was nearly transparent as it moved on the air to where Cadmus had stood.

The shape of his antlers became barely visible, and she knew that it was Malor responding to her unspoken request. He stood in an exact copy of how Cadmus had seconds before, his palms facing the sky.

The lake's water nearly sloshed high enough to drown any one of them on land, but it hadn't broken over its shores yet.

Cadmus watched this all, his eyes moving from the lake to the form of Malor standing in his place before him.

"We've opened it," Alys called. "It will take us to the other side. Don't falter!"

Before the wall of water broke from the lake on all sides, Cadmus stepped into Malor's empty form. The water's pull felt inexorable as the wave grew twice as tall as any of them.

It was all Anova remembered before water flooded her mouth and nostrils, and she was dragged forward.

Anova wasn't sure how much time she'd spent falling through to the bottom of the lake before she broke the surface. Sweet air filled and left her lungs too fast, and the world shifted against the bobbing motion of the water.

Her body hit the land that tapered into the lake, and she coughed up water as she dragged herself ashore. Arms pulled her upright and squeezed her in a tight hug.

She breathed in Cadmus's smell. "I can't believe it." Anova looked to the night sky above, and the sight took her breath away.

The moon was full above them. It was strange, however, in that she didn't feel a pull to the heavens as she usually did when it was high above.

"We got here because of you," Cadmus said, interrupting the thought. His eyes were bright.

As they pulled away, she saw Hellmyr and Alys on the shore nearby. As soon as she could, she took some of the remaining magic from the blood crown to dress the air in an insulating barrier for them.

Hellmyr was looking at the woods that surrounded them. The four of them were alone in the small glade.

"Do you feel it?" Hellmyr asked, nodding to a cleared area of forest beyond the lake that hadn't been there before.

The more she looked in that direction, the more she realized the pull of the moon was coming from there and not above her. She was certain that was where they'd find the physical token of the moon. All they had left to do was to annul the spell holding it to this realm and take it back with them.

As they walked there, Anova looked to the forest that surrounded them. The last time she'd been in this place, there had only been darkness beyond the glade where Rietvar had been.

Now, moonlight partially illuminated the dense forest beyond. If she concentrated hard enough, she could see the faint outline of movement through the branches. She stopped to look closer and realized the forest was full of some ... *things* moving through it.

But they didn't move like people, animals, or anything else she knew. A whisper slipped through the sound of wind moving through the glade.

"Anova."

Cadmus pulled her to him. "Don't focus on them," he said.

Anova blinked at the shapes moving through the trees. She knew what Cadmus had said to be logical, but she couldn't help but stare. She'd thought she'd heard something.

"Nove."

She froze in her path. She hadn't imagined that. It was the nickname that her mother had given her. Her heart bounded faster.

"Anova, please," he said. "We have to keep moving."

"Just a moment. I think I see something," Anova muttered as she pushed away Cadmus's hold on her.

She hadn't seen or spoken to her for six long years. Six years she'd lived with the hole in her heart that her mother's passing had left. She'd never gotten to tell her good-bye or that she loved her a last time.

"Anova, she's gone," Cadmus said more forcefully. Her hands shook, but she didn't look away. She couldn't—it would be like losing her again.

"Look at me," Cadmus said as he brought her face to his. Anova blinked as her sight focused on his face.

"I ..." The words dried in her mouth. Just beyond them, Hellmyr and Alys had stopped walking towards the moon's pull, as well. They'd nearly reached the shrouded forest around them.

"It got them, too," she gasped. She ran to take Alys as he went to Hellmyr.

"He took her," Alys said through her teeth when she'd reached her. "He took her and used her and killed her when she became useless to him."

"Let her rest, Alys," Anova said to her. She spun the witch around so she faced Anova. "Remember why we're here. Remember what we need to do yet."

Alys fell back several steps as she blinked. Hellmyr's hands were raking through his hair, but at least he wasn't looking at the forest anymore.

Cadmus turned to address them all. "The dead sleep around us in the shrouded forest, but their dreams are too inviting to listen to for long. If we are to leave this place, we *cannot* pay attention to them."

Hellmyr looked at him strangely. "And why aren't you affected? Care to share that?"

Cadmus just smiled back. "Because I remember my own dreams, Hellmyr." The smile fell from his face. "But we have a bigger concern than the dead's dreams, I'm afraid." He nodded towards the clearing.

They were close enough now to enter it. A pine tree taller than she'd ever remembered seeing met the night sky above. Like the rest of the woods, darkness shrouded much of it in shadow.

Circling and twisting around its trunk and branches was a vine that stretched along most of its height. The vine dressed the tree in a rash of heart-shaped verdant leaves like a cascading dress. But only one flower bloomed along its length.

It was a single white blossom, a moonflower.

When she saw it, Anova knew that this was the token of the moon.

It was too bad that a tail curled around it leading to a thick, white-coated body which was neither a wolf nor a bear.

CHAPTER SIXTY-NINE

Rietvar was supported by the tree's needle-coated branches while he slept in his animal form. As he breathed, his chest rose and fell in regular intervals. In that moment, he looked too much to Anova like an animal of the woods and nothing else.

Cadmus addressed the others. "If we are to free it from his clutches, it's time to perform the annulment."

The four of them came before the pine tree, their footfalls softened by Anova's magic as they moved.

"I forsake the bargain-spell made between myself and the creature known as Rietvar," Alys said, "by invoking it as incomplete and presenting its elements."

Alys pulled a vial from her pocket that looked to be water. She uncorked it and poured its contents into one of her palms. In it reflected the image of the moon, full and coldly unmoving at its zenith.

"The moon, trapped with the dead," she murmured.

Anova knew her barrier kept their sound from waking Rietvar, but she kept an eye on him and a hand on the pommel of her sword regardless. His breath moved slowly in and out of him.

Hellmyr stepped forward next, a knife in one hand as he opened his other to the starless sky. Briefly, his eyes flicked to Alys's. "I'm trusting you, witch."

"And I, you," she answered.

He paused some seconds before making a shallow cut in his palm that beaded immediately. At once, the scent of fae blood laced the air, and she wondered if Hellmyr's blood truly was stronger than that of the average fae.

"The lifeblood of a being of powerful magic," Alys said. After she approached Hellmyr, she focused on the water pooled in her palm.

"And magic to close the loop of energy." Light glowed in her hand as the water's surface began to tremble. "By thus, I render this spell annulled."

Alys clasped Hellmyr's hand, and the light within their grip faded to nothing.

The four of them stood in silence. Other than a breeze that stirred the leaves of the forest beyond, the glade remained still.

Anova waited and counted the breaths of the dread wolf of the night. *One. Two. Three.*

The breeze turned from soft and meandering to gracefully insistent. The white petals of the moonflower ruffled in the wind until the bloom fell from the vine.

"Someone protect it," Hellmyr hissed.

It drifted down, and Anova rushed forward to catch the sudden gift from the tree. In the moment before she nearly crumpled it in her palm, she loosed a bubble of magic that swallowed the flower whole when they met.

Anova barely breathed as she looked upon it. "This is it, isn't it?" she whispered. "I can feel ... *life* in it."

"It's what gave all fae life," Cadmus said next to her.

"I can't believe it," Hellmyr said in a half-laugh. He glanced at Alys and shook his head. "It actually worked."

Alys smiled back at him. "I don't *always* trick fae. Only sometimes."

"Although I trust in Anova's silencing spell, we should leave," Cadmus said. He pulled Anova closer to him, and their gazes went to Rietvar still sleeping in the tree branches before them.

And yet, it was from another direction that a voice spoke.

"My lord told me there would be intruders soon."

She walked from the clearing where they'd entered into this world. Her clothes, a tunic and pants, were somewhere between deepest blue and black like the shifting color of the night sky.

Her hair, a striking black color, had been braided and pinned against her head. Eyebrows lifted above piercing brown eyes that seemed too familiar to Anova. She was too lithe to be anything but fae, and as the light of the moon found her, Anova saw her pointed ears clearly.

Beside her, the others slipped weapons into their hands but didn't dare move.

She tilted her head in response. "Yes, I can see you, if that's what you're wondering."

But that wasn't quite what Anova was concerned about. She stepped towards her.

"Who are you?" The words barely left her throat.

The girl smiled with all the arrogance in the world, and Anova's heart froze. She'd seen that expression a hundred times before.

"He said you would ask such questions."

She drew two swords that had been sheathed at her waist.

"Get out of our way," Hellmyr said between his teeth. The girl took a few more steps towards them.

"But you're the wrong age," Anova whispered.

Alys stepped in front of their group. She'd drawn her own blade, and a black fire had sparked along its edge.

"Step out of our way, and no harm will come to you," Alys said. "We're leaving this place with what belongs to our world."

"Then he said you would claim to know me." It was then that Alys lunged towards her in an attack.

Before Anova could do anything, Cadmus darted between the two of them, blocking Alys's flaming sword with his own.

"What are you doing?" Alys yelled.

"Don't attack her," Cadmus managed to say against the strain of keeping her magic from spreading.

Anova stepped forward. Distantly, she heard Hellmyr curse under his breath. She wondered if he'd realized it, too.

Anova kept her voice steady even as her soul trembled.

"Elissa, do you know who I am?"

The girl with Cadmus's face looked back at her until something glimmered in the girl's eyes.

"And he said you would be *liars*."

It was then that the ground itself shook from the weight of a great beast landing behind them. At the same time, the girl who wore the face of their daughter rushed forward in a deadly strike.

CHAPTER SEVENTY

Cadmus twisted around just in time to see the girl's strike for him. It wasn't an attack meant to injure an enemy or make them yield.

Anova's blood ran cold, and she twisted to face Rietvar. He stood before them on all four limbs as the white wolf-beast.

A vile feeling rose in her. "You stole her from me, Rietvar."

"I don't take what doesn't belong to me, Anova of the blood crown." Teeth peeked through his wide maw when he spoke. "Besides, you were the one who gave the infant up freely."

Anova couldn't move as the thought crossed her mind.

He's right. But I thought her gone from this world already.

White blurred in front of her, and someone pushed her back, causing her to stumble to the ground.

"Anova, guard your moon," Alys said. She saw belatedly how claw marks had scored the dirt.

Rietvar narrowed his eyes at his missed meal. Anova breathed and tried to do as Alys had instructed her, but the sounds of Cadmus and their daughter dueling nearly stole her concentration again.

"Why is my daughter here like this, Rietvar?" she demanded as the wolf started to circle them.

"I don't know what you mean. She is not your daughter, at least any-more." His coal eyes were dull. "Now, return my possession to me."

"She ..." Anova breathed. "She should be dead. Tell me the *truth*," she hissed.

"She is my servant, now. But a baby cannot serve me." A quick, surpris-ing smile jumped to his lips. "It was lucky, then, that I had traded with a human to gain the years of her life."

That's why she's older, Anova realized with a sick feeling. He'd given her daughter Anova's eighteen human years. In the warped space of the afterlife, it must have seemed that much time to her in the second that Rietvar had given her infant Anova's own time.

Rietvar bounded forward before he was done speaking.

This time, she was ready for his lunge. She started to swing with her sword in one hand just before feinting to the opposite side. An arrow of searing light formed in the air above her just as she released it with a flick of her sword. It dragged across the side of his face, barely missing more flesh.

Rietvar snarled at the injury. "You will suffer for such disrespect. Your souls will be *mine*." He crouched low before he became a blur in the air again.

Ice spears the size of her forearm soared above her head. Alys joined Hellmyr in trying to stop Rietvar as she spread black flames from her palms, but none of their attacks touched him. A shriek pierced the air, and Anova turned to see Alys bleeding from a gash along her arm.

Some paces behind her, Cadmus's breath was coming shorter and short-er. By whatever magic Rietvar had changed their daughter, it appeared she'd gained unending stamina.

For just a moment, he met Anova's eyes.

Anova cradled the moonflower closer to her heart as she understood several things.

First, their daughter hadn't been dead when she'd passed her to Rietvar—at least enough for her soul to move to the shrouded forest beyond their reach. Otherwise, she'd likely have been lost to even Rietvar.

No, it was the moon's presence here that had sparked enough life in her for her first cry. From there, Rietvar had given her the years of Anova's human life to form a servant who could be trained.

Second, she understood that if one of their group died before they could reach the gateway, the moon would remain in the unliving world forever.

The war would continue. The fae realm would fall.

With enough days of darkness, most of the fae folk would die.

With enough days of warfare, humankind would forget that they'd been anything but pillagers and murderers.

It was then that Elissa's thin, sharp blade pierced through to the center of Cadmus's heart. He fell backwards into the dark forest behind them, and his sword clattered to the ground as the light of his magic faded from the steel.

Anova ceased to think.

She ran to Cadmus's side, but a low mist had already swept in from the forest and gathered about his body.

"Cadmus," she shouted. He didn't respond. "Cadmus!"

"Face your enemy or die facing the ground," Elissa said suddenly as she came for her. Anova's heart tangled in her throat, but she pushed a white blast of magic from the blood crown at her.

Elissa was thrown against the ground far from them, and Anova only took a second to see that she hadn't been seriously hurt before turning to heal Cadmus.

But he was gone.

Anova's heart drummed faster and faster as she scrambled among the brambles. A mist swirled about her fingers where she searched through the leaves and grass. He simply wasn't there anymore.

She came to her feet, and her gaze jumped among the moving shapes inside the shadows beyond the glade.

"Cadmus. Cadmus, please," she begged in a low voice. Nothing answered her but the whistling of the wind through the shadowed branches. "Cadmus, come back."

"Anova!" Alys shouted.

Anova turned in time to see Elissa paces away from her, her sword high above. Anova's blade protected her and the moonflower, but only just so as Elissa's steel glanced off hers.

"Don't you realize who we are?" Anova said through her teeth. The hurt of what she'd done to Cadmus still coursed through her. She was afraid that if she paid too much attention to it, it would bowl her over. "We're your parents, Elissa."

"I have no parents." Elissa's brown eyes—ones that resembled Anova's and her own mother's—looked upon her with a coldness. But there was a truth there, too, she realized. "I was abandoned before Lord Rietvar gave me shelter and training. I owe him my life."

Anova stared. It all sounded suspiciously familiar.

It's what I used to think before I escaped the Rosebud. It's what I thought after Mother died.

I blamed her for dying.

She looked to Rietvar. Hellmyr and Alys were now both bleeding from their fight. They couldn't last much longer like this, but she knew what to do now.

Hellmyr tried to stagger to his feet where he'd been thrown against the pine tree that touched the sky. Rietvar had left Alys gasping in the dirt behind him when he turned and sprinted to finish off the fae king.

Rietvar's jaws opened to swallow Hellmyr whole. Anova drew from the energy of the moon in her palm until she couldn't take it anymore. The magic from the moon exploded from her in millions of tiny spikes landing in Rietvar's fur.

The force pushed him from his deadly path enough to give Hellmyr the chance to run. She met him before Rietvar could continue his rampage. She forced the orb with the moonflower inside it into his arms.

"What are you doing?" he panted. "I can't guard this and fight him." He straightened as the rest of the battlefield came into focus. "Where's Cadmus?"

"Hellmyr, do you trust me?" Anova said. She could barely keep her face from betraying what had happened.

Or from what she was going to do.

But she couldn't risk him stopping her.

"We don't have time for this, Anova." Hellmyr's hand ran through his hair and came back bloodied. But there must have been something about her expression, because he added, "Yes. Now, what is it?"

"Give me your brooch. Guard the moonflower and get it back. I'll take care of the rest," she said in a rush.

Hellmyr had already given her the brooch before she'd finished speaking, and she was running again before he had the chance to respond.

Elissa was back for the remainder of their duel, and it was all Anova could do to avoid her next attack even with her other hand freed. Every single strike aimed for her head or her heart.

Rietvar had trained her in only deadly dueling, it seemed. Anger and grief tempted her to a bottomless abyss. How effortless it would be to fall here, she considered.

No. The world she knew was worth fighting for.

Suffering for, even.

Maris, Della, and Nerium. Lycastsa and Leander. Juras and Hellmyr. Elissa.

They deserved to live in safety and happiness.

"Elissa, I'm not your enemy," Anova said.

"Don't use my name," she said on the other side of her severe blade. "You can't trick me into believing you know me."

"I knew you first," Anova said. A light smile came to her lips as she remembered holding her for the first time.

But Elissa had pierced the air where she'd been a second ago. Anova's body could only last so long on her feet like this.

"Did you ever wonder how you got your name?" Anova asked as Elissa drew blood from a laceration on her shoulder.

"Don't," she warned Anova. "Don't speak your lies anymore!"

She's in there. I know it, Anova thought. *I have to believe it.*

"You were named for your father's mother. Her name was Eleris Wolfsbane." Tears blurred her vision, but her voice was steady. "I didn't get a chance to give you your second one. It would have been my mother's. You have her kind brown eyes."

Elissa stopped and stared. Her eyes were wide, and Anova recognized the emotion there with a jolt.

"I can't," Elissa said suddenly. "I can't listen to you. He'll hurt me."

She held the edge of her sword at Anova's throat, frozen between them.

Slowly, Anova extended her hand until it met the one Elissa used to hold the weapon's handle. She swallowed.

One wrong move, and it would be over.

She squeezed her daughter's hand.

"I love you, Elissa. Never forget that."

Anova pushed the bee's stinger into Elissa's wrist.

CHAPTER SEVENTY-ONE

Elissa slackened and fell into Anova's waiting arms as she kicked her daughter's deadly sword out of reach. Elissa's steady, even breaths tickled Anova's face.

Hellmyr had explained how the brooch worked during their ride through the Eastwoe gloom woods. Someone skilled at measuring their own magic could deliver a specific amount of the paralyzing toxin within the enchanted bee.

With this amount, she'd ensured her daughter had fallen into unconsciousness. If Anova were correct, she wouldn't remember any of this wretched place when she returned to the living realm and was shed of her artificial age.

Rietvar circled her two injured companions. Though they'd gained the power of the moon back and the source of their fae magic, it was only a matter of time before Rietvar devoured them like a cat playing with terrified mice.

I need your help, she said as she closed her eyes and focused her energy. *I need someone to guard her.*

Malor morphed from a phantom image to a solid presence before her, and she shifted Elissa into his arms. His red eyes were dull.

"You're certain you want to do this?" his strange voice asked her.

"Yes. You won't hurt her," she said, though she knew he'd meant it in another sense, as well. Malor nodded. He knew her heart, so he knew what to do next.

Nearby, Hellmyr had been knocked to the ground. He was panting, and one of his pant legs had been torn to reveal sticky blood running from an ugly gash.

The moonflower was cupped in his palm, and it casted a gentle glow across his bloodied face.

Alys stood between him and Rietvar as her black flames lashed at him like solid whips. They had no ground to give as they were pushed against the shrouded forest.

Rietvar pawed the ground around them, slowly closing the distance. "I never thought to see it. A witch protecting the king of Fae. Last we spoke, you were mortal enemies."

"I was wrong," Alys said. In her eyes was a dark expression. "Now allow me to show you something else you've never seen, dread wolf."

One of her whips slipped past his claws and found his neck, wrapping tightly around it like a noose. Her hand turned to a fist as it closed around the other end of it as the whip snaked through his fur. Rietvar clawed at the magicked whip, struggling as it tightened further.

Just as Alys helped Hellmyr to his feet, Rietvar gave a trickling laugh. He tugged on the whip past the black flames that seared down it, bringing Alys dragging across the ground.

Anova was already running, but it was too late. Rietvar had already grabbed the witch in one of his clawed hands. The razor tips touched where her ribs were, primed to dig deep into her flesh. Alys struggled, but he'd pinned her hands against her body.

"It's over for you," he said to Hellmyr. "Drop the flower. It's too late to pretend you don't care if she dies."

Anova's heart galloped faster than she could keep up. Slowly, Hellmyr crouched to the ground, his teeth bared at the monster before him. But he placed the token of the moon between them as he'd ordered.

No more, Anova chanted in her head. *No more of them will die.*

I vow it.

Before Rietvar could reach for the moonflower, Anova launched the sword she'd made of light and fire through the arm that held Alys prisoner. He twisted in a rare show of pain and shock as he dropped the witch on the ground. He hadn't expected her to live from her duel with Elissa, she realized grimly.

"Leave," she shouted at the other two. "You have to go *now*! Malor is at the lake already. He'll help activate the gateway with some of my magic."

"You're not coming," Hellmyr said simply. He stared at her. Between Cadmus's disappearance and her request for the bee brooch, he seemed to have pieced together her plan.

Tears beaded along her eyelids, but she had to focus on getting the three of them out of here, no matter the cost to herself.

"Go!" she said to them. Anova barely dodged Rietvar's next lunge.

As they ran past with the moon's token, Alys's hand found her shoulder, and Anova held it there for a moment. They didn't have time for words anymore, but this was important.

"Ask Nerium to look after her," Anova said.

Alys nodded to her before sprinting after Hellmyr to the lake. Rietvar turned to follow them, but Anova blocked him with her body and loosed a bolt of searing heat.

He snapped his teeth, and her magic dissipated before it touched him. "She is mine by rights, Anova."

She had to distract him long enough to give them a chance to leave this place, but she was precariously close to surrendering to grief.

Do it for her.

At least I'll be with Cadmus soon enough.

It was only these thoughts that kept her from running after Alys and Hellmyr.

Rietvar bounded after them. At the same time, she felt Malor draw energy from her for the spell and nearly sank to her knees as she formed a cord of light in her palm. Dizziness assaulted her, but she pushed past it.

She tried the same tactic Alys had by throwing the looped cord after him but missed Rietvar's neck by a wide margin. Instead, the cord of light snagged on one of his hind legs. His razor teeth easily bit through the magic, but it had had the desired effect.

A dark emotion flared in his gaze. He began to round on her, pushing her towards the shrouded forest.

His teeth showed in what looked oddly like a grin. It was out of place for this body, though.

"You always were one of my favorite mortals, Anova. I had wanted the chance to shape and mold my own servant, but ..." Darkness gleamed in his eyes. "With all the hours of eternity you face here, I think it will make little difference after I'm done with you. The only question is will it take one lifetime to form you? Or ten?"

A chill gripped Anova, but she couldn't give into it, now. He hadn't struck her yet, though she knew the attack would come anytime.

It would be something to disable her and keep her from fleeing, she realized. Otherwise, he would have ripped her apart by now.

"When I was trying to understand your motives for our bargain, I came across an old fae tale that told of how Death came to be," Anova said.

At her words, Rietvar's smile fell from his face.

"I couldn't fathom what you wanted," she continued. "You'd denied the blood crown as an offering, but you were interested in such things like the years of my life as a human or the lifeblood of the fae king."

"I am Death, Purveyor of Souls. Why wouldn't these things please me?"

"That's not what I mean." Anova shook her head. "In the fae tale, the hunter won the contest but was tricked into taking on the burdens of

Death for an eternity. He was taken from his life as a mortal, from his rivals, from his family."

Mist pooled at her feet as she took another step back. She had no farther to go, now.

"You are envious of the lives of mortals. Of the warmth in our lives," Anova said. She shook her head and clarified. "You bargained for a baby because you were lonely."

Rietvar's lips pulled back to show all his teeth.

"You will not *taunt* me."

He aimed a crushing bite not at her face, but at her legs. It was then that the magic from the blood crown left her entirely.

CHAPTER SEVENTY-TWO

As Rietvar's wide maw opened to rip her apart, a body launched from the mist-drenched forest behind her and stuck a sword inside the dread wolf's throat.

At once, Cadmus released the blade as he pulled Anova against him. Her fingers scrambled over his skin until she found what she was looking for: a heartbeat.

"Cadmus," she whispered. "You're here. You're really here."

"I know. I'm sorry I was gone. It was a maze I thought I'd never get out of." He held her back tightly. "I almost ..." He shook his head.

She pulled herself from him suddenly. "You have go. You'll miss the gateway closing!"

Cadmus stared back at her. "You're coming with me."

Rietvar spat out the blade and an odd sludge that must have been his blood. He crushed the blade like brittle leaves under his claws.

He smiled, though there was an edge to it. "Oh, which one to keep and which to dispose of? We can't have the both of you here."

Without warning, Anova lunged forward to grab a shard of the broken sword to stab at Rietvar. It was the only way she could think of to give

Cadmus an opening. There was no magic left inside her, and that scared her more than death in that moment. But she had to try.

She had to give Cadmus this last gift.

"Anova, no," Cadmus shouted and shoved himself between them as Rietvar raised his hand tipped in razors. It would be a killing shot.

Suddenly, Rietvar froze before them. A golden, searing light enveloped him.

It wasn't until Anova saw the fae hovering behind him that she understood. Her golden tresses spread from her like rays of moonlight. Her eyes were like jewels of the sea as she stared through to Anova. On her head was a crown that matched hers exactly.

It was the fae princess of legend, the first possessor of the blood crown and the one who had began the curse by killing her father in retribution for her human lover.

Rietvar struggled against the magic before saying, "Leave me to my business, Princess. You are but a phantom."

"No, Rietvar," she said. "What I am now was caused by you. But a phantom *that is not.* As I sank from the weight of my stones, bearing my curse with me into death, you took the bloodied crown from my head and gave it to another fae. I have persisted for far longer than I needed, watching countless crowned fae sicken themselves with hunger, greed, bloodthirstiness, and paranoia."

Rietvar tried to say something, but cords of light had been bound about his mouth like a muzzle. Her hands turned to fists.

The fae princess stared down at them. "Go. Leave this cursed place and the misery here. I am strong enough to hold him only for so long."

Anova beheld the princess. Past the boundless fury, grief was plain on her face. She recognized it so easily now.

She wasn't sure what spurred her to speak, but the words were free before she could stop herself.

"You couldn't join with him. Not even in death," Anova said. She knew she should be running, but her heart ached for their doomed love and the nightmare the princess was condemned to for eternity.

"Because of the crown, I am denied rest." She looked to the shrouded forest where darkness moved at her gaze. "I can't dream of *him*."

The ends to Rietvar's claws started to twitch where he was frozen before them. Cadmus pulled her away some steps, but Anova stopped and set the crown on the earth.

This was the answer, she realized. She hadn't known until she'd heard the princess speak. Golden light surged where she placed the artifact down.

"So long as I am allowed to keep the life granted to me by it as well as safe passage through your lake, I surrender my hold on the blood crown," Anova declared.

The fae princess's eyes filled with golden tears before she closed them. Anova remembered what the fae princess had told her once before.

"I want to break the curse."

The fae princess had stared back at her. "Such a thing is impossible."

All this time, she'd lived a hundred lifetimes. Watching fae murdering their own brothers for the cursed object that kept her from a peaceful death.

She spoke now, blurring with Anova's memory of her. "I was wrong to doubt your hope, Anova. But this means my form will linger only a little bit longer. I can help you no more."

This time, Anova ran with Cadmus across the glade where the princess's lake was. Though their friends were gone by now, a gentle mist had risen above the surface of the water. The shadows in the trees moved faster now, as if they too knew what was happening.

"Hold tight to me, no matter what. We'll go in—together," Cadmus said breathlessly to her. "I love you so much."

"I love you, too, Cadmus," she said back as their hands wound tightly together. They stood on a sharp ledge just above it.

Together, they jumped into the black depths of the lake.

EPILOGUE

Six months later

Juras was laughing at Anova's sour face as she pushed away the pint of ale. She should have known by the smell not to try it, but she hadn't wanted to insult him by not drinking what he and Hellmyr had brought them as gifts.

In her defense, she hadn't had human food in months. It didn't help that it was swill from The Last Chance.

She was tempted to remind him that it was possibly bad luck to laugh at a bride on her wedding night until she remembered something.

"Sweet Delen," she cooed, recalling the alias he'd once used in their cons. "Who is that strange figure you've brought down with you from our room?" She pretended to gasp as Hellmyr raised his hands before him like claws and exposed his teeth like a monster.

The Gloom King of Fae smirked at her fake reaction. "I have stolen your fiancé for my own, poor human girl."

Hellmyr and Anova laughed until a smile came to Juras's lips. They were seated along a wide table with drinks, fruits, breads, skewered meats, cheese spreads, and more arranged along its length. The moon had just risen, and she felt the magic surge in her at its fullness.

"Wasn't it you who once told me that the worse it tastes, the better it works?" Juras asked her.

Anova was about to open her mouth to answer when she smelled something familiar. This time, Anova stood before Della assaulted her in a bone-shattering hug.

"I trust the three of you are doing well," Anova managed to gasp.

"Better than we deserve," Della said. "Congratulations, Anova! We're so happy for the two of you."

Despite having just arrived on the Wolfsbane property, Elissa was already gleefully in Maris's arms. In only a few months, the two had developed a deep bond.

"Thank you," Anova said after she'd been released. She tickled Elissa's nose until she made her laugh. "I see Nerium found the other two."

Elissa had been with Cadmus while Leander had helped prepare him for their ceremony. Lately, she'd been enamored with Cadmus's ability to form bubbles on the air.

Anova frowned as she remembered how Leander had arrived to Wolfsbane manor alone. She'd invited Lycasta by butterflywing—a token of amicability on her part, or so she'd intended—but she felt the fae lady wasn't coming.

"How is the Thorn and Bramble?" Anova asked.

Maris moved Elissa to her other side. "We've done quite a bit of work on the building. I don't think you'd recognize it, even. Many of the others are staying on to run it."

Anova smiled at that. She and Juras had given the deed to the Rosebud to these two, who had then given the remaining profits to the workers and closed the brothel. From there, they'd started work to reopen the building as a breakfast-themed inn. She'd heard they'd even partnered with Mara's bakery.

Della added, "We've decided to stay in Fae for the next few months and for your coronation. We figured you'll be busy enough as a new queen and king that this one could use another playmate or two."

"Cadmus will be delighted to hear it. I know he's missed Nerium," Anova said. She squeezed their hands. She still hadn't gotten used to the titles of Spring King and Queen of Fae. Their coronation was only a month away, and this would likely be the last night she'd see so much of her friends before she was officially crowned as one of the rulers of Fae.

Fae were at work renovating the old facilities in Westvalde for a castle that would become the heart of their court. Anova still wasn't convinced she was ready for the position. Her hand flew to her head in a familiar gesture, but there was nothing atop it. She covered the movement up by replacing a stray hair back inside her elaborate braid.

It'd been six months since the five of them had woken on the shore of a calm lake in the Sorrelands not far from here. Elissa had cried immediately, and Anova's heart had nearly hammered out of her chest to hear it.

By how she'd understood the rules of the blood crown, she'd assumed the specter known as Malor had returned to the crown as nothing more than mist again. It'd been her single regret from giving up the blood crown.

But Leander had related to her whispers of an antlered fae spotted in Farstar. It was one of the many things on her list of things to investigate after their lives calmed again.

Maris pulled closer to Anova. Elissa grabbed for Anova's free hand, and she let her pat her palm. "A certain witch we know is tied up in negotiations with the human king, though she sends her regards tonight to the Spring Queen and King."

Anova held her shoulder. "Have they agreed to it?"

A ceasefire had been called months ago, but the humans had been slow to declare aggressions over entirely. They were reluctant to trust such claims of restructuring within Fae society, and Anova knew why.

Never before had Fae had more than a single tyrannical ruler. By splitting Fae into two courts—Farstar and Eastwoe in one and Westvalde and the Sorrelands in the other—they had established two separate houses of power.

Maris said, "Still not officially, but views are changing, even in Irbess. The dissolution of the tariffs seems to have made the biggest difference, as has Alys's voice."

Anova nodded. It was going better than she could've hoped, she knew, but she dreamed of how reality could be.

One day, Anova hoped that the border between Fae and the human lands would become little more than a formality or line on a paper rather than the strictly guarded area it needed to be for now.

Already, they'd established laws protecting humankind in Fae, but the real work would begin after her and Cadmus's coronation.

Soft, feathery wings brushed against her face until insectile legs found hold of her nose. She looked up at Viridia and greeted her. It wasn't until she saw that Viridia had her new friends behind her that she realized they had a new guest.

A trail of three gray moths took to the air as her butterfly friend followed after them, leaving Anova's face.

Lycasta stepped down from her oversized moth, her lilac dress following in a cascade. The others' conversation had quieted, but Anova went to her side and greeted the fae lady.

"Please, share our table. They should be down soon," Anova said.

"Thank you, Anova," she murmured. She sat across the table from Hellmyr and Juras as her moths came to rest their wings in her hair.

Before she could reseat herself, a frenzied rhythm of gallops upon the earth caught her ear. The last three of their party broke into her line of sight as they crested a hill behind the estate.

Though it was difficult to tell from this distance which was Cadmus, she knew with a certainty which figure he was as he came down the valley before the others. Nerium had almost overtaken him in the last few seconds with a silver-maned horse, and Leander trailed just behind them with an ebony steed opposite to his brother's white and gray one.

Cadmus's laugh was sharp on the air as he accused them, "It's not a fair race if you've allowed me to win."

Nerium's smile was dazzling. She felt sure that he could feel Della and Maris's gaze on him. "It was never fair. You're forgetting who taught you how to not fall off a horse."

He was breathtaking, and all over again, she remembered how she'd fallen so deeply in love with Cadmus. As he approached her, she could barely think.

His dark hair had been tousled by the wind, but no other part of him seemed fatigued from the ride. He wore a gardenia bloom pinned to his inky blue jacket that matched the ones in her hair.

When his eyes met hers, he ran to her, swirling her skirts around them as they kissed.

As their guests reveled in the moonlight and delight that laced the air, the moon had nearly come to its zenith. It was time.

None of the others seemed to notice when Cadmus and Anova slipped out from the center of the celebrations. Hand in hand, they walked from the riotous joy in their honor until they could hear them no longer.

Cadmus led her under a flowering crape myrtle tree. Ruffled petals scattered along their hair and shoulders as they dedicated promises to each other in silver moonstream. At the end, Anova kissed him fully and deeply, and her heartbeat scattered like it was the first time they'd done so.

When they pulled apart, she stilled.

"What is it?" Cadmus asked.

Dancing in the air above them were two luna moths. The moonlight fell on them, and for just a moment, golden light followed after their quivering forms like phantoms. These were no ordinary moths like the ones following Lycasta.

It reminded her of the aura that had surrounded the fae princess when Anova had seen her for the last time. Anova clutched Cadmus's hand close.

"I think ... it can't be, but I think it's them," Anova whispered.

The fae princess and her human lover.

The breeze carried more ruffled petals, but it didn't seem to affect the luna moths. They watched as the two floated higher and higher until they could be seen no more.

* * *

The End

* * *

ALSO BY JOY LEWIS

A Thorn among Fae (Fae Crown Book 1)
A Crown for the Cursed (Fae Crown Book 2)

* * *

The Lost Princess (A Sleeping Beauty Retelling)

* * *

Wither Thorn (The Crest of Blackthorn Book 1)
Soul Sworn (The Crest of Blackthorn Book 2)
Marrow Blade (The Crest of Blackthorn Book 3)
Blood Prophecy (The Crest of Blackthorn Book 4)
Heir of Thorns (A Crest of Blackthorn Prequel)

* * *

A Curse of Silver

About the Author

From the time she "borrowed" a floppy disk from her school's computer lab at the age of 12 to type her first story, Joy Lewis has been dreaming up tales of adventure and danger for most of her life. In 2017, she graduated with highest distinction from Middle Tennessee State University with a B.A. in English. She lives in Tennessee where she can be found in her garden when not writing.

Sign up for her newsletter for a free book at www.joylewisauthor.com.